THE LOST GOD

SHEILA MASTERSON

THE LOST GOD

SHEILA MASTERSON

hardback: 9781960416049

paperback: 9781960416032

ebook: 9781960416025

Cover Design: Andrew Davis

Hardback Case and Map Design: Mike Sisak

Editing: Lisa Gilliam

Proofreading: Mike Sisak

To all those who will never be too old for a good bedtime story.

A NOTE FROM THE AUTHOR

Dear Reader,

This book includes some content that might be challenging for certain readers. Please be advised that these topics have been treated with the utmost of care, but I always want my readers to be prepared.

This story includes self-harm for magic (cutting of a hand), fertility issues, parental death, violence, and explicit sex. Please proceed with caution.

Happy reading,
Sheila

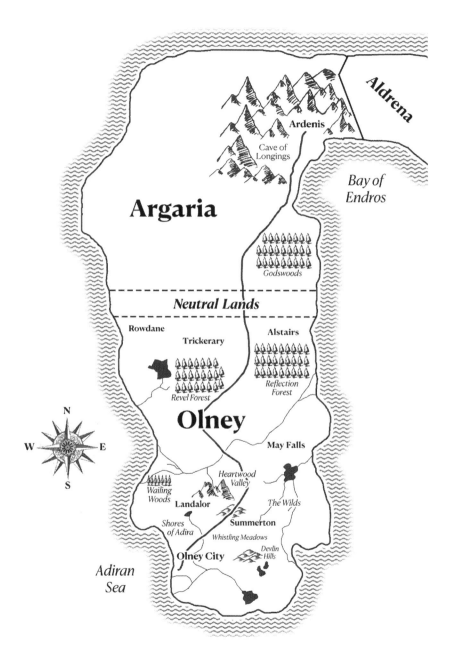

BEFORE

The cave stretched dark and wide before her, like the mouth of a beast waiting to swallow her whole.

Hours of honing her magic, volumes of reading, and grueling practice sessions over the past twelve years had prepared Cecilia Reznik to tuck away her fear and walk into the dark alone. Pulling ancient wisdom from these caves was what memory witches were born to do. Plenty had done it before her, and if she succeeded, no one would need to do it after her.

She stared into the void, the first of many stops required to complete the Gauntlet and release the power of the Lost God back to her people.

Rainer took her hand, brushing his thumb along her inner wrist.

"Are you nervous?" he whispered.

Cecilia shrugged. "Not really."

"We've already done the hard part. We got here safely. You're ready for whatever is in there, Cece."

All day, he'd been practically vibrating with excitement, flooding every silence with animated chatter, but now he was notably quiet. She knew Rainer dreaded that she'd have to go in without him. They did everything together, and it was his job to protect her.

She closed her eyes, reaching out to test her memory power. It rushed up to meet her. A familiar and perfectly preserved memory began to play out.

Cecilia sat in a chair across from a beautiful witch who studied her like she was a puzzle. Cecilia's powers had only shown up days before, but her father, the Olney huntmaster, was eager for guidance. He told her they were going to visit the seer to have her bonded to a guardian.

The seer placed a hand on Cecilia's shoulder. "Yours is not an easy road, girl. It is hard to carry memory. It makes the mind chaotic. You will need a will of iron to forge the path that needs to be taken. The whole world will try to tell you who you are, but it's your choice if you want to believe them. Fear will be your catalyst, and only you can decide who fear will make you."

The seer gestured to the boy with bright green eyes who sat on Cecilia's right. "This boy is kind, strong, and a hard worker. He will need to work to be the best, but he has that potential. He's also a worrier, which means he'll always be prepared."

"But is he the best match?" the huntmaster asked.

"Don't rush it, Huntmaster. This is a serious decision. These bonds are for life," the seer scolded. "He is more than just a protector. He is a friend and confidant, and he would have more than just a usual guardian bond with your daughter. The two of them have soul bond potential."

"What's a soul bond?" Cecilia asked.

"A soul bond is a connection on the deepest level, and it's quite rare. A regular bond will let your guardian know when you're afraid, in danger, or hurt, and help him find you if you're separated. It's what most memory witches and guardians have. With a soul bond, you could feel everything the other feels. It requires a great deal of trust. Each soul bond is as unique as its duo, offering as much risk as protection. It can be a distraction as much as an advantage. It is a trade—an exchange. Like all magic, it requires balance."

Cecilia laughed herself back to the present moment. At six years old, a soul bond sounded exciting. She and Rainer couldn't have imagined how hard it would be to experience each other's feelings so acutely that at times it was impossible to tell who was the source of the emotion and who was the echo. It had taken years for them to become attuned to each other's ebbs and flows without being overwhelmed. Despite its pitfalls, she wouldn't have given up a direct connection to Rainer's heart for anything.

That day, he'd promised to protect her with his sword and strength, and she'd promised to protect him with her magic. It was an agreement that could be undone only by death or an excruciating process called severing.

She looked into the same green eyes she'd been looking into since that day in the seer's suite and smiled.

"I can do it," she assured Rainer. "I'll be back in no time."

She squeezed his hand and made her way closer to the entrance. Wisteria wound around the cave, blooming wide and littering the ground with tiny purple petals, the sweet scent of the flowers in stark contrast to the damp, mossy smell that wafted from the darkness. Energy pulsed around the cave as if somewhere inside the very heart of magic beat in a steady hypnotic rhythm.

Cecilia was drawn to it on instinct. *Remember*, it seemed to whisper.

She knelt in the flowered dirt, silently requesting permission to enter, and an eerie collection of whispers crept into her mind, forming one strange discordant voice—the voice of the ancients.

Cecilia Reznik, what do you seek? the voice asked.

She replied as she'd been taught. *Wisdom, memory, magic.*

The words were a shorter version of the vows made by every witch and guardian in Olney based on the principles that Clastor, the god of all matter, had shared when he created the Gauntlet. Wisdom to know that power is best when shared. Memory of our mistakes, as to not make the same ones again. Magic to restore peace and prosperity to the kingdom.

The ancient voice buzzed into Cecilia's mind again. *You may enter.*

Cecilia stood, pulling her dagger from the sheath on her thigh.

All magic required an exchange. She'd learned that repeatedly over the years. To obtain the cave's magic, she would need to pour her blood over the sacred medicinal plants that would later be harvested

3

by healers and earth witches. She was part of an ecosystem that kept magic alive. A cut on her palm was a small price to pay. Especially when she could heal the wound as soon as she got outside.

She snapped her fingers, summoning a flame to her fingertips as she walked into the cave.

The farther she walked from the entrance, the more oppressive the darkness became, devouring the light from her flame until she could see only a foot in front of her. She felt a buzz of anxiety through her bond with Rainer and sent a bit of calm back so he would know she was fine.

She worried she had walked too far when she felt the sudden urge to stop. Looking down, she found a crop of vibrant plants.

Make your exchange, the ancient voice whispered.

She released the fire magic, allowing her eyes to adjust to the inky blackness of the space as she cut her hand without flinching. Blood given with fear and resistance led to less potent magic, but blood given freely created robust power.

She dribbled the blood over the plants. Moments passed, and she breathed deep, keeping her heart rate low and her mind clear.

A thread of fear that the magic might somehow overwhelm her bloomed in the eerie silence.

That's enough, the voice said.

Cecilia wrapped linen around her palm and turned toward the voice.

Hold out your hand. An ancient spirit appeared, a faint and flickering light in the dark. She placed her palm over the spirit's.

There was a gentle brush against her mind, and she let it in despite her fear. She closed her eyes and waited for a memory to come to life behind her lids.

Only you can decide who fear will make you, the seer had said.

Cecilia let it make her a warrior.

PART I:

THE END OF AN ERA

1

Freedom was expensive.

Though all of Cecilia Reznik's life revolved around exchanges, none were as costly as the bits of freedom she carved out for herself. She paid in uncomfortable dresses, tedious conversations at afternoon teas, and exhaustive hours of magic and combat training.

At the moment, liberation would cost only a headache—a price she'd gladly pay to prove a point to the man who had lifted her off the ground. She huffed a breath, swinging her legs up and thrusting her head back into the side of his face.

It wasn't a direct hit, but it was enough to get him to drop her. Cecilia spun to face her opponent. She took a swing with her right fist, but he ducked out of the way. The next few minutes were a maddening dance, as hardly a single punch or elbow connected. He knew how furious it made her when he picked her up and counted on it making her sloppy.

Rainer gave her a teasing grin as he put his hands up and stepped away to let her catch her breath.

Cecilia learned to fight from the time she was young. Her father insisted on it, even though it was frowned upon for a lady of the court to be formally trained in combat in the kingdom of Olney. His chief concern was that she knew how to defend herself.

Personally, she just enjoyed seeing the shocked look on a man's face when she took him to the ground.

"Let me hear it," she said.

"Stop dropping your right shoulder, Cece. You give away your movement every time. You take a breath when you're about to move. If your shoulder doesn't give you away, your breathing does. Smooth it out and try again. We have a month before we leave. I know you remember how to do this."

Cecilia's magic had always been about remembering. Remembering ancient magic and rituals. Remembering how to summon memory, healing, fire, tides, earth, and storms. And today, remembering her close-combat training if she had a prayer of taking Rainer down and wiping that smug grin off his face.

"Of course I remember," she huffed.

"Could have fooled me," Rainer countered. "You got so mad during training this morning in the practice ring, you summoned a storm in front of everyone. You're distracted, and it shows. Take me down once, and I'll let you sleep in tomorrow after the Godsball."

The thought of being able to sleep in for one blissful morning was extremely enticing. He had her on a relentless training schedule leading up to their final Gauntlet run, and she was exhausted.

Rainer made everything look maddeningly effortless, even though he spent hours perfecting every movement and skill he learned. He was a master swordsman, a great shot with a bow, and so good at close combat, he could beat most of the guardians in the kingdom. On top of all of it, he was handsome, friendly, and liked by everyone.

The late afternoon sun cut through the branches of the wisteria above them, highlighting the russet and gold in his dark hair from hours of training outdoors. He settled in across from Cecilia, green eyes blazing—daring her to take him down.

In their sixteen years of practicing, it was still rare that Cecilia bested Rainer. As he loved to point out, the more hits he landed, the more reckless she became. Despite her speed, he had significant size and strength advantages, standing a full foot taller than her. That didn't stop her from trying.

She focused on Rainer's feedback as she settled into her stance. She kept still until the last moment, catching him on the side of the face. He laughed and ducked away as she summoned earth magic to raise roots from the soil, hoping to trip him.

He anticipated the move, jumping out of the way. The energy drained out of her with the wasted magic. It was stupid of her to conjure while fighting when she'd already spent so much energy earlier in the day, but at least earth magic burned through her reserves slower than most of her other elemental magic.

Rainer's ease at evading her only infuriated her more. They traded blows until Rainer caught her in the ribs and she stumbled over the roots she'd conjured. Her head hit the grass with a thud, her vision darkening momentarily. When she opened her eyes, Rainer's concerned face peered down at her.

"Cece, are you all right? I didn't mean to take you down that hard."

"You didn't. The roots did. I would have still been on my feet."

They primarily drilled in a scenic spot off the main road in the wild. The training grounds in Olney City Center were much more convenient, but Rainer preferred the grove because in the field they battled unpredictable terrain along with enemy hunters. So each time they fought, she risked rolled ankles, skinned knees, and rogue tree roots.

Cecilia sat up too fast, nearly falling over from the head rush. Rainer's rough hands cupped her face as he looked into her eyes. Her stomach flipped as he let loose a barrage of questions.

"Rain, calm down. Don't be such a mother hen. It's just a bump on the head."

She wanted him to stop fussing but not to stop touching her. Though she'd become better at masking the emotions that flowed through their bond, it was hard to hide the immensity of her affection. Beyond their connection, her expressive face meant that her crush on Rainer was the worst-kept secret at court. He was good enough to pretend not to notice.

Sometimes she appreciated it. Other times she wished he would just acknowledge it.

Rainer sat next to her in the grass. "Looking forward to being out on the road again?"

"Our whole lives have been about completing the Gauntlet. It's strange that it will finally be over."

She brought her hand to the knot already forming on her head and summoned healing to ease the ache. The tingling power settled in her body, and she made a mental note to eat something extra at the party.

All magic required an exchange, and healing was no exception. It burned through her energy quickly. She'd be exhausted if she didn't replace the spent calories before a night of dancing.

She sighed as she met Rainer's expectant gaze. Four years had passed since she stood in front of the first cave to enter the Gauntlet. Her mind spun, tugging at the strings of perfectly preserved memories detailing the struggles and adventures of completing the first seventy caves. Her memory magic was always itching to break free and pull her into a vortex of memories, both her own and others.

"These final seven stops are supposed to be the most challenging. We have to go farther into Argaria than we ever have," Rainer said.

What he failed to say was that every other duo had either quit or died pursuing those last few caves.

"We could finally be the ones to do it, Cece. It's a big deal," Rainer said with a proud smile.

It *was* a big deal. Though the stories of the Gauntlet's creation diverged and there were many tales, their magic theory classes explained that before he died in the War of the Gods, Clastor—the god of all matter—infused some of his power into the caves with the help of four ancient witches. Each cave held a page in a living grimoire written in the language of memory. The witch who completed the route would release the Lost God's power back to the witches of their kingdom. Though even their finest scholars didn't know exactly how the power could be used.

For Cecilia, the Gauntlet had always been a special type of torture in the patriarchal world in which she lived. She felt like a kite, flying high enough to see the world but tethered to the place she started, and always forced to return. It was the sweet illusion of independence that made coming home to Olney sour.

As dangerous as it was, the Gauntlet was the most freedom she'd ever experienced. Once completed, she'd be expected to go from a life of daring adventure to one of wife and mother. What little choice she had would end with that final cave. The thrill of finishing their life's work was overshadowed by the claustrophobic feeling of the walls of her life closing in.

A persistent restlessness settled in her bones. She refused to grow roots in the very soil in which she'd been planted. Olney was home, and it wasn't. She loved the beautiful seaside scenery, wild blooming florals, and the bustling pace of Olney City. She loved her quiet cottage haven on the bluffs above the Adiran Sea, but some part of her always felt aimless and unsettled. Each morning, as she stared out over the bright blue water, she longed not for the sea but for adventure beyond the horizon.

There had to be more options for her. Still, a lifetime of chipping away at herself had left her with little idea of who she was outside of someone who sacrificed for what little power the kingdom allowed her.

"You don't seem excited," Rainer said.

"Well, I know it's really important to *you*, Rain. I know you have people to impress." Cecilia tried to be delicate, but she was as Rainer often described her—subtle as a sledgehammer.

A shadow passed over his face. "It's not about that."

Everyone Cecilia knew longed for parental approval, but she sometimes wondered if Rainer being adopted by the hardest-to-please man in the two kingdoms made that desire more intense.

"Maybe it's a little bit about that?"

He sighed and looked away. Most people were put off by the way she cut to the truth so quickly, but Rainer had always insisted he found it equally disarming and comforting.

"Maybe a little," he admitted with a shrug.

Cecilia typically left worrying to Rainer, as it came so naturally to him, but the disquieting thought that she and Rainer might return from the Gauntlet to yet another tepid reaction from his father dogged her. Raymond McKay's bullying had turned Rainer into a relentless perfectionist. Even if they succeeded, he would only notice how Rainer's success could benefit his social stature at court. It infuriated her that anyone could ever look at Rainer as currency instead of someone kind, steady, and unbearably lovable.

It made her grateful for her own father, who took such pride in both of them and was generous with his time, attention, and praise. Leo Reznik was both the current leader of the Olney hunter army and a celebrated war hero, and Rainer worshipped him.

As a father, Leo was warm and funny. He'd trained her to hunt, track, spy, fight, and use a bow from the time she was old enough to hold one. He marveled at her skill. By the time she was six, she had accuracy that rivaled hunters who'd been training for longer than she'd been alive. He took special pride in her natural skill. She thought he'd been a bit disappointed when her memory witch abilities showed up, but he always told her how proud he was of her.

"Regardless of what happens, we've made it farther than anyone else. We're a good team," Cecilia said, placing a hand on Rainer's knee.

The sun lit the crescent-shaped scar on the outside of her left palm, making it appear like a bright white moon.

"I wouldn't want to save the kingdom with anyone else." Rainer gave her a dazzling smile.

She rolled her eyes, but the sentiment made butterflies take flight in her stomach.

"What about the huntmaster? He must be proud," Rainer said.

"It's strange. Usually, he's such a mixture of nervous and proud when we go out, but this time he seemed oddly somber. It could be all the rumblings about Argaria assembling around our borders, or maybe he's thinking about what comes after." She hesitated, twirling her fingers in the grass. "Do you ever think about that? What comes next? We save the kingdom by unleashing this old Lost God magic, and then what? It's all downhill from there. You go train some guardians. I train some memory witches. Is that all there is?"

"I like to think that you and I are always going to be having some type of adventures together."

She liked the sound of that dream, but it was just that—a dream. When the Gauntlet concluded, they would both be expected to get married and start families. Everything would be different. They had been the biggest fixture in each other's lives for sixteen years.

They studied, trained, and grew up side by side. Rainer looked out for Cecilia, and in her own way, she looked out for him, too. Imagining a world without him as such a constant in her life was painful.

"I've been thinking about what it's going to be like when we get back and we're not together all the time," Cecilia said.

"Cece, I won't let that happen. You're my best friend. Nothing is going to change."

She looked at him skeptically.

"Worrying won't give you answers. It'll just give your mind a thousand paths to go down with no ends to any of them. Trust me, I know. Nothing will ever take me away from being your best friend, Cece. You and me are a pair, so whatever very lucky bastard you end up with better get used to that idea."

Cecilia laughed. "Oh gods! You're going to be such a nightmare once I actually have suitors."

"Do you want suitors? I've never heard you talk about it before."

Cecilia twirled a curl around her finger. "No one's ever really shown an interest in me. They just make offers to my father. Plus, you've scared off the few who have flirted with me, Rain. Hardly anyone talks to me except you. I don't think anyone notices me. It doesn't help that I'm always standing next to Sylvie."

"Trust me, Cece, they notice. Wicked bow skills and those big blue eyes. I think you could have pretty much any guardian at court."

Rainer was so earnest, but the only guy's attention she wanted was his.

"But how could anyone compare to Rainer McKay?" She faked a swoon.

"Well, obviously no one can, but you can't hold that against them. If you want suitors, I will send them your way."

Cecilia frowned. Suitors were the last thing she wanted to worry about with the ball in just a few hours. "If you send me suitors, then I won't be there to be your buffer when you inevitably upset your next conquest."

"Good point. Perhaps the husband-hunting will have to wait a bit." He smirked.

She slapped his arm.

Rainer laughed. "Come on. I should get you back. You're covered in mud, and we're going to be late for Godsball. Wouldn't want you to miss your first dance."

She cringed, thinking about her inevitable first dance at the ball, hundreds of eyes fixed on her as she stumbled her way through the steps with whatever hunter had won her father's solstice contest. For the winner, it was a great honor, but for Cecilia, it was a palm-sweating nightmare.

"I still don't see why I shouldn't be able to compete for my own hand to win the honor of not being scrutinized by the entire court," she grumbled.

In fact, she'd done just that when she'd turned eighteen and been permitted to attend the dance for the first time. She'd ended up in the arms of the runner-up anyway.

Rainer laughed. "And deny all of those hunters the ability to embarrass you in the one place you don't excel?"

Cecilia covered her face with her hands, thinking about it.

"Don't stress. What you lack in grace, you make up for in pure enthusiasm," Rainer said, biting back a laugh. "Race you back?"

She was already mounting her horse.

Cecilia beat him back to the stables. She stood there gloating in her mud-stained boots and leggings when he arrived a minute later.

"I think you should just go to the party in that," Rainer teased, pulling a stray pine needle from her hair. He tucked a loose lock of hair behind her ear, sending her heart racing.

If only he wasn't so handsome and so sweet to her. Perhaps then it would be easy to remember that he was entirely off-limits. After all, witches of the Olney Court were forbidden from having anything other than professional relationships with their assigned guardian.

Years ago, after too many witches and their guardians became distracted by romance, King Hector Teripin had banned dalliances between them. The idea was to focus duos on completing the Gauntlet instead of each other. Now, any witch and guardian relationship that was discovered resulted in the immediate severing of their bond by a seer—a rare but excruciatingly painful process. One of them would be banished while the other was forced to remain in Olney in shame. Although the rules were selectively enforced, they were enough of a deterrent to most duos. Nevertheless, some witches and guardians got away with pretty obvious relationships.

Cecilia couldn't imagine the pain of being separated from Rainer that way. As far as she knew, there was only one soul-bound duo who had been separated. It ended in tragedy when the witch was so distraught from the loss of her connection and the banishment of her guardian that she leapt from a cliff into the Adiran Sea.

It was just one reason she didn't press the issue of romance with Rainer. Though it didn't diminish how much she wanted to.

She smiled at him. His eyes sparkled, and his messy dark hair was wild from riding.

"What?"

Cecilia snapped herself out of her daze. "You look like just as much of a mess, too."

"I guess it's a good thing I don't have to look like an elegant lady then, Lady Mudpie." Rainer faked a bow.

She slapped his arm. He threw her over his shoulder, carrying her out of the stables. She squirmed, trying to get out of his grip, pounding her fists on his back until he drew up short. When she craned her neck, she saw her father standing in front of them.

"Good evening, Huntmaster," Rainer said.

"Rainer, do you want to put my daughter down so she can at least attempt to be on time for once?"

It didn't matter that he had a soft spot for Rainer. Leo Reznik was the kind of man who could put the fear of the gods into the fiercest of warriors. Rainer slowly lowered Cecilia to the ground.

"Hi, Dad," she said.

Leo's eyes washed over her muddy attire.

"Your Aunt Clara is going to be livid," Leo said. "We need to talk."

He tried to sound stern, but his smile broke through. He loved that she was wild, loved that she was more skilled than he with a bow and equally fearless.

Rainer took his dismissal. "Save me a dance, Cece?"

She rolled her eyes. Rainer had no problem getting women to dance with him. They loved his gregarious personality and startling good looks. What he wanted was for her to protect him from whichever court lady he'd pissed off that week. Rainer broke hearts, and Cecilia helped him manage the damage.

"Only if I can sleep in tomorrow."

Rainer nodded and then dashed off to his apartment as Cecilia relished the small victory.

Cecilia turned to her father with a grin. "If this is about my first dance tonight, I swear I practiced all week, and I'm ready."

Leo pursed his lips and said the last words she wanted to hear. "We need to talk about your marriage prospects."

2

Cecilia groaned and threaded her arm through her father's waiting elbow. She watched him out of the corner of her eye as they walked past the gardens toward the main house on their estate. His brow pinched in sorrow, his dark eyes focused on the vibrant garden around them instead of her face.

"Times like these, I wish your mother was here. Rosalee was much better at getting to the heart of things than I have ever been."

Grief washed over her at the mention of her late mother, extinguishing her fiery spirit. She leaned her head on her father's shoulder, sensing the murky flow of his grief mixed with her own.

Cecilia had always sensed emotions, but it was a gift she kept to herself for much of her life, afraid of further alienating herself. Sincerity was warm and bright like sunshine. Anger was sharp and burning hot like a forge. Grief was sluggish, like being caught in molasses. There was a language to the feelings that surrounded people that took her years to learn, but it always showed their truths. Her instructors wrote it off as generic empathic gifts, though they hardly felt like gifts to Cecilia at the time. She couldn't control picking up on them, and she struggled to learn what belonged to her and what belonged to people around her.

"Cece, I have raised you to be a smart, talented, strategic young woman. I like to think I've given you your fighting spirit, if nothing else."

Cecilia laughed. It was the only thing she had in common with either of her parents. Where they both had tan skin, dark eyes, and light hair—her father's even lighter now with more streaks of silver—Cecilia's skin was fair and dotted with freckles, her eyes were bright blue, and her hair was a mess of wild dark curls that grew redder in the sun. Sometimes she caught him staring at her, as if trying to find himself or perhaps her mother in her face.

"I've given you a lot of leeway these past few years because you've earned it, but it's time that we have an honest conversation about the future," her father said. "You know that I have had more than a few offers for your hand. I need to know if there's anyone I should hold out for."

Cecilia smothered a giggle with her hand. "You think I have some secret love affair *you* aren't aware of?" She stopped and forced him to face her head on. "Why not just say what you mean?"

"I love Rainer like a son. He's a good man, even if his father is a conniving weasel. He's grown into a tremendous warrior, and it brings me peace to know how he looks out for you." Leo hesitated, rubbing his chin. "But it would do you good to get some distance through this next Gauntlet run."

Cecilia crossed her arms. "Rain is my friend."

"Whom you're in love with."

She looked down at her feet, drawing a sad face in the mud with her boot. "Please don't ask me to do this."

"You will likely find your circumstances changed once you return from your trip. I don't want to see you heartbroken or ruined. Your reputation will be delicate as we navigate these next few months, and you can't keep fixating on the one guardian you can't have when there are plenty of others you can."

"Why the sudden urgency to marry me off?" Cecilia asked.

"You're twenty-two, Cecilia. This is hardly your first marriageable season. I have postponed this inevitability as long as I can. I would like it to be a decision we make together and not one I make for you. Will you work with me instead of against me?"

The request was a betrayal. The very man who had stoked her fighting spirit into a vicious beast that snarled inside her chest wanted her to settle. Frustration swelled inside her, her skin a size too small for her wild soul.

No matter how much the kingdom relied on her strength in the field, when she married, she'd be expected to act powerless. A good Olney wife was humble, supplicant, and obedient—qualities she found unnatural on a good day.

Though Cecilia regularly walked into caves full of unpredictable ancient magic, she found marriage a more terrifying prospect. She'd woken one morning and suddenly people expected her to want what every other lady in the kingdom did, but the tameness of that life made her feel feral. Marriage seemed a tool used to contain women, all while convincing them they'd gained valuable proof of their worthiness. Yet every other courtly lady seemed content to think of love as a magic that only existed in exchange for ownership.

She'd always been someone else's—first, the huntmaster's daughter. Next, she'd become some man's wife. She would never belong to herself. The wildness inside her reared up at the thought of being caged in such a way.

For years she'd collected memories of exciting lives and adventures, held them in the vault of her mind like they were her own, but she'd done so little living. To know what was out there, then be told to stay still, was maddening.

Leo swallowed hard, his face clouding with grief. "If Rosalee were here, I know she'd have a more delicate approach."

Cecilia's instinct was to fight, but the mention of her mother guilted her into silence. Her father was doing his best. He'd put off every offer he'd received for the last four years.

"You're so good with the young witches in training. Don't you want to have children of your own? I'd love to have some grandchildren to train."

"Maybe I'm not cut out for mothering," she muttered.

The words were deflection. She loved children and wanted a family, but she wanted adventure before she settled down. Not to mention that every time she tried to picture her future family, the only person she could imagine beside her was Rainer.

Her father's face grew grim.

"What aren't you saying?" Cecilia asked.

Leo cleared his throat. "There have been more disturbances than usual along our borders. King Hector may ask me to head out and see to it myself soon. I'm aware that you can take care of yourself. I'd simply feel better seeing you settled with someone I know will be good to you."

Her whole life, her father had managed the military training and strategy while the fieldwork was left to his battalion captains. Imagining him on the front lines at his age was filled Cecilia with dread.

She swallowed hard. "What do you need me to do?"

"Just for tonight, please try to appear interested in your suitors. Dance with someone who isn't Rainer. I'm not asking you to marry them. I'm asking you to present the appearance of a woman who is interested in her prospects instead of one who resents them for even attempting."

"But I'm not interested in any of the offers I've received—"

"You don't have to be. Cece, I am asking you to trust me. Have I ever led you wrong before? Have I ever made decision for your future without consulting you?"

Cecilia crossed her arms. "Why should I have to consult you about *my* future?"

Leo sighed heavily. "I don't make the rules. I'm just an old man trying to navigate them as well as I can for my beautiful, willful daughter. Please, my little storm." The term of endearment hooked into her heart. "Just for tonight."

She reluctantly nodded. "Fine. I'll dance with anyone who asks. I'll wear whatever dress Aunt Clara has made, and I'll act like all the other empty-headed ladies at the dance."

Leo chuckled. "Nothing would make me happier. Now run along

and get washed up. Your Aunt Clara is very excited about your dress and mask, so don't give her a hard time."

Cecilia kissed him on the cheek and ducked into the manor to get ready.

———

Cecilia stared into the looking glass as her Aunt Clara fixed her mask in place, tying the golden ribbons into her elaborate coronet braid before weaving in some greens and white flowers.

"It's perfect. You look so beautiful," Clara said, stepping back to take in the full look. Her eyes were glassy with unshed tears.

Leo's sister, Clara had helped raise Cecilia, stepping in after Rosalee died. Now she seemed to think it was her personal responsibility to fuss enough to make up for Rosalee's absence.

"Don't start," Cecilia said.

Cecilia frowned at her transformation from muddy huntress to proper lady in an itchy seafoam-green dress with organza flowers at the top of each shoulder. Perhaps it was a good thing she didn't look like herself—the dress like armor for facing down the assault of courtly judgment.

She ran her fingers over her mask—the same shade of green with golden embroidery of a bow and arrows dotted around the edges to pay homage to Sayla, goddess of the hunt.

Each year, the Godsball masquerade kicked off the Olney summer solstice festival, and all who attended honored the gods by dressing in the likeness of their favorite. Sayla was an easy choice for Cecilia because of the goddess's talent with a bow. The costume also allowed her to carry her dagger on her thigh and pretend it was part of her costume.

"I think you'll break some hearts tonight," Clara said, clapping her hands.

"Here's hoping," Cecilia said, morosely following her aunt down the hall to the front door.

"Run along. I'm sure Sylvie will delight that you're fashionably late," Clara said, shooing her out the door. "We'll see you at the ball."

Cecilia stepped outside and nearly ran into Rainer.

"Cece," he said breathlessly. Though she'd seen him an hour before, the vision of him in a fine hunter-green tunic with golden embroidery and his hair neatly combed was devastating. "You look nice."

Her cheeks heated as she took in the detail on his tunic and mask. Stacks of books and map markings dotted his clothing.

"You're Devlin." Cecilia laughed. "So bookish."

Rainer's outfit honored logical Devlin, god of wisdom and reason, who'd helped the kingdom chart their geography and record their history.

Rainer became obsessed with mythology around the time they started the Gauntlet, taking a particular interest in Devlin's writings. He never explained his sudden fascination, but Cecilia found it adorable. Sometimes she asked him questions about the gods just to listen to him launch into complex stories about them.

He held out his arm to guide her down the walkway to the Brett family estate to pick up her other best friend, Sylvie.

While Rainer and Cecilia had the natural closeness of their bond, she and Sylvie connected over magic. Like Cecilia, Sylvie was a memory witch and understood the way that trying to complete the Gauntlet and fit in at court felt like switching between two oppositional identities, though Sylvie had always managed it with more ease.

"So, did you get in trouble for being late?" Rainer asked.

Cecilia shook her head. "Nope. Just Dad being Dad."

Rainer looked at her expectantly, but she took the rest of the walk in silence. Sylvie was waiting in her garden with her younger sister, Vera.

"Gods, Cece, you look gorgeous," Sylvie said.

"You say it like it's a surprise."

Sylvie grinned. "Are we going to act like you didn't try to wear pants one year?"

"Pants?" Vera said, her eyes wide. "Why would you wear pants?"

"To be fair, it was pants with a sheer dress overlay. That dress was a masterpiece that looked like a swirling tempest. I still don't see why I couldn't go to the ball as the Storm Prince."

Rainer sighed. "Not this again."

Cecilia grinned at Vera. "I was your age, Vera. It was my first Godsball, and I loved the story of the Storm Prince, and while I know he's not technically one of the gods, some of the stories claim he's Endros's son, so I thought I could get away with it. But Rainer, being the fun-sucker that he is, shared my plans with my father, and I was forced to go as Sayla instead."

Sylvie pursed her lips. "Who you've gone as every year since."

"You're one to talk. You always go as Desiree," Cecilia said.

"That's because I enjoy reminding men that my beauty rivals the goddess of love. Plus, Vera was already going as Adira, and we couldn't both go as the goddess of the sea. I wouldn't want to outshine her in her first season," Sylvie said, ignoring her sister's eye roll.

While Cecilia thought of marriage as a cage, Sylvie saw it as a chess game. Memory magic was far from Sylvie's only power. She moved the men of the court around her like pieces in an elaborate game to win her heart. She wasn't cruel, she just knew how to use the considerable assets the gods had given her, and Cecilia didn't blame her for using men's weaknesses against them in a world that provided them such startling advantages.

Sylvie was the master of her own form of combat. It took place not in a training ring but at balls, teas, and other social gatherings. She was stunning—tall and curvy, with shiny blonde hair, clear blue eyes, and a natural elegance that made her very popular at court. Where Cecilia swung between extremes, Sylvie was temperate. Where Sylvie rarely left the dance floor, Cecilia clung to the edges of the ballroom. And while Cecilia couldn't seem to shake her feelings for the one person she couldn't have, Sylvie held command of her heart.

"Are we waiting for Cal?" Rainer asked.

"He said he'd meet me at the ball. He knows I prefer to make an entrance on my own," Sylvie said.

The foursome followed the short trail to town and entered the large white tent in the Olney Castle courtyard. Humidity hung in the air, even as the sun sank low on the horizon. Olney summers were brutally hot and humid, and the evenings brought little relief.

The Godsball kicked off a weeklong festival honoring the gods and the history of Olney.

Inside the tent, Rainer tapped his fingers to his forehead, lips, and heart in respect as they passed shrines to the gods. Cecilia mimicked him, more out of habit than devotion. She had faith, but most of these events felt like a performance rather than true homage.

All of Olney's living gods died centuries ago in the War of the Gods that divided Olney and Argaria, or shortly thereafter. Though many people claimed to feel their influence in the world, Cecilia had never looked at the raging sea and seen Adira's anger, or felt Sayla's steady hand on hers when she was practicing with her bow on the shooting range, and she'd certainly never witnessed Desiree's inspiration coaxing Rainer to reciprocate her feelings. In Cecilia's mind, the only true godly magic left in their world was woven through the Gauntlet caves, and the war that the last living gods, Endros and Cato, stirred up along Olney's northern border with Argaria.

Walking into the tent was like walking into a whole new world: hundreds of colored lanterns scattered hung from the roof of the tent, and each table had large floral centerpieces sprinkled with candles. It was beautiful but over the top.

A servant guided them to three thrones where King Hector Teripin, Queen Elena, and their son, Prince Marcos, waited.

"Lady Cecilia Reznik and Guardian Rainer McKay," the servant announced.

Cecilia dipped into a curtsey and Rainer bowed.

"Oh, darling, doesn't Cecilia look so lovely," Elena said, patting Hector's arm. "Both of you do. I wish your mothers were here to see. They would be so proud of you two. All grown up and so accomplished."

Cecilia smiled at the queen. Elena Teripin, Rosalee Reznik, and Rainer's mother, Maura McKay, had been close friends growing up. Elena had been a fixture in Cecilia's childhood, though less so since her mother had passed and then hardly at all once Rainer's mother passed several years later. Still, the queen's affection was always apparent when she saw them at court events.

"We hope you'll save a dance for Marcos," Hector said, pointedly giving the prince a side eye. Marcos shifted uncomfortably in his seat, hardly meeting Cecilia's eye.

"I would be honored, Your Grace."

The king waved a hand, dismissing them, and as they turned to enter the fray, her shoulders relaxed.

"I need a—" Before she could finish her sentence, Rainer placed an ice-cold glass in her hand. She sucked it down in a few desperate sips.

"Slow down, Cece. You're going to be drunk before the dancing even starts."

"Not drunk, but hopefully pleasantly buzzed," Cecilia countered as Sylvie and Vera joined them.

"Are you really nervous about your dance?" Sylvie interrupted.

"What dance?" Vera asked.

"When the dancing starts, the king and queen have the first dance, then Marcos will dance with the Solstice Princess—the lady selected for her poise and grace," Sylvie explained. "Then, because she's the esteemed huntmaster's daughter, Cecilia will dance with whichever hunter from her father's army won the solstice hunt games." She looked at Cecilia. "I don't understand why you're so nervous. It's just a hunter."

"It's not that. It's the weight of every eye in the room focused on me."

"I'm still not seeing the problem." Sylvie grinned, stepping up behind them.

"Maybe he'll be handsome," Vera said dreamily.

"Ugh, Vera. That's not the point. It's not as if Cecilia can marry a hunter. She can only marry guardians...or princes," Sylvie said with a feral grin. "I heard the king."

Cecilia blanched. "Oh gods, don't start. Marcos is like a brother to me. I can't think of him that way."

"Is Rainer like that too?" Vera asked, looking from Cecilia to Rainer.

"No," they said in unison.

Rainer looked across the room. "I think I see someone I need to talk to." With that, he was off to hunt down whichever conquest was topping his list for the week.

As soon as Rainer was out of earshot, Sylvie gave Cecilia a delighted grin. "He's so bent out of shape about talk of you marrying someone else, he ran away."

Cecilia crossed her arms. "He is not."

Sylvie's grin grew wide and knowing, but the gods were smiling on Cecilia when Sylvie's guardian, Cal Bennington, saved her with his abrupt entrance.

"Are we talking about McKay?" he asked.

Cecilia shook her head. "Gods, give it a rest, you two."

Sylvie and Cal grinned at each other. The duo were bonded and had a great relationship. They'd secretly dated when they were teenagers, even though it was against the rules, getting the tension out of their systems. They'd lucked out and weren't caught, though it seemed the king was selective in enforcing the rules. Now they were the best of friends, with no awkwardness at all. Cecilia marveled at them.

"I think everyone knows Rain is a stickler for the rules and that he spends a lot of time pretending he doesn't want to break them." Cal smirked.

Cecilia slapped his arm.

Cal shrugged. "I call it like I see it, Rez."

"It's not like that."

Sylvie elbowed her. "Maybe when Rainer sees the competition tonight, he'll finally come to his senses and stop sleeping his way through the court."

Cecilia's cheeks heated. "Sylvie, we can't do that."

"What? There's not a person in the Olney court who doesn't know that Cecilia Reznik loves Rainer McKay. And he sure spends a lot of time and energy trying to pretend he's not in love with you," Sylvie said.

It might have been true, but a crush didn't break the rules. An actual relationship with Rainer would.

"He's not in love with me."

Playing dumb while making people uncomfortable was one of Sylvie's most potent court skills. Cecilia loved watching her do it to other people, but she didn't enjoy being on the receiving end.

A horn blast from the dance floor saved her from Sylvie's taunting. The king and queen made their way to the center of the floor for their customary first dance, and Cecilia grabbed another glass of bubble wine from a passing servant.

King Hector stood in the center of the floor, looking regal in his Clastor regalia. "My loyal Olney family, Queen Elena and I are thrilled to hold this ball in honor of the gods. Although it's been many years since our living gods walked among us, we honor them tonight for the blessings they've given. Though the threat from our northern neighbors is ongoing, we hope to have the power to end it soon with the completion of the Gauntlet."

The crowd erupted into loud cheers, and the king preened in the attention as he signaled the band and he danced with the queen.

Cecilia glanced at the costumed crowd. The masquerade allowed everyone to blend, but they still congregated in classist groups. The masks gave a false illusion of anonymity, since it was easy to pick out status by the quality and extravagance of their dress.

While some dresses gave nods to Goddess Adira of the Sea, most marriageable ladies in the kingdom wore various shades of pink and violet—gowns wrapped in florals and ribbons meant to evoke the spirit of Desiree, goddess of love and beauty. And there was Cecilia dressed in green as the goddess always ready for a fight. She didn't fault other women for being eager to marry and mother, but she resented the idea that there was only one way to be a lady.

To her right, against lush silk drapery and cushioned seating, sat the ladies of the court, the older nobility, and the guardians—most were sons of the wealthiest Olney families, who could afford swordsmanship tutors and hours of training, but some had earned their way in for their elite fighting skills.

Across the tent, in more modest surroundings, stood the elevated common folk: merchants who were in favor with the Teripins and officers Leo Reznik's hunter army.

Though hunters were not marriage material for Cecilia, it didn't keep them from trying to bed her. Her father forbade any of them from coming near her, which only made her more desirable. Hunters thrived on the challenge of conquest, and they knew her well since she trained among them. For the most part, she avoided them, not because she was a snob but because it was difficult to take their intentions seriously, and even socializing with them brought her virtue into question.

She scanned the room for Rainer, wishing he hadn't left her alone so soon. He had a way of soothing her when she was nervous, and he had to feel her anxiety through their bond. She closed her eyes, trying to remember the movements of the dance she'd need to do in mere moments. While the royal duos would each do slower dances, Cecilia and whichever hunter had won her father's contest would do a quick and complicated step dance that was a common choice for bars and folk festivals.

The crowd applauded as the king and queen finished, and Marcos and the Solstice Princess made their way to the center of the dance floor.

Cecilia's heart pounded in her ears, drowning out the music. She frantically searched the crowd for Rainer and spotted him on the far side of the dance floor, next to a beautiful woman in a lilac dress. He bent low and whispered something into her ear, and she laughed daintily.

Cecilia silently begged Rainer to look at her, to close the space between them and comfort her. He knew how nervous this dance made her, and yet he seemed compelled to stay as far from her as possible.

She dried her clammy hands on her dress. She would have rather been in a fighting ring facing off against the biggest burliest hunter than about to step onto that floor.

Her father appeared on the opposite side of the dance floor, just a step away from Rainer, as the crowd applauded Prince Marcos and his partner. Then the huntmaster stepped onto the floor. He looked regal and strong in his blue mask and shirt, which paid tribute to Clastor.

"Ladies and gentlemen, it is my great honor to call my daughter, Cecilia, to the dance floor for her traditional dance with our Solstice Hunter."

Cecilia's eyes flicked around the edges of the dance floor. She searched the crowd for a friendly face, but the smiles of the ladies on the edge of the dance floor turned to sneers as they took in her dress. Worse were the appraising glances from the guardians, eyeing her up as a marriage prospect.

What did they see when they looked at her? A hefty dowry? A spirited girl to be broken? She couldn't imagine any of them would think of her as a partner, and the more they looked her over, the more angry she felt. She clung to her rage like a shield.

It was easier to focus on anger than the fact that some naïve part of her hoped for a love that would sweep her away and rid her of the ache she felt every time she looked at Rainer.

A hunter appeared beside her, dressed in a vibrant scarlet tunic woven through with golden thread. Her father looked momentarily furious as his eyes settled on the hunter, though she noticed nothing unusual about her partner but the fine quality of his clothing.

Leo left the floor, and the musicians lifted their instruments. Cecilia's heart pounded as the hunter took her hand, and panic set in.

3

Cecilia stared at her hand, which looked pale and insubstantial in the hunter's. He said something, but she couldn't hear him over the rush of her heartbeat in her ears.

She gasped as his other hand came to her low back and he pressed her body to his. It was not the starting position for the Olney Step. There should have been plenty of space between them.

The hunter spoke again, but all she could hear over the murmur of the crowd was her thunderous pulse.

"*Cece.*" His insistent voice finally cut through the din. "Look at my eyes."

She met his gaze, and her senses sharpened. She tuned in to the feelings around him, sensing the buzzing of his excitement, and a hint of curiosity.

"Good. Now keep looking and don't look at anyone or anything else until we're done."

Cecilia didn't mind letting him take control when she felt moments from fainting, an embarrassment from which she'd never recover.

"I paid the musicians to change the song," the hunter said. "We'll be doing a Reldan, and I'm leading, so you have nothing to worry about."

She couldn't wrangle the words to argue. The Reldan was a dance of seduction. It was slow and sensual, and she hadn't practiced it in months.

"No, that's stupid." Cecilia's words came out like a dying gasp.

"You'll be fine. Trust me," he whispered as the first note sounded.

"I wouldn't trust you if my life depended on it."

His lips quirked up in a grin as he led her through the first few steps of the dance. She remembered enough to be a passable partner as the hunter guided her into the first dip. He spun her back against his chest, and his lips brushed her ear, sending shivers scattering over her skin.

"You're stiff as a board, Cece. Relax and let me have control. I promise I'll make you look and *feel* good," the hunter whispered as his fingers skimmed up the bare skin of her arm.

All of her nerves dissipated as she spun back to face him, pressing her hips flush to his. She relaxed into him, letting him truly lead for the first time. He was a graceful, confident dancer and certainty seemed to bleed from his body into hers. Her shoulders relaxed, and her grip on his hand and shoulder loosened as she allowed herself more flourishes.

Cecilia ran her fingers down the hunter's chest as she spun away. He pulled her back against him. His hand skimmed over her neck as she leaned her head back on his shoulder, closing her eyes for a breath before he twirled her back. She hooked her leg over his thigh, giving a flash of skin through the slit in her dress as they leaned, then took two quick steps back. Their bodies moved as one, as if made to dance with each other, and her heart quickened more from the desire stoked by his touch than the dance itself. Her skin heated, the buzz in her body growing to a fever pitch with every brush of his fingers.

People claimed the Reldan was a dance of passion, and for the first time in her life, Cecilia understood how simple steps in a dance could seduce and entice. It was like his body was teaching hers something it didn't know yet, but wanted to.

As the music ended, she dropped her head back as the hunter dipped her, before she tucked her chin, meeting his warm hazel eyes again. She couldn't help but smile.

"Gods, you're beautiful," he whispered.

Her cheeks heated, but a hard yank on the connection she shared with Rainer startled her so much she nearly fell right out of the dip. Cecilia's eyes went wide as she remembered an entire room of people were watching.

The hunter pulled her up to stand. She quickly curtseyed, and he bowed to her as the crowd tentatively applauded.

The hunter bent to kiss her hand, meeting her eyes. "Your body moves like it was made for mine, Cece. Find me later if you want to know for sure."

He strode off, leaving her speechless.

The band broke back into song, couples took to the dance floor, and Rainer was on her in seconds.

"Really, Cece, a Reldan?" Rainer whispered, yanking her against his body in the illusion of dance. "I can't believe the way you let him touch you in front of the entire kingdom."

Cecilia intentionally stomped on his toes. "It's a beautiful and sensual dance. What's wrong with changing things up? It was awfully stuffy in here."

Rainer's mouth tugged into a perfect smirk that made her eager to do reckless things. "It hardly sends the message that you're looking for serious suitors."

"Neither does dancing with you." She slammed her foot down on his toes again, and he winced before tripping her and then catching her around the waist before she could fall.

"Don't bullshit me. I know you liked it. I could feel how much you wanted him from clear across the room."

"Perhaps I was just attracted to his confidence."

Rainer rolled his eyes. "Yes, and perhaps he's just attracted to your skill with a bow."

"Well, I wouldn't blame him. I'm an unparalleled talent."

"And so modest," Rainer quipped.

"You don't need to be modest when you're the top-ranked archer in the kingdom."

"Fine, but for someone who has the magic to read people's emotions all the time, you sure miss a lot."

Cecilia grimaced. "Just because I can read people doesn't mean that I do. I have boundaries, and walking around reading people all day would be an exhausting invasion of privacy. I only really notice things from people when what they say doesn't match how they feel. The dissonance between feeling and expression is what I read—like when Nora Belani walks up to me and says it's good to see me, but I feel that she doesn't like that I'm there and wishes she had you to herself."

Rainer rolled his eyes as he moved her around the floor in slightly stilted movements. "That hunter looked like he was moments from sweeping you off to his bed."

No one else would have seen it, but she'd been studying Rainer McKay her whole life. She knew all the secret things written on his face, like the words to their favorite fairy tales. Rainer tried to keep his emotions in, but jealousy snuck through. She felt a thrill of satisfaction in turning the tables on him for once. She pressed on, even though she didn't understand why some wounded part of her wanted to lash out at the person she loved.

"Perhaps I should have let him."

Rainer's grip tightened on her hand. "Is this what happens when I leave you alone too long? Someone swoops in and steals you from me?"

"I'm not yours, Rain." She wished the words were true.

They stood suspended for a beat. It was satisfying seeing him disoriented for once. Rainer had a way of making every stumble look like an intentional choice.

He quickly recovered, pulling her back before spinning her. "I know that, Cece, but it doesn't mean I like someone else having you."

Fury burned through her like a fever, the heat of it opening their connection wide, the way powerful emotions always did.

"You're angry," he said.

She pressed her lips together, willing herself not to say anything, and failing. "Rain, you have *everything*. You sleep with a different girl every week and then use me to insulate you from the chaos you leave in your wake. Every time you sense anyone getting close to me, you feel a need to step in and yank me back from any happiness that might be just my own. You can't stand the idea of someone taking my attention away from *you*. Rainer McKay has to be the center of everyone's world. Why can't you just let me have this one thing without cheapening it?"

She didn't care that her words hurt him. Maybe it was the wine, or maybe the hunter's offer made her bold. Maybe it just felt good to have something to get her mind off the fact that she couldn't have Rainer.

"I was nervous, and he made me feel at ease. I thought you'd want that for me."

As the song ended, he pulled her close, his breath hot on her ear. "I've never seen you look more lovely. I saw you tonight, and I hated the idea of anyone else having you when you look like you do right now."

The words kicked her heart into a frenzy. She suspected he said it more to keep her attention on him than to show genuine interest in her. Rainer could be so vain.

Cecilia turned on her heel and stormed away, ignoring him when he called after her as she walked out of the tent into the maze of the queen's garden. She breezed by exotic orchids, ivy walls, and rare tropical florals until she reached her favorite spot on a bench by the queen's roses.

For once, she was actually trying to improve her chances of making a match, and yet she'd made a fool of herself already. Tears threatened, and she blinked her eyes, trying to force them back with deep breaths. A cool wind kicked up, rustling the trees and bushes in the garden, and clouds churned overhead.

Oh gods, not now, she begged. *Please don't let me conjure with my humiliation. That's a step too far.*

She'd already summoned a storm by accident during morning

training. Twice in one day would be a record. Pulling back hard on her magic, she let out a growl of frustration as nothing changed.

Then, mercifully, the storm dissipated.

"Bad night?"

The deep, warm voice startled Cecilia.

"Just a bad moment, but I'd rather not have any company right now, hunter." Cecilia blinked rapidly and kept her gaze straight ahead. A hunter seeing her in tears would only add to her humiliation.

"I could be anyone. What makes you think I'm a hunter?"

She still didn't turn to look at him.

"Only a hunter would hide out in the queen's garden during the party."

"Is that so?" The hunter sat down on the bench behind her, but she still didn't turn to look at him. If she'd met one hunter, she'd met them all, and they were a rakish lot.

"You walk like a hunter. No footfalls. Silent as death," she said.

"Very impressive. And what should I call you?" he asked.

"Not for you."

She smiled in response to his warm chuckle.

"If you were any good at your job, you'd know who I was. If you don't know me, I'm definitely not interested in getting to know you because you won't last long in your line of work," she started.

The words were harsh but true. Hunters relied on sharp instincts and being well informed.

"And if you do know who I am, you must have a death wish because that would also mean you know who my father is."

"I know who you are. I make it a point to know the most beautiful woman in the room, Cecilia Reznik."

"If my father caught you talking to me out here, he'd—"

"Do no worse than you could if I got out of line," he finished. "Your reputation precedes you, Lady Reznik. Plus, you have your dagger on you, correct?"

She heard the smile in his voice. She wanted to turn around and see it, but she enjoyed the mystery.

"How do you know about the dagger?" she asked.

"Lucky guess. You usually wear it. Can never be too careful with all these drunk hunters running around."

Cecilia laughed and finally turned to look at him and met the same hazel eyes that had held hers throughout their dance. "You," she breathed. "I'm not here for what you suggested."

Just voicing the words aloud seemed to heat the air between them. Desire buzzed around both of them like the crackle before a storm, and she couldn't tell who was generating the feeling.

The corner of the hunter's lips twitched. "Oh?"

Cecilia searched frantically for anything to take the heat out of the moment. It was not appropriate for her to be alone in the queen's garden with any man, but especially not a hunter.

"Endros," she stammered with a breathless laugh. "Of course your mask is for the god of war."

It was a bold choice. Endros and his son Cato, the god of manipulation and influence, were the last of the living gods who still inhabited their realm. Although they'd been involved in the kingdom's creation, they'd sided with Argaria in the War of the Gods, and almost no one in Olney had the guts to honor them at the Godsball. Still, it was an appropriate choice for a pompous hunter looking to make a statement.

"Who else would I be?" he asked, brushing his hand down his fine scarlet tunic.

"I don't know. You seemed plenty prepared to flirt. Perhaps you should have gone with Desiree, like so many ladies of the court."

The hunter grinned. "Would you prefer to think of me as more of a lover than a fighter, *Cece*?"

He spoke her name like it was a dirty word. She was glad for the darkness to hide her heated cheeks.

"I'd prefer not to think of you at all."

The hunter was unfazed. "What brought you out here in such a huff if not to find out if our bodies move together just as perfectly in the dark?"

Cecilia blushed, feeling foolish for even considering pouring her heart out to a stranger.

"Is it your guardian, who enjoys toying with you so much?"

"Rainer does not toy with me." *Yes, he does.*

"Looked like he did in there. Just one dance and you went from glowing to crying."

Cecilia bristled. "Don't you have better things to do than watch me all night?"

"It was impossible to keep my eyes off you while we were dancing. If you're looking for advice—"

"I'm not."

"So that's why you're still talking to me?"

"I'm not," Cecilia huffed. "I just wanted some air. You're the one driving this conversation, and apparently, watching me all the time."

"I only watch you enough to know how much you like these roses. You come here when you're upset. Why is that?"

Cecilia pressed her palms to her eyes. Over the years, her father had assigned several hunters to monitor her, and he must have been the latest. She kicked herself for not noticing sooner.

She flushed. "You sure ask a lot of invasive questions. What's your name, anyway?"

"Cece!" Sylvie called, drawing Cecilia's attention to the garden trail.

When she turned back, the hunter was gone. She wondered if she'd imagined him. In his place was a lemon cake atop a cloth napkin with a tiny, folded paper bird that read: *Didn't want you to miss dessert.*

She had no clue when he'd found a moment to steal her dessert or write a note, but she was charmed. Cecilia fought a grin as her gaze darted around the periphery for the hunter, who had clearly been watching her enough to know her favorite dessert. She tucked the note into her dress.

"Cece, what are you doing out here alone? It's not safe," Sylvie said as she sat down beside her on the bench.

"Just trying to cool down." Cecilia sighed, giving up her search for the hunter.

Sylvie took Cecilia's hand. "What did Rain do now? I saw him jerking you around the dance floor."

"He's infuriating. It's like he has a sense for when I'm even the least bit distracted by someone else, and he has to ruin it."

"He's jealous." Sylvie sighed. "You two constantly circle each other. You get close, he runs away. It's like the world's most exhausting game of tag."

Cecilia shook her head. "That's ridiculous. If he cared for me the same way, he wouldn't tell me about all of his conquests."

"I love you. Normally you are so wise, but Rainer is your blind spot. He only tells you about other girls to keep you at a distance, because if he doesn't, he's going to just keep getting closer and closer until the two of you finally lose it and give in to what you both so obviously feel."

Cecilia shook her head, but Sylvie pressed on.

"He sleeps in your bed every night. He wouldn't be there if he didn't have feelings for you. Cal is my guardian and best friend, but you won't find him cuddling with me. It's not a job requirement. Rainer's obsessed with his duty now, but what happens when you finish the Gauntlet? In theory, he's no longer sworn to you except in battle. Would it really be out of the question for you two to be together?"

Sylvie sounded so certain. Cecilia had avoided thinking too much about what came next, mostly because this portion of the Gauntlet was so dangerous that it felt like tempting fate to make future plans. Although Rainer slept in her bed every night, he did nothing other than tell bedtime stories and leave before dawn so no one would know he'd been there.

"I don't think that's it, and even if he felt that way, he's such a stickler for the rules," Cecilia said, picking at a loose thread on her hem.

"My dear friend, love makes fools of the best of us. Sometimes I wonder how much you know your own heart."

"Can you ever really know your own heart?"

Sylvie sighed. "I don't think you give yourself enough credit. Your heart is your true north, always. Follow it and see where it leads. It might be somewhere surprising. Now, do you want to go home, or do you want to go back inside and dance with a very long line of guardians who saw that extremely sensual Reldan you did with the hunter and are dying to dance with the loveliest Goddess Sayla at the party?"

Cecilia laughed and stood, lacing her arm through Sylvie's as she made her way back inside. Rainer might have spoiled one dance, but she refused to give him the satisfaction of ruining her entire night. She'd promised her father she'd see what was out there, and she was a woman of her word.

4

The Olney City Center Amphitheater was alive with whispers and bustling bodies rushing to their seats. Torches burned bright along the perimeter, illuminating rows of seats cascading down the hillside toward the stage as night two of the Olney summer solstice festival kicked off with a performance of *The Gauntlet's Creation*.

Normally Cecilia looked forward to seeing her favorite childhood story performed on stage, but the heat, and the constant attention and Rainer's lateness wore on her. She shifted in her seat, patting down the puff of organza flowers on her one-shoulder gown. She kept catching glimpses of them out of the corner of her eye, evoking the memory of the hunter from the previous night sneaking up on her.

Her gaze settled on three women from court around her age who sat two rows in front of her. Though modesty was expected of courtly ladies, there was no shortage of skin on display. Nicola Logan, Fiona Ratel, and Angeline Flynn were all perfectly coiffed, and Cecilia wondered if they were just as uncomfortable.

"In her fourth season and she still has no suitors," Nicola whispered to her friends. "It's just not heard of for a highborn woman with so many resources and properties."

Normally Cecilia avoided court gossip, but she leaned closer, curious who they were speaking about.

"I know her father is the huntmaster, but she's always out rolling around in those filthy fighting rings with the men, so what does she expect? How could anyone see her as a wife and mother when she insists on being a brute?" Fiona whispered with a disgusted sneer.

Angeline giggled. "Truly. Who does she think she's fooling with a few new dresses? She's more wild beast than lady. Remember when it came out that those hunters took bets on who could claim her virginity and the huntmaster had them all banished? Even they would only approach her for sport."

Cecilia sat back, her cheeks burning. At least on the battlefield she could learn to work around her shortcomings. At court they were forever on display—her height lacking, her breasts ordinary, her backside too large. Her flaws were endless, and other ladies were delighted to offer them in whispers behind her back or as underhanded compliments to her face.

She thought sitting in the back of the theater rather than her father's box next to the Teripins up front would allow her to escape scrutiny. She'd appeased her father enough by dancing with fifteen guardians the night before, her cheeks still aching from the smile she'd plastered on her face all evening, but she hadn't fooled the cruel ladies of the court.

She swallowed the lump in her throat as Rainer filed into his seat next to her, tugging on their connection, trying to feel out her mood.

"What's wrong?" He unpacked their basket of snacks, handing Cecilia a lemon cake.

"Nothing."

He lifted an eyebrow.

"You came in after I was asleep last night and left before I woke up," Cecilia murmured, keeping her voice low.

"I figured you were still mad since you danced with other

guardians the rest of the night. I thought I would give you some space," he whispered.

"So you were too chicken to face me?" She tried to make it sound light.

Rainer gave her a sheepish smile. "You're scary when you're mad, Cece."

"Big warrior like you afraid of a little witch like myself?" she teased. "I missed story time."

Rainer grinned at the mention of the nightly tradition they hadn't grown out of since they were children. The tension eased in his broad shoulders.

"I'll make it up to you tonight. I've got a good one I'm working on." He looked over the crowd with the same caution he did when they were out in the wild.

"Afraid an Argarian hunter is going to pop out of the audience and attack?"

Rainer's face relaxed. "Perhaps just the hunter you shared that dance with last night."

"He's hardly a threat."

Rainer shook his head and sighed. "Maybe not to your life."

Cecilia opened her mouth to speak but immediately shut it when Nora Belani entered their row and gracefully tucked herself into the seat on the other side of Rainer. Nora's dark hair was perfectly styled in a sleek updo and stood out against her purple dress. He turned to welcome her with a warm smile.

Cecilia frowned and waved down a whiskey vendor, grabbing two and dropping coins in his jar.

"Cece, a courtly lady wouldn't be drinking two whiskeys at a time," Rainer teasingly scolded.

She combined them into one glass, handing him the empty. "Call me a problem solver."

"Hi, Cece," Nora said. "I hope you don't mind me sitting with you two. Rain invited me."

Cecilia forced a smile. "It's nice to see you, Nora. I didn't realize you'd be joining us."

Rainer turned to Nora. "I was just getting to it."

Cecilia turned her attention back to the stage. A hush fell over the restless crowd as a man in an elaborate robe strode to the center to the stage.

"Long ago, when our world was young, the gods descended into mortal form and lived among men, helping to build the kingdom of Olnargaria. For a time, there was peace, and then—as it always did—greed made fools of wise men and gods alike. The result was a war between gods, a kingdom split in two, and the series of seventy-seven caves holding ancient magic that became the Gauntlet."

Behind the narrator, six actors stepped onto the stage, two in godly costumes and four dressed as the four witches who created the Gauntlet.

"Ash Rivers, Raven Whitewind, Petra Ryan Light, and Selene Carrick traveled through the kingdoms with Clastor and Cato at their side. Cato, the Trickster, had convinced Clastor that to find peace, he would have to sacrifice some of his power so he would be equal with Endros. But Clastor was wise. He knew Endros didn't want peace. The god of war only wanted him weak. Still, the witches filtered Clastor's magic into each cave, leaving behind a series of memories meant to be used to access it. They hoped that the first person to complete all the caves would release that power back to the people of his or her kingdom. Seventy-seven stops through all parts of the split kingdoms, they ensured neither kingdom would have easier access to the power of the Lost God and that it would eventually bring peace."

The players took over, portraying the Gauntlet's creation and the witches' return home to realize they'd failed in stopping the war. From there, the story became political, and Cecilia's mind wandered until the intermission torch was lit and the spectators stirred.

"It always struck me as strange that Clastor would accept Cato's help in creating the Gauntlet since they were on opposite sides of the war," Nora said.

She looked expectantly at Rainer as if she was trying to follow a script on engaging a suitor in pleasant conversation.

Cecilia deserved an award for not rolling her eyes.

Rainer smiled at Nora indulgently. "Some scholars believe it was a trick of his own. That Clastor allowed Cato to believe he'd done something when Clastor only pretended to give up his power."

"Okay, Scholar McKay," Cecilia teased. "Where do we sign up for the next lecture?"

Rainer's cheeks pinked slightly.

"That's so interesting. Tell me more," Nora said.

Rainer nodded and continued with more detail. Nora laughed at perfect intervals, and Rainer preened. Flirtation came naturally to Nora, and Cecilia couldn't understand why Rainer wanted the performance of it. Of course Cecilia thought he was smart, but she didn't fawn over his intelligence.

Cecilia stood abruptly. "I think I'm going to get some air before the second act." She hustled out of their row, whiskey in hand, without waiting for a response.

The tension finally released from her shoulders once she made it out of the theater. Shops, bars, and boarding houses lined the busy streets, and though most were closed for the festival, people spilled from taverns and brothels that were busier than ever. Tents lined the streets in front of the businesses that sold food and beverages, each offering special solstice-based delicacies—bright summer wines, delicious peach tarts, lemon cakes, light summer ales. Cecilia passed them all by, making her way into the queen's garden until she reached her favorite bench.

Her heart pounded in anticipation, imagining the hunter following her. The way the hunter's attention stoked Rainer's jealousy was thrilling, and part of her wanted a taste of rebellion to prove that she still had it in her after appeasing her father the night before. It was easier to reckon with those two parts of herself than to admit she was also inexplicably drawn to the hunter.

She ran her hand over her bodice and looked up at the hazy night sky. The humidity stuck to her skin, but it felt good to be away from the crowd in the theater.

"Good evening, Cece. Were you looking forward to another chat?" The voice cut out from the dark behind her.

She spun on the bench to find the hunter. Tonight, he wore a hunter-green uniform along with the same mask he'd worn the previous night.

"That's presumptuous." She smiled. "Maybe I just really enjoy the roses."

The hunter laughed. "I suppose you're right. You are your own woman."

"I wish." Cecilia sighed. "I wish I was my own anything."

This hunter might have enjoyed her company, but the men in her father's army didn't like being bested by a woman and never treated her like anything but a nuisance.

"Why are you here?"

"Curiosity," the hunter said.

"Still hiding your identity, I see. You must be hideous," she teased.

The hunter scoffed. "Hardly." He closed the distance between them, sitting on the bench behind her.

They sat in silence for a moment.

"Did you always want to be a hunter?" she asked.

"No."

His quick response surprised her.

"What did you want to be?" She took a long sip of her whiskey. The warmth spread through her, and she felt a bit drunk.

"A prince."

Cecilia laughed.

"That's funny?"

"It's just more of a career you're born into than one you can choose."

The hunter shrugged. "Yes, I suppose that's the problem. It sounded like fun to me. You get all the benefits of being royal without the pressure of having to run a country. You're rich, and you get to choose how to spend your time."

She took another gulp of whiskey. "So hunter was the next best choice?"

"It was what I was good at. Did you always want to be a memory witch?"

"No. I wanted to be a hunter like my father. I think he wanted me to be one as well. It was a surprise when my magic showed up."

"And do you like it now?"

Cecilia set her half-empty whiskey glass beside her and played with the hem of her dress. "I wish I had more control over my life. I think if I could choose anything in this world, I'd choose to be a man, regardless of profession."

He laughed. "You think that would give you more options?"

"Of course," Cecilia said. "We're all victims to our place in this world, but men run the kingdom. People listen when they speak. They choose who they marry. No one tells them what to wear or how to act. People excuse their violence and destructive behavior. They decide the laws and how the world runs."

"So, you value choice."

"Don't you?"

"I guess I've never bothered thinking about impossible things. Being a dreamer doesn't suit me."

"Other than dreaming of being a prince?" Cecilia quipped.

The hunter grinned, drawing her attention to the dimples in his cheeks. "I like to think I at least have the charm of a prince."

"Perhaps you are more of a dreamer than you give yourself credit for," Cecilia teased.

The hunter chuckled, his laugh as smooth as her whiskey. "I enjoy your quick wit."

"I'm glad someone does. It's not often an attribute the court values in a lady. Truly though, hunters have the most choice of anyone. You choose where you're stationed, your specialty, and you can marry who you want. There are no expectations of building some kind of alliance or trying to raise your station through marriage."

"But we only have the choice at our own level. I couldn't ever ask a lady for her hand."

Cecilia turned away to hide her heated cheeks, at a loss for a clever comeback. He was so still that if she hadn't felt the heat of him so close behind her, she might have thought he left.

"It's frustrating that I spent my whole life pursuing the Gauntlet, and then when I get back, I'm expected to just surrender all agency and get married and have babies. I know that's all most women are taught to want, and it's not that I don't want those things, but wouldn't it be nice if women could be driven by their own desires instead of others' expectations? I'm sure there are many who would make the same choices to embrace marriage and motherhood, but they'll never know unless given an alternative."

"I think everyone should have that agency. What would you change if you were queen?" he asked.

"I have no desire to be queen, but if I were in charge, I would put women in places of power. There wouldn't be any more wars, just diplomacy, less foolishness and fighting."

The hunter's lips quirked up. "I like your ideas. I hear Prince Marcos is still looking for a wife. Maybe you should go after him."

"I'm not going after anyone," she sighed.

"Perhaps you should. I expect you could lay the world at your feet, Cece." He grew quiet. "You're not what I expected."

"How so?" Cecilia asked. "I thought you'd been watching me. Perhaps you are a terrible hunter."

"You get so flustered around your guardian. I didn't expect you to be so bold talking to a stranger."

She took another sip of whiskey, trying to think of a response. "Rainer knows me best, which means he knows exactly how to push me over the edge." She was quiet for a moment. "I'm not sure how I feel about you monitoring me so much."

The distant sound of trumpets startled them both.

"What is it?" the hunter asked.

"Probably just King Hector making one of his self-important speeches." Cecilia clapped a hand over her mouth. "Oops, did I say that out loud?"

The hunter laughed. "Would you prefer I stop watching you?"

Cecilia thought about it. She enjoyed their battle of wills, and she didn't want to give it up yet. "No."

As much as she wanted to know his identity, Cecilia liked the idea of this hunter as a personal confidant and was unprepared to give up the illusion yet. She spread her fingers wide on the cool granite bench and tipped her head back, glancing at the sliver of moon in the dark sky.

"It can't hurt to have someone else watching my back," she said. "Also, I like the challenge of trying to figure out who you are. Have we met face-to-face before?"

"Only on the dance floor."

His large, calloused hand slid over hers. She jumped in surprise but didn't pull her hand away.

"My turn to ask a question," he said. "Why did you slip your guardian to come talk to me tonight?"

"Who says I did it to talk to you? Maybe I was just tired of the crowd and didn't want to watch Rain flirt with Nora Belani."

"I don't think that's it. You watch him flirt with other ladies all the time."

Cecilia cringed. "I just like being able to be myself. It's exhausting playing the part of *Lady Reznik*. Even with Rain, he's my best friend, but he's always fit in so easily. He doesn't understand that loneliness. Everyone at court has an idea of me—each one defined by my relation to the men in my life or the power I could bring the kingdom. No one really sees *me*."

The hunter drew his thumb soothingly over her hand.

"I see you, Cece."

Cecilia rolled her eyes. "You don't even know me. You're just trying to get me into bed."

"Well, if you're offering, I wouldn't turn you down."

She burst into giggles.

"I know what you mean about feeling lonely at court," he whispered. His voice sounded so different.

"You feel that way too?" she asked, finally meeting his gaze.

"Yes. I'm far from home. I have been for most of my life. I miss my family. Although listening to you reminds me, I always felt like you did when I was at home. Like everyone had their own agenda. I used to feel pretty isolated."

"I'm sorry. It must be hard to be so far from home. How long have you been in training?" Cecilia asked.

"Since I was fourteen."

"So young," she said. "I know family is complicated. Gods know mine is."

"Is it hard with your father being so visible?" he asked.

"Yes and no. If he wasn't, I wouldn't be nearly so well trained, which makes me feel much better in the field. However, there are always so many eyes on me and so much pressure to be a certain way. I'm a passable lady at best. I don't sing or play instruments, and I'd rather restring the bow of every hunter in my father's army than sew a stitch of needlepoint. There's a lot of pressure on my father to find me a good match. I'm sure I'm not helping by brutalizing half of the guardians at court."

"I find you very charming, especially when you're holding a weapon," the hunter said, a flirtatious edge returning to his voice.

"That's a little twisted."

"Perhaps."

"Why did you come to talk to me again, hunter?"

"I like how your mind works. You're easily the most interesting person at court."

She frowned. "I doubt that."

"I don't. You have your own ideas. You're not blinded by what you've been taught. You don't feel superior to people around you. Instead, you see the structures of this country and the people as they are. You are wise. Most people are not like that their whole lives, and yet you are even though you are so young. You're a lady and also a hunter who reads people. You assess situations, and you understand influence. I find you very interesting, Cece."

His hand caressed her arm, but she didn't move. Goosebumps followed in the wake of his touch. Her heart kicked up, and her breath grew shallow. She wondered if she'd had too much whiskey. His breath breezed over her skin as his fingers trailed over her shoulder, up the side of her neck, resting above her pulse.

"Your heart is racing," he whispered.

"Yes."

"I thought you would knock my hand away or break a few fingers. Maybe you've had too much to drink."

"Or not enough," she whispered.

Cecilia couldn't believe the words had come out of her mouth. The hunter went completely still behind her. His fingers traced back down her neck and shoulder all the way to her hand, sending a chill through her body. His touch was both soothing and exhilarating.

"I want to know—" She choked on a gasp as his lips brushed against the back of her neck.

"What did you want to know?" the hunter taunted.

She wanted to know who he was and what it felt like to kiss someone she felt so drawn to. The Gauntlet ending only stoked her urgency. Cecilia hadn't had more than a few stolen kisses here and there—hardly the kind of experience that satisfied her curiosity.

"I think you want me to kiss you. *Really* kiss you. The way no one else has," he whispered, his lips brushing her ear. "The way you deserve to be kissed."

"I don't know what you're talking about," Cecilia stammered.

"I think you do. You say you want to take back the power in your life, but now you seem content to defer to me. Why?"

She shrugged.

"I think you want to know what I'll do. You like how I touch you."

She didn't bother denying it. His hands spread mesmerizing warmth through her body.

"You deserve to feel that, Cece."

"Feel what?" Her voice sounded so small.

"*Desired.*"

His arm wrapped around her, pulling her back against his chest.

"Too many people have made you feel small and unimportant. I would treat you like a queen."

She gasped. No one ever spoke to her that way. She felt dizzy. The hunter placed another light kiss on her shoulder. She brought a hand to his cheek. Leaning into her touch, he turned his head, kissing her palm and the inside of her wrist. He brushed his fingertips along her lips and down her neck, leaving goosebumps in their wake.

"Do you want me to kiss you?" His fingers glanced along her collarbone.

"Yes," she rasped.

Suddenly she felt so exposed she wanted to yank off his mask so she could really see him. The hunter cupped her cheek, cradling her face, and placed his other hand on her low back. He drew her close until their lips were an inch apart. Her heart thundered in her ears.

"You're smart and talented, and you deserve to be cherished," he said.

His lips brushed lightly over hers—less of a kiss than the promise of one. Then he froze and drew back, sighing heavily.

"Your friend is back. How does he always seem to find us like this?"

"Cece?" Rainer's voice cut through the silence from beyond the nearest hedge.

She'd punched Rainer many times in training, but she'd never wanted to hit him as much as she did at that moment.

"I promise the next time I see you, I will kiss you like you deserve to be kissed, and I won't stop until you're trembling and your knees are weak," the hunter whispered.

Before she could say more, he ducked beyond a hedge.

"I hope you keep your promises," she whispered.

She smiled as she turned, and Rainer rounded the hedge.

"Cece?" Rainer stopped on the path a few yards away. "What is it with you and this garden?"

"I like the roses," she mumbled.

Rainer plopped down next to her.

"Hey, are you okay? You're shaking. I felt you through the connection. You were anxious or something. I didn't recognize it."

Yeah, I was turned on. Cecilia held her hands to her warm cheeks.

Rainer frowned. "You missed the end of the play."

"I already know how it goes by heart. The War of the Gods split the kingdom in two. Legendary guardian Zelden Novaris and his battalion held off Endros to give the Argarian army time to assemble. Clastor was killed in battle but not before he wounded Endros and

Cato so badly they took years to recover. And we were forced to spend our lives pursuing the Gauntlet to release the power of the Lost God so that Olney can finally stand up to Endros and Cato and stop Argaria's aggression once and for all. I spared myself the propaganda and the nausea-inducing flirting you were doing with Nora." She hated how petulant she sounded.

Rainer sighed, reaching out a hand. "I get it, but your father sent me. Did you hear the king's announcement?"

Cecilia shook her head.

"Argaria attacked. They've sent hunters beyond the neutral lands. They probably assumed the solstice festival was a good time to pick a fight, but we are going to be heading into enemy territory." Rainer's face was grave. His anxiety snaked through their connection. "Endros was spotted on the front lines along with several battalions of Argarian hunters."

Dread rendered her speechless. She stared at him, trying to figure out what to say, but nothing seemed appropriate. Endros and his son, Cato, had long aligned themselves with Argaria, but the god of war hadn't been spotted in combat for years. Now he was stepping out of the shadows just as she was about to finish the Gauntlet and release the very power that could defeat him.

"What about Cato?" Cecilia asked.

Rainer shook his head. "No one has seen him, but with the trickster god, that might not be a good thing." He hesitated. "We're leaving this weekend."

"They moved up our departure?" she asked, dumbfounded.

"King Hector said if we're going to war, we'll need the Gauntlet magic now more than ever."

Cecilia's blood turned to ice in her veins. Rage, fear, and confusion warred in her mind. Rainer ran a hand through his perfectly styled hair.

Though the southern, summer kingdom of Olney and the northern, winter kingdom of Argaria had been on the precipice of war her entire life, the last year had brought a series of Argarian attacks, annexing bits and pieces of their borders that meant

Olney's geography constantly shifted, which meant violence was imminent.

Now war was upon them, right when they needed things to be calm. Right at the moment they would need to cross into enemy territory to finish the Gauntlet.

"I know it's scary, but I promised two years ago I would never let anyone hurt you again, and I meant it." Rainer cupped her face in his hands. A chill ran through her at the memory of the day she almost died.

"I should take you home," Rainer said.

She nodded as he took her hand and led her home in silence.

Inside her cottage, she flicked her hand, lighting candles with fire magic as she circled the room. Rainer untucked his shirt and stretched, revealing a glimpse of his muscular stomach. Cecilia flushed and looked away, walking into the washroom to change.

She slipped her dagger and its sheath from her thigh, untied her dress, and pulled on soft linen pajamas. She tossed the dress on the floor. Rainer sighed, instantly gathering it and hanging it in her closet. Cecilia slumped on the edge of her bed to unpin her hair.

"Gods, Aunt Clara put about four hundred hairpins in here. It will take me all night to get them out," Cecilia said.

Rainer sat behind her and carefully started removing them. He was so gentle, making sure not to pull or tug too hard at her hair. When they were all out, he ran his fingers over her scalp in a light massage.

"Oh my gods, that feels good. Never stop doing that." Cecilia dropped her head back.

"I like you best like this. You look more like yourself," he whispered. Rainer's fingers moved down to the base of her neck, and when they touched her bare skin, she leaned into his touch.

"Did you have too much whiskey, Cece? You're normally much jumpier." He let his fingers slide along the nape of her neck, over her shoulders, and back up.

"No, it just feels nice to be touched right now."

"That sounds more like yes." Rainer laughed, peeking over her shoulder.

Her eyes drifted to his lips involuntarily.

He swallowed, then shook his head like he wanted to rid himself of a bad idea. Hopping up, he fetched her a glass of water, which he promptly made her drink. Then he lay down next to her, drawing a sheet up over her legs. They lay face-to-face in her bed, the way they did every night. She slid her hand into his open palm.

"Now, I promised you a good story," Rainer said. "Where were we? The red maiden is about to take her first trip into the dark wood, right?"

Cecilia nodded. She loved this secret tradition of theirs.

What started as a game, making up fairy tales after Rainer's mother grew tired of telling them each night, turned into a tool for comfort for them even as adults. It was the last vestige of the joy of childhood. They were both unwilling to surrender it, each tale further embedding them into each other's lives. Listening to Rainer spin a story was the time she found herself most acutely aware of her love for him.

Something numinous passed between them in those quiet moments that was impossible for outsiders to see. Rainer's hands were the hands that picked her up when she fell—the hands that cleaned her cuts and bruises and protected her since they were children. The two of them were an ecosystem. No matter how she might try to explain it to an outsider or even to herself, there was no language for it.

Every warm moment stretched out forever in her mind. She could not rid herself of the sweetness of each one because it was a sweetness that was for her alone. When she tried to speak it to someone else, it burned out in the air with a crackle and fell flat before their ears. There were no words to describe what she and Rainer had. It was just the human noise of one heartbeat matching another in a quiet room where no one else could see, and that was everything.

This is what love does, she thought as her eyelids grew heavy. *It binds you together recklessly, whether you're ready or not.*

Love needed no permission to grow roots and bloom.

5

Daylight blazed through the windows of Cecilia's clifftop cottage, the waves crashing hard on the beach below. A salty breeze ruffled the curtains as she lay in bed.

Most Olney ladies were required to live with their parents until marriage, but the loophole of her cottage being a family property on the edge of their estate allowed Cecilia freedom and privacy. Leo had bought the cottage as a studio for Rosalee, who was an avid painter. Though Cecilia did not inherit her mother's artistic gifts, she shared her love of quiet.

It was a small space: one room with a corner kitchen, fireplace, and a small washroom with a pump for well water and a beautiful bathtub.

Cecilia kept the cottage as it was when her mother died, her art still hanging on the walls.

It had been a haven for Cecilia and Rainer growing up. Rainer had built shelves for her many books of fairy tales and his history books about Olney warriors. Scraps of paper and dried flowers stuck out from pages, marking their favorites.

The windows were the real glory of the space, taking up most of the back wall and offering views of the cliff's edge, the beach, and the

Adiran Sea. Rainer loved watching the fishing boats coming and going as he woke up to sneak out at first light and would wake Cecilia when ships from Novum came to port because Novumi fishermen were the best storytellers.

Cecilia rolled over in bed, feeling the soreness of a week of heavy training. Both her body and magic felt a bit rung out from the extra practice, the days a blur of preparing for the Gauntlet trip.

Tension ran high among the few duos leaving, but it was just another day for the rest of Olney City. The threat of war had become so ordinary, it ceased to feel real or immediate. The people of Olney were immune to the fear of it.

A loud knock on the door startled her to her feet.

"Cece, open up. My hands are full," Rainer called.

She opened the door to find Rainer with a bunch of maps in one arm and a platter of lemon cakes in the other.

"Where did you get those?"

His mouth drew up in a grin. "Aunt Clara let me borrow her kitchen this morning."

"How long have you been up?" Cecilia asked, noting the dark circles shadowing his eyes as she took the plate and led him inside.

"No 'thank you'? No 'Rain, these are my favorite, you're my hero'?"

She threw her arms around him. Surprise bubbled through their connection as he hugged her back.

"You feeling okay this morning?" he asked, pretending to feel her forehead. "My friend Cecilia only gives out sarcasm and takedowns for free."

She put tea on to boil, ignoring his teasing. "I'm fine. I just thought it was very sweet of you, that's all."

Rainer had a map spread in front of him, his brow creased in concentration. He did this for every Gauntlet run. He'd drilled their route into her for weeks, but he soothed his anxiety by going over it again as if having the entirety of Olney geography committed to memory could spare them from complications. Rainer mumbled about the Reflection Forest and opened a book, *The Magical History of Olney*.

She took a bite of lemon cake and ran her fingers through his hair, and for once, he let her muss it. "Rain, I know you're nervous, but we're ready. You already have this stuff memorized."

"But do *you*?"

"Why bother when you do it for me?"

He sighed, leaning into her hand in his hair. "Because we could get separated."

"We've never been separated on these trips, and this time will be no exception."

"This is the most dangerous trip so far. Please take this seriously. It would make me feel much better." His eyes pleaded with her. "Recite the stops."

She went through them forward and backward and named the closest Olney army outposts to each one.

"And, of course, if we get separated, you are to go straight home. Minimal stops," he said.

"I'm not doing that."

"Cece, this is how it works. You have to. If I get hurt or taken, go home."

Cecilia shook her head. "I'm not leaving you behind. You wouldn't leave me."

"It's my *job* not to leave you behind, Cecilia. I have to protect you, no matter what. I need you to promise that if something happens to me, you will go straight home."

"You know I won't do that. If you want me to lie and pretend, fine. This can be like putting on a play. One where I'm a helpless girl who can't save your stupid, stubborn ass, and you pretend to be my hero."

Rainer looked like he was unsure if he wanted to laugh or yell at her as she poured tea.

"Rain, you know I won't ever leave you," she said. "Yes, it's your job, but you feel what I feel, and I feel what you feel. Remember how you felt when I almost died?"

He cringed, and his face clouded over. He hated when she talked about it.

"I could never leave you if I felt that," she said. "I would still feel everything you feel if I went all the way home. It would be so much worse. You can't ask me to do that."

"Why are you so stubborn?"

"Why are you such a hypocrite?" Cecilia sat down, pulling her chair close to his. She blinked rapidly, trying to ease the press of tears.

Rainer's face softened. "I'm sorry. I shouldn't ask you to. They should postpone this or send Cal and Sylvie with us. It feels reckless to send the two of us into enemy territory with the open threat of war. If we're caught, I doubt they will use us as hostages. They'll have a slayer take your memories, and they'll kill me."

Cecilia shivered at the thought. Years ago, Argaria found a shortcut to having their witches complete the Gauntlet. They trained powerful memory witches as warriors called slayers. Aided by hunters, they searched out Olney duos on their way to the caves, killed the guardians and stole the witches' memories before killing them as well.

Cecilia and Rainer had only ever run into one slayer, and he had wounded them both in the fight.

"I'm sorry. I'm making you worry." Rainer sighed.

"No, that's not how this friendship works," she said, taking one of his hands in both of hers. "Your worries are my worries, remember? We share the burden."

Rainer shook his head. "You're much braver than me. Maybe you should have been the warrior, and I should have been the witch."

"Maybe." She looked away to hide the flush his compliment brought.

"How do you feel about your conjuring?" he asked.

"I would have liked another month to practice, but I've been trying to master my conjuring for years, and this might be as good as it gets."

Most witches could conjure one or two elements, and the kingdom had long since taken to pushing anyone with even a hint of an affinity for memory in that direction. Cecilia could conjure every element, but learning to control them too was exhausting work.

Summoning memory was her primary and most efficient modality, but she could also conjure fire and earth with moderate effort. Healing required more energy and meant burning through her magic quicker. Conjuring storms and tides was a mess—she'd get either a ripple or a tidal wave, a breeze or a tempest, all of which blew through her energy at an alarming rate. No matter what she conjured, she'd need to eat afterward to rebuild her energy, or she risked passing out mid-battle.

Then there was conjuring death. She'd been able to communicate with spirits since she was a child, but conjuring and controlling them was completely different. It was rare magic that only a few living witches possessed. She'd mostly avoided learning about it because it wasn't as practical in combat.

That ability had always freaked Rainer out. He was more superstitious, and it unnerved him when she became suddenly distracted by a spirit. Conjuring that element also came with the death whispers— a warning sound that came before someone died—so chilling, she shivered remembering them. She'd heard them only a few times, when Rainer's mother was dying, and again the day Cecilia almost did.

It wasn't her favorite gift, but it had its uses. Sometimes, the dead came to her in dreams and warned of traps along their route or Argarian hunters hidden in the woods.

As if reading her mind, Rainer asked, "What do the spirits say about this trip?"

"Nothing yet. No news tends to be good news with the spirit world. In any case, I have been getting my witch tea ready," she said, holding up her flask.

Rainer blanched. "That stuff is disgusting."

Cecilia laughed as she funneled the extremely sweet mixture of tea, lemon, mint, and sugar that acted as a quick boost of energy if she had to burn through a bunch of magic quickly. It was invaluable to her in the field.

A light tap on the door startled them. Cecilia hopped up and opened it but found no one. She went to step out and nearly tripped on two dozen of the most beautiful pale pink roses she'd ever seen. She picked them up and took a deep breath, inhaling their scent. Her eyes widened as she realized they were the very roses she'd been staring at the night before. Another paper bird was tucked between the stems.

––––––

Beautiful Cece — I always keep my promises. Safe travels.

––––––

Cecilia couldn't stop smiling. She was sure her hunter was watching from the shadows.

Rainer froze when he saw the roses. She pushed by him, back into the cottage, busying herself looking for a vase and putting the roses in water to hide the flush creeping up her neck.

"Cece, those look like those roses from the queen's garden that you're always looking at," Rainer said.

"I suspect they are," Cecilia said.

"Who are they from?"

Rainer's eyes burned into her, and she couldn't think of a lie.

"They're from that hunter, aren't they? I knew he was trouble after that dance, but stealing roses from the queen's garden—" Rainer blew out a breath.

"He knows how much I like them." Cecilia couldn't stop smiling.

"I can't tell if he's romantic or insane."

"Probably safe to say he's a bit of both."

"What did you do to inspire that kind of show of affection?" Rainer asked.

"I haven't done anything—yet."

"Did you ever figure out who he is?"

"Not yet." Cecilia shivered, remembering his lips grazing hers and his hands all over her skin. She wished she'd had more time with him.

"Well, I think if he really knew the way to your heart, he would have shown up with two dozen lemon cakes, not two dozen roses."

Rainer's jealousy was so new to her. She didn't know what to make of it.

"Why do you like him so much?"

Cecilia sighed. "He has a sense of humor and no pretense. He says what he means. We just talk. It's nice to be myself."

"I talk to you."

"Yes, but you don't have those kinds of feelings about me. Everything you think about me is related to risk analysis."

Rainer looked offended. "That's not true. I love talking to you."

Butterflies fluttered in her stomach. "I don't know how to explain it. He puts me at ease. He's funny and charming."

Cecilia looked at the roses again and set the little bird note on the table. Rainer read it.

"What did he promise, Cece?"

"That's between the two of us."

They were both quiet. Rainer looked over at the roses again and said, "He must really like you to take a risk like that."

She shrugged, delighted by the flirtation but unwilling to give too much credit.

They went back to studying their plans and reading about the obstacles they might encounter on their way to the last seven caves, the entire Gauntlet culminating with the Cave of Longings, the farthest cave, deeper in Argarian territory than any of the others.

Morning tipped into afternoon, sliding into evening as she finished packing her clothing into a satchel just as they needed to head out for a goodbye dinner with her father and aunt.

At dinner, her father was especially quiet, but Cecilia was relieved Rainer didn't bring up her hunter in front of him. Aunt Clara made light conversation about fall plans for her garden. Cecilia was so distracted by her father's somberness, it was hard to keep up with the small talk.

Back at the cottage, Cecilia and Rainer were quiet and tense as he tucked an extra map in his bag.

"Will you show me a memory?" Rainer asked. "I think we're both nervous, and it always seems to calm us down."

Throughout their lives, whenever they had a moment they both wanted to remember, Rainer would share the memory with her. All she had to do was hold his hand and pull a copy. He would still retain it, but her power allowed her to preserve it perfectly.

The memories were immersive, infused with smell and emotion. Recalling them truly felt like being back in the moment.

"What do you want to see?" Cecilia asked.

"Surprise me."

They sat together on the edge of the bed. She closed her eyes, considering which to show him, reaching for his hand. She pressed gently on his mind. He let her in. An image of Rainer at thirteen flashed into their minds, which meant they were in the memory of eleven-year-old Cecilia.

Rainer dashed ahead, taking the ropes course on like it was nothing. He was taller and faster; his grip strength was better. She was terrified of letting him down.

"Cece, hurry." Rainer sighed, impatiently looking back at her from where he stood halfway across the ropes course.

She looked down at the ground. The fall wouldn't kill her, but she'd watched a guardian fall and break a leg earlier. She reached for the next post, but it was too far. If she were taller, she could reach it, but she was still so tiny. Rainer hadn't even needed the support rope to get across. He'd been able to jump it, and now he was sighing impatiently in front of her. She swung as hard as she could and let go, landing on the platform with him.

"Come on, you're slowing us down too much. We'll never come in first with you being so slow," he huffed, swinging across the longer distance to the next platform.

He swung the rope back to her. She caught it but hesitated. She heard other guardians snickering. A fresh rush of tears blurred her eyes. Frustration set in.

Rainer was already reaching for the next rope—leaving her behind. Cecilia swung, letting go at the apex of the arc through the air, but missed the platform.

She screamed as her hands flailed for purchase. Her left hand clamped onto a steel support just below the platform. It sliced into her hand, but she didn't let go.

"Rainy!"

The strangled cry didn't even sound like her. Blood slid down her wrist from where the metal bit into her hand as it grew numb and slick. She slipped.

Suddenly Rainer appeared above her. His hand clamped around her wrists, and he pulled her up. She landed in his arms and clung to him.

"We have to go, Cece. We're almost there," he soothed, helping her to her feet.

She nodded and blinked back tears. There was only one element left. He scooted across the rope first, one footstep at a time, holding on to the balance rope for support. When he was across, she followed, ignoring the pain in her hand as she clung to the balance rope. By the time she crossed, every muscle in her body felt wrung out.

Guardian McIver frowned at the two of them. "Very sloppy, McKay."

Rainer looked like he wanted to shrivel up and die. Cecilia felt a sharp anger in her chest. She lifted her palm, ready to heal it.

"Not so fast, little witch. There won't be any healing this wound. This is meant to remind both of you of the cost of not working together."

"But, sir, Cece is a lady. She's the huntmaster's daughter," Rainer stammered.

"So she should be treated differently than everyone else?" McIver asked.

Neither of them had a reply as he clasped an Unsummoner bracelet on Cecilia's wrist, and she felt the connection to her magic sever.

"How long?" she asked, looking up at Guardian McIver and trying to keep tears from her eyes.

"Just three days. Until it's sure to scar. A scar is a lesson learned."

Cecilia looked down at the crescent-shaped cut on the outside edge of her left palm and swallowed hard.

She followed Rainer down the ladder to the ground. As they walked by *the guardians who'd been snickering the whole time, Anders Everett stepped forward.*

"It's such a shame, Cece. You were pretty before, but now you're ruined," Anders teased. "Boys can get away with scars because it shows they're tough. Girls with scars are ugly."

"Shut up, Anders," Rainer said, guiding Cecilia away.

Rainer took her to her cottage and cleaned and wrapped the wound. He tried calming her down, but she wouldn't stop crying.

"It's going to be okay, Cece. It's a small scar," he said.

"But I'll never be pretty again. Anders says scars are ugly on girls. He said I'm ruined."

"Cece, you aren't ruined. Anders was being an asshole. I still think you're really pretty." Her heart skipped as he reassured her. "It's just your hand. No one will even notice it."

Cecilia sniffled. "I'll notice it."

"Scars are just reminders of the things we've survived. This is just a sign that you are stronger than the thing that tried to break you, Cece. When a boy sees this, he will know that you are brave and strong, and you don't want anyone who doesn't like that, anyway."

She smiled through her tears. A serious crease formed in Rainer's brow.

Cecilia reached up, running her thumb over the line. "I found a worry, but I'll fix it in a hurry," she whispered.

Rainer's face instantly relaxed at the familiar rhyme she spouted off whenever he was tense. "This was my fault. I shouldn't have rushed you. I should have realized how far a leap it would be for you. You're so quick at everything. I just assumed you would be all right, and that was wrong. We're supposed to be a team, and today I let you down. I won't do it again. Here."

He grabbed the dagger from the sheath on her thigh. He unwrapped her bandage and held up her hand so he could see the wound. Then he took his own left hand and grimaced as he cut almost the exact gash into it. She stared at him in shock. He held his hand next to hers. Two crescent-shaped wounds, nearly identical marks to remind them both not to make the same mistake twice.

"Now we match. Am I ugly?" he asked, wiping a tear from her cheek with his finger.

"No." She sniffed. "You look the same."

"And so do you." Rainer smiled. "From now on, anytime we really mean something, we will make it a crescent promise, okay? Crescent promise that you will stop worrying about a little scar."

She couldn't help but smile back. "I crescent promise."

He rinsed his wound and cleaned it. Then he wrapped his hand and rewrapped hers. Cecilia flopped down on the bed, and Rainer lay down next to her. They stared at each other as Rainer told a story.

"Hey, Rainy?"

"You really need to stop calling me that. I hate it," Rainer huffed.

"You're my best friend."

"You're my best friend, too, Cece."

———

Cecilia wiped away a tear as Rainer blinked his eyes open.

"Why that memory?" he asked.

"I always watch it when I feel anxious. It's the memory that makes me feel less alone."

Rainer was quiet for a moment. "I never hated that nickname," he rasped.

"I know."

What Rainer did that day reminded her that whatever wounds she might be dealt, there was someone there to bear witness to each one and share the burden. As cruel as Guardian McIver was, that scar did teach Cecilia an important lesson: a wound doesn't need to leave a scar for it to go on hurting. She'd experienced more pain in her life from invisible scars than ones the world could see.

6

Rainer helped Cecilia carry her bags to the stables and secured them to her horse, a shiny black stallion with a spectral white marking on his head that earned him the name Little Ghost.

Fanfare of the send-off reached all the way to the stables. Several duos were riding out along with them in case Rainer and Cece were unsuccessful. She knew it was a contingency, but it made her uneasy, even though they were all headed to cover different parts of the Gauntlet.

"Rain, if you check those supplies one more time, I'm going to scream." Cecilia sighed. "We have everything."

"It's soothing," he said, though he finally stopped. "I guess there's only one thing left to do."

Cecilia grinned as they walked to the entrance to the stables like they did before every Gauntlet run. It was a tradition Rainer started with her when they were young, any time she was nervous about a test or upcoming challenge.

When they assigned him to Cecilia as a boy, Rainer didn't understand the complexity of the job. He was unaccustomed to handling Cecilia's emotional extremes. It took a lecture from Captain McIver to explain that guardians handle both their bonded witch's physical safety and emotional well-being. Storytelling was how he helped settle Cecilia when she was overwhelmed.

They pressed their palms together and interlaced their fingers for the ritual that had become more superstition than necessity.

"Once upon a time, there was a guardian," Rainer started.

"And a witch," Cecilia continued.

"Who went on a Gauntlet run," Rainer said.

"And both came back safe, healthy, and happy," Cecilia finished.

Rainer hugged her. She stayed there for a moment, enjoying the feeling of being held.

They walked to their waiting horses. Rainer pointed at a rose among the arrows in Cecilia's quiver.

"Looks like your secret admirer has struck again," Rainer teased.

Cecilia tried to hide her heated cheeks as she pulled out the rose and the attached bird note.

———

Beautiful Cece. Be safe. Packed you and your guardian a surprise.

———

She shoved her hand inside her satchel and found a package of freshly baked lemon cakes.

"That's unnerving. We only walked away for a second," Rainer said, his eyes shifting around the stable.

"He's very unnerving," she agreed.

Rainer ignored the comment and boosted her onto her horse before mounting his own. They rode to the royal dais in silence. Leo Reznik, Captain McIver, and the royal family waited amongst cheering townsfolk. Cecilia hopped down and hugged her father. They received disapproving looks from some of the aristocracy, but Leo smiled and kissed Cecilia on the cheek.

"My little storm, you have your dagger?" Leo asked.

Cecilia patted her thigh where she always wore the dagger her father had gifted her when she was just a girl. It was light and balanced so she could use it up close or for throwing. She also suspected that it held an enchantment of some sort, because every time she touched it, she felt a magical resonance in her body.

Leo nodded. "Good. Be brave and careful. Take care of Rainer. I will see you soon. I have faith in you."

There was a hint of sadness in his eyes.

"You'll be here when I get back?" she asked.

Leo frowned. "You know I can't promise that, Cecilia. But I'll do my best."

She kissed him on the cheek and mounted her horse before she had time to cry in front of the crowd, waving as they rode off into the morning.

Cecilia was quiet for a while, trying to settle her worry over her father and focus on the change of scenery from the bustling downtown of Olney City to the tranquil farmland.

The heat was oppressive, and while Rainer thrived in the humidity, Cecilia couldn't stand it. Her hair clung to her neck, and the wisps around her face sprung into tighter coils. She could never get cool enough. She complained endlessly, though Rainer didn't seem to mind.

They'd be in Olney territory for several days, so Rainer was more relaxed than he would be the rest of the trip. Cecilia loved seeing him enjoy the peace and beauty of the forest. Once they were close to the border, he'd become anxious and edgy.

The first few days brought them to familiar places as they passed through Olney vineyards, several hunter army outposts, and the Whistling Meadows, one of Cecilia's favorite places. In the summer, the meadow was full of wildflowers in a kaleidoscope of colors, and the wind slid through reeds along the far edge, creating a soft whistling sound.

There were few travelers on the road. The threat of war appeared more real to people in the country than in Olney City.

In the quiet, Cecilia's mind drifted to her time in the garden with the hunter. She wasn't sure what she was doing with him. She kept telling herself it was just for fun, but that didn't explain why she couldn't stop thinking about it.

"Do you think I'm being stupid?" Cecilia asked.

Rainer laughed. "I never know what is going to come out of your mouth after those long silences. About what, exactly?"

"The hunter from home."

"What does Sylvie say?"

"I had little time to talk to her about it before we left, but you know how she is. Any attention is good attention to Sylvie," she said, trying to smooth the sweaty hair away from her face.

"I don't think you're being stupid," Rainer said. "I'm not sure what exactly you're doing. You've never been terribly interested in casual relationships, and I'm not sure what kind of long-term prospect a hunter would present."

"Have you ever given a girl flowers?"

"Only if I was trying to bed her."

Cecilia rolled her eyes.

"I'm kidding," Rainer said. "I guess I've done it a few times, but I've never stolen two-dozen roses from the queen's garden and left them with a love note, if that's what you're asking."

"It was not a love note," she said.

"*Beautiful Cece*. Sounds like a love note. Plus, he sneaked those lemon cakes into your bag. That requires a certain level of genuine interest unless you made him really desperate to get you into bed."

"Doubtful." She sighed.

Rainer frowned. "I'm surprised you want to slum it with a hunter."

In the past, Rainer had never been a snob when it came to hunters. Although Rainer was part of the aristocracy like all the other guardians, he never acted like he was entitled to the advantage. He practiced relentlessly and even spent considerable time training with the hunters, though it wasn't a requirement.

The two styles of fighting were very different. Guardians were, as their name suggested, protectors of the witches of the kingdom and the royal family. Hunters were spies, trackers, ghosts who haunted the forests of Olney, waiting for their unsuspecting Argarian counterparts. They moved in shadows and acted as the foot soldiers of the army, able to work as a unit or a brutal solo weapon.

It was easy to see the differences in their fighting styles just by watching them. Guardians with their careful strategic battle plans and defensive moves, trained to protect a moving point. Hunters trained to be a weapon of swift death—all attack and little defense.

"Since when is that slumming it? I don't know what I want. I'm just intrigued," Cecilia said.

"I've intrigued my way up quite a few skirts myself, Cece. I just want to make sure you know what you're getting into."

"No one is getting up my skirt." He relaxed a bit, so she added, "Unless I want them to."

It was worth it to see his relief die a quick death.

"Cecilia!"

"You're not the only one who deserves some fun, Rain."

"That's not what I meant."

Cecilia frowned. "Being your buffer for the last few years has taught me plenty. I have my eyes wide open. Not everything has to mean something. I'm allowed to do something just because it's fun."

"You have little experience with men, and I know how they can be," Rainer said.

Frustration boiled inside of her, stoked by the oppressive heat. Her thirst and exhaustion only made her more impatient with Rainer.

"When we get back from the Gauntlet, you'll be able to do whatever you want. Sleep around or choose a wife—who becomes your property, by the way. But I'll be expected to get married right away, and my ownership will pass from my father to my husband. What little freedom and choice I have will end with the Gauntlet. This is my last chance to mess around, to make my own mistakes. I've spent the last couple of years helping you have fun—at times, more than you can handle. I'm not even asking for your help. I'm just asking for you not to be such a judgmental ass about it. As my friend, I thought you would want that for me. If I want to kiss some hunter in a dark garden, who are you to say anything about it but 'Good for you, Cece, you deserve some godsdamn fun!'"

He stared at her in stunned silence. "You're right. You do deserve some fun. I just worry you'll get your heart broken."

She rolled her eyes. "My heart has nothing to do with this."

Rainer ran a hand through his hair. "I want to meet him."

"Absolutely not." She laughed. "Rain, remember last year when I made out with Kyle Brennan, and then you beat the crap out of him at training? None of the guardians would go near me for months afterward. I couldn't even get anyone to *dance* with me. You're way too overprotective. I wanted to make out with Kyle, and you scared him off."

"He was trouble."

"Kyle was a perfect gentleman."

Rainer arched an eyebrow. "I doubt that."

Cecilia giggled. Kyle hadn't been a gentleman at all, but she hadn't wanted him to be. Rainer showed up at her cottage before she could do anything more than kiss him. She suspected that was why Rainer had done such a number on him. Rainer played it off as a frustrating day, but when Kyle came and apologized to her out of the blue, with his face bruised and swollen, she knew.

"I didn't want you to get a reputation, and Kyle's not exactly discreet."

"A reputation for what? Being fun?" Cecilia taunted.

"You know what I mean."

"Plenty of witches do much worse than I did with him."

"Yes, but I'm not in charge of them," Rainer said.

She shook her head. "You're in charge of keeping me safe."

"From any and all threats."

"And should I protect you from the lips of all the ladies at court?" she asked.

"It's not your job to protect me."

"Yes, it is. It's the part of our vows that everyone pretends doesn't exist. Your job is to keep me alive, but I'm also supposed to protect you. We're supposed to be a team. All of this to say, I don't think I want you to meet my hunter."

"So now he's *yours*?" Rainer asked.

"He's a mystery. I'm going to figure it out when I get back."

"I could help," Rainer suggested.

"No. Definitely not," she said firmly.

Rainer frowned. "Cece, if you're going to be seeking marriage prospects, you'll have to be careful about how things look."

"Why is that a standard only applied to women of the court? Why don't you have to worry about your reputation?"

"I'm not saying it's fair, but it's the reality."

"Maybe that wouldn't be such a bad thing." She sighed.

Rainer looked perplexed. She didn't understand why he couldn't encourage her to embrace her last small bit of freedom before being tied to a stranger for life.

"How many women have you been with?" she asked.

Rainer was so surprised by the question he nearly fell off his horse.

"We should stop for the day soon. The horses probably need to rest," he said.

"Don't change the subject. You've never actually told me."

"I don't think we should talk about this."

She persisted. "How about you just tell me if I'm close? Five?"

"Cece—"

"Ten?" Her eyebrows shot up as she turned to look at him again.

He blushed. "I'm not going to—"

"Twenty! Good gods, Rain. I knew you've been busy, but that's a lot."

"I will not talk about this with you," he said.

"Why not?"

Rainer tightened his grip on Zeke's reins. "Because I... I don't know. It's not appropriate."

"But sleeping in my bed every night is the height of propriety?"

He sighed. "We do nothing but tell stories and sleep."

"It's still not allowed," Cecilia said. "Especially for a rule follower like yourself."

"I don't like being away from you. How can I keep you safe if I'm not there?"

"Is that all just a convenient way to keep me from bringing anyone else to my bed?"

Rainer smirked.

"Oh my gods! Is it?"

Rainer laughed. "No, it's not. I just like being there. I like story time. I like falling asleep knowing you're safe."

Butterflies took flight in her stomach. She was completely surprised by the words, and even if her brain knew he meant as her friend, her heart didn't care.

Rainer grinned at her. "Rare that you're speechless."

"I like falling asleep knowing you're safe, too. But it begs the question: If you sleep in my bed every night, when are you finding the time to bed all these other ladies?"

"Gods, Cecilia! You are so stubborn."

"It's part of my charm."

"Is it?" he asked with obvious annoyance.

"Don't pretend you don't love it. Give me a range at least," she insisted.

Rainer sighed heavily. No good would come from this, but she wouldn't drop it. "Probably not as many as you think."

"You always make it seem like a lot. You make such a point of mentioning who you're currently pursuing," she said.

"That doesn't mean I'm always successful or that I want to be."

Anxiety buzzed on both sides of their connection, as if they both knew this was dangerous territory.

"Then why am I saving you from awkward interactions with someone new every other week?" Cecilia asked.

"Because most of the ladies of the court want something I can't give them."

He shut down the connection between them so she couldn't read him. She wanted to push, but she'd already led him well outside his comfort zone.

"How do you turn off the caring?"

Rainer smiled knowingly, as if he'd expected that very question. "I just do. I'm not like you. It's easier for me to shut that down. You feel everything. I know you like to play tough, but I think you would have a hard time having a casual relationship. That's why I worry about you."

"You don't know everything about me, Rain." Her voice turned sulky.

"The way you feel everything is beautiful. I think it's actually really grown up, but I worry about you getting your heart broken by someone who doesn't know how special you are. I know how the other guardians are, and I sure as shit know how the hunters are. You're beautiful and talented and smart, and I trust your judgment, but I'll always worry about you."

She tried not to feel thrilled at the words. "I can handle myself."

"I know." He pulled back on the reins, bringing Zeke to a stop.

She drew Little Ghost up next to Zeke. They were in an area more open than they usually camped out in. It was a hillside open to the path below. A copse of birch trees stood at the top of the hill, but rather than tuck themselves in there for cover, they set up on the side of the hill so they could watch the Summer Firestorm meteor shower, an annual tradition.

After dinner, as darkness closed in, Rainer lay down beside Cecilia, looking up into the night sky. Once their eyes adjusted, the sky illuminated with shooting stars. Cecilia couldn't stop staring at the stunning array of lights. In all their time in the wild, they'd seen so many wondrous things—glorious winter sunrises, gorgeous mountains, sparkling caves, and sandy beaches. But the Summer Firestorm meteor showers were her favorite.

"Do you think we get multiple wishes or just one?" Rainer asked, breaking the silence. He blindly reached for her hand, folding it into his.

"I think just one good one," Cecilia said.

She kept her eyes on the heavens so she wouldn't look down to where their hands intertwined or over at his handsome face and want more than he could give her. She wondered what he was feeling from her through their connection at that moment.

"What will you wish for?" he asked, his gaze burning into her.

"You know I won't tell you, or it won't come true," Cecilia said. "I never tell you. Why do you ask every year?"

"I don't know. I just want to know what goes on in your head. How about this—is it a new wish or an old wish?" Rainer asked.

She thought about it.

A new wish could be for more time, more freedom. She could wish for the power to make her own choices—to choose adventure, or romance, and not feel guilty for putting her own wants above what was expected of her for once.

Or she could go with her old wish. The one she usually settled on. The same one she'd wished every year since she was old enough to know what lived in the quiet of her heart. She could wish for Rainer —to have his heart, to give him hers. It was a silly, foolish wish, but wishes were supposed to make people believe in impossible magic.

"I think maybe a new one," Cecilia whispered.

Rainer's thumb ran over the inside of her wrist. She closed her eyes, basking in the sensation. She wasn't sure if he'd started doing it because he thought it would soothe her, or if she found it soothing because it was something he did all the time. It had become so habitual that she clasped her hands and rubbed her own wrist whenever she was nervous and alone.

"What about you?"

"I think it's going to be a new one this year," he said.

She felt his gaze, even with her eyes closed.

A surge of emotion flowed through their bond, and her eyes snapped open, meeting his. She sensed something that usually originated on her side of the connection. She knew it well because it was the same thing she held back every time she looked at him, every time he was close, every time he touched her hand, or brushed hair out of her face, or tucked her in at night.

Rainer felt a longing so strong Cecilia nearly mistook it for her own. There was no way to know what it was for. Maybe for the open road. Maybe for a bigger life. In the back of her mind, the tiny nagging voice of hope wouldn't let her let go of the thought that it might be longing for her.

For a moment, neither of them moved. Cecilia felt as if she were standing at the edge of a cliff, about to step off into free fall. Her stomach dipped. *Look away, Cece, just look away.* She tried to make herself break eye contact first, but she couldn't. She didn't want him to stop looking at her like he'd rather see her than a stunning meteor shower.

The buzz of crickets chirping around them grew louder. Rainer abruptly looked back at the stars.

"I win," Cecilia whispered.

"What do you win?" Rainer laughed breathlessly.

"The staring contest you sprung on me."

She hated herself for making light of the moment. She was quick to dispel any awkwardness between them, never forcing him to explain. Cecilia was constantly tending to their friendship like it was hers alone to care for.

Another swipe of Rainer's thumb on her wrist settled her mind. They lay in silence for a while.

"I have a different wish I'll share with you," Cecilia whispered. Rainer looked over at her again, but she kept her eyes on the sky. "I wish I could remember all the stories we've made up over the years. They aren't all winners, but I fall asleep in the middle of them a lot, so they aren't all locked in my mind. I wish I had them to go back to."

Rainer's grin grew wide. "I was going to wait until your birthday to tell you, but I may as well just tell you now. I've been writing them down. Not all of them, but just over the last few years. When I got up at dawn every day, I went back to my place and wrote. On nights when we were on the road, I wrote it down while I was awake on watch."

She turned to look at him. "Are you serious?"

Rainer looked suddenly self-conscious. "Yes. Is that stupid? I thought maybe it would be a good gift—that you might want to remember some of the stories or that maybe someday you would want to read them to your kids."

She swallowed hard around the lump in her throat.

"Okay, it's stupid. I should've thought of something else—"

"No, it's not stupid," Cecilia whispered. "I just can't believe you wrote them all down. That's such a sweet gift."

He blew out a breath. "You like it?"

"I love it. It's perfect."

"Happy early birthday, Cece. I'll give it to you when we're back home."

She looked back up at the stars. "I want to keep this memory. Will you share yours with me?"

It had been a while since she'd asked to keep one.

"When you copy one of my memories, does it come with my thoughts? I never thought to ask before," he mumbled. A hint of nervousness buzzed through their connection.

"No, they don't come with thoughts, just feelings and smells and sounds and vision. Think about when I share a memory with you," she whispered.

She practiced a lot with Rainer when she first learned how to use her power, but now her sharing was fewer and farther between. He knew she liked to capture her favorite things from him so they would have a complete memory with his side and hers.

"Okay," he said.

She took his hand. She pressed against his mind, and he let her in. They watched the memory play out, and when it finished, she squeezed his hand.

"Thank you."

They looked at each other for a long moment.

"It's your turn to start the story tonight," she finally whispered.

Rainer launched into a story about a village where it rained stars for one night every year, and all who lived there collected them in jars so they would have them anytime they needed to make a wish.

As she listened, Cecilia wondered what it would be like to feel that full of hope and promise. She imagined having a jar full of wishes she could count on coming true and what she would ask for if she did.

7

————————

Three caves and one week later, Cecilia stood in front of yet another Gauntlet cave, staring into a whole different darkness. She tilted her head, narrowing her eyes on the wildflowers that framed the cave mouth, bending away from the abyss within.

"What's wrong?" Rainer asked.

She wordlessly filed through her grimoire of memories. Though nothing appeared wrong with the cave, the magic that pulsed from within felt strangely stagnant. Most of the cave magic felt like it was reaching for her, like it was something that belonged to her. This cave just felt sluggish and heavy.

Finally, her magic snagged on a suspension spell.

Cecilia gasped and took a step back. "It's a trap."

Rainer was so eager to stand between her and danger that he stepped right into it. His eyes went wide as he tried to move and found himself frozen.

"Don't panic. I'll pull down the enchantment in a moment and you'll be able to move again," she whispered.

Spellwork differed from summoning in that any witch with any affinity could practice it. It simply required knowing the words to the enchantment and making a worthy exchange for the cost of it.

Cecilia's natural affinity benefitted her in that she could easily sort through memories of spells she'd learned and find the right one with ease rather than needing to carry a physical grimoire. As long as she had the memory of reading or learning a spell, she could undo it as well. She focused on the memory in her mind and watched the spell play out, then she opened her eyes and set about doing the spell in reverse to pull it down.

Though blood was her exchange of choice for the Gauntlet since her memory magic felt more like something that channeled through her body, spellwork felt more external, so she preferred to exchange herbs or her hair since she had such a wealth of it. She unbound her hair and cut off a lock in offering, closing it in her fist as she recited the words to the spell in reverse. After several painstaking moments, the enchantment released, and she felt the familiar surge of normal Gauntlet magic from within the cave. Rainer sagged in relief, finally able to move again. Cecilia opened her palm and found nothing but ash, which she shook into the dirt at her feet.

"No sign of trouble still," Rainer murmured, his eyes darting around the periphery.

"Will you be okay if I leave you alone?" she asked.

"Of course," Rainer scoffed.

She didn't want to wound his pride, but once she started the cave ritual, she wouldn't be able to come out until it was done, even if she felt him in trouble.

She knelt at the cave mouth and waited for permission from the ancient cave spirits. When it came, she glanced back over her shoulder at Rainer. He gave her a nod, and she continued into the dark.

The ritual was second nature after doing it seventy-three times before. She walked until she found the sacred plants, cut her hand and dribbled her blood over them. Then she held out her hand, and the ancient cave spirit's touch ghosted over her palm and her mind lit with a memory.

There was an intimacy in sharing memory. It wasn't lost on Cecilia how much of themselves the four witches who created the Gauntlet had given to help Clastor and Cato create it.

Each memory had a different texture, a different emotional signature. After so many caves, Cecilia had learned the differences between them. Ash Rivers's memories were curious and seeking. Raven Whitewind's spells were full of calm, intuitive knowing and trust that could only be born out of being a seer who knows what's coming. Petra Ryan Light's were illuminating, mercurial, woven through by her fiery nature.

This cave had a memory from Selene Carrick, whose signature felt compassionate, vulnerable, and full of fierce courage that left Cecilia feeling like she'd looked too closely at something too personal.

She finished the memory retrieval and met Rainer outside. He cleaned the wound on her hand before she healed it, and they got back on the road again.

They rode through the afternoon without incident, cooled by the shade of the forest canopy, the smell of honeysuckle in the air, the shadows stretching long as daylight faded.

As they settled in to camp for the night, Cecilia's body still felt incandescent. Each time she completed a cave, she felt exhilarated, not because she was closer to completing the Gauntlet but because her magic swelled with each success, bubbling through her veins with ecstatic energy so bright she struggled to sleep most nights on the road.

Even more than the magic that kept her wired, her mind kept turning over and over what Sylvie had said to her before she left. Was it really possible that she could come home a hero and demand authority over her life? Would Rainer even want to be with her if he had the option?

Cecilia lay awake, her gaze trained on the moonlight passing through the canopy of pine branches. She sat up and found Rainer watching her.

"Can't sleep?" he asked.

"I can't stop thinking about what happens after this," she said, trying to close off their connection so he wouldn't feel her anxiety.

"What do you mean?" Rainer asked. "Like, what we'll do once we get home and we have all this magic sorted out?"

"Yes. Technically, we'll still be bound to each other. We'll still fight together in any battles or against any threats to Olney, but we won't see each other nearly as much, right? We won't have reason to."

Rainer looked baffled. "Can't the reason just be that we want to?"

"But when we get back, my father expects me to marry." Cecilia looked down at the grass.

"I haven't given it much thought. I've never heard you talk about this before. Is this about that hunter? Why the sudden interest in romance?" he teased.

"Because I'm staring down marriage, and it's somehow scarier than this trip. I'm afraid of finishing the Gauntlet because of what comes next. I just wonder sometimes—" She trailed off, working her fingers through her tangled braid, the curtain of hair acting as a buffer between them.

"You're fishing for something," Rainer said, eyeing her suspiciously.

"I'm wondering what happens for you after our official duty is done. What's next for Rainer McKay?" She tried to sound casual but only succeeded in sounding desperate.

"I always thought we'd still be spending all our time together like we already do. I don't want things to change between us," he said.

"How will that work when I get married? Are you going to move in with my husband and me? Still going to sleep in my bed every night?"

"Cece." His tone changed, and the look in his eyes heated her blood. Something silent had shifted between them, fissures forming in the truce that had existed for so long.

"I'm just trying to understand how you picture things. You think I'm just going to be there for you whenever you want while you chase every pretty girl in court and come back to me when you're bored?" she said bitterly.

Rainer stepped back like she had slapped him. "That's not what I do."

"My mistake. What do you do?"

Rainer let out a heavy sigh and turned away from her. His hands ruffled his hair and then clenched at his sides.

"This idea you have in your head is lovely, but it's not realistic. It's the same as the stories we tell before bed—a beautiful fairy tale, Rain."

"I don't want to talk about this anymore," he grumbled.

Her chin jutted out defiantly. "Well, I do."

"Please don't be like this right now, Cecilia." He dropped his head back and sighed.

"Like what? Questioning the great Rainer McKay? Are you saying you have no one in mind for marriage when we return? You seemed awfully cozy with Nora before we left."

Rainer's face shuttered, and she knew she'd get nothing else. She wanted to pry the truth out of him, but it was no use when he was in this mood. This was business Rainer. His eyes skimmed the perimeter, searching for a threat.

She itched to press him more, but instead, she waited in the awkward silence for sleep to take her away.

———

Cecilia woke up splayed across Rainer's body like he was her own personal bed. She went rigid with embarrassment.

"Rain?" she rasped, her voice still thick with sleep.

"It's okay. I think you were cold, and I didn't want to wake you," he whispered. Rainer rested a hand on her neck, running his thumb along her jawline. That combined with the slow movement of his other hand on her low back settled her.

Awake Cece might have kept distance between them, but Sleeping Cece was clinging to him like he was a life raft and she was lost at sea. She was a little embarrassed, but she had a strange dream —the same one she'd had for days, of darkness chasing her.

"Don't be embarrassed," he said, reading her through their connection. "Honestly, I was cold too, and it was nice to have you as a blanket."

His stubble scraped against her forehead, and she knew that when she looked up at him, it would be torture. At home, Rainer was always perfectly groomed, but when they were out in the wild, his hair was messy and a bit of stubble grew in. He looked so good like that.

Cecilia felt into their connection again. Rainer was nervous but happy. She felt the warmth of contentment that they both felt lying there. Then, underneath that, she felt a powerful longing and the sharp edge of desire. She shifted down his body in surprise, feeling the physical desire in him. Her eyes went wide, and he shifted her back up, tucking her close.

"Sorry about that," Rainer mumbled.

Humiliation rushed through their connection. It didn't embarrass Cecilia at all. Instead of hiding it like she normally did, she left the connection open between them.

"Cece." He said her name like it was a curse.

She sat up, straddling him. Her breath caught when she saw the look on his face, because it echoed her own feelings. She rolled her hips. The tension stretched out between them, leaving them both breathless.

"Cece," Rainer gritted.

His hands flexed on her hips. She was too inexperienced to make sense of the chaos in her body, but she didn't want it to stop or slow down, so she rolled her hips again, and they both groaned.

Rainer's eyes went wide in surprise and he gasped, gripping her hips firmly, though she couldn't tell if he was trying to stop her movement or encourage more of it. She rolled her hips again—the friction eliciting another breathless gasp and a flex of the hips from Rainer.

He shifted quickly, flipping so that she was beneath him.

"You think I want this?" he gritted through clenched teeth. "You think I want to be some itch you scratch before you settle down?"

Cecilia narrowed her eyes. "What? You don't want to be used the way you use all those women you parade around? Or you don't want to be used by *me*?"

Rainer's eyes lit with anger. He moved to get up but suddenly froze.

Cecilia's heart leapt into her throat when she saw an Argarian hunter with a knife at the back of his neck. A second hunter stood behind the first, sword drawn.

"Stand up, Guardian. No sudden movements, either of you," the hunter said.

Sliding her dagger onto the ground so it was hidden under her leg, Cecilia eyed up the second hunter while the first was distracted subduing Rainer. Both wore vests with Argarian red emblems.

It would have been easy to surrender to the rising tide of panic in her body, but she'd learned long ago that she had to master her fear. Fear was poison. The more she let it in, the less clear her mind would be, the weaker her will would be. It wasn't about ignoring it. Conquering fear meant walking beside it as a constant companion. Her life required it, but beyond that, she remembered what the seer said to her many years before. *Only you can decide who fear will make you.* The words grounded her in the most tumultuous moments. She refused to let fear make her a coward.

"Spicy morning for you two." The hunter laughed. "I almost let you go just to see what would happen."

The hunter hauled Rainer away from Cecilia and turned back to her.

"Goodness, she looks mad with lust," the hunter said.

Cecilia flushed as she studied the two hunters, looking for weapons and weaknesses.

"What do you want?" Rainer asked. Shame slunk through their bond. She wished she could wipe it away for him.

"To kill you and bring your witch to our slayer so that he can drain her memories and steal her Gauntlet magic, of course. Maybe we'll have some fun with your witch first," the other hunter said. "What are your names?"

A spike of rage from Rainer shot through their connection.

Cecilia ignored it and searched the hunters for any mistakes. In the past, hunters would have killed Rainer immediately. She wondered why the change in plans.

"I'm not a witch. I'm a huntress," she said, climbing to her feet. She held the dagger behind her leg, angling her body away from them.

"Why would a huntress and a guardian be traveling together?" the first hunter scoffed.

"To serve as backup to a duo trying to complete the Gauntlet. The king is desperate to have it completed with the coming war." She lied so smoothly, she almost believed herself.

Doubt swept over the hunters' faces.

"You don't believe me. I get it. Why should you? If you want to see a demonstration, I can show you. I can hit an apple on that tree down there from here. Right through the center," she said, gesturing to her bow.

"First, a witch could do that with magic. Second, we aren't giving you a bow. Third, why aren't you in a hunter's uniform?"

Cecilia rolled her eyes. "No witch can do that with magic. You probably shouldn't give me a bow. You're right about that. And I'm not much for uniforms. Too stuffy for me."

"Witch, what are you playing at?" The hunter closest to Rainer had relaxed his hold on the knife.

Cecilia looked at Rainer and then at the knife. He gave her a subtle nod. She was buying them time.

"I'm not a witch. I'm a huntress, and I'm excellent with a bow. Know what else I'm good with?" She laced the words with as much innuendo as possible, and the hunter's gaze dropped to her lips. "A blade," Cecilia said, letting her dagger sail. It landed right on target, buried in the hunter's chest.

Rainer punched the other hunter, disarmed him, and cut him down with his sword in seconds. He stood over the two bodies, breathing hard, before turning to Cecilia.

Cecilia took no joy in killing, but she never hesitated in defending herself or Rainer. Although it pained her to hurt others, it was such a regular part of the world they grew up in she'd become accustomed to the feeling.

Rainer dropped his sword and held her face in his hands. His green eyes were wide with concern, but she just grinned at him.

"Are you hurt?" he asked.

"Rain, stop. Everything is fine. There's not a scratch on me."

Rainer pulled back, looking with wild eyes for more hunters.

"We have to go. I shouldn't have done that. I was distracted again, and you could have been hurt," Rainer said. He gathered up his sword and started putting away their supplies on the horses.

"Rain, slow down. Everything is all right. We're both okay."

"Cecilia," he huffed, exasperated. "That was a momentary lapse of judgment. I shouldn't have done it. I shouldn't have made you believe there was more between us."

"I felt how bad you wanted it. Now you want to say it was a lapse of judgment?"

Rainer threw his hands up. "You said yourself how this ends. We will go home, and you'll be expected to marry someone. And I'll—" He swallowed hard. "I'll never do anything to risk your safety again."

"I'm standing here in front of you without a scratch on me."

"That's not the point! You could have died, and it would have been my fault. It was all I could think about the whole time. It was like watching the same thing play out. I was terrified. I still am." He brought her hand to his pounding heart as a fresh wave of fear passed through their bond. "We have to go."

They mounted their horses and took off into the woods. She could still feel his warm hands on her skin as she fought angry tears. She should have known better, but for a moment, it seemed he was truly going to let it happen. Any chance to break through the walls he put up was lost the moment the hunters surprised him.

She should have spent the rest of the day feeling grateful that they'd escaped the Argarian hunters unharmed, but she was angry at the system that would bind two people together with a soul bond and not allow them to love each other.

8

Cecilia blinked her eyes open to a handsome face hovering over her. Fear tore through her as she shuffled back, grabbing her dagger and holding it out in front of her to ward him off. She wildly looked around for Rainer. Though she was in the same place on the forest floor where she'd fallen asleep beside Rainer, he was nowhere to be found, and the sky was still dark.

"I thought you might never wake up. You sleep like the dead," the man said.

He was handsome, his jet-black hair falling over his forehead, shading his light gray eyes, and the scar across his right eyebrow.

"Who are you? Where is Rainer?" Cecilia asked.

The air filled with the scent of pine and leather. A tingling spread through her body. *This is some sort of strange dream magic*, she thought. It wasn't anything she recognized, but there were plenty of old spells to travel through dreams that she'd never learned because she had no practical use for them.

"Easy there. I'm not here to hurt you."

All the fear she'd felt before faded to the back of her mind and was replaced with curiosity and confusion. She fought against the artificial calm, to no avail.

"It's creepy to watch a lady sleep," she huffed, crossing her arms and leaning back against a tree.

"Good thing you're not a lady then," he said with a grin.

She laughed involuntarily. "Who are you?"

"You don't recognize me, Cecilia?"

Cecilia frowned. "Should I?"

"Let's just say I'm a friend."

She rolled her eyes. "I have enough friends. Just tell me what you want."

"I wanted to get to know you. I've been waiting for you," he said.

"Get to know me? What do you want to know?"

"I like to know what makes people tick."

"Is this a type of dream magic?" she asked.

"Of sorts."

Cecilia rolled her eyes. "So you're a witch. Do you ever answer questions directly?"

"Occasionally." He smirked. "I've been curious about you and your motivations. Do you seek love or power?"

It startled Cecilia how the words echoed what the seer, Raven Whitewind, had said to her years before.

"Does one have to choose?" Cecilia asked.

"Always."

"Then I chose love," Cecilia said plainly.

The man frowned. "Well, that's foolish. Why would a witch with so much power want such a blatant weakness?"

"You see love as weak?"

He sighed, sadness passing over his eyes. "You see it as a strength, but really it's an exchange. It may make you feel more confident or happy, but even the powerful are ruled by what they can't bear to lose."

The man ran a hand through his dark hair, moonlight glancing off the scar on his eyebrow. "My turn. Why are you so frustrated with your guardian?"

His question snaked inside her, the scent of leather and pine wrenching the words from her mouth. "I've loved him for years. I've waited for him to come around, but he's never going to."

"Sounds a bit spoiled to me. You don't get what you want, and so you toss him away."

"I don't want to, but I've accepted that I can't change his mind," Cecilia started. "I need to move on. This is ridiculous. I don't even understand why I'm telling you this."

Talking to the stranger was confusing. She still didn't understand why she felt oddly at ease with him, as if she'd known him forever. He had a way of drawing complex feelings and thoughts out of her. She couldn't seem to shut up.

"I'm trying to get to know you," he said.

"Why?"

"Because I find you fascinating."

"What are you?" she asked.

"I'm like you."

"A memory witch?" she asked. His power felt different.

He laughed. "No. Just another lonely soul. I know what it is to be different. To feel isolated. I know what it is to feel like no one else understands."

"No one else does. Not even Rain." She flinched as the intimate thought was ripped out of her.

"I do," he whispered.

"You don't know me."

"But I want to," he said. "I suspect you're the only person who I can truly relate to in the entire world."

"That must be lonely."

Her response seemed to surprise him because it was the first time the cocky look on his face faltered. It was only for a second, but she watched the flash of surprise and then something else before he fixed his face back into a smirk.

"You would know."

He smiled at her, but she could see an edge of pain behind it. She nodded.

"Tell me this, Little Dove, if you're so in love with the guardian, why did you let that hunter touch you in the queen's garden?" he asked.

The hairs on the back of Cecilia's neck stood on end. "How long have you been watching me?"

"Answer the question," he insisted.

"He barely touched me, and what I feel for him has nothing to do with love." Again, the words flew out of her mouth unbidden.

"So it was just physical attraction?"

"If you're going to be so nosy, then I want to ask questions, too."

His gray eyes lit up. "I suppose that's fair."

"How long have you been watching me?" she asked.

"Many years. I keep my eye on all the powerful witches in Olney. You're not the only one. I've also been watching your friend, too, the pretty blonde one."

"Sylvie? How?"

"Spies. Friends. Allies. My own brand of magic. Does it matter?" he said. "My turn to ask you something. Why do you love the guardian so much?"

Cecilia thought about it. It was hard to give voice to the depth of emotion. She opened her mouth but then closed it.

"It's all wrapped together with our history and memory," Cecilia said. "He's always been my person. He's kind, and he's taken care of me my whole life. I share my dreams with him, and he never makes me feel silly, no matter how strange they are. I can always be myself with him."

"And yet he keeps you weak and ensures that you'll always need him," the man said.

Cecilia recoiled. "That's not true. He taught me how to fight. He trained me."

"But he doesn't let you choose for yourself. He doesn't trust that you can protect yourself, always making you stand behind him instead of beside him."

Cecilia stared at him. It was as if he had looked into some place in the back of her mind that she didn't like to go. He called forth something she knew but didn't want to look at closely.

SHEILA MASTERSON

"He plays with you. He says he wants to let you go, but as soon as you wander, he draws you back in. You received roses from your hunter, and he wouldn't stop questioning you about it. He won't hold on to you, but he also won't let you go. He keeps you imprisoned, and he likes you weak, just like everyone else."

The stranger knew too much.

Cecilia sighed. "He does not."

"I know fear, and he's full of it. Afraid to give in to what he feels. Afraid of failure. Afraid of the depths of his longing. He's weak-minded. You fell in love with the first person who showed you kindness in a world that made you feel other. Haven't you ever wanted more for yourself? Someone who would really see you?"

The words hit her like a punch in the gut, but she kept her face placid. "Well, after all that talk of me letting go too easily, you sure seem to want me to let him go."

"I merely ask questions so that you can think about what you really want, Little Dove. So that I can understand your mind."

Cecilia leaned away from him. "Talking to you reminds me of playing chess."

He laughed. "It probably should."

"What do you want from me?"

"Cecilia, I know you are used to all the relationships in your life being transactional, but I just wanted to get to know you."

She glared at him. "I don't believe that for a second."

"Well, maybe you're smarter than I gave you credit for." His eyes had a mildly hypnotic quality, and she had the feeling she could get lost in them if she looked much longer.

"What do you want most right now?" he asked.

Cecilia thought back to her wish, lying under the meteor shower with Rainer. It felt too personal to share with a stranger.

"Freedom," she said. It wasn't a lie. It was at the core of everything she wanted.

"From what? Your broken heart? Your mission? Your home? Marriage?" he asked, looking genuinely curious.

"To make my own decisions when I want to. To have power over

92

the course of my own life. To wander alone or with whomever I wish."

"Interesting," he said, considering her response. "You're not what I expected."

"And what did you expect?" she asked.

He grinned. "I thought you'd be taller."

"So now you've got jokes?" She laughed.

"You're just freer than I think you give yourself credit for. More spirited than I expected."

"I'll take that as a compliment," she said.

"It's meant to be one. He's going to wake you up soon. I'll give you one last question."

"What should I do to get what I want?" Cecilia asked.

Laughter sparked in his eyes. "Say yes to the hunter."

"From home?" She frowned at him as he stood, turned away, and disappeared into the dark, leaving her with more questions than answers.

And then Rainer's voice dragged her from her dream until she blinked her eyes open into the bright morning light, finding herself next to him, exactly where she'd fallen asleep.

9

The reflection of the full moon rippled in the water's surface as Cecilia's feet slid along the cold stone riverbed. She was so desperate to be clean after a long day of riding in the sun that she didn't mind the icy water or that the area was more exposed than she would have liked.

The evenings were cooler the farther north they traveled, but the days still sweltered, and the humidity never broke. She'd spent most of the day bickering with Rainer, the exhaustion of the frenetic pace finally wearing on her. He left her alone to bathe, but she knew he was nearby if she needed him.

She stopped when the water reached her waist, monitoring the nearby trail for Rainer's return. She sucked air through her teeth, goosebumps rising on her skin as she adjusted to the cold. Unraveling her braid, she relaxed for the first time all day, enjoying the moment of solitude.

Her bathing gown tangled around her legs, the thin green fabric catching on the dagger strapped to her thigh. She hated the gown but couldn't bear the awkwardness of Rainer wandering back early and seeing her naked. Then again, that might catch his attention.

Cecilia worked the soap into a lather and washed her hair and body. She floated on her back in the gentle current and stretched her arms up, picking out constellations she knew. She was about to get out when she felt a shift in the air. Someone was nearby.

She jammed her feet down and stood in the shallow water. Her dagger was in her hand before she saw him.

"Moon Goddess, I didn't mean to startle you."

On the shore, a man leaned against a boulder in the shadow of the thick pine trees along the trail. His dark hair fell over his forehead, and a slash of moonlight highlighted his cocky grin. He was tall and broad—not quite Rainer's size, but he looked strong. She couldn't make out the emblem on his vest or its color: Argaria red or Olney green. She didn't know if he was a friend or an enemy but assumed that if he was disturbing a woman while she bathed, he was trouble at the very least.

Pebbles bit into Cecilia's feet as she stepped onto shore, trying to get a closer look at the vest. The man stared back. She was grateful she hadn't forgone the bathing gown, though she realized the fabric sticking to her skin left little to the imagination. His gaze swept over her slowly.

"It's not polite to stare," she said.

"Or to startle a goddess while she's bathing," the man said with a sly smile.

"I'm not a goddess."

"You sure look like one worshipping the full moon. Though I suppose no mortal would be blessed with such beauty. It would make the gods jealous."

Heat rushed to her cheeks.

His gaze sharpened on her dagger. "Of course, I don't know if a moon goddess would carry a blade, so perhaps you are a mortal after all. What should I call you, then?"

Cecilia knew how powerful men used fear to rule over women. *Only you can decide who fear will make you.* Rather than show how frightened she felt, she took a step toward him.

"I think the better question is, what should I call you? Raised with no manners and startling a lady while she bathes."

She took another step, gaze narrowing on the emblem on his vest: the hunter's mark of a bow and arrow with crossed short swords. She couldn't make out the color to tell if he was friend or foe.

Cecilia backed away, bending her knees to center her body in a fighting stance. If he didn't mean her harm, he wouldn't have startled her.

"Where's your guardian, Goddess?" the man asked, assessing her like prey.

Her heart thundered in her ears. Where *was* Rainer? He should have been back already.

"Closer than you think, hunter." She spit the words out like they were poison.

"Then why do you look so frightened?" he asked, another smile passing over his lips.

She noticed a dimple on his right cheek. *Stop looking at his dimple before he kills you, Cece.*

"I'm not afraid," she huffed.

"I don't want to hurt you," he said, amusement dancing in his eyes.

"Well, the feeling isn't mutual."

Cecilia brought her hands to the slit in the side of her gown and tugged on the fabric to deepen it so she could move easier. It split almost to her hip. The hunter looked startled.

"What?" she said.

"Are you trying to distract me?" he said, eyes tracing the slit. "Because it's definitely working. How could I possibly fight when all I can think about are your beautiful legs?"

Heat prickled across her skin. *Where is Rainer? What if this hunter already took care of him?* The thought clamped down on her heart. She channeled her fear and panic into anger. Anger would help her focus. Without looking, she flung her dagger at the hunter's chest. He stopped it between his palms.

"How did you—" she choked, shocked by his speed.

"That was not very ladylike," he scolded.

"Maybe you just haven't spent time with the right ladies."

The hunter laughed. "Perhaps you're right. All the ladies I know are a bore. All right, Goddess: if you insist, we will fight, but no weapons."

The hunter dropped his sword and bow and tucked her dagger into the back of his waistband.

"I'll make you a deal," he said. "You get the dagger back, and I will let you use it on me."

"Well, I certainly don't need more motivation."

It would have been wiser not to engage, but she didn't know where Rainer was and didn't have a horse to get away.

They glided around each other. He seemed to float with supernatural grace, keeping his distance, waiting for her to strike first.

"Come on! You said you weren't afraid—"

Before he finished, she lunged and hit him in the right shoulder. He stumbled back, startled but smiling.

"That's good. I suspect there is very little you fear."

She lunged again, hitting him in the gut with a jab that sent a satisfying puff of air out of his lungs. To her frustration, he was still smiling. She swung again. He caught her wrist and twisted it behind her, pulling her back flush against the front of his body.

"Very sloppy," he whispered in her ear.

Cecilia slammed her head into his. He stumbled back, holding a hand to his forehead.

"Better." He laughed.

Nothing she did fazed him. The more she hit him, the more delighted he got. Hunters were known for their love of a fight, relishing the opportunity for conquest. They also had magically enhanced senses that helped them hear greater distances, smell poisons, or see in the dark.

His head snapped to the right. "Someone's coming."

"What? How do you know?" Cecilia asked.

He held her wrists and spun her so he was between her and the road. She saw a faint light down the trail but couldn't see or hear anyone.

"Goddess, do you trust me?" the hunter said.

He framed her face with his hands. They were warm and rough, but his touch was surprisingly gentle.

"Of course I don't trust you." Cecilia snorted.

"I need you to trust me. I'm here to keep you safe, but to do that, I need to do something right now that might make you want to try to stab me again."

She took a step back.

"Say you trust me. It doesn't have to be forever. Just for the next few minutes, and you can't forget it no matter what I do. Please."

"What are you going to do?" she asked.

"I'm going to kiss you."

She gasped.

"I know it's far from ideal, but I would need to have your permission," he said. "I'm not in the business of kissing beautiful strangers without their consent. We need to improvise, and it's the easiest cover story. They may already know we're here by scent alone if they're hunters. We have little time. Say yes."

He slid a hand across her cheek, tucked a stray hair behind her ear, and glanced down the road toward the light again.

Cecilia couldn't help but wonder what trusting him might cost her. Would he stab her the moment she let her guard down?

He pulled off his leather vest and tossed it aside. Anxiety flooded her mind. Her heart pounded, not so much from fear as anticipation. She made a split-second decision to go with her gut. If he'd wanted to hurt her, he could have waited and surprised her when she got out of the water. Suddenly the words from the man in her dream the night before came back to her: *Say yes to the hunter.*

A peal of faint laughter split the silence from farther down the trail.

"Yes," she breathed, barely a whisper, but he heard it.

"Thank gods," he said.

The hunter wrapped Cecilia in his arms and backed her against the boulder, the cool of the granite contrasting with his warmth. The kiss was gentle at first, then urgent and all-consuming.

She'd been kissed before, but not like that. Everything in her body came alive, every nerve ending firing like a million fireworks across her skin. He pulled her hips flush against his. A shock went through her body.

Cradling the back of her head, he drew her deeper into the kiss. His fingers grazed the skin of her neck. She felt like she'd been tossed up to the moon and was free-falling back to earth. She kept falling deeper into the kiss, weaving her fingers through his hair to pull him closer. He moaned against her lips, though she couldn't tell if it was desire, surprise, or part of his ruse.

What are you doing, Cece? Her mind spun wildly. It was madness kissing a complete stranger in the woods at night, and yet she'd let him do it and was enjoying it.

The hunter slid his hand down her side, his fingertips roaming to the slit in her dress before drawing her leg up. She gasped as a new riot of sensation whipped through her. She widened her legs and brought a hand to his hip, desperate to pull him closer.

Laughter trickled from the trail, much closer than before.

The hunter did his best to distract her, pressing his hips into her. She felt him hard against her. Her body went rigid. Her eyes snapped open.

The hunter pulled away, murmuring against her neck. "Apologies for being so improper. I won't hurt you, but they might."

He went back to kissing her neck and hit a spot that set her blood on fire. Her breaths were quick and shallow. She moaned and rolled her head back against the boulder. It felt so good she wasn't even embarrassed. Spurred by her response, he did it again, and she rolled her hips against him.

He pulled up her other leg, so both were wrapped around his waist as he pressed his hips against her. Her heart pounded in her ears, and her entire focus narrowed to the pleasure of being touched that way, like the hunter would die of wanting if she didn't let him have her.

"Hey! You there!" a voice called from the trail. "What are you doing?"

The hunter pulled away. Cecilia was shocked by the disappointment she felt at the loss of his frenzied kisses.

"Goddess, you have to let go," he whispered.

She released her hold, her legs shaking as he set her on her feet. He smirked and turned to look at the men heading their way.

She could tell by the emblem on their vests that they were hunters. Their torches highlighted the mark's bright Argarian red. They would kill her if they knew who she was.

Where was Rainer? The hunters came from his direction. He couldn't have been nearby, because he would never have let a stranger kiss her like that.

"Good evening. Apologies for startling you," her hunter said, his voice smooth like honey. He stepped forward, blocking her from their view. "I was just enjoying a romantic swim with my lady."

The stout Argarian hunter smirked, trying to peek around him.

"Doesn't seem like she's much of a lady if she's out here at night letting you tumble her up against a rock." One of the men laughed.

"Perhaps not," her hunter said. "We'd appreciate your discretion."

"What brings you out here?" asked the tallest hunter.

Cecilia tried reading their emotions and could tell the towering hunter had been drinking from his slurred words and muted quality to his feelings.

"We came from May Falls for a night swim," Cecilia's hunter said. "She loves the full moon."

"I'd like to hear from the lady," said the third man. "My lady, are you all right?"

Cecilia stole her dagger back from her hunter. She stepped out from behind his right shoulder, holding her arms behind her, the wet gown taut on her skin. The biggest unknown was if the man she'd just kissed was really trying to help her.

"I'm all right," Cecilia said.

The stout hunter's eyes roamed from her face to her breasts to the slit up her leg.

"More than all right, I'd say," the tall man said with a laugh.

"Are you sure you want to be out here with this man? I expect a beautiful woman like yourself could do much better than this rake," the lead hunter added.

"You think a hunter like yourself might be a better option?" Cecilia asked. She gave him a sly smile and stepped toward him. "What brings you to these woods so late?"

"We were hunting for a powerful memory witch and her guardian. I'm leading this group," he said, puffing out his chest in pride.

Cecilia feigned a gasp. "A memory witch? That sounds dangerous."

She hated him leering at her, but as long as he was looking at her breasts, he wouldn't be wondering what she was holding behind her back.

"Did you find them?" she asked.

"Not yet." He swallowed, looking her up and down again. "Although you are a welcome distraction, my lady."

"My love?" Cecilia's hunter called. She was very close to the three Argarian hunters now.

"Darling, you keep an eye on this tall fellow. I suspect he's had a few drinks and might be trouble," Cecilia said, winking at the tall hunter.

Hoping her hunter understood her meaning, she looked back at the man in front of her. "I've always had a thing for hunters."

The man grabbed her waist. She tried not to bristle but looked into his eyes and smiled.

"What's behind your back, miss?" he asked.

Cecilia stabbed the dagger into his throat and yanked it out. The man stumbled back, and she sent the dagger sailing into the chest of the hunter beside him. Before the tall man could react, Cecilia's hunter shot an arrow through his heart, and he crumpled to the ground.

"Cutting it a little close, Goddess," her hunter said.

"I had it under control."

The hunter smiled and shrugged on his vest. Cecilia could finally see the color of the emblem: Olney green. He was from home. Relief poured in as she retrieved her dagger. There was something familiar about him, but she'd met so many hunters as the huntmaster's daughter.

"My name is Xander Merleen," he said. "I thought you might want to know since you kissed me and all."

"Kissed you?" She whipped her head around to look at him. "You kissed me!"

"And you kissed me back."

Though she'd liked the dimple before, it made her furious now. "I was *pretending*."

"That's a lie that only you believe, love. I felt the way you came alive in my arms. The way you pulled me closer. I heard the way you moaned when I—"

"Stop—" She shivered, thinking about his lips on her neck.

Cecilia knew the name Xander Merleen, though she couldn't recall ever meeting him. Her father was often singing his praises and, according to Sylvie, so were the ladies of the court, though they were speaking to an entirely different set of skills.

"It's okay to admit you enjoyed it," he said with a wink. "I'm not afraid to admit that I did, but I'm sure you felt that. Your enthusiasm surprised me."

Cecilia's cheeks burned as she looked away.

"The way you blush in the moonlight makes me want to do it again," he whispered.

He struck like a viper, wrapping his arms around her. He was so focused on getting close to her, he missed what she was doing with her hands. She pressed the tip of her dagger into his neck.

"You are magnificent." He laughed.

His mischievous hazel eyes glowed like liquid gold. Something about his voice and the way he moved was terribly familiar.

"Magnificent? I could kill you where you stand," Cecilia whispered.

"I know. That's why I said it. I didn't see it coming."

She frowned. "You're a sloppy hunter."

His gaze dropped to her lips. "Maybe I'm distracted by the desire to kiss you again—maybe more than kiss you."

"You can't speak to me that way," Cecilia said.

"Who will stop me, Goddess?" Xander leaned in, allowing the blade to nick his neck. He looked at her mouth before meeting her eyes again.

"You're making me cut you."

"Then move the blade."

"If I move it, you will have me up against that rock again."

"All the more reason to do it." He smiled, letting his hand cup her bottom.

"Are you always this crude with ladies of the court?"

"Only when they want me to be." He laughed.

"I don't want that." She bit her lip to keep from grinning.

"Sure you do. That's why you haven't stabbed me, and it's why you keep looking at my lips. You're wondering what else they can do. I can tell you're the adventurous type. I promise, if you let them, they can do magical things. Would you like to find out?"

She gasped but kept the blade where it was. Xander smelled like bergamot and cedarwood. The scent evoked a memory. Her memory witch powers were mostly an advantage, but sometimes they were a distraction.

"I would like you to let go of me and take a step back," she said.

"Your lips say one thing, but your hips pressed into me, and you loosened your grip on the dagger. I suspect you would very much enjoy the way I would worship you. I could hear the way the words I said made your heart race."

Xander set her on her feet. She stepped back, annoyed at his magically enhanced hunter's hearing. She couldn't even get turned on without him eavesdropping on her heartbeat.

"What do you want?" Cecilia said, pulling dry clothes from her satchel.

"Other than another chance to kiss you?" He grinned. "Your father sent me to find you and Rainer McKay. Several duos have come under attack, so they're pulling hunters to protect the last witches pursuing the Gauntlet."

"Sounds like you're expendable. Perhaps I'd be better off without you," Cecilia said, crossing her arms.

Xander laughed. "On the contrary. The huntmaster requested me by name."

"How do I know this isn't a trick?" she asked, picking up her clothes. "Turn around."

"So bossy." Xander laughed but turned his back to her, and she quickly changed.

"How do I know you're telling the truth?" she asked, working on the buttons of her pants.

"I have a summons with instructions and a royal seal addressed to you and your guardian. Do you want to tell me where your guardian is?"

"You can turn around." Cecilia worked her long damp hair into a loose braid.

"I preferred your hair wild and loose. It suits you."

"Then I suppose it's good that I don't care what you prefer."

He laughed, sending butterflies scattering her stomach. "Your guardian?"

"I don't know where Rainer is. He always gives me space to bathe, but never more than a short time, and he's always within earshot in case I run into trouble."

"I suspect that it's rare you run into trouble you can't handle, Goddess."

"Don't call me that."

"Apologies, *Cecilia*."

The way he said it like it was a dirty word sent warmth pooling beneath her navel.

"How did you know it was me?" she asked.

"Your father described you and said you'd probably put up a fight, but I thought he was speaking figuratively. He knew the route your guardian planned and suggested I start here, close to the caves."

"Did he also suggest you kiss me?"

Xander's eyes lit with mischief. "No, that was improvised."

"I'm worried about Rain. Those other hunters came from the direction he went. What if he's hurt or—" She couldn't bring herself to say it. He couldn't be. She would feel it, but at the moment, she couldn't feel anything through their connection.

"Don't worry until we have to. I'm sure there's an explanation, although he really shouldn't have left you, even though you can defend yourself. It's sloppy work." Xander looked angry. Cecilia wanted to defend Rainer.

"He did nothing wrong. I like my privacy."

"I would prefer your safety to privacy."

"I would prefer you not pass judgment on things you don't know or understand," she snapped.

"Do you always just say whatever you think?" Xander asked.

"Is that a right reserved only for men?" She picked up her bow and satchel and walked toward him. "Let me see the letter."

She broke the Olney green wax seal on the letter, and read the message from her father.

Xander led her to his horse. "We have to find your guardian."

"How? I can hardly feel him," Cecilia said.

"I am a hunter. If you think I can't track your careless guardian, you are seriously underestimating your father's training."

She frowned and followed Xander to a beautiful brown horse.

"What's his name?" Cecilia asked.

"He doesn't have a name. I just call him 'horse,'" Xander said.

She patted the nameless horse. "That's barbaric. He needs a name."

"What would you have me call him?"

Cecilia thought for a moment. "Biscuit."

"Biscuit?" Xander asked. "Hardly a name for a warhorse."

"I think he's more of a lover than a fighter," she said.

"Much like his rider, then?" Xander taunted.

"Hardly. You strike me as quite a bit of both."

"And you strike me as a woman who'd like to find out."

Cecilia rolled her eyes, and Xander chuckled as he helped her onto Biscuit. She watched him warily as he hoisted himself behind her. She tried sitting straighter so they wouldn't be so close, but he wrapped an arm around her, pulling her flush against him. She longed for some space to think, but her own horse was gone, along with Rainer.

"You'll be less sore if you relax," he said, leaning so close that his lips brushed her ear.

She shivered, unnerved by the effect he had on her.

"You're quite stubborn. Want to know what I think?" Xander said.

She sighed heavily and said, "No, but I suspect you'll tell me, anyway. You seem to enjoy the sound of your own voice."

"I think you like me. I think you enjoyed that kiss. I think you want me to do it again, but you're not ready to admit it yet, and that's okay. I can be patient."

He brought a hand to her hip, and she tensed against him.

"Don't worry," he said. "I won't do it unless you ask. I know you will eventually, and when you do, I will be happy to oblige."

She shook her head, laughed. "I knew hunters had enormous egos, but I have never seen one that rivals yours. I do not want you to kiss me again, and I definitely will not be asking for it."

Cecilia was certain that wasn't true and afraid she'd be asking for it much sooner than she hoped. There was something about Xander that made her feel like she was right on the edge of losing control, and yet it was so exhilarating to run toward that feeling. Still, she was unprepared to give the hunter an inch, or he'd try to claim a mile.

"You lie so beautifully, Cece, but your body tells the truth. Twice now you've moved perfectly with me."

"Twice?"

"Tonight and during that Reldan."

"You're my hunter!" Cecilia craned her neck to see him, her cheeks heating at her word choice.

"Yes. *Yours*," he said with a smug grin. "I promised you I would kiss you the way you deserved to be kissed when I saw you again. You with your legs wrapped around me, all wet from your swim, moaning

—that was not what I expected. Did it live up to your expectations? It certainly exceeded mine."

She ignored the question. "Did you spend all your time at court stalking me?"

"No, but anytime you were around, I couldn't help but watch you. You have a way of pulling all the light in the room, Cece. I'm surprised you didn't notice. You're quite observant yourself, and I was very popular at court."

Cecilia pursed her lips. "So I've heard."

"I only really had an interest in one lady, though. She was thoroughly unimpressed with my nonsense, and I couldn't get her out of my head. I was desperate to win her over."

"Oh, please," Cecilia sighed.

"Why is it so hard for you to believe that I enjoyed your company, and the more I talked to you, the more I liked you? I should have kissed you as soon as you walked into the garden that last night. I regretted it. The way you responded to my touch. I've thought about it every night since."

Cecilia was speechless. Xander lifted his hand from her hip, ran his finger against her throat, and slid it up to her cheek. He turned her head toward him. She thought he might kiss her again, but he held her head pressed into his chest.

"You should try to rest, Cecilia. I'm sure you're tired, and I'm not sure how long we will have to ride to find your guardian," Xander whispered. "It's okay to let yourself relax. I will find the guardian. I will keep you safe."

She wanted to argue, but she was too tired. His voice was soothing, and he ran his thumb gently along her jawline. Her eyelids grew impossibly heavy. Despite the motion of the horse and the strangeness of being pressed against someone she hardly knew, she drifted to sleep.

PART II:

INT�he WILD

10

The morning light cut through a thick canopy of pines as Cecilia and Xander rode at an easy pace through the forest. Though he'd ridden all night with Cecilia asleep in his arms, Xander seemed no worse for the wear, thrilled with the challenge of a hunt.

"You realize the farther we get from where you were, the more likely it is that he's—"

"I would know if he's dead," she interrupted. She expected Xander to laugh or tease her, but he simply nodded.

"I hope you are right, Goddess. We could use his help for the rest of your journey," Xander said, kicking the horse into a trot.

"Why do you insist on calling me that?" she asked, scanning the horizon.

"Because it's been stuck in my head since the moment I saw you in the moonlight. You can call yourself whatever you like, but I prefer goddess."

"Some might consider that blasphemous," she taunted.

"I doubt they would fault me if they had seen what I did."

Cecilia expected to feel guilty, as if kissing Xander somehow betrayed Rainer. Really, she just wanted him to do it again.

She turned and expected him to smile in his usual teasing way, but his face was starkly serious. His eyes made her squirm like they could burn right through to her and see all the things she kept hidden. It had been easier to be herself when he was an anonymous hunter in the garden. Now she felt nervous and disoriented every time he shifted against her.

Cecilia focused her energy on reading Xander. His emotional signature was more unique than anyone she'd met. The air crackled when he moved—dangerous and thrilling, his emotions projected out in front of him like a storm front. The way he failed to guard his feelings was so similar to how she met the world.

"Were you disappointed to be pulled off your regular assignment for this?" she asked.

"They honored me with such an important task, though I'll admit I hadn't planned on having to rescue your guardian," Xander said. "I had the impression he was one of the best."

"He is."

"I admire your loyalty. I understand you two are close."

Her crush on Rainer might have been common knowledge, but she didn't like when relative strangers brought it up.

"You shouldn't believe everything you hear." She sighed. "We grew up together. We've trained together for years. Of course we're close."

"He's your best friend?" Xander asked.

"Yes."

"And your lover?"

"What? No!" Cecilia choked on the words. "That's forbidden."

"And who has that stopped?" Xander said with a laugh. "Many witches and guardians have physical relationships. The forbidden nature of it is what makes it so appealing. I didn't peg you for a by-the-book kind of woman."

"I'm not. I just understand the importance of not allowing emotions to cloud our work. It's safer that way." Just saying those words left a bad taste in her mouth.

"Is that what you believe, or what McKay believes?" Xander challenged.

Cecilia shifted, as if to give herself space from the truth.

Xander tightened his arm at her waist and pulled her back, pinning her against him. He dropped his head so his lips were at her ear. "He's a fool. You're stunning."

Years ago, Cecilia noticed the shift in men's gazes from the dismissive way they appraised a child to interest that came when they saw a pretty woman. Women in Olney weren't supposed to acknowledge their own beauty, even as the world held it up as the only currency worth having.

It was one reason her father taught her to fight.

There are greater dangers than witches and hunters, Cecilia. The minds of men can bring their own terrors, Leo had said the first time he taught her to hold a blade.

But no one ever looked at her the way Xander did. It was an admiration that made her more uncomfortable and intrigued than all the leering of the past.

"Well, we work together now, so you should probably stop telling me about the moonlight on my skin, and you should definitely avoid kissing me," Cecilia said, uncertain if she wanted him to listen.

"I'm quite certain I couldn't promise to do those things if my life depended on it," Xander whispered. He brushed her hair aside and planted a soft kiss against the side of her neck.

She flinched. "You said you wouldn't do that again unless I asked you to."

"Apologies. You reminded me of the moonlight on your skin and kissing you, and I had a momentary lapse of sanity."

"You have major boundary issues. Has anyone ever told you that?" Cecilia craned her neck to give him a dirty look.

"Gods, you have the most beautiful, expressive eyes. If you keep looking at me like that —" His eyes shot to the road. "We're close."

Her bond surged to life, searching for Rainer. When they were children, it made hide-and-seek rather boring, but it was extremely helpful in crowds and out in the wild.

Xander brought the horse to a stop and helped her down. He placed her bow in her hands and held a finger to his lips.

"Which way?" he asked.

Cecilia closed her eyes and focused on her connection to Rainer. She gave a gentle tug on the bond like she did when she needed his help. A moment later, relief rushed through her as a tug reverberated back.

She made her way through the thick ferns on the forest floor with Xander on her heels. After a moment, she tugged again, and a surge of fear and anxiety shot back through their bond. Rainer was trying to scare her off. She rubbed her sternum, trying to soothe the ache as she continued in the same direction.

The trees thinned, and the scent of woodsmoke filled the air as Xander and Cecilia came to the edge of the forest. From their vantage point at the top of the hill looking down into the valley, Cecilia counted twelve enemy hunters.

"That one is a slayer," Xander said, nodding toward a particularly burly man.

"How do you know?"

"I can see the emblem from here," Xander said.

"If you can move Rainer out of the way, I can take them out with a storm," she offered. "It's unpredictable power."

Xander considered it.

"That's not a bad last resort, but I would rather not let a group of hunters know that they have a powerful witch to capture, and I'd prefer not to be struck by lightning today," he said.

"Are you afraid, Xander? You've certainly been singing your own praises enough that I was expecting to be impressed," she taunted.

"I fear nothing, but that is an unnecessary risk." He brushed a hand over her cheek, but she swatted it away.

"If you don't help me save him, then you can just go home now and tell my dad he should have sent someone who isn't an asshole," Cecilia said, her eyes blazing with anger.

"There she is," he said, stifling a laugh. "I have a better idea. You're an excellent shot, even from horseback."

Cecilia nodded.

"Worst-case scenario, how many can you take out with their full attention on you?"

She stared at him, slack-jawed. "You're really going to let me help?"

Rainer would have never let her ride into a fight that outmatched. She would have done it anyway, but Rainer's plan wouldn't have included her putting herself in harm's way.

"I'm not *letting you* do anything." Xander frowned. "I need your help if I'm going to get him out of there. I'm good, but I'm not good enough to face off with eleven hunters and a slayer alone. So I'll ask you again. How many can you take out on the first pass?"

"Six, maybe seven? I'm more concerned about the slayer. Rainer and I fought one alone, and we barely made it out alive. I tried to counter his magic while Rainer fought, but some of them have powers I don't know how to handle."

"I've heard that as well. I want you to ride in and take out who you can. They won't be expecting two of us. While they are distracted, I will free Rainer and hope that's enough to even the score. Then I will go after the slayer," Xander said. "And you will ride away until you reach the next town."

"I won't leave you and Rainer behind," she said.

"We'll catch up, but it will be easier for both of us."

She shook her head. "Out of the question. I won't run, and I'm not a distraction. I want to help."

"Cece, it is possible to be both brave and smart. I can't do what I have to if you are there," Xander said.

"Why not?"

Xander took both of her hands in his, pleading with her with his eyes. "Because I find you exceedingly distracting, and I suspect your guardian will, too. I promised your father I would keep you safe. I need you to trust me like you did yesterday."

"You promise not to let anything happen to Rainer?" she asked.

"He's a guardian. He's not my responsibility."

Cecilia frowned. "Rainer being hurt would hurt me, and you promised to keep me safe."

Xander sighed heavily. "Fine, I promise to protect him as well."

They walked back to Biscuit. Xander handed her one of his vests.

"Put this on," he said.

"Why?"

"So they think you're a hunter and not a witch."

She tugged on the vest. It was too big, but Xander adjusted the laces so that it sat closer to her body. He rested his hand on her hip, ready to help her onto Biscuit. He hesitated, a mischievous smile passing over his lips.

"Cece, I wonder if maybe you want me to kiss you before we set out. This is a dangerous task, and you might not get another chance."

A fiery flush crept up her neck. "You are—"

"Charming? Handsome?"

"Overconfident," she countered.

"Very well. I suppose it's for the best. We wouldn't want you moaning like yesterday and letting them know we're here."

Cecilia took a swing.

Xander caught her arm and said, "I will just wait until after to collect my reward." He kissed her hand and swept her up on the horse. "Give me a five-minute head start, then charge in."

She nodded, and he disappeared into the woods with his short swords and bow. She waited with nothing to keep her company but the sound of the wind-stirred pines scraping needles together.

She adjusted her quiver so she'd be able to work quickly and, when it was time, took off at a gallop down the hill toward the Argarian hunters' camp.

The hunters were clearly surprised at the rescue attempt. Cecilia shot an arrow through the eye of the first hunter before he could even register that she was holding her bow. Before any of them could stand, she took down two more, narrowly avoiding an arrow as they returned fire. She did as she promised in her first pass, taking out seven of the hunters with little trouble.

Like always, Cecilia felt Rainer before she saw him. She found him in the fray. As she locked eyes with him, she felt fear through the connection.

"Cece! Look out!" Rainer shouted.

She wasn't fast enough. Before she knew it, she was on her back in the grass with the wind knocked out of her. She gasped, looking around wildly. Blinding pain tore through her ribs from the impact, but she didn't have time to figure it out if they were broken. The slayer stalked toward her. Her eyes narrowed on the emblem on his vest: an open palm holding flame and a dagger.

Slayers were the most fearsome warriors in the Argarian army, adept at both combat and magic. Worse, if he figured out she was a memory witch, he would drain her of all her memories and power, leaving her a brainless husk.

She pushed away the fear threatening to cloud her mind. She'd never faced off against a slayer alone, but if Rainer was hurt, she didn't want this man anywhere near him.

He brought down a sword, and she barely had time to roll out of the way before it split the earth next to her. Sweeping her leg, she brought him down next to her. She hopped back to her feet. Her ribs throbbed with every movement.

"Hunter!" he spat. "You shouldn't have come here!"

It took a moment for her to realize he was talking to her. Xander's plan worked. She'd taken out seven hunters on horseback with a bow, a decidedly hunter thing to do. A witch would have used her magic.

Cecilia's bow had landed several yards away, so she unsheathed her dagger, held it out, and settled into a fighting stance. The slayer was distracted by the commotion behind him. The clang of steel meeting steel cut through the air. Rainer was free, fighting alongside Xander.

The slayer winced, stumbling toward Cecilia. He reared up and wrenched an arrow from his back, then turned toward Xander.

Xander met her eyes and mouthed, "Run."

She ignored him, using the distraction to leap onto the slayer's back. She brought her hands to his temples. Although her memory powers weren't terribly useful in a fight over distance since they required her to touch someone, she could use them in close combat. The slayer bucked, trying to pull her off, but she called forth her power, and his body went rigid.

Although she could copy memories, she could also remove them with surgical precision or all at once, like a slayer. It was an unusual talent that she'd learned on instinct, since it wasn't taught in Olney's magic classes.

She pulled the memories from his head. They were laced with so much hatred and anger, they hurt to take in. When she had all memories relevant to his assignment, she pulled his memory of who he was, how to fight, and what he was supposed to do next. He crumpled beneath her, a feeble mess, and Cecilia landed hard on her knees, meeting Xander's wide eyes.

A hunter took a swing at him. He narrowly ducked. In her fear for him, she'd missed another hunter taking aim at her.

She turned at the last second as an arrow seared through her left side, grazing her ribs. Her hand flew to the wound, but she kept moving despite the stickiness of the blood on her side. Cecilia wasn't close enough to hit the hunter with her dagger. She had to keep charging. She prayed he was a bad shot.

A second arrow sank in just below her left collarbone. Cecilia yelped as she crumpled to the ground. The fiery pain sliced through her, blotting out everything else.

Rainer yelled her name from somewhere far away. His fear tore through their connection in echo to her pain.

Her assailant stood over her with eyes full of contempt. He straddled her. She tried to shove him away, but her left arm was weak, and when she moved, the arrow sent a jolt of pain through her body.

The hunter lifted his dagger high over her chest. She stared up at him, unable to move.

"Ready to die, hunter?" he taunted.

"Not a hunter," she sputtered. Her right hand rested on his thigh, and she looked up into his eyes. "A witch."

He brought the blade down, but she snagged his mind, and he froze in place, knife hovering over her. She used her memory magic to push the hatred from the slayer's memories into her attacker. He let out a loud, animalistic scream and rolled off of her.

He was lost in overwhelming anger. That much hate could drive a non-magical person mad if the overcrowding of memory in his brain didn't. He writhed on the ground, foaming at the mouth.

Xander looked baffled, and frightened. When Cecilia realized the fighting was over, she collapsed onto her back in relief.

Rainer slid down next to her, and pulled her into a hug. His anxiety was as suffocating as his arms. "Cece! You're hurt. You should have gone back to court."

"Don't be hysterical. It's a scratch," she grumbled.

He looked down at the arrow and at the blood on her side. "Only you would call a chest wound a scratch."

He leaned his forehead against her, his lips brushing her damp skin.

"It will heal," she said.

His eyes were wild and far away. She put a hand to his cheek.

"Rain, it's not like last time," she said. "It will heal. I'm more worried about you. Are you okay? How did they get you?"

Rainer shook his head. "I was tying up the horses downstream from you, and I checked the area, but the second I turned my back, someone hit me on the head. When I woke up, I was at their camp. I'm sorry I was careless and you got hurt."

Shame snaked through their bond. Cecilia touched the cut above his right eye. He flinched, then leaned his cheek into her palm.

"Goddess, you didn't run," Xander said as he knelt beside them.

"Cece has never run from a fight in her life." Rainer sighed. "She has more courage than sense."

Xander smirked. "I see that now. I probably should have known when she tried to kill me last night."

Rainer's brow creased in concern. "What happened?"

"We should head to your next location before someone else shows up," Xander said. "Before you try to send me away, McKay, they have assigned me to help you protect Cecilia. There have been some attempts at kidnapping our witches, and the Teripins and Commander Reznik personally assigned me to the two of you."

He handed the summons over to Rainer, who skimmed it warily before tucking it in his pocket.

"Is the huntmaster still in Olney?" Rainer asked.

Cecilia couldn't believe she hadn't thought to ask Xander the night before.

Xander's eyes narrowed on her. "I left a week ago, and he had not yet been dispatched to the front, but they were assembling his battalions."

Cecilia was running out of time. If she could finish the Gauntlet before he was sent out, perhaps he'd be able to stay safe at home. She took a shuddering breath, instantly brought back to the pain in her ribs.

"I need to heal my broken ribs and get this arrow out before I can ride," Cecilia grunted.

Rainer stopped her from reaching for the arrow. "I can do it, Cece."

"You're always too tentative. You'll make it worse."

Xander leaned closer. "I can do it. Goddess, do you want to rethink my offer from earlier?"

"Absolutely not," she said, trying not to blush. She willed him to be silent.

"Liar." Xander smirked. "It was very sexy watching you kill all those hunters."

He grabbed the arrow with one hand, bracing himself on her collarbone with the other as Rainer held her hand.

Xander leaned closer. She felt disoriented, lost in his eyes. Then he ripped the arrow out. She hissed out a breath and squeezed Rainer's hand before letting out a string of curses that made Xander chuckle.

"I'm sorry to surprise you. It's just better if you don't see it coming," Xander said. "It hurts less and does less damage to the muscle. I need to clean and cover it, Cece. May I tear your shirt to see the wound?"

She nodded. He untied and removed the hunter's vest. Despite Rainer's proximity, what was between her and Xander felt strangely intimate. He split the seam of her shirt and opened it, never taking his gaze from hers. He brushed her undergarments down her shoulder. Rainer tensed and drew her closer to his chest, but she couldn't look away from Xander.

"This will hurt. I'm sorry," Xander whispered, pulling out a flask.

He poured alcohol on her wound, and she hissed in pain. She leaned her head on Rainer's chest and listened to the sound of his heartbeat.

When the burning finally died down, Xander's fingers grazed her skin. She tipped her head back, her mind drifting to their kiss. He smirked, pulled a bandage out of his bag, and carefully wrapped the wound. She wondered irrationally if he could read her thoughts.

"Let's see your side now," Xander said, pulling at the hem of her shirt.

Rainer watched with distrust as Xander's fingers grazed up the skin of her waist. Goosebumps rose in the wake of his touch. He cleaned and wrapped the wound.

As Xander worked, Rainer ran his thumb over her inner wrist.

"You okay, Cece?" Rainer whispered.

"Yes. Now, what's this?" She reached her thumb up, brushing it over the crease in his brow. "I found a worry, but I'll fix it in a hurry."

Rainer's face softened into a smile as she covered the cut on his head with her hand. After a moment, the cut was healed, the dried blood the only sign that a wound had even existed.

"Gods, that's amazing," Xander said. "Should I have just let you do all this yourself?" He gestured to the wound on her side.

"No, I'm too worn out and in too much pain right now to heal myself. That was just a little cut. I used a lot of magic in the fight. I need to save up some energy for the damage from these wounds. I'll heal my ribs now, and I'll take care of the rest when we stop for the night or tomorrow."

Xander pulled her shirt back into place as Cecilia healed the broken ribs until they were nothing but a dull ache.

The Argarian hunters' horses had fled during the battle, and Cecilia's horse, Little Ghost, was living up to his name, having completely disappeared. Luckily, Rainer's horse, Zeke, and Xander's mount, Biscuit, wandered back.

Rainer retrieved her flask, and she took a long gulp of her syrupy tea to rebuild her energy before offering it to Xander.

He took drank, sputtered, and spit it out. "What is that?"

"Witch tea." Cecilia giggled.

"It's foul," Xander said, grimacing.

"It helps me rebuild my energy quickly in case we run into more trouble." Cecilia pulled a clean shirt from her saddlebag on Xander's horse and turned to find Xander staring. "Turn around."

He winked. "Of course."

Once she'd changed, Cecilia and Rainer rode off together, having not found her horse. Xander followed close behind.

She grinned as the wind whipped through her hair, relieved that Rainer was safe and relishing the familiarity of being by his side.

"What's with you and Xander?" Rainer asked. He tried to sound casual, but she felt the tension in his body.

"He found me bathing after you disappeared last night," Cecilia said. "I saw he was a hunter, but I couldn't tell who for, so of course I attacked him."

"Why would you risk that? That's Xander Merleen. He's at the top of his hunting class. You could have been hurt," Rainer scolded. "How do you not know him?"

"It was dark, and we'd never met face-to-face before." She shrugged.

"Cecilia." He only used her full name when frustrated with her.

"I was scared, and I kept waiting for you to come back, so I bought myself time. I knew you would know what to do, but then we were fighting, and these other hunters came along, and we had to fight them, and I was just in my bathing gown."

She turned and saw Rainer looking horrified. Xander smirked before riding ahead to give them privacy, or at least the illusion of it.

"It was fine. It was dark. No one saw anything. It just kept getting tangled around my legs, which was annoying," she said.

"I'm sure they saw plenty. No wonder he was looking at you like that today," Rainer said.

"Like what?" she scoffed.

"Like he was picturing you naked. And what's with the nickname? Goddess? That's a bit much, no?"

She felt it then, in a quick surge through their bond. "Rain, are you jealous?"

"No, but it's my job to protect you from all threats."

"And now a kiss is a threat?" She laughed.

"A kiss from him is. His conquests are—prolific."

"That's hypocritical coming from you, isn't it, Rain?"

"Maybe, but I would hate to see you hurt," he whispered.

"Nothing happened."

He sighed. "You're lying."

"I'm not."

"I always know, Cece."

"Maybe you're getting rusty."

Rainer leaned close to her ear and said, "I don't trust him, Cece. I just want you to be careful."

It astonished her how simple things like that could startle her. Her heart raced at his proximity.

"If you don't trust him, why are you letting him come with us?" she asked.

"Because we were ordered to, and when it comes to your safety, I'm willing to get all the help we can, especially with the way you can't help running toward danger. You know, he told me his plan for my rescue, and it's exactly what I would have done. I trust him to keep you safe, but I don't trust him beyond that. Be careful how much you show him of yourself."

"Is that literal or figurative?" she asked, trying to make a joke.

"Both."

"Rain?"

"Yeah?"

"I'm just so glad you're all right."

He hugged her, and she leaned her head back against his shoulder. For a moment, their tension eased. They fell into a comfortable silence, Rainer stuck in his own head and Cecilia too tired and sore to carry on an idle conversation.

11

When they finally stopped for the night in a dense group of trees, Cecilia practically fell into Xander's arms as she climbed off Zeke. They'd been on high alert all afternoon. The vigilance was draining but necessary since Rainer decided they should stay on their initial route to have a prayer of making it in and out before full war broke out.

The temperature dropped as the sun went down, and since they were at a higher elevation as they entered the more mountainous region, a chill hung in the air. She hadn't noticed when they were riding because Rainer's proximity kept her warm.

She shivered, but before she could even look at her satchel, Xander handed her a sweater. She fought a smile as he helped her put it on over her wounded shoulder. It smelled like him, a pleasant blend of cedar and bergamot.

"Just as I suspected." He smiled at her, pulling her hair out of the collar, his fingers lingering on her neck.

"What?" she asked.

"You look just as lovely in blue as you do in green. It brings out your eyes."

Her gaze darted to Rainer, worried he'd catch her fawning over the hunter, but he was busy starting a fire.

"I still owe you that kiss," Xander whispered, brushing his thumb over her bottom lip.

"I didn't ask for it." She refused to give Xander the satisfaction of knowing how interested she was.

"Yet," he teased. "You will."

"Funny that you're the only one bringing it up," she said casually.

"But not the only one who's been thinking about it."

Cecilia enjoyed the flirtation. It reminded her of their time in the garden. "I should go help Rain."

"He can handle a fire," Xander whispered. "He's had you to himself all day. I've missed you."

She rolled her eyes. "You barely know me."

"And yet I already pine for you. All day, the only thing I could think of was kissing you." Xander sighed.

"Oh, please," Cecilia scoffed. "I'm not just some empty-headed woman who will swoon over your poetic ramblings. The moonlight on my skin, thinking about kissing me all day? You must think me a common fool."

"Of course not. I think you uncommonly lovely. Would you prefer hand-to-hand combat as courtship? I'd be happy to oblige, but seeing as you're wounded, it seemed inappropriate today."

Xander tucked a stray hair behind her ear with the same familiarity usually reserved for Rainer. His hand lingered on her neck.

"How are you feeling? It frustrated me when you didn't run. I was so distracted worrying about you, I only killed three hunters."

Cecilia smiled sardonically. "I'm fine. So sorry I distracted you from your murder spree."

"But I hate to see you in pain," he said, guiding her chin up so she met his eyes. "What did you do to that slayer?"

"It was just some memory magic."

"It was like no memory magic I've ever seen."

"I'd expect a hunter wouldn't have seen much," Cecilia said pointedly.

"I suppose." Xander smirked.

His fingers roamed down the back of her neck, and she shivered. They stared at each other. She wanted him to kiss her again. Though she wouldn't admit it, her body leaned toward him involuntarily. Xander's eyebrows shot up in surprise.

"Cece? Can you help me?" Rainer called.

"I'm winning you over, Moon Goddess," Xander whispered.

"You keep telling yourself that," Cecilia said over her shoulder as she walked toward Rainer.

"Nice sweater," Rainer mumbled as Cecilia squatted down next to him and conjured a small flame to get their fire started.

"Thank you. I was cold."

"Why do you let him touch you like that?" Rainer asked.

"I like the way he touches me." She paused, questioning whether she should tell Rainer. As much as his jealousy thrilled her, it also confused her. Rainer didn't want her, but he also didn't want her moving on.

"Rain, he's the hunter from home, the one who left the roses," she said.

Rainer's eyes went wide in recognition. "Well, that's just—"

A feeling she didn't recognize flowed through her bond with Rainer. It felt like a sinking regret and nauseating envy. He opened his mouth to say more and then shook his head, thinking better of it.

Rainer said little for the rest of the night. They ate dinner in silence before settling in to sleep. Cecilia could barely keep her eyes open, the blood loss and exhaustion weighing heavily on her.

After the attack, they decided they were no longer safe to all sleep at the same time. Someone would need to stay awake to watch for threats.

"I'll take the first watch," Xander offered.

"But you were up all night riding," Cecilia argued.

"She's right. I'll take the first watch," Rainer said, picking up his bow and sword and stalking away.

"I guess it's just you and me, Cece. Let me tuck you in." Xander pulled a blanket up, and she grinned. He lay down a few feet away.

"You're staring," she whispered.

"Just making sure you're okay. You look cold."

"I'm fine," she said. The temperature had plunged further, and her breath came in little puffy clouds in the cold air. She shivered under the blanket.

"You know. I would be happy to help keep you warm if you wanted me to. You just need to ask," Xander whispered.

She closed her eyes, pulling the blanket tighter around her. After a few moments of quiet, Xander spoke again.

"Your teeth chattering could wake the dead."

Cecilia opened her eyes, annoyed at the amused look on his face. "I'll adjust."

"Are you afraid to let me close? I promised I wouldn't do anything you didn't ask me to do. I can behave myself."

"It's hard to fall asleep when you won't stop talking or staring at me." She sighed. Cecilia closed her eyes again and tried to keep herself from shaking.

"It's my job to keep you safe. If you freeze to death, I won't have done my job, and that will be hard to explain to your father. I promise I'll behave myself," Xander said.

"Will it shut you up?" she asked.

"Yes, and I'll be a perfect gentleman."

"I'm certain you have no idea how to do such a thing."

Xander pulled her against his chest. Warmth flooded her body. He wrapped the blankets tight around them. After a few minutes, she stopped shaking.

"Is that better?" he whispered. She was warm but wide awake. "Relax, you're as tense as you were when you first started riding with me."

"I'm just not used to sleeping so close to a stranger," she whispered.

"We're well-acquainted now, aren't we? After all our time in the gardens in Olney and on the road here? After our kiss?"

Cecilia sighed. "I suppose we are, but I've always struggled to sleep when I'm not at home."

"You seemed to sleep quite well in my arms last night," he countered.

"That was unusual."

"Perhaps I just have a soothing effect on you, and you aren't willing to give me credit for it," Xander suggested.

"Or perhaps your endless self-important droning bores me to sleep."

He laughed. Then his face grew serious, and he looked down at her lips again.

"I think you were right about how tempting I find your proximity. Now that you're pressed up against me, all I can think about is you pressed up against me last night."

Her breath hitched as he pulled her closer.

"That was quite surprising, you know. Not just that you let me kiss you but that you kissed me back," he whispered.

"Well, I hope you enjoyed it, because it won't be happening again," she said, closing her eyes.

"I enjoyed it, and I look forward to doing it many more times."

She stifled a nervous laugh. "But not tonight."

"There's always tomorrow," Xander said.

———

Trying to take off layers of clothing with a shoulder wound in the freezing cold was a slow and exhaustive effort for Cecilia's already weary body. She'd woken stiff but warm at first light, her body pressed against Rainer's. Sometime during the night he must have changed places with Xander, but she'd slept so heavily she missed it.

Now, she was happy to have some alone time. She hadn't been on her own in weeks, and she needed to clear her head. Checking that Xander wasn't spying on her, she slowly changed into her bathing gown and removed the bandage.

The morning was cloudy, the air thick with the scent before snow. All the foliage in the forest seemed poised to curl in on itself at the first flakes.

She knew the water would be icy, but fresh water was hard to come by, and she was still caked in blood and sweat from their fight the day before. Hissing as she waded into the icy stream, she washed up quickly and was ringing out her hair when the crunch of leaves startled her. She drew her dagger and turned to find Xander watching her on the shore.

"Goddess, we have to stop meeting like this." Mischief danced in his eyes as his gaze passed shamelessly over the bathing gown stuck to her skin.

"I wanted some alone time."

"I told you before. I value your safety over your privacy," Xander chided.

She frowned at him, shivering as she stepped out of the water. He pulled off his tunic and started on his pants.

Cecilia gasped, abruptly turning away. "What are you doing?"

"Bathing."

There was a splash behind her as he moved into the water. Cecilia kept her eyes averted as she changed into her last clean set of clothes and Xander's sweater before glancing at him.

He stood with his back to her, waist-deep in the water. Cecilia took in his well-defined shoulders and back as water droplets slid down the path of least resistance along the lines of muscle. His skin was a ledger of combat written in scars. Cecilia's fingers itched to trace each mark and hear the story of how he received it.

She sat down on a log, facing away from the water. Lifting the hem of her shirt, she brought her hands to the wound on her side. She took deep breaths, drawing on her power. Tingling healing spread through her body as the wound knitted over to a pink scar and then, nothing at all.

When she opened her eyes, Xander stood next to her, wearing just his britches, loose on his hips. The muscles of his stomach rippled as he moved. She'd felt the strength of those muscles when he'd lifted her up the day before, but seeing them on display was mesmerizing.

"Xander!" she said, covering her eyes with a hand too slowly. "Can you put some clothes on, please?"

"See something you like?" he taunted as he pulled on a tunic.

Yes, everything. A flush spread up her neck to her cheeks. She'd only seen Rainer in such a state of undress after his morning swims in the sea beneath her cottage, and that left her similarly flustered.

She tried to ignore him as she brought her hand inside her shirt to the wound in her left shoulder. She breathed deeply, calling on the same power as before. Flurries began to fall around them as the wound slowly knit back together. It took longer since the injury was more serious.

After a few minutes, her shoulder looked normal, though the pain and stiffness would remain for a day or two. She moved her shirt so Xander could see.

"Amazing. You would never know," he marveled. He leaned in close and placed a feather-light kiss where the mark had been. She rose to her feet, and the blood rushed to her head, sending her stumbling into Xander's arms.

"Sorry, sometimes healing wears me out," she said.

"Not a problem." Xander swept her into his arms.

Cecilia swatted at him. "I can walk. It was momentary dizziness."

"Gods, I love the way you smell. Even in the snow, you smell like midsummer in Olney, lemons and lavender. How is that?" He tucked his face into her neck.

"It's magic." She laughed. "Rainer's mother was an earth witch, but she had a gift for scents. She and my mother were good friends, and she used magic to bind the smell of the day I was born. My birthday is in late July, when the lemon trees and lavender bloom."

"The scent is intoxicating, just like your lips."

"Put me down," she said, trying to squirm out of his arms.

"I dreamt about kissing you all night," he whispered.

"Well, it's good to have ambitious dreams. Gives you something to aim for."

He laughed, continuing to carry her up the hill to their camp. "Say that you want me to."

"I'm not in the business of lying," she taunted.

"That's funny, because I think if you were, you would be terrible at it. Your heart races every time I suggest it."

"Maybe it's because it annoys me." She fought to hide her grin.

"It's not." Xander smirked at Cecilia as he set her back on her feet and brought his hands to frame her face. Her heart beat wildly at his proximity.

"Are you feeling better?" he asked, concern wrinkling his brow.

She wanted to say something, but the exhaustion and the way he looked at her made her shaky, so she just nodded.

"Can I assist you with anything else?" Xander's gaze dropped to her lips.

Snowflakes dusted his hair, and she reached up to brush one from his cheek. The entire scene was like something out of a fairy tale. She wanted to resist, but she was also desperately curious to see if it would feel the same to kiss him again.

"Kiss me," she whispered.

Xander smiled triumphantly, tilting her chin. He placed a soft, sweet kiss on her lips—short and tender and over much too soon.

"That's it?"

"Goddess, you're already weak in the knees. I didn't want you to faint."

She rolled her eyes but froze when her gaze landed on Rainer, watching them from the top of the hill.

Xander followed her gaze. "Plus, your guardian is watching. He always seems to interrupt us. I don't think he likes me."

Rainer's hands clenched at his sides as she worked her way up to meet him. Before she reached him, Xander grabbed her wrist and spun her toward him.

"Here. Take my scarf. It will be colder as we climb higher in these mountains. It will keep you warm," Xander said.

She smiled as he wrapped the soft wool scarf around her neck.

"We're about an hour's ride from the next cave," Rainer said tightly.

Cecilia felt him quietly seething, his anger sending warm prickles snaking down their bond. He helped her onto Zeke before hopping up behind her.

They took off without waiting for Xander. Rainer urged the horse on faster.

"Rain, it was just a kiss," she said.

He slowed their pace slightly. "It wasn't. I saw the way you looked at him like a lovestruck teenager, like all the women at court do."

"And like they all look at you," she shot back. "It's a meaningless flirtation."

"It's not. You really like him."

She could tell he wanted her to disagree. "I don't know him or how I feel, but regardless, it's not my priority right now. I don't know why you're so bent out of shape. You've seen me kiss other people before."

"Not like that."

"That was a chaste little kiss."

"It wasn't the kiss. It was the way you let him sweep you up. You let him take care of you. I've never seen you do that. If he hadn't been there yesterday, you would have pulled that arrow out yourself."

"Can we drop it? I have to focus today, and if you're mad at me, that will be hard to do," she said.

Rainer sighed heavily. "All right."

He was still stiff, but after a few minutes, he finally relaxed. They rode in silence for a while, the sun cutting across the forest. The shadows of the boughs above them were long by the time they drew close to the next cave.

"We're close," she said, signaling for Rainer and Xander to slow down.

"How do you know?" Xander asked.

"I can feel it," she said plainly.

"How?" asked Xander.

"We should stop. Stop!" Cecilia said.

They both pulled up quickly, and she hopped down. She paused and listened as the two men hopped down behind her.

"What is it, Cece?" Rainer asked.

"They're saying you can't come beyond here. Wait here," Cecilia said.

The cave mouth was twenty feet away. She'd only seen a cave's protective magic like this once before, when there was a slayer hiding inside.

"Cecilia, I'm charged with keeping you safe. I'm not letting you out of my sight," Xander said.

"You can't come. You can try, but they won't let you, and you risk madness. It's witches only beyond this point. I'll be fine. Rain—tell him. This is how some of these sacred sites are."

"It's true. I've tried to follow, and they won't let me. I end up walking in circles. It's potent magic," Rainer said.

She knelt down in the fresh snow and bowed her head, listening to the pulse of the place. Slowly, the frantic energy around the cave softened. When she finally felt permission come, she looked back at Rainer and Xander.

"Someone was here recently. Keep an eye out. I'll be back soon."

She drew her dagger as she stepped inside and let the dark swallow her up.

12

Cecilia emerged from the cave, taking in the restless trail of footprints Xander had left in the snow. He paused his pacing, his gaze resting on her bloody palm.

Rainer tugged on their bond as soon as he saw her, clearly sensing her anxiety, though he said nothing.

Xander guided her to a fallen log, placing her palm in his lap. He pulled out his flask, cleaning the wound before wiping it with a piece of cotton and kissing it. As she healed it, Xander's eyes burned into her like he could tell she was hiding something.

"Would you like to ride with me for a while, Goddess?"

Her gaze darted to Rainer. "I don't think that's a good idea."

"Whatever you say. I'll ride ahead and scout. McKay told me where we're headed."

Cecilia felt a sudden sense of foreboding. "Be careful."

Rainer helped her onto Zeke before hopping on behind her. He didn't relax until they settled into a trot and Xander was out of earshot.

"What's wrong?" he whispered.

"Rain, there was so much blood in the cave." Cecilia's composure cracked. "Much more than a typical exchange, but there was no one there. I asked the ancestral spirits, and they showed me a memory. I saw Mandy Midkiff."

Mandy was a sweet, quiet witch a year behind Cecilia in the memory witch training program.

"She was wounded when she entered the cave and told the spirits she was separated from her guardian because they were attacked," Cecilia continued. "He sent her to the cave, knowing that hunters wouldn't be able to enter. The last thing the cave spirits showed me was a slayer entering. The same one we fought before. I think she—"

Cecilia couldn't bear to say the words.

"Her guardian is Peter Quibly," Rainer said solemnly. "He's very capable, but if they ran into the same group I did—"

They'd narrowly avoided the same fate since the Argarian hunters hadn't caught them together. Rainer held her close as she cried.

"Deep breaths, Cece. I've got you." He ran a thumb over her cheek, brushing away tears. "Why didn't you say something in front of Xander? You don't trust him?"

"It's not a matter of trust. I might bend a lot of rules, but I take the rules of magic seriously. I'm not even supposed to tell *you* about what I experience in the caves, so I definitely shouldn't be telling a hunter."

They took off at a gallop, trying to catch up with Xander. Cecilia used the rhythm of the ride to clear her mind. Suddenly, the energy in the forest seemed to shift, all the spirits in the woods charging toward them, away from whatever was around the bend in the trail.

"Rain, slow down. Something is wrong," she said.

He'd become accustomed to Cecilia's sudden commands. He pulled the reins and eased the horse to a stop.

"I should leave you here and come back," Rainer said, eyes darting around the periphery.

"Hilarious that you would even suggest that." Cecilia grabbed her bow and quiver.

"Xander is probably already in trouble," Rainer said.

"I'm not letting you walk into this alone as well."

He pulled out his sword. "If things get crazy, you know you'll have to leave."

"If things get crazy, I will bring half the forest down with a storm, so you better get out of the way," Cecilia said.

She didn't have to look at him to know he was smiling. They came around a curve and saw the first hunter up in a tree.

"Scout!" Rainer called.

Cecilia was already firing. The man hit the ground behind them with a thud. The clank of steel cut through the forest. When they crested the hill, they saw Xander fighting with three hunters. Three additional hunters were making their way through the forest toward the fight.

"You've got this?" Rainer asked.

She nodded and took the reins. She slowed Zeke so Rainer could hop off, then sped up and attacked, putting an arrow through the eye of a hunter standing near Xander.

She didn't realize her mistake until she rounded the curve in the road and found three hunters waiting. Dropping back to lie flat on Zeke as their arrows whooshed past, Cecilia loosed two arrows from her backbend, killing one hunter instantly and wounding another.

Cursing herself for the sloppy second shot, she turned Zeke around and charged back. She fired again at the wounded hunter, taking him out for good.

Cecilia didn't anticipate the hunter knocking her from Zeke and tackling her to the dirt. The fall knocked the wind out of her. Wheezing from the fall and the hunter's weight on top of her, she could only turn her head as his fist connected with her cheek. She jabbed the heel of her hand into his chin, surprising him enough to scoot from under him.

Scrambling to her feet, she tried to catch her breath as she turned to face the hunter with her dagger in her hand.

"Deadly with a bow. Let's see how you do with a dagger, hunter," the Argarian hunter said, a hint of humor in his voice.

Cecilia had forgotten she was wearing Xander's sweater with the hunter logo. It wasn't the first time a man with a considerable size advantage had underestimated her. She didn't want to use magic and tip her hand as a witch if she didn't have to.

She assessed the hunter's weapons—a sword in his hand and a dagger strapped to his waist. She waited for him to strike first, the way confident men always did. He lunged, and she slid down on her knees, spinning past him and gashing his side with her dagger. She relied heavily on everything her father taught her about fighting someone with a longer reach.

Cecilia, when you're small, you must run toward the blade to deplete your opponent's advantage. Her father's voice rang in her head in every fight.

The hunter slashed with his sword, narrowly missing her. Cecilia spun behind him. They moved in fluid movements. Strike. Parry. Counter. She knew she just had to avoid him until she saw an opening. She chipped away at him, sensing his growing frustration with every blow.

"You're not bad for an Olney hunter," the Argarian hunter taunted. "Most of you are poorly trained and impatient. I haven't fought many female hunters."

"Clearly, or you wouldn't still be breathing." Cecilia winked.

She lunged left. He blocked with his sword, leaving his body exposed. He hadn't noticed she'd stolen his dagger until she shoved it into his ribs and twisted before pulling it free.

He dropped his sword, falling to the ground. His face clouded over, and the last breath left his lungs.

That was the part of the job she hated. It hurt her to hurt others. As much joy as she got out of vanquishing an enemy, it vanished the moment she saw their pain. She shoved the guilt away as she ran back to Rainer and Xander.

"Rain?" she called.

He was fighting one hunter but looked to be in control.

"Go find Xander," Rainer said, swiping at his opponent. "He's wounded. I lost sight of him."

Cecilia tried to breathe through the surprising panic that clamped down in her chest. She ran toward the sound of steel clashing. At the bottom of the hill, by a small stream, Xander was slumped with fatigue and covered in blood, an Argarian hunter on his heels.

Cecilia raced toward them, trying to stay quiet. Xander fell back. The hunter stood over him, about to plunge his sword down.

Fear descended. She wasn't going to reach them in time. She reached beyond memory magic and seized storm magic. It flew through her. A bolt of lightning struck out, slicing into the hunter and sending him flying.

The relief she felt vanished when she realized the jolt blew Xander back, too.

She knelt next to him. "Xander! Oh my gods! Did I hurt you? I shouldn't have done that. He was too close, but I knew I wouldn't reach you in time."

"Goddess, it's fine." He winced. "You saved me."

"Where are you hurt?" Cecilia rested a hand on his cheek.

Xander pushed her hands away, grimacing as he tried to sit up. "It's just a scratch."

"Let me fix it," Cecilia said.

She lifted his shirt and gasped at the deep gash running across his chest. Blood oozed from the wound, pocking the dirt with crimson.

"Gods, that's vicious," Rainer murmured as he stepped up beside them.

"You've lost a lot of blood, and I can tell it hurts," Cecilia rasped. She was crying because she was overwhelmed, not because she cared about Xander.

"Goddess, don't cry. I won't die," Xander said, brushing away her tears. "I haven't kissed you enough to give in to death yet. Grimon would have to drag me to the Underworld himself to get me away from you, and I'm not sure the god of death could manage that with the way I feel. I know what would heal me even better than your powers, Cece."

He winked at her. She laughed through her tears. Hearing the name Grimon pulled forth a childhood memory, but she couldn't afford any distractions when Xander was so hurt.

She leaned down and kissed Xander hard, certain he could feel her desperation. She didn't know if she was driven by frustration with Rainer, desire and fear for Xander, or a yearning to do something for herself for once.

"If you die. I will kill you," she whispered as she drew away.

Xander laughed weakly.

"I can't fix it all right now, but I'll do my best." She closed her eyes, trying to calm her emotions. Summoning all the healing power she could, she gently placed her hands over the wound. It was painstaking work, and it wasn't long until her power sputtered and a rush of dizziness forced her to stop. Although she'd made progress, the wound was far from healed.

"That's the best I can do right now. I'll try again when we stop for the night. We should clean you off," she said.

"I'll go get the horses," Rainer said, leaving the two of them alone.

She helped Xander clean off the blood in the creek, using his ruined shirt to wipe dirt from his face.

"I think the way you rode in and shot that hunter through the eye on horseback was the sexiest thing I've ever seen," Xander said.

Cecilia shook her head. "I'm certain it's not, considering the company you keep."

"I assure you it was. Cece, you are exceptional."

She fought an urge to smile.

"What really happened at the cave?"

"What do you mean?" She couldn't hide her surprise.

"I could tell something was bothering you. That's why I asked if you wanted to ride with me."

"I had a bad feeling about the day. Turns out I was right."

Clearly, he didn't believe her, but he didn't push. She used his flask to clean his wound as Rainer made his way back with the horses. She shrugged off Xander's scarf and wrapped it back around him.

"With the blood loss, you're going to be cold, and you need it more than I do now. Don't argue with me. You'll lose," Cecilia said.

Xander brought the scarf up to his nose and smiled even bigger.

"It smells like you," he said. His eyes narrowed, and he tipped her chin into the light. "You're bruised."

She brushed his hand away. "It's nothing. It will heal."

Rainer cleared his throat, startling both of them. "We'll stay in town tonight. It's a risk, but we need good sleep and to have the horses tended to. Ride with Xander this time, Cece."

She couldn't tell if he was trying to make her feel better or make Xander feel inadequate. Xander climbed clumsily behind her with substantial help from Rainer.

"Are you going to be okay? I would ride behind you, but then I won't be able to see anything," she said.

"The pain is well worth being close to you," Xander whispered.

He was stiff, so she made a point not to lean into him. They rode to a discreet boarding house on the outskirts of town. Cecilia and Xander stayed behind while Rainer ventured out to find food and have their clothes cleaned.

Cecilia propped Xander on one of the two beds in the small room before adding a log to the fire. The room was plain, with creaky wooden floors, a threadbare rug, and worn linens, but Cecilia was thrilled to be in from the chill of the mountain and the hard forest floor.

His eyes glowed golden in the firelight as she sat on the edge of the bed, checking his wound.

"Cece, why don't you trust me?" Xander asked.

"I don't know you."

"I'm an open book," Xander insisted.

"You are a calculating liar, and it's your job to be. It's not personal, but if you were one of my father's spies, then I already know where your allegiance lies. I would not insult you by suggesting you should hand it to me. Beyond that, I'm not supposed to tell anyone what happens in the caves except my peers and the elder witches."

"But you told Rainer. He's been on edge ever since he saw you walk out of that cave." Xander sighed. "I want to know you, Cece. Not Lady Reznik or the huntmaster's daughter. *You.* You told me before that no one sees you, but I feel like perhaps you just don't let them.

Maybe that space is already taken up by Rainer, or perhaps you won't let me because I'm a lowly hunter."

A fresh wave of shame rose in her chest. She'd been concerned about how Rainer would fit into her life once she was married to someone else, but she hadn't considered that Rainer's presence blocked anyone else who might want to get close.

"I don't think you're beneath me, and you know it, and I'm hardly concerned with marriage prospects when I'm just trying to survive this trip," she quipped.

The crease in Xander's brow softened. "How is your cheek?"

"I will heal it after dinner. How are you feeling?"

"Fine."

Cecilia glared at him. "You want my trust, all while you lie effortlessly to my face."

"Only so I can impress you with my fortitude."

"I'd be more impressed by your honesty. I'll work on it again after I eat. Right now, I'm too tired."

"How can I get you to trust me?" Xander asked.

"You can't."

"Why?"

"Because you want it too bad," Cecilia said. "Anyone who wants my trust that much, that quickly, has their own angle."

"Fine. Ask me anything."

She reached her senses out to him. He was receptive, curious.

"What was your childhood like?"

Xander closed his eyes and smiled.

"I was always getting into trouble," he said. "There was a lot of love in my family, mostly from my mother. My father was too busy to pay much attention. I followed my older brother around, and he was trouble. But because he was the oldest son, he could do no wrong. He had such a way of getting out of it. He's very charming."

"More charming than you? Is that even possible?" she asked sarcastically.

Xander's face lit up, and the crack in his flirtatious facade fascinated Cecilia. She wanted to see it again, but it was gone in a flash.

"Yes, much more charming. He once convinced a local farmer's daughter that he was the Olney huntmaster's second-in-command when he was just sixteen years old. Gods, he was so much fun!" Xander's gaze was far away.

"Are you still close?" she asked, smiling at him.

"Not so much. I've been away from home for so long, and time changed him, made him bitter."

"Do you miss home?" she asked.

"At times. I miss the land and my friends Evan and Teddy. We were always getting into trouble. Evan is the serious, broody one, Teddy is the light-hearted dreamer, and I was the one with all the bad ideas and the charm to get us out of them. As the second son in my family, I've always felt expendable, like I need to prove myself. I suppose it's like that in most families. I'm taken more seriously away from home. And I've been in hunter training in Olney since I was a teenager."

Cecilia nodded. "I know what you mean. My father wouldn't let Rain and me go on solo trips until three years ago. Before that, he made us go out with other duos. Sylvie and Cal were nice about it, but I could tell they didn't want to be babysitting me, and I was frustrated being an adult with babysitters."

"Why did he do that?" Xander asked. "After all the time he trained you and with all your magic?"

"He was always overprotective. My mother died when I was young. Looking back, I think he felt so powerless after her illness that he wanted to control anything he could. He started training me like I was one of his hunters, and I was only six."

"I'm sorry about your mother," Xander said softly.

"Thank you. It was a long time ago. I only have fragments of things because my powers weren't active yet. I wish I could have known her as an adult."

"Was she a hunter as well, or a witch?" Xander asked.

"No, she was just a lady of the court. But there are quite a few of us witches with non-magical parents." She was quiet for a moment. "Speaking of natural talents, how did you train your reflexes to catch my dagger so easily that first night?"

"A very talented healer enhanced my senses," Xander said. "I can hear sharper than most people—heartbeats, voices from far away. I can smell things more clearly so I can sniff out poisons or track people or animals by scent. I also heal faster than most people, and my muscles are enhanced so I can react faster in a fight, like when I caught your dagger."

Cecilia was familiar with the process. All witches had healing abilities, but those who had it as their main power usually became healers who worked within the kingdom, their talent healing wounds, bones, disease, or mental ailments, as well as those who specialized in enhancing senses. It was a popular procedure for hunters who tried to achieve any edge they could in battle. If it wasn't so expensive, most of the hunter army would likely have it, but the ability to enhance senses was a rare magic that took a lot out of the witches who could wield it.

"Why didn't you ever speak to me until the Godsball?" Cecilia asked.

Xander worried his lower lip with his teeth. "You're the huntmaster's daughter. I have great respect for him, and I knew better than to go near you. I watched you from afar, and it was obvious how much you were in love with Rainer. One only needs to watch you when you think no one else is looking."

She wanted to deny it. "Why speak to me in the garden, then?"

"Because you went with the Reldan even though I thought you might slap me and walk off. I wanted to get to know you, but I had to appeal to your curious nature. It surprised me you let me get so close. I thought for certain you would stab me that first night."

Cecilia laughed. "You caught me at a strange time."

"I was so fascinated by you I couldn't help but come back. I couldn't stop thinking about kissing you. That's not a line, Cece. It's the truth. Getting so close to your lips and being interrupted—gods! It killed me. When your father tasked me to find you, it felt like an opportunity from the fates themselves. I knew I couldn't waste it. That's why I kissed you instead of having us both hide when those hunters were coming. Now maybe you can answer something for me —what would have happened if the hunters hadn't noticed us? Would you have stopped me?"

"I don't know," she said, surprised by her honesty.

"It didn't feel like you would have. It felt like you wanted me to keep going." Xander sighed. "I've never felt that way. I'm so drawn to you. Did you put some sort of spell on me?"

She laughed. "Love spells don't exist."

They stared at each other for a moment. It felt like a lightning current passed between them, leaving a crackling sensation in the air.

"Rainer's back," Xander whispered.

The door banged open. Cecilia hopped to her feet as Rainer walked in, his face pinched in worry.

"What is it?" she asked.

"I was picking up some supplies for the rest of our trip, and I over-heard some Argarian hunters talking. They're looking for me by name. They said they needed to capture Rainer McKay and his witch."

"Why would they be looking for you by name?" Cecilia asked as she helped him pack their supplies.

"I don't know. It didn't seem like they knew who you were, just that I was a guardian to someone important. They must have a spy in Olney. I don't know how else they could know that."

"I assume they don't know what you look like, then," Xander said.

"I'm not known to leave witnesses," Rainer quipped.

The two men stared each other down.

"Can you guarantee none of them knows what you look like?" Xander challenged.

Rainer's brow creased with worry. He cursed and turned away, staring into the fire. The room grew silent. Rainer's anxiety buzzed through their bond.

"Can you finish healing him tonight?" Rainer asked without looking away from the fire.

Cecilia walked over and stood next to him. She wove her fingers through his and leaned her head against his shoulder. "Yes. He might be a little sore, but it will be healed."

"We need to split up," Rainer said.

"What?" Cecilia dropped his hand and stepped back. "How did you go from not trusting him at all to sending me off alone with him?"

"My distrust is less for your safety than your virtue, Cece," Rainer said stiffly. "If I have a target on my back, I won't be the one responsible for bringing you down with me."

"By all means, continue to speak about me as if I'm not sitting right here," Xander grumbled.

They ignored him.

Cecilia held Rainer's gaze. "But who will keep you safe?" She blinked back tears as Rainer rested his hands on her shoulders.

"I will, Cece," Rainer murmured as he hugged her. "I know you're not crying right now. Tough woman like you?"

Rainer kissed the top of her head, and she buried her teary face in his chest. The birthday scent spell his mother had cast on him smelled like spring in Olney. The combination of fresh linen, ocean air, and lilac made her homesick. "Cece, it's going to be okay."

"I've never been away from home and away from you," she mumbled.

"It will just be for a bit. Tomorrow we will pass through the Reflection Forest together before I split off and take the long way around the mountains. I'll meet you at the Cave of Longings. You and Xander will take the shorter main route, although you should expect more hunters with how things have gone so far. Can you do that?" He turned to face Xander.

"I would be honored to," Xander said, sneaking a glance at Cecilia.

Rainer dished out potatoes and chicken, and they ate in silence. Cecilia's appetite was gone, but she forced herself to eat because she hadn't had a warm meal in days. She needed the energy to heal Xander.

When they were finished, she sat down on the bed next to Xander and worked on healing his wound. It took a long time and a lot of concentration, but eventually, it was a pink scar and then nothing at all. Xander watched her face the whole time but said nothing.

"Are you well?" He tucked a stray curl behind her ear. "Would you like to cuddle?" He patted the bed next to him.

"No." She giggled, the tension she'd felt all night finally breaking.

"Now you've wounded me again. Who will heal me?" he teased.

Instead, he lifted her hand to his lips and kissed her palm. It was such an intimate gesture. She was suddenly hyperaware of their proximity and the way it made the room feel too warm and small.

"Go to sleep, Xander," she whispered.

She stood up and climbed into the only other bed in the room, next to Rainer. He pulled her close. Whatever tension had grown between them was washed away by the reality of the situation.

"Where did we leave off?" Rainer whispered.

"The red maiden was wandering the halls of Wolf's Keep, searching for clues," Cecilia whispered.

Rainer nodded, continuing the story. She tucked herself against his chest and listened to his soft whisper. As Rainer spoke, they held on to each other, as if the familiar storytelling ritual could weave them together even as their paths were splitting apart.

13

In the distance, sunlight danced over the canopy of the Reflection Forest. The way the light glittered on the leaves was a visual warning of the powerful boundary magic within its shade. Cecilia's concern was that boundary magic wasn't terribly discerning. It confused friend and foe, and many entered the forest, never to be seen again.

When they came out the other side, they'd officially be in the neutral lands between Argaria and Olney. Cecilia felt the familiar flutter of nerves in her stomach.

"We should stay close once we get inside," Rainer said. "The path through is short but the magic here is very tricky. Many a rider has been driven mad."

Although Cecilia would be more aware of the magic, it was more likely to affect Rainer and Xander since they didn't possess magic of their own. *Magic sings to a witch's soul, and a witch's soul sings back*, as they said in her magic classes. The boundary spellwork was created by Olney witches years before, when Argaria encroached on Olney territory. It was designed to lure riders from the trail and into madness.

They slowed, and Xander brought his horse alongside theirs on the tight path. Rainer's arm tensed around Cecilia's waist. There was a strange stillness to the Reflection Forest. The place was devoid of the usual animal sounds and the gentle chatter of the forest spirits. Lush ferns and mosses bracketed the trail. Ivy climbed up trees, choking the life from lower branches.

The air was heavy with enchantment, like humidity in Olney right before a summer rain. She could practically feel the magic brushing her skin like phantom fingers. Xander went rigid next to them.

"Are you okay?" she asked.

He nodded, but his muscles remained tense. They rode on in silence. After a while, mist grew thick on the trail ahead.

"That doesn't look good," Rainer said.

"It's not bad. It just feels like anxiety," Cecilia said.

Xander still looked uneasy.

"I don't feel anything," Rainer said, pulling Cecilia flush against him, his arm firm and protective around her waist.

The mist blotted out the sun as they neared the center of the forest. The magic's weight felt so oppressive that it was hard to breathe.

Out of nowhere, a bright light flashed, blinding them. Zeke bucked up, sending Rainer and Cecilia to the dirt. Blinding pain rang through her head, and everything went dark.

————

Cecilia woke in a cave filled with the sounds and briny smell of the sea. She squinted at the sunlight peeking in through a crack in the ceiling. Spinning wildly, she looked for an exit.

Instead, she found a crack where seawater poured in.

She'd triggered either a portal or an illusion spell in the Reflection Forest, and she did not have the expertise to dismantle it since the boundary magic blocked her own. The water rushed in faster. Cursing herself for relying so heavily on memory for spellwork, she jumped to her feet. She screamed for Rainer and Xander but heard nothing but the sound of the sea.

She tried to summon the tide. It was a reflex, even though she knew summoning wouldn't work in the Reflection Forest. Taking a deep breath, she searched frantically for a way out, the rough cave walls scraping at her palms.

The water rose to her thighs. Panic overwhelmed her. She was terrified of drowning. She slammed her hands against the walls of the cave, but there was no way out. By the time she tried all the walls, the water was above her waist. Her mind desperately grasped for anything she could remember about illusion magic. There was something about how it only had power over a person if they believed it, but it was very challenging not to be compelled by the cold water soaking her clothes, the salty smell of it choking her, and the bone-deep fear she felt.

Cecilia closed her eyes and prayed as the water rose to her chest and higher.

She started treading water. Fear and frustration overwhelmed her, and she choked out a sob as her hands pressed against the ceiling of the cave.

As her head went under, all she could think about was how she was letting an entire kingdom of people down. If she didn't complete the Gauntlet, Argaria would invade with the power of Endros behind them.

She thought of her father fighting in battle and her Aunt Clara left behind without Cecilia or her father. Her lungs burned. She thought of Xander and Rainer and prayed they were all right. Her vision went white. Finally, she accepted it. She closed her eyes and opened her mouth, waiting for the water to rush in.

Instead of a lungful of water, Cecilia breathed in air and landed heavily on the ground. She opened her eyes. The gray-eyed man from her dream—the one she thought she imagined —stood in front of her. She startled, scooting away from him, her eyes darting around yet another large cave as she sucked in lungfuls of air.

"You said yes to the hunter. Got yourself into quite a mess, Little Dove." He chuckled.

Cecilia took a shaky breath as water dripped off her, puddling on the ground.

"I thought you'd be happier to see me, considering I just saved you from a deadly illusion."

Cecilia swallowed, her mind bursting with questions. "Thank you."

He smirked. "My pleasure, but you should get going if you want to save your friends."

"I thought you were just a figment of my imagination. Who are you?"

"A friend." He winked.

"What is happening?"

"One of you triggered an illusion spell woven into the boundary magic of the forest. You should be careful what company you keep. Anxiety triggers this kind of magic. It brings deep fears to life. Yours —and theirs. The only question is, who should I save first?"

She followed his gaze as pulsating light deeper inside the cave illuminated Rainer and Xander. Rainer was holding what looked like her bloody body, and screaming her name. Xander was locked in a sword fight with a relentless opponent.

"It's not real?" Cecilia asked.

"It's just an illusion meant to cause madness. Decisions, decisions, Little Dove," the gray-eyed man said, nodding toward her companions.

She stepped toward Xander because he seemed to be in more danger. But then she heard the strangled way Rainer said her name and ran to him.

"Release Rainer," she said.

The man snapped his fingers, and the illusion of her dead body disappeared.

"Rain!" she shouted.

Rainer looked up at her with confusion and tears in his eyes.

Cecilia froze. She hadn't seen him so emotional since she'd almost died two years before.

"Cece? Am I dreaming? Is this a cruel trick?" he rasped.

"No, it's really me. It's just magic. I'm okay." Cecilia knelt next to Rainer. He pulled her into a tight hug, buried his face in her hair, and took a deep breath.

"I thought you were gone. I thought—wait, why are you all wet?"

"I almost drowned," Cecilia said plainly.

Rainer cringed. He'd spent hours teaching Cecilia to swim in the sea by the cottage when they were young so she wouldn't be as afraid.

"But you're fine?"

"I'm fine. I thought your worst fear was falling from a great height," she whispered.

Rainer blushed, wiping his eyes on his sleeve. Seeing him so wrecked by losing her should have been satisfying after wishing for his affection for so long. Instead, it was a reminder that he only expressed his true feelings once he was certain she was gone. Thrilling in his regret was like celebrating a raindrop when she needed a river.

Cecilia turned back to the gray-eyed man. "Fix Xander."

Rainer looked confused, as if she expected him to do something, but she turned her attention to where Xander was still fighting his opponent.

The gray-eyed man snapped his fingers, and the man fighting Xander disappeared. "I must leave you now, Little Dove. Head toward the light at the cave mouth to get out."

Cecilia nodded, her gaze fixed on Xander. "Are you well, Xander?"

Xander turned to face her, wavering on his feet as he bent forward to catch his breath. "He just kept coming."

"Who was that?" Cecilia asked.

"I don't know, but he was good."

She frowned. "Your worst fear is a sword fight?"

"*Being bested* in a sword fight," Xander said. "Why, what happened to you and McKay?"

Xander looked from her to Rainer, as if he could see the increased tension between them. There was a question in his eyes, but Cecilia gave no voice to the origin of the awkwardness. Xander had already made enough commentary on their one-sided romance.

"Who were you talking to?" Rainer asked.

"The man with the gray eyes," Cecilia said.

Rainer stared at her, his brow creased in concern.

"You didn't see him?"

Rainer shook his head. "I only saw you."

A shiver rippled up her spine, but she didn't want to linger in the cave looking for answers.

Cecilia took their hands, unwilling to risk being separated again, and walked toward the light as instructed. When they exited the cave, their were horses waiting. Her eyes adjusted, and she realized they were on the other side of the Reflection Forest.

"Well, that's creepy," Rainer said.

"I'd heard rumors, and obviously there's what the books claim about this forest, but it's quite another thing to live through it," Cecilia said breathlessly.

A breeze ruffled Cecilia's damp braid, chilling the back of her neck. She pulled her satchel from Xander's horse and began rummaging for dry clothing.

"Now that we've taken care of our daily chaos, I'll head into town and grab some supplies, and try to find you a horse, Cece. You two lie low. I'll be back in a bit," Xander said.

Cecilia watched him go. Rainer gathered firewood and she changed into dry clothes.

Rainer wandered back to build the fire. The air between them felt as raw and brittle as the kindling he'd gathered, like a single spark might burn down the surrounding forest.

The setting sun cast orange light through the trees, stretching their shadows into something menacing. Cecilia was less unnerved by their spooky surroundings than Rainer's pensive silence and a torrent of questions pulsing inside her.

"Rain."

He said nothing, continuing to poke the fire.

"Rain," she said louder.

He still didn't look up.

"Rain, what was that back there?" Cecilia's voice was shrill. "You're afraid of losing me? What happens between us when we go home and we're both expected to marry other people?"

Rainer swore quietly. "Keep your voice down."

"No!" The word was a flex—a test of a new power she'd not thought herself capable of wielding. "I am so tired of you living in your fantasy world and leaving me out here to face reality on my own. I shouldn't have to do this alone. You're supposed to be my best friend!"

Rainer clenched his jaw and flinched like she'd landed a painful blow. Frustration pulsed through their bond. She should have let it drop, but once the words started flowing, there was no stopping them. All the bitter aching in her heart poured out in a flood.

"You act like my friend, but then you parade around all these girls, and you chase off anyone interested in me so my attention doesn't stray. You have it so easy. You can have anyone you want."

"No, I can't," he said, his fists clenched at his sides. "Cece, cut it out. There could be Argarian hunters nearby. I promise this isn't a conversation you want to have now. Not tonight."

Cecilia knew she was being irrational, but desperation burned through her like a forest fire. Every word suddenly felt more dangerous than anything they'd faced so far on their trip, as if one misstep could end their friendship forever.

Still, she wanted to rip out the truth, even if it tore them both to shreds.

"No! I want to know why. Why keep me hanging on while you sleep with a different girl every week?"

Her eyes blurred with tears. She rubbed them away in frustration. Rainer's face softened. He scrubbed a hand through his hair and cursed. All the fight in him evaporated.

"I chase anyone I'm not legitimately interested in because it's the only way I can keep myself from kissing you every time I see you," Rainer rasped. "Do you have any idea how hard it is to see your face every time I tell you about one of those girls I care nothing about? It's the only way I've been able to keep any distance between us."

She took a step back, eyes wide, nearly falling down.

"That's what you wanted to hear, right?" He looked terrified and frustrated.

"I wasn't expecting—"

Frustration surged through their bond. They were so wound up it was impossible to tell who it originated from.

"Cece, you have knocked me off-balance ever since we were kids. I saw you with your little bow, in your fancy dress with the hem all caked in mud, hitting every target perfectly at the Olney Tournament. We were so young but you were so small and brave. I wanted to be just like you," Rainer said. "You mesmerized me. I've never stopped feeling that same sense of disorientation every time I'm around you. I've just become better at operating within it. It's like taking target practice after a couple of whiskeys. I can't truly be how I want to be with you. Seeing you with Xander, I've had a taste of my own medicine."

"You knew how I felt," Cecilia sobbed. "I've been humiliated for years, the entire world knowing how I feel. Why wouldn't you just tell me?"

"Because I won't risk our connection being severed," Rainer said, desperation creeping into his voice. "I won't risk being separated from you. You're my best friend. I would never do anything to threaten your safety because I care about you too much. It seemed obvious. I sleep over almost every night, right next to you."

"I thought that was just a habit because you're used to sleeping next to me these past few years when we go out into the wild," she murmured.

"It is, but it's also because I can be close to you. You finally relax, you curl into me, you talk to me in your sleep—gods, it's so cute. I think that's why I stopped bothering to sleep anywhere else. Do you really think I enjoy getting up at first light every day so I can sneak back to my apartment so no one will know I stayed?"

"Kind of. You *are* a morning person."

Morning people were as fantastical as dragons to Cecilia.

"I have spent the past few years doing everything I can to keep you at a distance so that I don't break a rule that would put your safety at risk."

She shook her head. "But if you already feel this way, how is admitting it going to change my safety? Whether it's spoken or unspoken, it still exists."

"Because I think about what happened two years ago, and it kills me," Rainer snapped.

Two years ago—the only time in their adult lives he'd ever even come close to kissing her. They were doing a short cave run to a region well within Olney borders. It was supposed to be a safe, easy trip, but they paired up with Sylvie and Cal because her father heard rumblings of unrest in the region, and he didn't want her and Rainer out there alone.

They found the cave without incident. She and Sylvie did their work, and they were on their way back to court. They stopped for a break in the Revel Forest. Cecilia and Rainer had been going through a flirtatious time in their relationship. Each of them constantly daring the other to do more.

They were by the stream filling up their canteens when Rainer caught her around the waist and spun her around. His lips were only inches away. After what felt like an eternity, he leaned in. The softest brush of his lips just as searing pain tore through her back. She couldn't even scream around the hurt, but Rainer felt her entire body tense.

They'd been so distracted, they missed three hunters sneaking up on them, and Cecilia was shot with two arrows through the back. Rainer returned fire. Cal heard the commotion, and came running with Sylvie.

One arrow punctured Cecilia's lung, and she struggled to breathe. Everything after that was blurry, but as Sylvie told it, Rainer lost his mind. He freaked out so badly that Cal had to walk him away so Sylvie could try to heal Cecilia. She got the arrows out, healed the punctured lung, and stopped the worst bleeding. Cecilia got an infection, and despite the healers that worked on her when she got back home, she was sick for days. Even magic had its limits. Those wounds were still her only two scars from combat. Sylvie did her best, but it was more important to heal the damage at the moment than to make it look good.

Rainer stayed by her bed the whole time she was sick and barely let her out of his sight for the next two months.

"Rain, that was two years ago. Is that the reason you won't get close to me?"

"You mean the fact that the one time I did, you almost died? I almost lost you! You collapsed against me, and I couldn't breathe. I still can't when I think of it."

Rainer swallowed thickly.

"I was just out there with Cal trying to talk me down, making bargains with all the gods. I promised I would never kiss you again if it meant keeping you safe and alive. I never want to live in a world without you in it." His voice was tight. "It was my fault because I was distracted. I promised I would never let it happen again. I've spent the last two years trying to keep that promise, but gods, if you don't make it damn near impossible, Cece."

She wiped tears from her cheeks and pressed the heels of her hands into her eyes out of frustration.

"I'd like to give you a real offer, but I can't." Rainer sighed. "The last thing I want is for you to hurt. I just thought it would make this too hard if I told you. I wouldn't give up our connection for anything."

Cecilia was furious at the entire situation. She hated the kingdom that forbade their relationship and the girls he used to distract himself. Most of all, she hated Rainer for hurting her and lying to her for so long.

"When will you give up the stupid court rules? They run everything about our lives. They shouldn't get dominion over this." She felt pathetic begging, but she was desperate to get through to him. "Please," she rasped.

His eyes searched the surrounding woods. She felt his fear, cold and tight in contrast to the prickling heat of desire.

She took his face in her hands, pressing onto her toes as her gaze dropped to his lips. He bent down to meet her until they were sharing the same air. Every nerve in her body surged to attention, her entire being ready to breathe a sigh of relief.

Finally.

Rainer was finally going to give her what she wanted for so long —what he finally admitted he wanted too. The air between them sparked, the forest noise drowned out by the whooshing of her heartbeat in her ears.

Finally.

Her whole body trembled with anticipation as she pressed to the very tips of her toes.

Right as their lips were about to brush, Rainer turned his head. His stubble scraped along her mouth and cheek until he dropped his forehead against her shoulder, breathing heavily.

"I can't," he rasped.

Cecilia felt frozen in place, so shocked by the rejection that time seemed to have stuttered. An icy breeze rustled the pine boughs above, snapping her from her daze.

She recoiled from the rejection, stumbling away from him as if he'd struck her.

"You'll never give me more," she whispered as the understanding settled like a chill in her bones.

"I can't, Cece. I promised I would always keep you safe. If that means that I have to lose you to someone else, I can accept it."

The words pierced her like a well-aimed arrow.

Cecilia had always given Rainer full access to her while he kept his deepest feelings carefully tucked away. Even if he'd never said so, some part of her—the part Cal and Sylvie and so many others had validated—had hoped they were on the same page. For the first time, she realized he'd never felt the same. He might have cared for her in his own way, but it was not the grand sweeping way that her love for him had drowned out all reason.

He gave her scraps to stave off her hunger, but never enough to feel full. Now she was starving to connect. Every time she advanced,

Rainer retreated. It was infuriating how easily he withheld, as if all she'd shown him of her heart wasn't bait enough to lure him. Rainer remained stubbornly controlled, no matter how wild and reckless she became.

He was willing to lose her.

She felt breathless and unmoored, as if anchoring herself to the illusion of their equity had tilted the world on its side, and now she no longer knew how to move forward. She'd only imagined that her soul and Rainer's were mirrors. She'd conjured a fairy tale that only she believed in.

Cecilia brought her hand to her heart as if it could act as a barrier in their bond. Rainer had no right to her grief.

She would never have more than she had now. All because he made a deal with himself when he thought she was dying, and unlike her, Rainer could force his feelings to submit to his will.

She didn't realize until that moment how much of her future, how many secret parts of her heart, she'd reserved for Rainer. Now that Xander had shown her how it felt to be wanted, to be chased eagerly, she had something to measure Rainer against, and he fell short.

Fury burned through her veins. All the hurt and heaviness in her heart. All the quiet moments spent crying over him when he wasn't looking, worrying he'd never feel the same. It all came out at once in a wave of rage.

"I know how you feel," he whispered, as if sensing the rising tide of her anger.

"You have no idea how I feel," she said bitterly. "To have everyone know what's in my heart while you run around with whoever, just so you can push me away and be a good little soldier. I don't want your scraps. You're a coward, Rainer. You'll never care about anything the way you care about being a guardian."

"That's not true. There's so much more you don't understand."

Her anger festered in the silence, growling inside her like a beast, too wild for her to hold back.

"You know, you're already the best at what you do, and your father still doesn't care," Cecilia said. "Finishing the Gauntlet won't make you enough for him, but you've always been good enough for me."

Rainer recoiled. It was a low blow, even if it was true. She still didn't know the full depth of the damage Raymond McKay had done to his son, but as soon as she saw Rainer's face, she knew she'd been too harsh.

Rainer's shoulders slumped. She instantly wished she could take it back. It was so like her to deal damage and immediately regret it.

"I'm sorry I've hurt you so much, but I'm more sorry that I can't be who you want me to be right now. I swear I will tell you everything the moment we're home safe. Maybe I'll learn something from you about courage. You've always been much braver than me," Rainer whispered. "But for now, that's going to have to be enough. Can that be enough for now?"

His eyes were full of such desperate hope that it almost drew her back in.

Want less, she begged herself. It was the same thing she'd told herself for years. *Want less, Cece.*

Maybe she was a person who would always feel unsatisfied with what the world offered her. Maybe it made her ungrateful for having so much that others didn't. Maybe she was a person who would feel offended each time she was given less than she knew she could live with.

Want less, Cece.

A war tore through her as she met Rainer's eyes. She'd put too much on the line to convince herself that later was enough. She'd been patient with him for so long, but she was tired of waiting for the love she wanted. It would be too late once she was back in Olney.

In the depths of her heart, a voice bellowed for more. Perhaps it was foolish to think she could get that in a world so set on mediocrity. Perhaps she was a dreamer who needed to wake up and accept less.

But less wasn't in her. She was a witch, a huntress, and a lady, and she needed someone who could handle all of those sides of her. Someone who wouldn't make her feel like she had to put a limit on her desires. Someone who would look at her and beg to see all of her, consequences be damned. Someone who would dare to want more right along with her.

The wanting was built right into her soul. She couldn't rip it out. Rainer wouldn't give it to her, even when she put her heart on the line. In trying to save her life, he was just killing her spirit slowly. The revelation broke her, sending her into body-shaking sobs.

Rainer tucked her in and held her in his arms while she cried. His grief reverberated through their connection as an echo of her own, but it still wasn't enough to move him.

When Xander returned a short while later, Rainer joined him by the fire, letting Cecilia pretend to be asleep under her blanket.

Alone in the darkness, Cecilia promised herself she would never want less again.

14

Cecilia hid her grief behind a mask of calm. The chill of the morning was welcome, as it helped wake her up.

She shivered against the icy breeze as Xander helped her fasten her satchel and supplies to Biscuit. Much to her frustration, she was stuck sharing his horse. Xander had tried to get one for her in the village on his supply run but only found an old mare who would never make it up the steep mountain passes ahead as they ventured deeper into Argarian territory.

Cecilia was uncertain how to see Rainer off when she could barely meet his eye.

The humiliation of his rejection was still fresh in her mind. She wanted space, to not feel his eyes on her and be reminded that he didn't want her, but now that she was getting it, panic gripped her. Rainer could be hurt miles away from her, and she'd feel it with no chance to get to him. She could be captured, her mind wiped to a blank slate with no memory of him. Her unrequited love cut deep, but not enough that she would give up the life they'd built together even if it would never be the same.

Rainer took her left hand in his, tilting her chin so she'd hold his gaze. He kissed the crescent scar on her palm, cupping her hand with his so that their two moons lined up.

"Cece, remember to be smart with Xander. I'm trusting you over him. If it comes down to it, or if he gets handsy, stab first and ask questions later. You can always heal him if you're wrong," Rainer whispered.

She laughed in spite of herself. "Crescent promise you'll be careful."

A crease formed in Rainer's brow, and he squeezed her hand. "I crescent promise. I'll do my best to get back to you, but if I'm not there in four days, you need to go home without me."

She blinked tears from her eyes. "I don't think we should split up. We're safer together, Rain."

"I don't think we are, Cece. Plus, you could use the space, and it's only for a short while. I'll be careful."

Cecilia tried to be brave, but her courage fled. Rainer wiped a tear from her cheek and hugged her.

"I can be brave if you can be brave too." He echoed the words he said sixteen years before when they were bonded together. "I know you could do this whole thing without either of us. That's how confident I am in you. I'll see you in a few days. I promise."

She sniffled and tried to wipe away her tears, but they kept coming. She felt stupid and soft, a sorry excuse for a warrior. Rainer smiled and kissed her forehead. He placed her hand over his heart again and sent a whisper of peace through their connection.

He looked at her like he was trying to memorize her face. So many unspoken words passed in that one glance, the silence between them holding all the fear and longing in both of their hearts.

Then, he turned and walked over to Xander. He whispered something in the hunter's ear, mounted his horse, and rode off without looking back.

Xander made his way to their horse with a smirk on his lips.

"What did he say to you?" she asked.

"He told me to keep my hands to myself and promised me a slow, painful death if I did anything to hurt you." Xander chuckled.

"And that's funny?" she asked.

"No, I believe him. The one time I think Rainer McKay could beat me in a fight is one over you." Xander sighed. "I respect it. He's looking after someone he cares about. We all would do crazy things for those we love." They were quiet for a moment as she watched Rainer ride away. "Are you ready, Goddess?"

She nodded as Xander helped her onto Biscuit and climbed on behind her. They rode in silence for a while.

"Why is finishing the Gauntlet so important to you?" Xander asked. The question surprised her.

"No one ever has. This is what I've been training for my whole life. Olney is on the brink of war with a kingdom that has the power of two living gods. The power of the Lost God might be enough to save lives and even out the scales in a fight between the two kingdoms."

"Do you ever resent being a pawn for the kingdom?" he asked.

She blanched at the question. "Do you?"

"I don't mean to offend, but that feels like the answer you're supposed to give. I'm curious what actually motivates you. You seem so eager to be known, but when I try to get beyond the surface, you shy away from me," Xander said.

Cecilia rubbed her thumb over her inner wrist, trying to soothe the agitation that rose at his words. What was she holding back for? She'd been trying to ignore her growing feelings for Xander because acknowledging this eagerness in him confronted her with Rainer's indifference. What did she have to lose in letting go?

"On a personal level, I'd prefer not to see my father ride into battle against the god of war, but I also know what people expect of Rainer and me. I know how important it is to him. He always feels like he has something to prove to his father, who is a total asshole, by the way, but it goes beyond that. Not only will finishing it release the power that will hopefully protect my father on the front lines, but I think in the back of my mind, finishing the Gauntlet will give me some sort of goodwill or freedom."

Xander's arm tightened around her waist. "It always comes back to that for you, doesn't it? What would you buy with that freedom?"

"Time. Adventure that doesn't end in me slicing into my palm to try to pull magic from a bunch of ancient caves." She was surprised by the anger that crept into her words. "Traveling for fun instead of necessity. There's so much beyond these two warring kingdoms. I want to see the Moonrise City of Estrellas in Novum and the summer auroras that paint the sky colors. I want the power to make my own choices. My whole life has been about what other people expect from me. I want to choose for myself. I want the freedom to love who I want and to marry only if and when I want. You think that's silly?"

"No, I think that's a much better answer," he said.

"Why are you so pushy?"

"I like getting to know you, Cece."

"Why?"

Xander grinned, his smile brushing her skin as he kissed her temple like a habit. Without Rainer standing between them, she noticed how Xander read her body and mood without the benefit of a bond. There was a current running between the two of them that surged to life whenever they were close.

"Because I find you as charming and fascinating as you are beautiful. It's a rare thing. Most women are satisfied with just looking pretty, but you don't seem satisfied with anything."

Excitement bubbled in Cecilia's stomach. "What about you? Why come all the way out here? Why risk your life for me? You can't tell me it's just because of meeting me in the garden or wanting to save Olney from war."

"It's because I'm the best. I wanted to prove it to everyone else."

"Why do you care what anyone else thinks?" Cecilia asked.

"I wasn't finished," Xander chided. "I was going to say I want to prove I'm the best to everyone else and to you. I wanted you to make it back safe so I could keep getting to know you. Maybe I wanted your father to think I might be worthy of you—and of course, I wanted a chance to finally kiss you."

She laughed, the tension finally easing from her shoulders. "Who was the man you were fighting in the cave back in the Reflection Forest? I don't believe you didn't know him."

"What makes you think that, Goddess?"

"You were only making defensive moves. You didn't want to hurt him."

"How long were you watching before you figured that out?" Xander sounded genuinely impressed.

"Only a minute."

Xander sighed. "Did you get a good look at him?"

"No."

"It was my brother."

"Oh." She was quiet for a moment. "That's horrible."

"It was."

They rode on toward the town of Alstairs, and Xander filled the time with idle chatter about his childhood.

"I was the black sheep. I had talents my family didn't understand or see value in. They wanted me to be something I wasn't. When they realized I wouldn't be, they still spent a lot of time trying to get me to fit in. I think I would have been better off if they'd just embraced me the way I was. Maybe I would be an even better hunter—like you and your magic. You were lucky to have resources to train you. I had to learn so much on my own when I was young. I wanted to prove myself, so I traveled to Olney City to join the army, and I got my senses enhanced. I could already track, but I wanted every edge. My parents didn't understand why I would want that life when I could have had a comfortable life in their world."

"On a farm?" she asked.

He laughed. "Yes, a large farm. You have to understand, it's the only life they knew. They were happy with the work and used to it. I wanted more—to prove myself. I wasn't like my brother. It didn't come naturally to me, but to them, being there was just what was expected. It was the safe route, but that's often a trap. It took a while to convince them to let me do something else."

Cecilia turned to look at Xander, studying the hint of sadness in his eyes. They were more alike than she'd thought. Both from families that didn't quite understand them, both longing to make their own choices.

"You must miss them," Cecilia said.

"I do, especially my mother."

"What's she like?" Cecilia asked.

"Beautiful and kind," Xander started. "Sometimes, I wonder how she ended up with my father, though I suppose women so rarely get a choice when it comes to marriage. My father can be so hard and cold. I am fortunate that she writes a lot. She was the one who could see how I struggled at home. She advocated for me with my father, convinced him it was a good idea. I owe her a lot."

"She sounds wonderful. You're lucky to have her."

"I am," he sighed, and she could tell he meant it. "What were you and Rainer whispering about the other night as you were falling asleep?"

Cecilia hesitated. She'd told Xander he didn't know her well enough, but he was clearly trying to. What she had with Rainer was sacred and private, but she needed to let him go, just as he so easily let her go. If she were going to move on from Rainer, she'd need to open up to someone else. Xander was so earnest in his questions. He clearly wanted what Rainer had turned down, and she couldn't deny the attraction between them.

Xander had a way of drawing her in. She wanted freedom, and he could provide it, but embracing that freedom required a different type of courage than she was accustomed to.

"It's a thing we've always done. When we were young, we begged Rain's mother to read us every fairy tale and myth in the kingdom. We were relentless. Eventually, she would be too exhausted or busy, so she told us to take turns making up our own. So, we did, and we just never stopped. I know it probably sounds childish, but it reminds us of home."

"I think it sounds sweet."

"I can't tell if you're making fun of me," Cecilia said, turning to look at him.

"I'm not. I can see how much you two care for each other."

They came around a curve that brought a breathtaking view of the world below. Their vantage point from midway up the Argas Mountains allowed them to see miles of pine forests below, as well as the brighter foliage of the Reflection Forest in the distance.

"I know you're trying to distract me from worrying about Rainer," Cecilia whispered as Biscuit lumbered on up the rocky trail.

"Is it working?" Xander asked.

Cecilia smiled and kept her gaze on the path stretched out before them.

———

By nightfall, they reached the outskirts of Alstairs. Xander found space in a boarding house on the edge of the main town and sneaked her inside. Cecilia was relieved the room had two beds, and she almost cried when she saw there was a private washroom with a hot bath already drawn by the boarding house staff.

She couldn't wait to take a bath. As if reading her mind, Xander handed her a towel and robe and offered to take her clothes down to be laundered overnight.

By the time she came out from her bath, he had warm stew and fresh bread waiting for her. Xander disappeared to take a bath and let her eat in peace with nothing but the sound of the crackling fire for company. She was startled by how easily he read when she needed the distraction of conversation and when she needed alone time.

Cecilia tried not to think of Rainer, but she couldn't stop herself. She felt into their connection and sent a little spark of warmth. A moment later it reverberated back, and she finally relaxed.

When Xander returned in his robe, she was already tucked into bed. He whispered goodnight and settled into the bed across from hers. Cecilia's exhaustion weighed heavily on her, but the more she tried to will herself to sleep, the more she tossed and turned.

"Goddess?" Xander's voice startled her. "You're rocking back and forth like a boat in a storm. Can't sleep?"

Cecilia sighed heavily. "I'm not sure why. I'm tired, but my brain won't shut down."

"It's understandable. You're worried, and you don't typically sleep alone."

It didn't occur to her until then that he was right. She had only slept alone a handful of times in the past few years.

"I didn't really think about that," she said, meeting his eyes across the firelit room.

"I would be happy to keep you company if you wanted." A sly smile tugged at his lips.

"That won't be necessary." She laughed, looking up at the ceiling. There was no way she was going to let him into bed with her when she was in nothing but a robe.

"I would be a perfect gentleman, Cece."

She frowned. "I haven't seen any evidence of that so far."

"That may be true, but I would never do anything to make you uncomfortable. I promised I would take care of you. You won't be at your best if you're exhausted, and neither will I," Xander said seriously.

"Fine, but if your hands wander anywhere, I will kick you out of this room," Cecilia huffed.

"I wouldn't dream of touching you anywhere inappropriate, unless you asked me to, of course." He smirked.

She shifted to make room for him in the bed.

The bed sagged as Xander climbed in behind her, wrapping an arm around her waist and pulling her close. She went rigid, suddenly aware of how thin her cotton robe was. It felt like no barrier at all, and she felt much too warm.

Xander propped himself on an elbow, and she turned to look up at him. "There you are," he whispered, stroking her cheek with calloused fingers. "It's so rare you let me see you."

"Nonsense. You've seen me every day since you got here."

"On the contrary, Cece. You only let me see bits and pieces. It's so rare you let me see more than what you wish to present."

Tears filled her eyes, and she looked away. She was certain he'd been following her at her father's behest. Instead of being angry about it, she felt overwhelmed that Xander was drawn in by what he saw in her when no one else was looking.

"How do you know?" she rasped.

"The same way you know when you're really seeing me," he whispered.

There was something inexplicable between them, but she knew exactly what he meant. Sometimes he was giving a performance, but now, he was open to her, and his hazel eyes lit with doubt.

Cecilia brushed the tears from her eyes. "You must think me a silly, weak girl."

"On the contrary. I find your honesty quite lovely and fierce. It's a different kind of strength to feel so much so deeply." He wiped away her tears, letting his thumb brush back and forth soothingly over her jaw before settling in behind her again.

"Relax, Cece. I'm just going to hold you. Go to sleep," he said as he pressed a kiss to her neck. "Would you prefer I tell you a story?"

"Do you know any stories?" Cecilia asked.

"I know many that aren't appropriate for a lady's ears, but of course I know the story of the Gauntlet's creation, or 'Goddess Sayla and Wailing Woods,' or the 'Tale of the Storm Prince,'" Xander whispered.

"I was at that play about the Gauntlet before we left, and I've thought about it enough over this trip, and the Wailing Woods and Sayla will give me nightmares," Cecilia said, shivering as she remembered the tale of a huntsman who disappears in the woods said to be haunted by the specter of the goddess. "How about the Storm Prince?"

Xander's arm squeezed her tighter. "On a cold winter day, high in the mountains, a baby was born in the heart of a storm. The wind tore through the peaks, battering the castle walls with rainy fists, begging to be let inside. Lightning flashed across the sky in vicious fissures. The queen had labored for hours, and despite the plea of the head healer to let them take the baby to save her life, the queen trusted her intuition. She felt the shift in her body, just as the storm shifted outside. The rain turned to snow, the wind died down, and the queen pushed hard. As the snow settled, coating the castle grounds in white, bringing a sort of calm after the storm, the prince's cry broke through the silence, heralding his arrival to all who awaited."

"You're a good storyteller," Cecilia murmured, her eyelids growing heavy.

"I think by now you should realize I'm good at everything, love."

His pride was almost endearing.

"Nine years passed in the blink of an eye. The prince was returning from visiting his grandmother when he and his escort were surprised by an enemy ambush. The boy was pulled from his horse. Down to his last two guards and surrounded by enemy hunters, he surprised them all when, in his panic, he summoned a storm. Lightning rained down with brutal precision, wiping out all but the prince and his two guards."

Cecilia wanted to stay awake for the rest of the story, but the steady crackling of the fire and Xander's soothing voice in her ear lulled her into a pleasant sleep.

15

X ander and Cecilia rode most of the morning in easy silence, enjoying the view as Biscuit carried them higher into the Argas Mountains.

"I've been debating asking you something because I'm not sure if it will make you want to try to stab me again," Xander said.

"Maybe you should think better of it."

"I probably should, but my curiosity is getting the better of me," Xander said. "It's clear that Rainer is attracted to you and that you really like him. Why not act on your feelings?"

There it was, laid out plain as day by someone else. The question she asked herself countless times. Usually, people asking about it frustrated her, but she could tell Xander really wanted to know.

"Stop the horse for a moment," she said.

Xander brought their horse to a stop. Cecilia pulled off her sweater, leaving just her green undershirt. She loosened the ties at her neck.

"Pull the collar down my back until you see the scars," she said.

Xander pulled the shirt down and revealed two arrow scars.

"I thought those who could heal didn't scar," he whispered.

"Usually they don't, but they were critical wounds, and Sylvie had to work quickly."

Cecilia told Xander about the day she almost died. How Rainer almost kissed her. How she was wounded. How he lost his mind. How Sylvie healed her.

Xander ran his fingers over her scars, sending a shiver through her. He grew quiet, his hand still resting her bare skin. She shifted and shrugged her shirt back into place.

"I suppose I can understand his hesitation," Xander said. "I certainly find you distracting. I wouldn't let it keep me from being with you, though."

"Clearly." She laughed and pulled on her sweater. "Are you jealous of Rainer?"

"No—" He shook his head. "Well, maybe. Have you ever kissed him like you've kissed me?"

Cecilia laughed. "I haven't kissed anyone like I've kissed you."

"But you've kissed him?"

"Once, when we were teenagers—just a first kiss. I certainly didn't know what I was doing." The memory tugged at her mind, filling her with an urgent nostalgia. "Are you jealous now?"

"That depends. Did you like it?"

She considered lying. "Yes." She had really liked it. Though it was years ago, she remembered it perfectly. Kissing Rainer felt like coming home to something familiar after being away for far too long. She wished she could forget it.

"Then I am definitely jealous. I will just have to remind you what you're missing later." Xander kissed the side of her neck, and she shivered. "Would you like that?" He continued a line of kisses as goosebumps rose on her skin.

"No," she gasped as she pressed back against him.

"I love the way you lie even while you lean in for more," he whispered against her skin, making her arch against him again.

Xander froze, his arm tightening on her waist as he looked back over his shoulder.

"I would love to continue this conversation because I really enjoy where it's heading, but I hear quite a few riders coming behind us, and I suspect they aren't friendly."

"How many?" she asked, looking back over his shoulder.

She could barely make out figures in the distance, and once again, she was impressed by his excellent hearing.

"Ten or more. It's hard to tell at this distance. I can ride hard, but they may catch us in the Godswoods, where the roots are wild and I'll have to slow Biscuit down."

"Then I suppose I will have to take them out before we get there." She grabbed her bow and quiver with determination. She started to turn toward him.

"Cece, what are you—"

"Stay focused on the road ahead," Cecilia said. "I'm going to turn around to face you so that I can shoot. I'll need you to hold on to me so I don't fall. Keep riding."

Before he could react, she took the reins. She lifted her right leg up and around him and twisted herself quickly so she was straddling him, facing the back of the horse. Then she handed the reins back to him.

"Gods, you want me to focus now when I'm between your legs, Cece?" Xander hissed.

Seeing him flustered made her giggle.

"Bring your arm here." She wrapped his hand low around her hip so she would have the room to take aim over his shoulder. He instinctively brought his other arm around her waist.

"You have to pull me closer."

He grinned. "You don't need to tell me twice."

He pulled their bodies flush to each other, and a rush of desire tore through her. She swallowed hard as she tried to ignore it and focus on the road behind them.

"Have you done this before with Rainer?" Xander asked.

"Only when it was necessary. Why?"

"Because if you sat on him like this and then killed a bunch of hunters, I don't understand how he could have avoided falling in love with you immediately."

She bit back a smile. "Don't flirt. I'm trying to concentrate."

"Goddess, I will always make time to flirt with you," Xander said.

The first rider moved into range, and she loosed an arrow, sending it into his throat. Off target, but she knew it would be harder to aim when she wasn't controlling her own horse. *Whatever takes them down.* That's what her father always said.

"The good thing about being in this position is that you get to use my body as a shield for any arrows." Xander laughed.

She shot two more arrows.

"If I pull you over me, go with it," she said. Several hunters returned fire, arrows flying wide of them. She took aim and shot another arrow, taking down the closest hunter.

Her hair whipped against her cheeks as the men kept coming. Three Argarian hunters took aim at once, close enough that she could see the hatred in their eyes. Without thinking, she wrapped her arms around Xander and leaned back, pulling him flush on top of her.

"You're going to be the death of me," he grunted in her ear.

Arrows whizzed by, just over his back. She pushed him back up to seated and quickly unleashed five arrows in quick succession. She took down the three closest riders, but more quickly replaced them.

"You have to go faster," she said.

"I'm going as fast as I can. Perhaps if you didn't wiggle against me so much."

"I have to take aim," she said, pressing her legs down into his to get some leverage.

He cursed as she rubbed against him. Cecilia took out two more riders. She pulled him down on top of her again to avoid another assault of arrows. She wrapped her legs around Xander's waist as she leaned to the side and fired off three more arrows, taking down several pursuers.

Xander made a strange sound in the back of his throat. "Are you hit?" she asked, patting his back.

"No, I'm just very interested in this position," Xander said quietly. He shifted his hips slightly, and she felt him hard against her.

"Now? Seriously?" she asked. Her cheeks flamed, but he didn't seem the least bit embarrassed.

"If not now, when, Cece?" he asked, pulling her back upright.

"Literally—any—other—time." The words punctuated the shots she took at the next three riders.

Her hand fumbled in her quiver for more arrows, but she was almost out. Praying she'd have enough for the last few riders, she kept shooting, ignoring the hair blowing in her eyes and the thundering horse hooves. She fired away, adrenaline pumping through her heart so fast she thought it might stop.

Finally, she shot the last rider just as they reached the edge of the Godswoods. Slumping into Xander, relief crashed over her. She tucked her face into his neck, wrapping her arms around him.

"Are you well?" Xander asked.

"Just letting the nerves wear off." She took deep breaths, trying to calm her racing heart. She waited for the adrenaline to pass. Her legs shook, and she didn't know if it was the strain of trying to get leverage to shoot or fear. Xander rubbed circles on her low back.

"You didn't seem nervous," he whispered.

"That's good."

"How many riders were there?"

"Fifteen."

Xander cursed.

"I was on my last arrow," she said.

They were quiet for a moment, considering how close they'd come to disaster. They slowed as they entered the shade of the woods. She tried to adjust herself to make some distance between them but only succeeded in rubbing against him more.

Xander groaned. "If you keep shifting like that, I'm going to lose my mind."

"Sorry." She leaned away from him.

Xander drew up, stopping the horse. He cupped her face with one of his rough hands.

"Cece, that was magnificent. I would really like to kiss you now because I could think of nothing else with you pressed against me like this. Please say you want me to kiss you."

Her breath caught, and she involuntarily found herself looking from his intense hazel eyes to his lips.

"Please, love. Let me thank you in the only way I know how to show the immensity of my gratitude." He pulled her legs up so they were wrapped around his waist, and there was no space between them.

"Kiss me."

Xander quickly jumped down from the horse with her in his arms and laid her back against a large boulder next to the trail. His lips crushed over hers, and once again, her body sprung to life. Her breath caught as his tongue gently tangled with hers.

At first, the kiss was tentative, as if testing how far she would let him go, but then it grew hungrier. He stopped holding back and pressed himself against her in a deep, passionate kiss. His hands tangled in her hair, and she slipped hers up his shirt against his warm skin, pulling him closer. He had a way of making her feel like she wanted more—like what he was doing was never enough. She felt like her body was burning from the inside out, but instead of pulling away, she drew him closer. She chased the flame, welcoming it, wanting to become a part of it.

Xander pulled back, searching her face. "We should stop. I would love to keep going, but if I do, I'm afraid this will go beyond just a kiss."

"What if I don't want you to stop?" she said, breathless. She felt hot all over, her body brimming with ecstatic energy.

"Don't look at me that way," he said, shaking his head.

Cecilia expected him to be fully on board with her idea. "Look at you what way?"

"Like the kiss isn't enough."

"Maybe it's not."

He sighed and dropped his head back, running a hand through his hair. "I don't think you realize what you're asking for. I'm afraid I will start something I won't want to stop."

Cecilia smiled coyly, patting her dagger. "Then it's a good thing that I know how to stop you if you get carried away."

"I'm more worried you won't stop me."

"Then what's the problem?"

Xander let out an exasperated sigh, but a hint of a smile tugged at the corner of his lips. "The problem is that you deserve more than this. I would love to be deep inside you right here in the middle of the woods, but I don't want your first time to be like that."

"It's not my—"

"You're a bad liar, so don't bother," he said, waving a hand dismissively.

A violent flush burned through her. *Is it that obvious that I'm so inexperienced?*

Although ladies of the Olney court were expected to preserve their virginity for their husbands, plenty of them discreetly parted with it before they walked down the aisle. Rainer had thwarted any chances she had of successfully parting with hers, despite her best efforts.

"You're much too good for me," Xander whispered, kissing her gently.

"We already know this, so what's the holdup?" she taunted.

He laughed and brushed a loose wave back behind her ear. She kissed him again, using the kiss as a weapon to erode his resolve. She reached her senses out to him and felt lust and a desire that pulsed like a current in the air around them. Still, a part of him felt hesitant and frustrated.

She drew back. "Why is there always some part of you that doesn't want to be kissing me?"

"Cece, I promise that all parts of me want to be kissing you right now," he said, pressing his hips against her as proof.

"Then why do you feel so conflicted?"

"Because I shouldn't want you. Because I can't have you—not in a tangible way. When we go back to court, you are you, and I am just a hunter. I have no right to you. I have no right to want what I want right now."

"And what do you want?" She couldn't stop herself from asking.

"All of you. Every part of you. Your time and attention. I want to please you. I want to hear the sounds you make when you're pleased. I want to see your flushed cheeks and bright eyes after I satisfy you. I want to know every secret beautiful thing you hide from the world. Please don't ask me any more questions."

Xander looked pained. His words sent a rush of heat through her body because she wanted the same thing.

She was certain she was losing her mind. Wanting Xander was dangerous, but she'd spent her whole life running toward danger. Why would this be any different?

"Well, then you're going to have to kiss me more because I have many more questions," she whispered.

Xander took to the invitation with vigor as Cecilia spread her legs wide and pressed her hips into his.

"More," she whispered against his lips.

"Cece, I will not have you here and now—not like this—but I will give you a taste," Xander said.

"Yes," she said breathlessly.

"You tell me if you want me to stop, and I will, okay?"

She nodded.

His hand drifted down her stomach. He slipped it up her shirt to the thin cotton of her bra and tweaked her nipple. She cried out in surprise, and a rush of damp heat settled between her legs. Her hips moved involuntarily.

"Gods, Cecilia, the way you respond to my touch undoes me. I've barely done anything, and you are already coming to life." He kissed her neck and moved his hand to her other nipple, giving it the same attention. She felt something building inside her. Something coiled deep in her belly, like a snake waiting to strike.

"More," she moaned.

He stiffened in surprise. She was certain she was losing her mind. They weren't even off of the trail, and she was letting him kiss her and more in plain sight of anyone who rode by.

He chuckled softly as he slid his hand lower, over her hip, and then between her legs. He watched her face as if waiting for her to stop him. Her boldness inspired his own.

"Do you want to know what I dream of doing to you?" he rasped.

"Yes," she whispered, meeting his gaze.

"First, I would kiss you here because I know how much you love it," he whispered as he kissed the spot on her neck that made her cry out.

Every thought exited her brain at once, and all she could focus on was the feeling of his lips on her skin and the teasing drag of his teeth. He did it over and over until she involuntarily lifted her hips against his hand and moaned his name. There was no space for hesitation or self-conscious thoughts to drag her mind from the riot of sensations in her body.

"Then I would do this."

He rubbed two fingers against the seam of her pants, right at the apex of her thighs. She gasped in shock, and he kept kissing her neck. The dueling sensations were almost too much. She felt completely out of control. The motion of his fingers brought ragged sounds from her lips she'd never heard before.

"Of course, when I do it, you wouldn't be wearing these pants. It would just be my fingers against your skin. Imagine that." He breathed the words into her ear, and she twitched against him. "I would do this until you were slick, and then I would push a finger inside you right here." He tapped a finger at her center, and she jumped. "It would be difficult at first because you would be tight, but you would also be wet and ready, just like I'm sure you are right now." He took a nip at her earlobe, and she cried out.

"Then I'd press in another finger, and you would start—"

As if he were a puppetmaster and she the puppet, she rose to meet the motion of his fingers. The drive to release whatever tension was building in her body was undeniable. She needed it. She didn't even know what she was running toward, but she couldn't stop herself.

Xander sighed. "Gods, yes! You would start riding my fingers like you're riding my hand right now."

He kissed down her jaw. He seemed shocked by her wildness, but she wasn't. This was what she'd been waiting for. She might have imagined it with someone else, but she was clearly in deeper with Xander than she thought. There was no fear or anxiety, only desire, heat, longing, and a driving momentum pushing her toward release.

"Then, when you were close, I would take my fingers away. I would kiss down your whole body. I'd kiss every inch of your skin until you were shaking and begging me not to stop, Goddess. And then I would bring my mouth between those pretty thighs."

He rubbed her faster, and the thought of his mouth all over her body and between her legs made her impossibly hot. His words were a wildfire burning through her.

"I would lick you long and slow, tasting all of you. Gods, Cece, I would have you bucking your hips like you are now, and then I would hold you down and lick you until you came so hard your legs shook."

He kissed her neck, and she cried out again. She was being much too loud, but she didn't care. A wolf could have walked up and taken a bite out of her arm, and she wouldn't have noticed. Her entire attention was focused on the driving force pooling low in her belly, the snake coiled and so close to striking.

"Xander," she breathed.

He smiled against her lips.

"You want me to stop?" he asked, pausing his fingers. His eyes were teasing, playful.

"No!" she said it desperately, and he chuckled.

"I know what you want. I can tell you're close. I'm going to give it to you." He rubbed her harder, and she let out a loud moan. "Then I would crawl back up your body and bring myself between your legs."

He shifted, and suddenly she could feel him, hard against her, along with his hand.

"I would push inside you. It would hurt at first. Just a little sting, but I would wait for you to adjust. And then when you did, I would push deep inside of you over and over. You would moan just like you are right now, and the sound would drive me as crazy as it is at this moment. I wouldn't stop until you came. You might wake a whole village, but I wouldn't stop. I would make sure that you felt the extent of my desire for you for days. Every time you sat down, you would think of me. Every time you felt the ache between your legs, you would imagine my mouth on you. And only once I was sure that you were very well taken care of would I finish deep inside you." He kissed her long and hard and claiming.

She felt as if she were on the edge of a cliff about to fall over. With a couple more hard rubs of his fingers, she plummeted over the edge with a sound that was somewhere between a scream and a moan.

It was like nothing she had ever felt before. Her entire body shook, and all of the tension that had built snapped at once. When the wave of pleasure passed, she was left panting, pressed against Xander.

Their eyes met. Xander was just as breathless, his face inscrutable. Something sacred passed between them. The forest was silent as if holding its breath. They'd crossed some invisible boundary to somewhere entirely unexpected that they couldn't come back from.

Suddenly Cecilia felt exposed and self-conscious. She flushed, and he smiled, cupping her face in his hand.

"Cece, you have nothing to be embarrassed about. The way you give yourself over to pleasure undoes me." He closed his eyes and shook his head. She couldn't quite read what he was feeling. It was a vortex of emotions. "I worry that doing this has made things much worse for me."

She looked up at him, confused. "How?"

"Because now when I look at you, I will see your face and hear the sounds you make when you fall apart, and it will drive me to the most pleasant distraction."

Heat rose on her neck and cheeks. Xander pulled her into a long, deep kiss. When he pulled away, she was shaking again. He leaned his forehead against hers.

"We should keep riding a bit longer before we sleep for the night."

She just nodded, unable to form words. She was in over her head.

This man, who never stopped forcing her to confront what she truly wanted, helped her push out past her comfort zone, and it felt like falling. It seemed impossible to like him so much in such a brief time, but without Rainer she was forced to confront her easy intimacy with Xander.

Her legs still felt unreliable as he helped her up. He lifted her onto the horse, and jumped up behind her.

As soon as the horse began to move, a shock ran through her, from between her legs all the way up her spine, and her whole body went rigid against him.

He chuckled in her ear. "You might be a little sensitive after that. It could be a fun ride for you."

His confidence chaffed her.

"You sure seem pleased with yourself," she muttered.

"It's okay that you enjoyed it, you know. You wouldn't be the first woman who found me frustrating but enjoyed what I could make her feel," Xander taunted.

"You are—"

"Dexterous? Talented? Charming?" he suggested.

"Tedious. Conceited. Annoying."

"And yet I still made you come so hard and loud with just two fingers that they probably heard you back in Alstairs."

A fierce heat rose to her cheeks at the crude words. He tucked his face into her neck and kissed her.

"I love to make you blush."

They rode for a few minutes in silence, and she let him stay tucked into her.

"For all your confidence, I am a little confused about something," she said.

"What's that?" he whispered.

"I asked you to take me, and you said you wouldn't. I gave you the opening. You keep saying you want to, but you wouldn't. Why?"

He sat straighter behind her, pulling away from her. When she craned her neck to look at him, he seemed lost in thought. Finally, he spoke.

"I told you, Cece. I can't have you. You're not for me. Unfortunately, it doesn't stop me from wanting you."

Those words broke him open, allowing her to see part of him that had never been available to her before. She finally recognized the warm longing that buzzed around him.

There was something between them that was as sudden as a lightning strike and so far beyond her comprehension. There was no rhyme or reason to the way she felt about Xander. It sneaked up on her and dug its claws in, and no matter how she tried to twist and turn away, she couldn't break herself from it.

She didn't want to stop running toward him. Each glimpse of him left her wanting for more. She tried to reason with her feelings for Xander, but the more she thought about it, the more she liked him. He made her laugh. He challenged her ideas. He asked her what she really wanted. Even her own father had never asked. She and Rainer talked about it, but he put her safety above her autonomy.

Xander wanted her right there beside him. He believed and guided her without coddling or telling her how to feel. He simply let her be herself.

For years her heart had belonged to one man. Now she was forced to admit she might be losing it to someone else who inspired her to boldly be herself.

In the fading light, she realized falling for Xander felt like freedom.

16

After almost two days of riding through the chill of the Argas Mountains, Xander and Cecilia came to a clearing with a remote cabin. She might have missed it in the heavy snowfall, but Xander seemed to expect it.

If Rainer were with them, he would have delighted in pointing out that she would have expected it if she'd paid attention to the maps he insisted she memorize. But Rainer was miles away, somewhere else on the mountain, hopefully dealing with less treacherous weather. Cecilia shivered, wishing she'd packed another sweater. Her clothes were soaked through with snow, and she was miserably cold. She couldn't believe she'd complained about the heat when they began the trip and now feared she'd freeze a few weeks later.

Xander had continued to surprise Cecilia. She loved his playful humor. He somehow sensed when she was worried, cutting the tension with a story or a joke. She was used to that comfort with Rainer, but that was because of their connection. Xander could read her with no magic bonding them together.

They hadn't shared more than a few sweet kisses since their time in the Godswoods, but Xander held her close every night. She wondered if he was caught up in the same relentless pull that she felt, as if some invisible tether drew them together.

Part of her felt compelled to resist Xander. Like surrendering to her feelings meant letting Rainer go for good. Everything about her feelings for Xander felt like being drawn into something consuming and unpredictable. It sneaked up on her like an Olney summer storm, blowing through her, unsettling everything that had always felt grounding and familiar.

Snow crunched beneath Biscuit's hooves as a gust of wind blew a startling flurry of flakes into her face, the bracing cold sending a jolt through her whole body. Xander's arm tightened on her waist, his breath puffing out in little white clouds against her cheek.

"Almost there," he whispered, his voice nearly drowned out by the howl of the wind.

Cecilia couldn't comprehend why Xander was so desperate to know her or why she felt so committed to resist. She'd wanted love her whole life, yet the moment it reached for her, she seemed determined to run from it. She'd told Rainer that her heart had nothing to do with what existed between her and Xander, but she'd long suspected that wasn't entirely true. Admitting she was falling for him meant surrendering.

Xander pulled the reins, stopping Biscuit in the small stable next to the cabin before helping her down. He took care of the horse as Cecilia let herself into the cabin and started a fire.

Once the fire was crackling and her body thawed, she poked around the small room. It was well-appointed for a simple hunting cottage, with plenty of wood stacked away by the hearth and a bed made with fine linens and a heavy down comforter. Plush robes hung on hooks by the door.

The best feature by far was the hot spring behind the cabin. When she discovered the outdoor tub in the house's rear with a pump to bring the hot water directly into the bath, she almost cried. Xander laughed and left her to bathe in peace.

Later that evening, when they were both bathed, fed, and sitting in front of the fire, she caught Xander staring at her lips for the third time in a half hour. She leaned into him, but he pulled back. He jumped, pretending to check on the snowstorm that was blowing through the valley.

"It's really coming down. We might need to stay an extra day," he said, turning to look at her again.

"Why won't you kiss me? Why do you insist on keeping your distance?" Cecilia asked.

She closed the space between them. He seemed tentative, almost afraid of her, as he brushed her hair back over her shoulders.

"Because you don't know what you want."

"That's not true."

When Cecilia left Olney, it felt like there wasn't a choice at all. It was only what her father decided for her. Now she was being presented with an option she hadn't considered.

"You don't." Xander sighed.

"I do," Cecilia hedged.

"Then enlighten me, Goddess."

She huffed and sagged back against the soft carpet. Frustration tied her tongue in knots. "I want—" she started. "I want you to—"

The corner of his lips drew up. "You can't even say the words, love. How do you expect me to take it seriously?"

She sat with a start. "Fine. I want you to take me to bed. I want you to do everything you talked about when you touched me in the Godswoods." She hid her heated cheeks behind her hands.

Xander's grin grew wide. "You're so lovely when you blush."

She rolled her eyes and sighed. "Fine, let's just wait out the storm talking to each other or staring into the fire. Hopefully, we don't die of boredom in the meantime."

Xander took her hand. "I never find conversation with you boring. I love how you say whatever you think. Most people have so much pretense, but you speak from the heart. It's refreshing."

"I'm glad someone thinks so." Cecilia sighed. "I know what you're trying to do, you know."

The corner of Xander's mouth quirked up. "And what's that?"

"You're trying to distract me."

Xander's eyes lit with amusement. "Perhaps."

"That would only work if you didn't look at my lips so much. I know you want me. I can feel it."

"How?"

"I can sense people's emotions. It's always been like a nonverbal language I can read on people."

"And I feel desire?" He took a step toward her.

"You feel conflict and desire. You want, but you won't let yourself surrender."

He pressed his lips together, considering it. "Well, that puts me at a disadvantage because I don't know how you feel."

"I feel like I want to be with you," Cecilia said.

"Why?" He closed the distance between them, cupping her face in his hands. "Why do you want me, Cece?"

"Because when I'm with you, I don't feel like I have to pretend. I'm not a memory witch, or Commander Reznik's daughter, or a lady of the court. I'm just Cece. It's liberating. Like I can do what I want, and you won't judge me. You bring something wild and free out in me I forgot I had. Something I forgot to want for myself. You make me feel things I've never felt, and I want more. You make me feel safe to be myself."

He looked surprised at her words. "You shouldn't feel safe with me."

"Why?" she asked.

"Because I don't trust myself with you from moment to moment. I've never wanted anything the way I want you. It kills me because I know I can't have you! Not for real. Not for any more than a moment."

Cecilia threw her hands up. "And that moment wouldn't be worth it? Gods, Xander! I have control over almost none of my future, but right now, I want to choose this just for myself. Maybe it's temporary, but at least I'm not afraid. You claim to be afraid of nothing. You charge into battle with no fear, but you won't even try to be with me for real, even if it's temporary."

She wasn't sure that she could handle another rejection. There was something seriously wrong with her to risk the humiliation, but she'd been so certain Xander would agree. Suddenly, she worried she'd miscalculated again, and he didn't even want the chance to bed her and give her an experience she so desperately wanted before she had to settle with someone else.

Xander laughed, running a hand through his hair.

"What?" Cecilia huffed.

"Goddess, you're so demanding."

"Don't call me that," she said. She turned away, annoyed.

He wrapped his arms around her from behind, kissing her neck. "You're right. You're much braver than I am. You're smart and kind and a little violent and so incredibly brave. I'm in awe of you." He hesitated. "I think perhaps you're the loneliest woman I've ever met, and while I'm happy to entertain you, I'm afraid we're unmatched in our investment in each other."

Cecilia met his hazel eyes over her shoulder. "How so?"

He looked suddenly vulnerable and uncertain of himself. "Cece, I am in love with you."

Her breath froze in her lungs. She pulled out of his arms and turned to face him. Her mind spun in a thousand directions.

She couldn't quite process his words. Clearly her fear of rejection was unwarranted, but now she felt certain she'd miscalculated. What was between them was only safe when it was flirtation.

She shook her head. "No."

Xander choked on a laugh. "No?"

"No, you can't be," she insisted.

It was much too soon. She'd clearly felt lust, desire, fascination in him, but he didn't know her well enough to love her.

"And yet I am."

"I forbid it," she said, lifting her hands as if to ward herself against his feelings.

Xander frowned, running a hand through his hair. "This is not how I saw this conversation going."

"You're mistaking what this is. I cannot be that for you. I don't want to."

She felt suddenly furious. How dare he complicate things this way when she just wanted to choose one simple thing for herself. Cecilia knew her limits, and if someone dangled the kind of love she wanted so badly to believe in, she'd be helpless to the pull of it. When she told herself it was just a physical connection, just an itch to be scratched, she felt confident she could keep her distance. Now Xander had ruined that, even if his confession sent a thrill through her.

"You don't want love?" Xander challenged.

"I don't want complications. When I finish the Gauntlet tomorrow, I'll go back to Olney and marry someone else. This was just supposed to be fun."

"You're using me?" he asked incredulously.

"I think that's a bit dramatic. Either way, you can't be in love with me. This game has been fun, but I don't want to keep playing," she said.

He assessed her cautiously. "I'm telling you the truth, Cece. Feel for yourself. Read me. You'll see it's true." He held her hand to his heart.

"I don't want to read you." She yanked her hand back.

"Not so brave all of a sudden." He took hold of her arm. "Feel it for yourself."

Cecilia shook her head. "It's an invasion of privacy. I won't."

"Then I will just have to make you feel it." Xander kissed her.

Her stomach dipped, and her heart thundered as sparks fired all over her skin. As he kissed her, she opened herself up to him. She felt the overwhelming warmth of his love, the sharp edge of his desire, the deep longing in his heart, and a hint of grief and fear she didn't understand. Xander kissed her expertly, and she felt unsteady when he finally let her go.

He searched her face. "I would do anything for you, so I will give you more if you want it. I just want to be sure that is what you want now that you know how I feel. This isn't a game to me, Cece. I'm in love with you."

She looked away, trying to collect herself. Her thoughts were a whirlpool that threatened to pull her under a stormy sea. She didn't want to think anymore. She just wanted to feel. His eyes reflected the apprehension she felt.

"This could ruin you, Cece. If anyone else finds out, you would never marry," he said solemnly.

She shrugged a shoulder. "Well, I won't tell if you don't."

Xander hesitated. She felt him right on the precipice of letting go. They both stood poised to descend into chaos. Somehow, it wasn't frightening. It was simply exhilarating. Want spread beneath her skin like a slow-blooming bruise.

"I want more," she whispered. She barely had time to say it before Xander swept her into his arms again in a scorching kiss.

They were graceless and needy, and there was nothing expert about it. They fumbled with their robes, driven mad by desire, as he kissed down her neck. She pulled back for a moment and let the white cotton pool at her feet. She stood naked in the firelight, fumbling awkwardly with her hair.

He was still as a statue as he took her in. His eyes moved from her face, over the curve of her breasts, down her stomach and hips, to her legs.

"Gods, you are so beautiful," he breathed.

"Are you going to do something or just stare at me?" Cecilia mumbled.

She'd never been naked with anyone before. Xander's gaze was too heavy.

"I'm going to do everything, Cece."

He laid her down on the rug in front of the fire, meeting her with another kiss. His fingers slid down her side, and goosebumps rose in the wake of his touch. He moved like he had all the time in the world, kissing her until she was breathless and shaking, and only then did he leave her lips.

He kissed down her body, just like he said he would, listening to the sounds she made in each spot, charting a map of her skin with his hands, lips, and tongue with a reverence that brought tears to her eyes. Finally, he made his way between her trembling thighs. She was breathless and flushed, and she was utterly undone already.

"Are you well?" he asked, smiling at her. She nodded. "Do you want me to keep going?"

"Yes," she whispered, only vaguely embarrassed by the desperation in her voice.

"Remember, you're in charge. If you want me to stop at any time, I will."

She appreciated that he kept checking on her, but she had no intention of stopping what she'd started. "I don't want you to stop."

"Goddess, remember the night by the river? I told you that you would enjoy the way I'd worship you if you let me. This is what I meant."

She cried out as he brought his mouth between her legs. Xander went to work with slow, torturous strokes of his tongue, using every sound he coaxed from her lips as a guide to what she liked. She could not believe the speed with which he mastered her pleasure, or how much she enjoyed being mastered.

He flicked his tongue over her as she moaned, weaving her fingers through his hair. There were so many sensations—the warm slide of his tongue, his soft lips pressed against her, and his calloused hands on her hips, grounding her.

Her legs trembled, breathing turned ragged as her hips moved to meet him. Her pulse pounded in her ears as desire and need rushed through her body. He wrapped his arms around her legs and pulled her toward him, burying his face between her legs like he was starving for her.

She was so close, her head spinning from overwhelm as he slid a finger inside her, and her whole body clenched around it. He worked her slowly with his finger as he continued with his tongue, then, added a second finger. Her heart thundered in her ears, pulse pounding like it wanted to escape her chest. She could hardly hear the desperate pleas from her lips and was too lost to sensation to be embarrassed about them.

Cecilia dug her fingernails into his forearms, and she screamed as her whole body shuddered.

It was like nothing she'd ever felt—as if she'd called in lightning from every corner of the universe. It struck at once, right at the center of her, and exploded as the pleasure of the release whipped through her body. She felt she'd been tossed up into the night sky and was gracefully floating back down to the ground. Her legs kept shaking, even once the aftershocks had passed. He kissed her inner thighs and met her gaze. His eyes were bright with triumph.

He crawled back up her body and kissed her on the lips. "Are you satisfied now?"

"No." The word shocked them both.

He bit back a smile. "No? Did you not enjoy that?"

"Very much, but I want more," she murmured.

"Are you sure you want this? There's no going back."

"Please, Xander. I want you."

"You already have me, love," he whispered.

He was so gentle as he slipped between her legs, pressing himself inside her. At first, she was afraid her body would remain unwilling to surrender to him.

"Breathe, love. I promise if you relax, it will be easier."

Cecilia took a deep breath as the pressure built. Her muscles relaxed, and he slid further. A strange ache stole her breath, and she froze beneath him, sucking in air. Her fingernails dug into his arms.

"Are you all right?" he asked.

She nodded. He kissed her lightly all over her face, waiting for her to relax again. She loosened her grip on him.

"I'll go slow," he whispered as he drew out and pressed into her achingly slowly again.

Her breath caught as she felt every inch. She felt an ache and fullness that she'd never known, and she wanted more.

"I'm all right." She smiled at him as he withdrew again and pressed back into her.

The sensation shifted from pressure to pleasure. He dropped his head and kissed down her neck as he found a rhythm. She wrapped her legs around his waist and lifted her hips to meet him, moving entirely on instinct. It felt good to be so in sync with someone else.

"Gods, Cece, you feel amazing," Xander groaned.

He kissed her again as he quickened his pace with her breathing. His hand slid between them, and he rubbed her with each thrust. Her body was a symphony of wild, powerful sensations as she clamped down on him. Everything in her was set to combust.

"Let go, love," he whispered, urging her on.

The closeness of him, the way it felt to be held by his strong arms while he was inside her and wide open to her—it felt like too much. She felt his love buzzing in the air around them like a cocoon—warm and bright and electrifying.

Cecilia trusted him completely. She felt pressure low in her belly and at her heart, and she wasn't sure which was more intense. The emotion was too much and not enough.

Finally, Xander pressed deeper, and she cried out, shuddering around him as another release tore through her body. It was lightning fast and split apart all the thoughts in her head. It was completely different from the others and so much more intense. When she settled, warm tears slid down her cheeks.

Every bit of tension in her body eased at once, and she felt overwhelmed by her feelings for him. She was dancing along a dangerous line. She promised herself that he was just for fun, and she'd feared she'd already broken her own promise.

"You're crying," he said, pausing. "Did I hurt you?"

He pulled back, his brow furrowed in concern as he brushed a tear from her cheek.

"No, very much the opposite. I feel amazing," she said.

"Then why are you crying, love?"

"I've never felt this," Cecilia rasped.

She'd found someone who wanted to give her everything she wanted just in time to have to give him up. The fates were cruel.

Xander's face softened.

There were no more words. He sat up, pulled Cecilia into his lap, and pushed back inside her. The angle and the new fullness of it were overwhelming. At first, she was tentative, but his hands on her hips guided her. They moved together, savoring every touch. He helped her find a rhythm with him. He held her close and kissed her as they moved. The closeness of skin on skin drove her wild, and she felt the tension building fast again. A storm of pleasure spun through her, and she welcomed it. There was no space between them and no room for fear.

Xander watched her face, studying her every expression. She couldn't believe she had anything left, but she was so close to another climax. He wove a hand through her hair and pressed his lips to hers.

"Cece, I can feel that you're close. I want you to finish with me," he whispered.

She looked into his eyes and saw so much love reflected there. He kissed her as he pulled her hips down harder. Her whole body clenched, bearing down on him. With one more thrust, he sealed their bodies together, and he shuddered as she cried out and fell apart. Lightning buzzed through her veins, shooting out into little sparks of pleasure throughout her body.

She tucked her face into his neck. They sat there for a few long moments, catching their breath, waiting for their bodies to cool, listening to each other's heartbeats slow.

"You were right," he said, kissing her temple.

She snuggled into him. "I'm always right, but what am I right about this time?"

"This was worth whatever else we have to endure."

"Well, maybe that will teach you to stop arguing with me and just give me whatever I want."

"I expect I will be helpless to all your demands from now on." He sighed. He tucked her against his side as they stretched out on the floor next to the fire.

As she drifted off, she realized that true intimacy, like all magic, required an exchange. She couldn't access the full breadth of it if she wasn't willing to sacrifice her pride and be vulnerable. So much of her life had been about faking strength and confidence when she didn't feel it, but this kind of connection was one that required enough trust to let him see the softest parts of her. It was against her nature as a warrior to reveal places where she could be easily wounded, and yet she wanted to show him every one.

17

Cecilia woke wrapped in warm blankets in bed instead of where she'd fallen asleep in front of the fire. Snow pelted the cabin windows as the wooden ceiling groaned in protest of the stiff wind.

Stretching as she rolled over, the soft linen brushed against her skin as she found Xander propped on an elbow, his hazel eyes glowing in the firelight.

"Were you just staring at me all night?" she asked.

"Could you blame me?"

"Yes, that's creepy."

He brushed a loose curl back from her forehead. "Nonsense. It's awfully hard to sleep with you naked next to me."

She tried to hide the warmth rushing to her cheeks with her hands.

"So shy this morning. You weren't very shy last night. First, you demanded I make love to you."

"I did not *demand*." Her eyes went wide, and her cheeks burned.

"Then you were wide open and so sexy."

"Gods!" She pulled the blanket up over her head, hiding from him.

He yanked it down and kissed her. "It's nothing to be embarrassed about, Goddess. You are incredible."

She stared at him like he wasn't quite real. "Are you just saying that?"

"No. Why would I?" Xander looked baffled.

Cecilia played with a stray thread on the sheet. "I know you've been with plenty of women, most of them more experienced than me."

His eyes lit up. "Are you jealous?"

She wanted to slap him. "Yes. Could you try to look a little less pleased about it?"

"I may have been with other women, but I have never felt anything like that in my life. I was so turned on by every little sound you made."

She couldn't meet his eyes.

"Cece, I'm serious. I've never felt so connected to anyone. All of my other experiences were purely physical. This was so much more. This was magic." She smiled at him, and he kissed her softly. "You are full of surprises. I hope you never stop surprising me."

She hoped he'd never stop surprising her, either. They stared at each other in silence for a moment.

"Are we leaving for the Cave of Longings today?" she asked.

"The weather is pretty bad. I don't think it's smart for us to head out until it clears."

"But what about Rainer?" She felt a sudden pang of guilt.

"He will figure it out when he gets there and sees the fresh snow. I'm sure he will expect us to be delayed."

"Are you sure this isn't just a ploy to keep me here in bed so you can make love to me all day?" she taunted.

"I like the way your mind works, and I'd love to take you up on that offer. There are so many things I'd enjoy teaching you." The way he said it sent warmth to her belly. "I promise this decision is entirely for safety. The weather in the Argus Mountains changes swiftly, and the visibility is poor right now." He frowned. "What has you looking so distracted?"

"I was curious about what things you wanted to show me. Since we have some time to kill and all."

His gaze heated as he sat up. His whole demeanor shifted. "Kneel facing the headboard," Xander said, his voice rough and commanding.

She followed his instructions. Xander placed her hands shoulder-width apart on the headboard in front of her. He pushed her hips forward, kneeling behind her. He ran his hands up her sides, and she shivered against his touch as he pulled her back so she was seated against him.

"What are you doing now?" Desire and anticipation wove through her words, making her voice husky.

"Well, love, last night I did everything that I promised I would, right?" He cupped her breast with a hand, running his thumb over her hard nipple as she gasped. "Today, I'd like to see you figure out what you like."

"But I liked everything that you did." She sighed as he kissed up her shoulder.

"Yes, but I want you to be in control. I want you to learn what you like so you know what to ask for. I can give you pleasure, but I want you to learn how to give it to yourself and how to ask me or anyone else you're with for what you want," he said as his breath ghosted over her ear. "You're in control."

His words, touch, and lips combined for a drugging sort of effect. Cecilia felt lost in it as she leaned into Xander.

"What do you want me to do?" She felt him growing hard beneath her.

"I want you to push yourself back on me, to ride me until you make yourself come," he whispered, nipping at the skin at the back of her neck.

She arched back, pushing her ass against his hardness. He curled an arm around her and reached between her legs, rubbing her. She rocked against his hand. Feeling powerful and vulnerable at the same time was a novel experience.

"But I don't know how," she said.

"This is about learning, love. I'll be right here to help, and as we go, I will touch you, and you can tell me what you like and what you want more of. There's no wrong way. This is about you, Cece." He continued to move his hand between her legs.

"Teach me," she whispered, pushing down harder. He cursed. "Teach me," she murmured again, and he groaned at the words.

He brought one hand to her hip and used the other to line himself up. "Push yourself down on me."

Cecilia sank down on him slowly, feeling the delicious way he stretched and filled her. She was sore, but she wanted everything his touch promised. Inch by inch, she pushed against him until he was buried to the hilt.

"How does that feel?" Xander asked, nuzzling her neck.

"So good," she whispered. She hesitated, but she wanted to know, so she forced herself to speak. "Tell me how I feel." She was surprised by the boldness Xander drew out of her.

"You feel hot and so tight, like you could tear me apart just by breathing, love. You make it hard to control myself," he said. His fingers tightened on her hips as if demonstrating the struggle. His teeth raked down her neck, and she moaned. "Now, put your hands on the headboard to brace yourself and move up and down on me."

His hands fastened on her hips, and she loved the feeling of him holding her from behind. She placed her hands back on the head-board, lifting off him slightly and pressing down again with a moan.

"Fuck, Cece. You're perfect. Keep going."

She slowly found a rhythm. Xander let her have full control. Now and then, she'd hear a grunt or gasp from him, and she took inventory of each sound to learn what he liked. One of Xander's hands slid up to cup her breast, rolling her nipple between his fingers, and she cried out. She moved faster as he touched her.

"Do you like that?" he murmured.

"Yes," Cecilia moaned. "More."

He brought his hand to the other breast so that they both received equal attention, which made the tension rising in her more urgent. She moved faster against him. She was panting and moaning uncontrollably, and for a moment, she tensed, feeling embarrassed by the noise.

"Don't be self-conscious, Cece. I love the sounds you make," he said. "I can tell you're close. Can I make a suggestion?"

"Yes."

He took hold of one of her hands and brought it between her legs. "Touch yourself as you move. It will help."

She imitated the way he touched her.

"You're almost there. Faster," he coached.

The tension inside her was impossible. It was too much sensation. She felt so overwhelmed—hot and breathless and about to break.

"I can't," she whimpered.

"You can, love. Tell me what I can do to help. Tell me how to please you," he whispered, kissing her neck.

"Move with me. Hold my hips and help me finish myself," she panted.

He took hold of her hips and rocked with her as she furiously rubbed herself. Her whole body wound tightly, and it was only a moment before she threw her head back and screamed, coming apart around him in a rush of warmth.

He slowed their rocking, holding her back against his body. He turned her head, pulling her into a kiss, still seated inside her.

"How do you feel?"

"Powerful," she sighed.

She felt strong and open and free, fearlessly chasing something she wanted. She'd held immense power in her hands her whole life, but being open and vulnerable and asking for what she wanted made her feel more formidable than anything else ever had.

"That's exactly how you should feel. All women should know how to ask for exactly what they want," he whispered, kissing her again. "What do you want now?"

"I want to feel you come. I want you to use what you learned to make me come again," she said, meeting his eyes over her shoulder.

His smile brightened at the challenge. "Hands back on the head-board. Remember, anything you don't like, just tell me to stop, and I'll stop right away. Hold on, because I'm going to do exactly what you asked me to do."

He brought his hands to her hips and thrust inside her hard and fast. He reached a hand up to play with her nipples. She met every thrust, pushing back against him and panting his name. He moved a hand between her legs, rubbing her as he thrust. A shock wave tore through her whole body. She thought she might explode again, but she stayed balanced right on the precipice of release. She squeezed so tightly around him.

"What do you want, Cece?" he grunted.

"Harder," she panted.

He brought both hands to her hips, driving into her harder and faster. Then he wound a hand around her hair and pulled her head back, nipping at her neck. She screamed, crashing over the edge and squeezing him so tightly that he followed her over, moaning her name. He held her against him, kissing her over and over as they both panted.

Sweat cooled on their skin, and their breathing settled.

"Did you like it?" Xander asked as he pulled her down to the bed beside him.

"I liked when you pulled my hair." Her cheeks heated with the admission.

"That's nothing to be embarrassed about, love. A bit of pain at the right time can make for an intense release. You're just experimenting. Learning what you like. That's what you're supposed to do." He smiled, brushing a stray hair back from her sweaty forehead.

"How did you know I would like it?"

"Because you told me. You said you wanted it harder, so I tried something rougher to see if you would like it, which it seems you really did."

"I did." She bit her lip.

"This is why I want you to learn what you like. It's only fun for me if it's fun for you, love. You should always enjoy yourself as much as I do. Sure, sometimes I like to be in charge, but I want to know everything you like so that I can perfect it. Plus, you should be able to enjoy yourself on your own as well."

Xander's hands trembled as he touched her cheek.

"You're shaking," she said, pressing up to her elbows to look at him. "Are you all right?"

"I am more than all right. I'm overwhelmed by you." He pulled her close so that her head rested on his chest. They were silent for a few moments.

"What are you thinking about?" he asked.

"I'm trying to figure out why people do anything other than eat, sleep, and fuck."

He barked out a startled laugh. "That's a good question."

"Gods, it's a good thing I didn't do this sooner, or I would have ceased doing anything else. How do you even concentrate?" Cecilia asked.

"I told you, it's not always like this."

"Well, I have nothing to compare it to."

"Then you'll have to take my word for it."

They spent most of the day in bed. Everything was so new to Cecilia, and Xander couldn't get enough of her. She was delighted to oblige him. He seemed determined to test the limits of both her endurance and her flexibility. He made love to her all over the cabin, in many positions, until she was too exhausted and sated to do anything but lie beside him and enjoy the soft caress of his fingers on her skin.

Xander drew his index finger over her shoulder, connecting the dots between freckles. "You are beautiful, far beyond anything I've ever seen. I wish you could see what I do. Feel what I feel."

"You could share the memory of all of this," she whispered.

"How does it work?"

"You simply hold my hand and bring it to mind, and I catalog it with my own."

"Will you know my thoughts?"

She laughed. "Why does everyone ask that? No, I won't know your thoughts, but I will feel what you feel."

"And when you have the memory, you can pull it back up anytime and enjoy it?" he asked.

She nodded.

"That sounds convenient," he murmured.

He placed his hand in hers and nodded. Her powers pressed gently against his mind, and he surrendered to it. They watched it all play out again.

When it was over, she smiled, but Xander's face clouded over with worry.

"Cecilia, we could go back to Olney now. We could send word to Rainer. No one would blame us. Something is clearly very wrong in the kingdom."

"Why are you saying this?" she asked, brushing a finger along his jaw.

"Because I'm in love with you, and I think that's the safest option," Xander murmured. "If Argaria truly has spies looking for you and they know how far you've come, that last cave is sure to be the most dangerous."

"I have a duty, Xander. I might be the only one who can get the last missing piece of our magic and finish the Gauntlet. I have a responsibility to our people. It's the only way—" She stopped herself, realizing it was the first time she'd voiced aloud the hope she'd carried with her since Olney.

"It's the only way what?" Xander asked.

"It's the only way I can earn my freedom," she whispered. "If I finish the Gauntlet and go back with everything we need, who could deny me what I want?" She expected him to disagree. It was a faint hope, and she was probably foolish to nurture it.

She'd wanted to make her own choices, and now her vision for her life had shifted. Maybe she could have a future with Xander, even if he was below her station. The only difference between hunters and guardians was wealth, and Cecilia had plenty of family money. Who could deny her happiness after her hard work?

"I'm worried I won't be able to keep you safe. We've been lucky so far, but they must know where we're headed. This is easily the most dangerous part of the trip," Xander said. His gaze grew even more intense. "Run away with me, Cece."

"What?" She choked out a laugh.

"You heard me. Run away with me. Be with me. We can move northwest. Live by the sea—gods, we could cross it and live in Novum —get jobs doing what normal people do. We can get married when you're ready, only if you want to, of course. I just want to be with you. I want to keep you safe from all of this. You deserve more than a kingdom that would use you for your power and then treat you like a prize for someone else."

Cecilia stared at Xander, trying to puzzle out if he was serious.

"If this is meant to be a proposal, it's a bad one, just in case you were wondering." She frowned at him.

He laughed, and joy brightened his entire face. "You're right. Let me try that again."

Xander knelt on the bed, pulled her up to a seat, and took both of her hands in his. "Cece, I am in love with you. I'm uncertain of the moment it happened. It might have been back in the gardens in Olney, or the moment I saw you bathed in moonlight in the river, or more likely when I missed you pulling your dagger on me. All I know is that I loved you before I even knew what was happening. I would like nothing more than to spend the rest of my life kissing you, making love to you, and trying to make you laugh every day. Will you have me?"

Cecilia was prepared to give a sarcastic comeback, but his face was so earnest she smiled involuntarily. People were relying on her. She knew she had a duty to her kingdom—lives were at stake, her father's included. There was so much responsibility weighing on her, but at that moment, all she could think about was Xander and the way she felt when she was with him.

"This is the part where you're supposed to say yes, love," he whispered.

Cecilia was at a loss for words. It seemed impossible to be sitting there with someone who wanted to be with her because he loved her, not for who she was or what a marriage to her could do for him, but simply because he saw *her*. Since they'd first spoken in the garden, Xander focused entirely on getting to know her. He wanted her, and he was offering her exactly what she wanted.

"This is crazy," she said.

"I know you don't feel quite the same, but I'm confident you will get there."

"So pompous," Cecilia said, shaking her head.

"I don't want to own you, Cece. I just want to be the person you share your life with," Xander said.

She'd never imagined anyone would offer her that option, not after Rainer made his position clear. She hated that he was the first person who came to mind when Xander told her he wanted to marry her. She'd always been a decisive person, but love had muddled everything in her mind.

"I can't imagine trying to live the rest of my life without you in it to put me in my place, to make me laugh...to seduce me." Xander winked.

She covered her face with her hands. The room was suddenly much too warm despite her nakedness. Raw emotion overwhelmed her, and she fought against the tears that threatened to break through. She met Xander's expectant gaze.

"Cecilia Reznik, will you marry me? Will you let me spend the rest of my life trying to deserve you? Will you let me whisk you away and keep you safe forever? Gods, I know you don't need me to take care of you, but will you let me try anyway?"

Xander didn't want her to *need* him. He simply wanted her love.

"Yes." The word was out of her mouth before she could think any more about home, or duty, or Rainer.

She'd been acting like she had no choices, like she had to wait for her father or Rainer or a suitor to decide her future. But Xander was asking her to choose him—to choose herself just once. He asked her like hers was the only permission he needed. He handed her the power, and she would have been a fool not to take it.

Tomorrow, she would step into the last cave in the Gauntlet, the Cave of Longings, and release whatever magic existed there. She tried to envision finishing the Gauntlet. It should have been her only focus, but when Xander smiled at her, all thoughts of the future narrowed to him. Perhaps his love was the balm to the pervasive loneliness she'd felt her whole life.

PART III:

THE EXCHANGE

18

The sun pulled ribbons of pink and purple across the mountain sky as Xander and Cecilia rode up the steep trail. Snow glittered on the world around them. The storm had settled to a gentle breeze. Snow-laden pine boughs groaned to life, filling the air with their sharp scent.

In the quiet of the wooded mountains, Cecilia's mind drifted to Rainer. She'd woken at first light with anxiety bubbling through their bond, and she worried he'd run into trouble. The fear of losing Rainer was so sharp it stole her breath. She did not know how he'd react to her plan to run away with Xander, and imagining a life away from her best friend was brutal, but she'd cross that bridge once they were safely back in Olney.

Xander drew her closer and kissed her cheek.

"Are you well?"

"I think something is wrong with Rainer." Cecilia rubbed her sternum, trying to tug on her bond with Rainer. She waited, but no feeling came in reply.

"What can I do to ease your mind, love?"

She shrugged.

"Should I tell you another story? I know we did the Storm Prince the other night, but I could tell the one about Goddess Sayla and the Huntsman in the Wailing Woods."

Cecilia nodded. It was a horrifying story about the vengeful goddess of the hunt, but Cecilia welcomed the distraction. As they climbed higher into the mountain pass, her stomach lurched each time they came to an overlook, but Xander's warmth and the rhythm of his storytelling soothed her.

"Do you think it's a true story?" he asked, bending down and tucking his warm cheek against her cool, rosy one.

"It's just a fairy tale, Xander. Just like the red maiden and the wolf. It's just a beautiful story parents tell their kids to inspire them to do great things, be brave when they're scared, or keep them from wandering into the woods alone."

"I always wanted that one to be true." Xander sighed.

"Wouldn't you worry you'd be punished for the trail of broken hearts you left back in Olney?" Cecilia asked.

"Glad you've been appraised of my reputation, but my under-standing is that Sayla only punishes men who have taken something, not those who accept things given freely," Xander said, nipping at her ear. "As I recall, you demanded that I give you what you wanted. I should think the goddess would side with me in the matter."

"Your ego is spectacular."

He chuckled. "I suppose it's good I can back it up."

They rode in silence for a long while. The only sounds were the crunch of the snow beneath Biscuit's hooves and the heavy pine boughs scratching against each other like claws on bark.

"So, what happens in this last cave?" Xander asked as they crested a hill. They were nearly to the top of the mountain, and Cecilia knew the cave was close.

"I'll go in and make the exchange, and then, according to the myth, the power of the Lost God will be released. The scholars think it means all the witches of Olney will be able to wield it once I complete the ritual, but it's possible that I will get some type of memory or spell to help release the magic back at home."

Xander shifted behind her. "Does it make you nervous to walk into these caves not knowing what to expect?"

Cecilia shrugged. "I've been doing it for so long now I don't feel the same nervousness entering the caves. That said, the only rule about the order of the Gauntlet is that the Cave of Longings goes last. Apparently, it requires a more involved exchange, and that puts me on edge a bit, since a bit of blood is usually enough. This will require more, and once I'm inside, I'll be compelled to follow through or my soul will be rended from my body."

Xander blew out a breath. "No pressure, then?"

Her stomach flipped. "Yes, no pressure. Regardless, I have to do this. Clastor stored the last of his power here before the War of the Gods. The Gauntlet was his way of taking care of the people of Olney, and I've come too far to be a coward now. If I don't release this power, Olney doesn't stand a chance against Argaria. They have the god of war leading their army, and gods forbid the trickster god gets involved. I won't have my father facing off against either of them."

Xander grew quiet for a moment. "Do you really think the power of the Lost God will be enough to stop Argaria? They have two living gods. The Olney army might be bigger, but even if Clastor put a god's power into those caves and the witches of Olney learn to wield it, do you think it's enough to level the scales?"

Cecilia shook her head. "All I know is that not releasing that power won't make things better, and if Argaria finishes the Gauntlet first, they'll have the power of three gods. That would be catastrophic. They've been picking away at our borders for years, invading lands and annexing small towns, forcing the people there to pay back-breaking taxes. I have to believe this will make a difference. I can't give up hope."

Xander sighed heavily. "Living gods. I always found it curious that they call the rest of the gods ascended instead of 'dead.' I suppose it's less bleak."

Cecilia shrugged. "I suppose. There are plenty of people who still see their influence in the living world. Like your fairy tale about Sayla. Most of the scholars think that the ascended gods are still with us, still lending a hand, but without physical bodies their power in our world isn't as strong as those of the gods who are still corporeal."

"And what do you think?" Xander challenged.

Cecilia sighed. "I think we're all on our own, and I don't intend to wait for some absent gods to save me. I've certainly never felt their intervention."

That wasn't entirely true. A pang of guilt wormed its way into her stomach as a memory of a strange spirit on the beach who talked with her after her mother died. She was certain it was just the imagination of a grieving six-year-old, and giving credence to fantasies wouldn't serve her on the most important day of her adult life.

"Are you worried?" Xander asked.

"I'm more worried about Rainer, and it will be strange walking into a cave without knowing he's waiting outside. We have done every other cave together."

"Well, I can't replace him, but I'll be there if you need me, love."

"I know." She smiled.

It was a relief to know that someone would be there when she came out. She was determined to do whatever it took to complete the Gauntlet. What was one last exchange for the power to save countless lives?

"Did you always know you were a memory witch?" he asked.

"I didn't know until just after my mother died."

Xander's body stiffened. "You don't have to talk about it if you don't want to."

"No, I want to tell you," Cecilia started. "I haven't talked about it in a long time. I was too young when my mother died to understand what was happening. I knew she was gone, but I could still feel her because I can feel spirits. So, at first, I was confused why my father was so sad. I couldn't see her, but I could feel her. I remember walking around corners expecting her to be standing there, but she never was. Still, I knew she was close. My father was deep in grief. Most people don't remember, but I think it's the only time he ever took time off. He barely got out of bed."

"That must have been difficult," Xander said. "How did she die with so many talented healers and your father's access to power?"

"Even healers' magic has its limits. She had a wasting disease. Even the most talented healers couldn't keep her body from attacking itself. Rainer's mother died of the same disease years later. It's an awful thing." She shook her head, trying to rid herself of bad memories. "When my mother was dying, I spent a lot of time in bed with her, telling stories and talking to her. She was exhausted all the time, and I just lay with her, holding her hand. I didn't realize I was picking up her memories, but it was like I knew she was going and didn't want me to forget. My powers worked without me realizing. My magic has always been very tied to my emotions."

Xander tightened his arm around her, and she was touched by the way his grief echoed her own.

"Anyway, I wanted my father to feel better. I wanted things to go back to normal, so I went into his room and sat next to him. My father lay there dazed, staring out the window at nothing until I took his hand and pushed a memory in. It was one from shortly before he proposed to my mother. He was helping her in the garden, and it was short and sweet. He sat up so fast, so panicked, that I almost fell off the bed. I didn't really know what I'd done."

"You must have been frightened," Xander said.

"I was. He cried, hugged me, and told me I was supposed to be his little huntress and it was too soon. I didn't know what was happening. The next day, he took me to Madame Costello, and I started my memory witch training."

"What was it like?" Xander asked.

"Intimidating. I'd already been attending the little school, but they had to fast-track my training so that I could learn to control my powers. I was too strong for my own good and thrown into upper-level magic classes with kids twice my age. Once, I got so scared in an exercise that I accidentally summoned the tides and nearly drowned the entire class. I reached out and pulled on whatever I could get hold of, unaware that I was summoning. It was terrifying."

Xander kissed her temple. "How did you learn to control it?"

"Practice and a lot of mistakes." She sighed.

They sank into silence, but Cecilia felt his anxiety around them like a heavy blanket. A haunting howl cut through the air before she could ask him what he was so worried about. Her whole body went rigid.

"What is it?" Xander asked, but she could barely hear him through the noise.

"It's a warning. The spirits are very loud here."

She brought her hands to her ears and cringed, trying to cut her senses through the noise. Slowly, the noise quieted.

"The Cave of Longings is a challenging test. The books all said that I have to acknowledge my greatest longing, which will be painful and hard to look at. They're warning me away," she said.

Xander's arms tightened around her waist. "Maybe we should turn back."

"We're already here. I've been training my whole life for this. I can handle it," she said.

She drew Biscuit to a stop and hopped down without waiting for Xander. He hurried down behind her.

She paused, looking into the dark maw of the cave. "It's the last step. I may as well complete it. Will you keep an eye out for Rainer?"

Xander nodded, his eyes scanning the area for trouble before resting on the cave mouth as if looking for magic.

From the outside it looked innocuous, surrounded by bright green moss and wavering layers of windblown snow. Still, no witch worth her salt wouldn't notice the power pulsing from within the darkness.

"Cece, wait." Xander caught her arm and spun her around, pulling her into a slow kiss.

It shocked her the way she'd kissed him so many times over the past few days, but she could still feel completely surprised by the flurry of sensations his lips brought forth.

She grinned, brushing his hair back from his forehead. "I'm coming back."

"I know. I just wanted to do that." He pulled her in for one more quick kiss.

"Remember, you can't come in. Witches only beyond this point. I'll be back soon."

She knelt at the entrance of the cave and waited for permission. A few minutes later, she felt like she was being called into the darkness. She snapped and brought a flame to her fingers and entered the dark. The silence in the cave was oppressive, the darkness swallowing up her footsteps and the light from her flame.

Uneasiness grew in her belly as she walked for a long while.

A voice cut through her mind. *Cecilia Reznik, what do you seek?*

Wisdom. Memory. Magic, she answered.

You're here for the pinnacle of the Gauntlet. Are you prepared to look at your deepest longing?

Yes, she replied.

She didn't know what would come forth for her, but she was less afraid than she was determined, despite all the warnings. She wondered what her longing would be. A week ago, she might have known for sure, but now she wasn't certain if she would see Rainer or Xander.

Walk forward to the well.

She walked deeper into the darkness that seemed to close in on her until she saw a well in the dim light.

Look within, the voice prompted.

She knelt at the edge and waited, looking down into the dark water. But what she saw wasn't Rainer or Xander. It was something much bigger—her history.

What you see surprises you? the voice asked.

She saw a scene from when she first started taking magic classes. She was so much younger than her classmates. Fear and loneliness were her constant companions since no one paid attention to her or took her seriously. Her only friends were Rainer and Sylvie, and she rarely saw them. She missed her mother desperately.

Then she saw herself as a girl and felt the way her mother seemed to be a little frightened of her.

Her parents whispering behind a closed door even before her powers showed up. Her mother's hushed whisper, "She might be too much for us, Leo."

Cecilia had always been too wild. The memories were a barrage of every lonely moment in her life in quick succession. Being bullied by Anders Everett and teased by the ladies of the court. Rainer disappearing with a new woman each week. Rainer's rejection and the revelation that their feelings had never been as similar as she'd imagined.

I don't understand. Cecilia brushed away tears.

What is there to understand? There is only what you feel and what you already know. Longing is made of memory, the voice answered.

I never fit in. I was always alone. My greatest longing was companionship—to be understood. A cure for my loneliness, Cecilia sobbed.

Correct. Can you face that it might always be true? the ancient voice asked.

Cecilia took a step back. *It's not.*

You speak of your lover?

Cecilia nodded.

He can try, but he won't understand. Not truly. You are solitary—the only one. Not just a lady or a witch or a huntress, but all of those and more. You will always be separate. That is the price you must pay. Can you live with that?

The tears poured down her face, and she sobbed. *I don't want to be alone.*

The voice continued. *You must accept it, or you will never release this great power, Cecilia. You can't fear it, or it will control you. You must accept that gifts have a price, and yours is a very specific type of isolation.*

Ragged sobs tore through her as she watched more scenes play out. Then, the image in the water shifted, revealing the price of the magic. It was a completely different type of loneliness, one that would strip her of her legacy despite her finishing the Gauntlet. The cruelty of the exchange was shocking.

Do you understand what the price is? Are you prepared to make this exchange? The emotionless voice was in sharp contrast to her extremes.

Knowing the cost of the magic was savage. It clawed at her. She knew in her bones what it was so acutely that she wondered if she'd always known. It was like remembering. She was completely unprepared for the sacrifice, but she shouldn't have been. Exchange magic was unpredictable. She knew it would be more than blood but didn't expect something so different from what she'd expected and would alter her entire future.

She had to accept, or her soul would be trapped between realms forever. She felt something splitting apart inside her, as if her soul and body were splintering.

You're running out of time. You must accept it.

Cecilia knew that fear could make her a coward or a warrior. She ran a finger over the crescent-shaped scar on her left palm—proof that she usually chose the latter—but she was beginning to wonder if courage was worth it.

She closed her eyes and took a long, ragged breath. *I accept it.*

Place your hand in the well water.

Cecilia put her hand to the water, and lightning surged through her body. She let out a yelp but kept her hand in the water as pain flowed through her. She felt as if the lightning burned right through her gut. The pain was so severe that she could do nothing but scream.

There was no memory released. Just the surge of energy and pain until everything went black.

———

"Cece!" Xander called to her from far away.

"Xander?" Her voice was weak.

She tried to get up from the cold cave floor. Every muscle in her body hurt, and she was dizzy. Suddenly, she felt Xander beside her, his calloused hands on her face.

"You can't be in here," she murmured.

"The Gauntlet's over. Are you all right?" He helped her sit up. "I heard you scream."

She could barely see his face in the darkness. "It was awful."

He pulled her into his lap and held her tight as she sobbed. She sobbed for the lonely little girl she'd been, the lonely young woman she had become, and the lonely old woman she would be. Xander whispered soothing things until she finally calmed.

"I'm sorry," she said, wiping her cheeks.

He kissed her forehead. "You're so brave, Cece, but you don't have be to with me." The words set her free, and a fresh wave of tears came to her eyes. "I love you no matter what."

Her breathing slowed, and a resolute calm came over her.

The realization that she completed the Gauntlet crashed down on her. "I did it. I finished the Gauntlet. Did anything happen? Did you see anything?"

Xander shook his head. "No, I saw nothing. I just heard you scream, and I came running. Do you feel different? Do you have any new magic?"

"No. I feel the same."

She felt mostly the same. The memory of what she sacrificed to release the Gauntlet power sprung to the front of her mind, but she quickly pushed it away. She wasn't ready to acknowledge the price she'd paid or its permanence.

After all the hype, the pinnacle of the Gauntlet was anticlimactic for all she'd given up, though she supposed things could have been much wilder back in Olney. Maybe they already had access to the power. She wouldn't know for sure until they returned home.

Xander helped her to her feet and picked up his torch. His gaze was heavy on her, searching her for injury.

"We should go find Rainer," he said, placing a hand on the small of her back and guiding her toward the entrance.

They walked back in silence, but when they drew close to the cave mouth, she felt a heaviness just outside the cave.

"Xander, wait—"

She reached for his hand, but he was just beyond her grasp. He stepped into the light and drew up short. Surprise and fury clouded his face, and he held out a protective arm to tuck her behind him.

When her eyes adjusted to the light, she saw twenty Argarian hunters waiting for them with bows drawn.

19

"**G**ood morning, Lady Reznik!" the leader of the Argarian hunters shouted.

Cecilia was startled that he knew her name. The man hopped down from his horse. He wasn't wearing a hunter's emblem, and Cecilia instantly worried he was a slayer.

"We already have your guardian. If you want him to live, you won't give us any trouble."

She tried to push Xander aside, but he stood firm. He looked stunned and fearful, with all the color drained from his cheeks.

"Xander?" she whispered.

He didn't look at her. He focused on the group in front of them, his hand on the hilt of his sword.

"The prince is dying to meet you, my lady," the man said.

"The prince?" she asked.

The leader grinned. "Yes. He's been following your progress for a long while now. He's been waiting for you."

"Where is my guardian?" Cecilia asked.

"As long as you behave yourself, he'll be released unharmed."

Cecilia looked at Xander, hoping he had a plan, but he was still as stone. His eyes scanned the group, searching for a way out. She reached out her senses beyond the hunters in front of her, trying to grab hold of something familiar, but she stopped when she heard stumbling and felt Rainer's proximity.

Another man dragged Rainer out from the tree line. Rainer looked distraught. He was gagged, his hands bound behind his back, but he was uninjured. Cecilia had to stop herself from running to him. He stood next to a tall, broad man who looked vaguely familiar.

"Cecilia Reznik, the famous daughter of the Olney huntmaster!" the second man said. "I have your guardian here and several excellent marksmen spread all over the area, all trained on him. You can try to pull some magical stunt, but I expect that one of them will kill him before you do much damage. I need you to agree not to summon anything."

"What do you want?" she asked.

"No summoning?" He smirked, looking from her to Xander.

"Fine," she said.

"I'd also like you to toss your dagger aside. I understand you're quite deadly with it."

"I could toss it right into your throat," she threatened.

"If you do, your friend here will be dead before he hits the ground."

She hesitated. "It was a gift. I don't want to lose it."

"I will have one of my men hold on to it," he assured her.

"Fine," she said, tossing her dagger into the dirt. "You have me at a disadvantage. You know my name, but I don't know yours."

"How rude of me. I'm so used to someone else introducing me. Forgive me, Cecilia. My name is Davide Savero, Prince of Argaria. I have a bunch of other titles, but I assume I can skip those."

His smile was familiar, and a terrible sense of foreboding set her nerves on edge.

She tried to remember what she'd heard about the heir to the Argarian throne. Stories of his cruelty and manipulation had made it to Olney, especially those that suggested he'd become especially brutal since his younger brother disappeared years ago and was presumed dead.

She appraised Davide. He was tall, handsome in a cruel sort of way, with a pinch in his brow and a strong jaw. It was hard to know what to expect based on appearance and gossip. She'd learned enough about court rumors not to believe everything she heard. Maybe she could reason with him.

Cecilia dropped into a mocking curtsey. "Ah, *Your Highness*. What an honor to have my guardian taken hostage by you and your men."

"You're funny, Lady Reznik. I'd heard that from my spies. Why don't you step into the light so I can see you better?" Davide said.

She stepped forward.

"We'll have to get a good look at you in something other than those grungy hunter's clothes but, he may have undersold your beauty when he talked about you."

"When *who* talked about me?" Cecilia asked.

Rainer mumbled around the gag. She felt his guilt through their connection, but she couldn't make sense of it.

Davide's lips tugged up into a lupine smile. "My brother."

"Your brother?"

Davide wasn't making any sense. Maybe the rumors that his younger brother had died years before weren't true. It gave her hope that if those weren't true, the rest of the rumors might not be.

"Yes, you know him well. He's been keeping you warm for me." He laughed, elbowing Rainer in the ribs.

Rainer looked wrecked. He sputtered desperately against the gag, his shoulders slumped in defeat.

Time ground to a halt. Cecilia's whole body was cold and rigid. It wasn't possible. Rainer was her oldest friend—the person who knew her best in the world. Rainer slept in her bed every night. He baked her lemon cakes when she was sad and told her bedtime stories. Rainer, who had almost kissed her.

That reality warred with a different one. Rainer was adopted. He was so unlike his father. He was always trying to prove something with his commitment to the rules. Rainer had been terribly private about the identity of his birth parents, and she'd thought nothing of it. He'd told her that they couldn't be together because there was so much she didn't know, and he'd asked her to just wait until their trip was over. He could have hidden in plain sight her whole life, and she missed it.

Rainer was an enemy prince.

Shock sent her mind spinning. Cecilia looked from Davide to Rainer. There was only a slight resemblance, but all the air punched out of her lungs.

She feared she might collapse. She wished the ground would swallow her, or that she could cease to exist. Her heart threatened to shatter as it kicked up in her chest.

"Rain?" She looked at him, confused.

Rainer looked like he was seconds from crying. She'd never seen him look so moved. The guilt and fear that surged through their bond stole what breath she had left, leaving her gasping as she stared at him in disbelief.

Davide laughed heartily, breaking her out of her trance.

"Oh no, love. You have it wrong." Davide was in stitches. "I was talking about my little brother, Prince Alexander Savero, or as some people like to call him, the Storm Prince."

She stared at Davide.

"The one who calls you *Goddess*," Davide said exasperatedly.

Everything in her body went still. She turned slowly, looking at Xander.

He'd trained under her father for years, an enemy prince right under their noses.

And then another revelation: Xander was the Storm Prince, and the Storm Prince wasn't just a fairy tale, which meant he could summon storms and who knew what else.

Xander's face crumbled as she stepped back. Fear, grief, longing all swirled around him. She couldn't let herself be drawn into it.

"Cece, I'm sorry. I tried—" Xander started.

She held up a hand, trying to ward against his words.

The moments dragged. Her brain couldn't seem to catch up.

Xander who had spent hours kissing her, making love to her, telling her how beautiful and special she was.

So he could string you along, you silly, stupid girl.

How foolish of her to think that someone so handsome, charming, and experienced could want her. Years at court should have sorted out that notion. But he'd seen her as a sad girl, and he'd preyed on her loneliness.

Alone. Alone. Alone. Her mind echoed with words spoken by the cave ancients moments before.

Her face was wet. She looked up at the sky, expecting rain clouds but finding none.

She turned back to Davide.

"Cecilia, you're crying. I understand you and Xander were close. That must hurt."

The air crackled dangerously. Davide turned toward Xander. She felt the storm close by. She wasn't sure if she was causing it because of her grief, but Davide spoke and answered her question.

"Careful, brother, I'm not feeling especially playful right now. Remember how much she loves her guardian," Davide warned.

Cecilia looked at Rainer, but he just nodded at her and Xander. It was permission to risk his life to get Cecilia out. Permission she absolutely would not take.

"Don't hurt Rainer," she whispered, looking at Xander.

Xander took a hold of her arm, but she spun him around and swiped his dagger, flipping him to the ground and knocking the wind out of him. She straddled him, holding the dagger to his throat.

"Cece," he rasped.

"You will let my guardian and I go, or I'll kill Xander right now," she said.

Davide clapped. "Oh, Cecilia, you are just as spirited as he told me. Go ahead! He's played his part. He delivered you here. We no longer need him."

She looked down at Xander, feeling both rage and pity that his brother would let him die. She pressed the knife into his neck.

"You won't even defend yourself, brother?" Davide taunted.

Xander stared up at Cecilia. The love in his eyes hooked into her heart.

"Cece, I love you. This changes nothing," he whispered.

"You lied to me! About everything! You led me into a trap! That's not love, Xander!"

Her voice was a jagged whisper. She fed the burning flame of rage that lived in her heart with everything she had. She leaned into the deep burning pain, trying to hold on to it. Anger would sharpen her will into a useful weapon.

"I promise there's nothing you could do to me right now that I wouldn't deserve. Hurting like this breaks my heart," Xander murmured. "I swear I tried to think of a way out. Anything but *this*. I thought I had more time. I thought we'd come out of the cave, and I could tell you, and we'd find Rainer together."

Cecilia tried her hardest to hold on to her righteous anger, but it faltered. She started to cry again.

"This is why you tried to get me to run off. This is why you kept trying to get me to turn around." She sighed.

She felt like such a fool for not seeing it sooner. The dagger shook in her clammy palm.

"Alex, were you stupid enough to fall in love with her, knowing she's promised to me?" Davide laughed. His words startled her.

"I am promised to no man," Cecilia barked.

Genuine fear flashed through Davide's eyes as she leveled him with her gaze, but it was gone as quickly as it appeared.

Rage flooded back into her body. She looked down at Xander. Something deep and unspoken passed between them. She felt lost in a sea of emotion. She wavered, her grip on the dagger loosening.

Xander pressed up to a seat, trusting that she would move the blade. She didn't understand why, but she dropped it as soon as he moved. He wrapped her up in his arms, running his fingers through her hair as he kissed her.

He kissed her like they weren't surrounded by other people—like he thought he might never get to do it again. He brushed the tears from her cheeks with his lips and whispered in her ear.

"I love you. I need you to trust me. I'll get you out of this. You have no reason to trust me, but I need you to." He pulled back and looked into her eyes.

Trust felt like something fragile that she'd lost the right to possess. Maybe trust didn't really exist. Maybe the truth was as mystical and fleeting as magic. Xander might have believed he would get her out of it, but she didn't.

"No more kissing my fiancée, little brother." Davide looked irritated.

"For the love of the gods, I'm not going to marry you!" she said, climbing to her feet. "I will go with you if you let Rainer go."

"I won't let the guardian go until you agree to all the terms I set forth, so for now, he's coming with us. I can compromise, Cecilia. You can ride into Argaria with my little brother if you wear this Unsummoner bracelet." Davide held up the silver band and handed it to a hunter who tentatively approached her as she rose to her feet.

She let him fasten the Unsummoner bracelet to her wrist, and her connection to magic fizzled out. Even when she wasn't actually summoning, she could always feel her power there, but now it was as if the flame that always burned in her chest had gone dark. She fumbled with the silver band self-consciously.

"Your weapons have all been removed for your safety and for the rest of ours, and you'll be flanked by hunters who will shoot to maim and not kill you. There's no way out of this right now, so please save us the trouble."

She climbed onto Biscuit with Xander, leaning away from him as they rode.

"Cece?" Xander's voice was agonized.

"Don't," she said firmly. "I feel like such a fool, like the silly girls at court that I always thought myself above. Now I am just another stupid girl who believed a man who said she was pretty. Gods! I was so careless. You literally told me you wanted to be a prince the first time we spoke. You came into the cave! I hit you with lightning back when we were in that battle in the woods. I should have known so many times." She shook her head. "You preyed on my loneliness. How ruthless of you to use love as manipulation. I bet you'll be laughing it up to your friends about how you charmed me into bed."

Cecilia didn't want him or anyone else to know how much it hurt. The grief felt like a well with no bottom. She didn't want him to have the satisfaction of knowing how broken her heart was. He'd been so convincing when they were together. Would he be able to hear the moment her heart broke and ceased to beat, all because of him?

Her chest was too tight to take a deep breath.

Xander's voice was rough. "That's not true, Cece."

"I trusted you. I let you—" She couldn't say it. It was too much to think about how vulnerable she'd been.

Xander clung to her desperately. "Everything between us was true. I love you!"

"That isn't love, *Alex*," she rasped.

"Don't call me that."

"Sorry, *Your Highness*."

"Cece, I fell in love with you. Everything I said was true except my name and title. I swear it. I know you don't believe me, but the idea that you could think that everything between us was a lie breaks my heart. You are the most stubborn, brave, clever woman I've ever met. You changed everything. It was impossible not to fall for you. I would have given up everything in my life for you. I should have told you the whole truth, but never doubt my love."

"There is *nothing* between us but ruin," she huffed.

She didn't want to believe him, but the words put chinks in the armor she was trying to fasten around her heart. She felt like she was a breath from falling apart.

A startling revelation crashed down on her. She'd completed the Gauntlet, and they could be taking her to a slayer to steal the Gauntlet magic for Argaria. But that didn't explain why Davide called her his fiancée. She was missing something.

"How long have you been planning this?" she asked.

"For about a year—ever since your father asked me to keep an eye on you," Xander whispered.

"Have you really been in Olney since you were fourteen?"

"Yes, Cece. Almost everything I told you was true except my real identity. My family life, my feelings, my time in Olney."

She tried to take a deep breath, but her chest locked up, unable to process his words with her world imploding. She wished Xander's betrayal would annihilate her love for him, but her iron will was nothing compared to the fierceness with which she loved. Why was it that she could summon love so strong every time he smiled at her but not hatred when he deceived her so completely? Her heart rebelled against her will—two immovable parts of her grinding futilely against each other.

Xander pulled her closer. "Cece, I can help. I can soothe you like I did the night we met. You'll just go to sleep. I don't want you to hurt like this." He cupped her face with a hand.

"It's magic?" she asked.

"Yes," he whispered. "My grandmother taught me. It's a soothing spell. Say you want it, and I will put you to sleep. You can avoid talking to my brother until morning. I will keep you safe."

It felt cowardly, but she couldn't deal with the yawning chasm of despair opening inside her. She was worried that it might kill her and then more worried that she might want it to put her out of her profound misery. She needed to feel nothing.

"Do it," she whispered.

Her eyelids grew heavy as he murmured the words of the spell. His thumb rubbed along her jaw, calming her. She relaxed into his body, and his arms wrapped tight around her.

For a second before she fell asleep, the bitterness of betrayal grew faint, and she felt safe.

20

"My love, wake up." Xander's voice dragged Cecilia from a heavy, dreamless sleep.

She brushed her hands down the soft silk of her nightgown, keeping her eyes closed. For one blissful moment, she wanted to roll over and snuggle, but then she remembered the day before.

"I'm not your love," she snapped.

"You will always be my love." Xander said the words with a reverence that made her traitorous heart skip.

She hoped he hadn't heard it. She opened her eyes for the express purpose of rolling them.

"Where's Rainer?"

The words cooled all the heat on Xander's face to icy jealousy.

Xander crossed his arms, his words clipped. "He's fine. I'll take you to see him when I can."

Afraid to trust him, she brought her hand to her heart and tugged on her bond with Rainer. When a tug echoed back from him a moment later, she sagged in relief.

Cecilia turned her attention back to Xander, trying to ignore how annoyingly handsome he looked freshly groomed in his fine scarlet tunic and leather breeches. She grabbed a heavy fur robe that he'd laid across the bed, pulling it on to ward off the chill. She took in the luxurious bedroom fit for a princess with fine golden candlesticks, elaborately woven tapestries of the Argus Mountains, and bright scarlet curtains. There were no weapons, not that she expected them to let her be armed. She'd have to improvise.

"What do you want, *Your Highness*?"

"Don't call me that."

"Would you prefer I call you Prince Alexander or Alex?"

"I'd prefer you call me Xander." He sighed, reaching to touch her cheek.

Cecilia slapped his hand away. "Where am I, and what's happening, *Your Grace*?"

She stood and strode across the room to put space between them, crossing her arms as if they could protect her heart from further wounding.

Xander appraised her with amusement. "I know you're trying to push me away, but, gods, you're so pretty when you're angry. Your eyes sparkle and your cheeks flush, and you look just like you do after I make you—"

"Shut up!" She threw a candlestick that sailed past his head. She knew he would read something into her inaccuracy, so she threw another. He caught it and carefully placed it on the table next to him.

"Love, just because you don't like it doesn't make it untrue."

She couldn't resist smiling at him. For a moment, she could almost forget that he'd betrayed her. He was back to being the charming hunter who kissed her in the woods.

Focus, Cece, she scolded. Cecilia knew she had to use him. If Xander's feelings were real, she could use them to her advantage.

"True, like a fairy tale, Xander. Like a lovely dream that disappears as soon as you wake up and realize how fucked you are!" she screamed, throwing another candlestick. It barely skimmed his shoulder before it clattered onto the floor.

The bedroom door burst open, and two men stumbled in.

Xander shook his head at them. "I'm fine. Cece is a bit upset."

"A bit?" She chucked another candlestick.

Xander ducked, and it sailed over his head.

"She's got good aim." The blond hunter chuckled. "Honestly, I never liked those candlesticks, anyway."

"Good point. I suppose she has a right to redecorate her rooms if she chooses," Xander said, grinning at the hunter before turning his attention back to Cecilia. "Love, if you break them all, it's going to be awfully dark in here tonight."

She barked out a scornful laugh. "Oh, suddenly you care if I'm in the dark?"

With nothing else in range, she grabbed a heavy book from the table and chucked it at the three of them.

Xander ducked away before holding up his hands in surrender. "Goddess, really? A book of scripture."

"Anything is a weapon if you throw it hard enough," she huffed.

The dark-haired hunter behind him sighed, shaking his head. "She is assaulting the prince of Argaria. Are we really supposed to let this slide?"

"Who are you?" she asked.

The dark-haired one spoke again. "Evan Farlan, my *lady*. The prince's guard and the one who should probably arrest you for trying to kill him with your tantrum."

Cecilia narrowed her eyes at him. "I assure you that my *tantrums* would bring this fucking castle down if your cowardly princes didn't collar me with this stupid bracelet," she barked, holding up her wrist. "And as for His *Highness*, I suggest you leave him to his own mess."

"She's tinier than I expected," the blond hunter said. "Quite a lot of fire in a little package."

Xander's grin grew wide. "She is that, Ted."

Cecilia looked back and forth between the two hunters. "You're his best friends. Evan and Teddy. He told me about you, though I'm not sure whether to believe what he said, talented liar he is."

They both nodded. Xander had been telling the truth at least a little bit.

"Does he also lie to you?"

231

Teddy shook his head, but Evan cocked his head and shrugged. "Mostly he lies to himself."

Cecilia scoffed. "I can think of a few lies he likes to tell himself. His cockiness is insufferable."

"You like my brand of suffering, love," Xander quipped.

"I like it a lot less today." She hated that the heated look in his eyes still sent a thrill through her.

"Leave us," Xander said, as if reading her mind.

Evan gripped Xander's arm. "You can't be serious."

"My fiancée is understandably upset—"

"Fiancée!" Cecilia barked. "I wouldn't marry you if you were the last traitor on earth."

The two men looked from Cecilia to Xander skeptically.

Xander sighed. "Do you really think I can't handle her?"

Evan stared Xander down. "I don't doubt you, but she's—"

Xander shook his head, cutting off whatever his friend was about to say.

"Just remember, your brother will probably be here soon. For the record, this is a terrible idea, and it's going to end poorly," Evan grumbled, turning to leave.

"You can be the first to tell me *I told you so*, though I don't think it will be this morning," Xander said with a grin.

The two hunters left, closing the door behind them as Xander turned his heated gaze on her. "My love, I know that look in your eyes."

"Hatred? I expect you see it often if this is how you reward trust."

"I think you'll find there's a very fine line between hate and love. Both are born of passion," Xander said, taking a step closer.

Cecilia turned away, pacing the room like a caged animal. The heat of the fire and the robe were too much. She tossed the heavy garment onto a chair and continued her pacing.

"Cece, what are you wearing?" Xander asked.

His eyes scanned down her body. She'd forgotten about the flimsy red nightdress she'd slipped into half-awake the night before. She didn't even understand the purpose. It was silk and lace, and the straps were so tiny she was afraid she'd rip them just by walking. She realized the way she was standing backlit by the window likely made the entire dress sheer.

"Don't look at me like that."

His grin turned coy. "Like what?"

"Like exactly how you're looking at me. You have dirty in your eyes, and I am not interested." She resumed her pacing.

When she looked back at him, he'd silently closed the distance between them.

"Don't, Xander—"

He reached for her. Cecilia ducked him and spun back toward the bed, but he was quick. He swept her up, his hands wrapped around her thighs, lifting her up, and he slammed her back into the wall. He laughed when he realized she had his dagger pressed to his throat.

"Well, this is familiar." Xander laughed. "And very hot."

"There is something seriously wrong with you," she said.

"Probably." He laughed. "Drop the dagger."

Cecilia couldn't ignore the way her blood heated at his touch. She grasped desperately for the anger she'd woken with, but her body seemed eager to betray her.

"I loathe you." She pressed it against his skin, drawing a few drops of blood.

He smirked, and he pressed closer. She tensed as blood trickled from a shallow cut, but she didn't move the blade. She bit her bottom lip, and his eyes dropped to her mouth.

"Goddess, don't play games with me right now. I want you. *Badly.* Let me have you."

"Not until you apologize." She shifted the dagger slightly but didn't pull it back when he winced. She should have plunged it into his throat and ended the ordeal, but her body seemed at odds with that desire.

He laughed. "Gods, you are so stubborn and sexy."

"You're disturbed."

"Maybe, but I'm also very aroused." He pressed his hips into her to prove it.

"Apologize." She tried to hold her ground, but the way he looked at her made her hot all over.

Finally, he relented. "Cece, I am sorry that I hurt you. More sorry than I could ever put into words, but I could make you feel it if you let me."

Cecilia's eyes went wide. "You wouldn't dare."

Xander smirked. "Wouldn't I? You're certainly squirming against me like you need something."

Cecilia froze. She had been subtly grinding herself against him. Desire was a reflex with Xander.

He leaned toward her, allowing the dagger to cut him deeper. "You're beautiful and charming, and I love you very much."

She softened, and he struck as quick as lightning. One hand came off her thigh and knocked the blade away. She cursed. He pressed his hips into her, pinning her to the wall harder. The movement sent a surge of heat through her body. She kept expecting to reach some final edge—the edge of the world of wanting—but each time she encountered an obstacle, a new bridge was built, and the desire renewed, no matter how foolish it might be.

"First of all, Cece, I know you could get out of this if you wanted to." His gaze dipped to the neckline of her nightgown.

"Perhaps I don't want to be thrown in a jail cell for assaulting the prince of Argaria," she quipped.

He laughed and rolled his hips against her. She gasped. Her desire to scream at him was being replaced by a different desire altogether.

"I don't think that's the reason, love." He leaned down and kissed her neck, and she jumped. "You're wound tighter than a bowstring. You need to relax."

"Tell me to relax again and I'll risk being thrown in that cell," she huffed, giving his shoulders a futile push.

"I'm not telling you to relax. I'm going to help you relax." His lips grazed her ear as he spoke. He pulled back, and his eyes were smoldering.

"But I'm furious with you," she rasped.

"I know. I'm frustrated with you as well."

Cecilia frowned at him. "What? Why?"

"For yelling at me and teasing me with this skimpy little night-gown that makes it impossible to think, let alone argue with you."

He bent his head low and caught one of her nipples through the fabric. He flicked his tongue over it. She gasped in surprise.

"But do you know what's great about this? We can work through all of our aggression, and maybe you will finally relax," Xander murmured.

He moved his hips against her again, and she stifled a groan.

"I can tell by the way you've let me hold you here that you're at least curious. If you say yes, I will make you a very happy woman instead of a very grumpy one."

She wanted to slap him, but she restrained herself.

"Just say yes, Goddess. Please. At this moment, I'd give my kingdom to be inside you."

Xander's words unraveled her resolve.

"Yes," she whispered.

He freed himself from his pants, hiked her nightgown higher, and then quickly thrust into her. She gasped as the momentary discomfort shifted to pleasure.

The fullness was so different with this new angle, and it felt amazing. She squeezed her legs around his waist as he drove her against the wall again, catching her in a rough kiss. He picked up his pace, moving harder and faster. She bit his bottom lip so hard she tasted blood, but he didn't seem the least bit bothered by her roughness as he yanked her hair and kissed down her jaw and neck.

The cold stone of the wall bit into her low back, but she didn't care. She was entirely focused on every movement he made. She tried to keep quiet, but it was all too much—her anger, the look in his eye, the way he drove into her. A crackling, static sensation surged through her veins as she scraped her fingers over his scalp and yanked on his short hair.

The pain only spurred Xander on. Cecilia clung to him, pushing down against him. There was no reason anymore. She was driving toward something she didn't totally understand but needed badly.

They were wrapped up in the frenzy of it. She was right on the edge of letting go, so he pushed hard against her with three quick thrusts, and she smothered her cry against his neck, bearing down on him. Lightning pleasure whipped through her, shattering her into a thousand little sparks. As soon as it crashed over her, it built again with more intensity than anything else she'd felt before.

He kept up his frantic pace, his fingers bruising her hips, his kisses rougher. Pleasure tipped the scales, and she had the distinct feeling of losing ground to him.

"You're so good, Cece. I'm going to live between these thighs," he groaned.

The filthy words sent such a powerful wave of pleasure through her she cried out, and he rode over the edge with her.

They stayed there for a moment, just trying to catch their breath. Cecilia tucked her face into Xander's neck, trying to hide from the guilt and weakness she felt for giving in to him. All the tension left her limbs at once, and she felt like she might just melt onto the floor.

She was addicted to Xander's eagerness—compelled by the way he devoured everything she gave him and still went searching for more. She hated herself for it.

He carried her over to the bed, sitting down on the edge with her still wrapped around him. He took her face in his hands, kissing her until she was dizzy and exhausted and ready to collapse.

Xander leaned his forehead against hers. "Do you feel better?"

"I feel distracted." She sighed, running her fingers through the damp hair at the nape of his neck.

"Same thing."

"It is not," she huffed.

"You're still mad." He ran his fingers through her hair and kissed her bare shoulder.

"Mad doesn't cover it. I am furious. If it weren't for this gods-damned bracelet, my rage would conjure a storm even the illustrious

Storm Prince could not settle. What am I doing here? What is going on?" she asked.

"Well, you've met my terrible brother. I'm sorry about that. I was really hoping we could avoid it. In fact, I sent hunters to stop Rainer and send him the wrong way, but he was predictably immovable. I really tried to stop this, Cece."

She swallowed hard. "How long was this going on?"

He hesitated. "Since we met back at court. I did really get a summons from your father, but that was just the opening I needed to make this happen. Then, I fell in love with you—or maybe I was from the beginning. Honestly, I don't know. I started sending smaller and smaller reports to my family, trying to delay or stop everything that was in motion. I had more hunters attack us, but instead of deterring you, it spurred you on. I think Rainer was considering turning back, but he wouldn't do it without you. I tried to stop what I'd started."

She sniffled, horrified to realize she was crying. Xander made her feel chaotic and foolish. She extricated herself from his grip and crossed the room, trying to get a grip on her feelings.

"Cece, I am so sorry. Seeing you hurt breaks my heart." Xander's long steps ate up the ground between them until he was just behind her, the heat of his body brushing against hers.

She turned to look at him.

"Was any of it real?" She wished she could pull back the humiliating question.

Xander pulled her into his arms. She didn't fight him. She felt defeated, alone, and terrified.

"All of it was true. Except for my name. What I told you about my family. The story of the Storm Prince. How I felt about you. Everything between us—*especially* everything between us. I am crazy about you."

She sobbed against his chest. "How do I believe that? You took something from me when I didn't even know who you were."

Xander looked down at the stone floor, shame splitting the air around him. "Because I know you felt it. You can feel how much I love you. Can people fake how they feel around you?" He pulled back, placing her hand over his heart. "Read me, Cece. I know you'll see it's true."

She didn't want it to be true because if it was, it would prove that love was nothing more than another weapon. It would prove what the gray-eyed man in her dream had suggested, that love was merely a tool to control the powerful.

"I am so in love with you. I wish I could undo the hurt I've caused you," Xander whispered.

Cecilia couldn't listen to any more of it. Love pulsed in the air all around him, and she knew it was real, but she refused to let herself be a fool in love anymore. She could pretend until she figured out how to get Rainer and herself out of Argaria.

"Why does your brother want to marry me?" she asked.

Cecilia walked over to the mirror in the corner of the room and dried her blotchy face on a handkerchief. She started brushing out her hair. The pain of untangling the knots focused her mind.

She needed razor focus. *Think like a hunter, Cece. Figure out what they want. Figure out the loophole. You know how Xander feels. Use him like he used you.*

"That was always the plan. Well, that was always my father's plan. I suspect Endros and Cato had other plans. They've been looking for you a long time."

He'd truly been honest with her almost the entire time.

"That's why you kept saying that I wasn't yours? But why would Davide want to marry a memory witch? He already has a storm witch brother. You're much better in a fight. Are Endros and Cato here? Are they going to kill me before I can bring the power of the Lost God back to Olney?"

Xander frowned. "That's not the full story. Cece, I promise I will tell you everything, but we don't have a lot of time—"

The door flew open, and Prince Davide walked in. Teddy and Evan both stood in the doorway looking flustered.

"It's all right." Xander sighed.

Cecilia frowned at Davide, not bothering to curtsey. "Your Highness, I don't know about Argarian customs, but in Olney, it's expected that a man will knock before entering a lady's chamber."

Davide smirked. "I see no lady here."

Xander made his way between Davide and Cecilia.

"Little brother, we already talked about this. Am I going to ban you from my fiancée's quarters?" Davide asked with an edge to his voice.

A storm of poisonous emotions swirled around Davide, shifting from envy, to anger, to jealousy.

"I'm not your fiancée," she said.

"Not yet, you're right. I should propose properly, but first, why don't you get dressed, and we will take a walk and talk."

"I have nothing to change into."

"You have a full wardrobe in the closet over there," Davide said, gesturing toward a door on the far side of the room.

"How?" she asked.

Xander turned to face her. "It just took some flirting with the seamstress who made your dresses for the solstice festival. I sent your measurements ahead so you would feel more comfortable."

"No part of this is comfortable," she snapped. "I need to see Rainer before I do any negotiating."

"Fine." Davide rolled his eyes, tugging on the sleeves of his tunic. "Get dressed and meet us outside. We need to talk."

Cecilia shook her head. "I'd rather not."

"I'm sorry, *dearest*. If you'd prefer to go like that and show off what the gods gave you, I won't stop you," Davide said.

Heat licked Cecilia's cheeks as she quickly crossed her arms over her chest.

"If you'd prefer, I could dress you," Davide threatened.

"What is it with the Savero brothers and watching women dress? Good gods!" she muttered as she stormed to the dressing room.

21

Portraits of all the past Savero kings lined the corridor outside of Cecilia's bedroom. She trailed behind Xander and Davide, taking in glimpses of their ancestors. The entire line of men shared Xander's dark brown hair, strong jaw, and olive skin. Clearly the Savero genes were strong. At the end of the row of portraits was Damian Savero, Xander's father, who he bore only a slight likeness to.

"Worried our children will wind up looking too much like me?" Xander's whisper startled her, but his words cut through her like a knife.

She swallowed hard. "How dare you even suggest something as ridiculous as children?" The words made her feel sick with grief and self-loathing as she tore down the corridor to catch up with Davide.

He sighed impatiently, already aggravated at the compromise of taking her to see Rainer before she would discuss marriage.

After several more twists and turns, Cecilia felt a stronger sense of Rainer's proximity. They climbed stairs to the next floor and came to a stop in front of a large wooden door. Davide nodded to a guard, who unlocked it, and they made their way inside.

Rainer was already up against the bars, waiting for her.

"Rain!" Her voice broke, and she fought against the tears that stung her eyes. She was so relieved to see him looking exhausted and bruised but no worse for the wear.

He pulled her into his arms through the bars, kissing her forehead.

"Are you all right? Do you feel different? How was the cave?" A crease formed in Rainer's brow as he searched her face.

She ran her thumb over his brow until the line softened, and he smiled.

"I found a worry, but I'll fix it in a hurry," she whispered. "I'm fine. The cave was intense, but nothing I couldn't handle. Are *you* okay?"

Rainer nodded, but the crease in his brow returned. "There's something you're not saying. I can feel your grief."

She almost broke down. The unbearable weariness of the past day felt unmanageable. She wanted to climb into his arms and cry for hours.

"Let him go," she said, steeling herself as she turned back to Davide.

Davide shook his head. "I need you to agree to my proposal first."

"What is it?" she asked.

"Marry me. Be my queen. Have a few of my heirs. And then you can do whatever you want. You can keep your guardian here to visit for all I care."

Cecilia bit back a laugh. "I thought you were supposed to be charming, but this is the second gods-awful proposal I've received from a Savero brother, so I'm doubting it. There must be women in this kingdom eager to marry. Why do you want someone who can't stand you?"

Davide laughed scornfully. "Alex, you haven't told her?"

"I was getting to it when you interrupted us," Xander said, frustrated.

"Did you think his little nickname for you was just a fluke, Cecilia?"

Cecilia's eyes darted to Xander, but he stared at the floor. It was as if Davide took the spine right out of him. Cecilia barely recognized him as the sexy, confident hunter that seduced her so effortlessly.

"You didn't find it strange your magic showed up so much younger than every other memory witch at court? That you could also commune with the spirit world? That even as a child, you could summon storms stronger than advanced witches?" Davide said.

She shook her head in confusion. "Madame Costello said that with more practice, I'd have better control, but they divided my time between combat training and magic."

Davide's grin grew wide and cruel. "You didn't find your seemingly supernatural ability to hit a target strange? That neither of your parents had witches in their family lines? That you rarely got sick or seriously injured despite all your fighting?"

His words stirred up uncertainty in her heart.

"The story of the Gauntlet, it's your favorite, right?" Davide said. "You like hearing about the power of the Lost God?" Davide sighed, shaking his head. "Did you know Olney was working with a poor translation of the texts about the Gauntlet? The actual word in the old language is *gredi,* which has no gender and could translate to god or goddess. The stories were just written by men, so they made it god. The Gauntlet wasn't meant to release a power to the witches of your kingdom. It was meant to unbind the power of Clastor's youngest child—the Lost God. It's funny how we all recognize ourselves in stories, isn't it... *Goddess*?"

The word was too loud, like someone banging a gong right next to her ear. Cecilia felt dizzy and lightheaded. *Goddess.*

She wanted to deny it, but Davide's words had tilted her world on its side, and she could not get her bearings.

"I can't be a goddess. My mother was a lady. My father is a hunter," Cecilia said.

"Your parents who are both blonde with dark eyes and tan skin. Here you are with your dark hair, blue eyes, and fair skin. You look nothing like them, and that's because you aren't really their daughter," Davide taunted. "Your real parents are Clastor and Selene Carrick."

Selene Carrick, whose name Cecilia knew because she'd helped create the Gauntlet—whose memories Cecilia felt connected to on instinct when she watched them in each cave. Selene Carrick, who was featured in the few stories the huntmaster told her about a memory witch known for her fierceness in battle. Selene Carrick, who Cecilia had once seen a painting of and was startled because the face looking back was so similar to her own. She wanted to shake it off, but it felt as if some part of her had always known.

Cecilia had called up the few memories she had of Rosalee Reznik so many times, trying to see herself in the face or mannerisms of the woman who'd raised her. But try as she might, she'd only felt empty and certain she was falling short of the standard Rosalee had set. She didn't share her mother's temperament or talent in art, nor did she have her father's self-control. She was a wild, reckless, emotional thing that bore no resemblance to the people who raised her.

Her mind rebelled against the information. Cecilia was much too young to be a daughter of Clastor. She was an excellent shot because she practiced. She didn't get sick because she took tinctures and herbs. She was just lucky.

The shadow of doubt grew from moment to moment. Scenarios that she'd written off made sense now. The time she'd jumped out of a tree, and Rainer was shocked she hadn't broken a leg. The time when Rainer had the pox, and she didn't get it despite lying in bed with him for hours. The way that her memory magic was more robust than any other witch. She'd considered that the translation could be incorrect, but never in this exact way.

"But the Gauntlet is so much older than me. The War of the Gods was centuries ago," Cecilia murmured. She looked at Xander for support, clinging to the last bit of dissonance. "How could you possibly know this if even I didn't?"

"Cato figured it out," Davide started. "Apparently, it has always nagged Cato the way Clastor had him manipulate the populace of both kingdoms to believe the War of the Gods happened long ago, instead of when it actually did, just twenty-three years ago."

"But how?" Cecilia asked. "There are people alive who fought in that war."

Xander met her gaze. "Cato's power of manipulation gives more weight to the story than people's memories, so that even when they notice the variance between the two, their instinct is to look away."

Cecilia shook her head as Davide continued.

"Cato couldn't figure out why the timing would matter to Clastor until he overheard a conversation between two of the witches who created the Gauntlet about how foolish it was for the world to believe witches could wield a god's power. Magic has laws that can be bent but never broken. Cato realized he'd been duped, but it took him longer to realize that the Gauntlet was a part of it and not just a performance. If Clastor had just hidden his youngest child in Olney, wouldn't the child's magic give them away?"

Xander shifted beside his brother. "After searching all of Argaria and forcing every child in the kingdom's boundaries to present themselves for testing at court just to be certain, we knew the Lost God had to be hidden in Olney. Of course, we were still operating under the assumption that it was a god and not a goddess. When we had no luck, our focus shifted to the Gauntlet."

"How is this even possible?" she asked.

"It seems Clastor didn't trust Cato when the trickster god convinced him that sacrificing his power would bring peace, but he let Cato *believe* he did," Xander said. "Instead of creating a power that could be released to witches of the kingdom like they taught you, he bound the power of his youngest child to those caves, only to be released when that child visited each cave. The four witches who created the Gauntlet made sure that anyone else who attempted was fated to fail, either by dying or retiring from active duty."

Cecilia felt suddenly ill.

"That's when Argaria started training slayers to steal memories from Olney witches and guardians. That's when Xander was sent to Olney to be a good little spy," Davide taunted. "But there were so many memory witches, it was easy for you to fly under the radar until a year ago, when you rose above everyone else as the most likely candidate to finally finish the Gauntlet."

Cecilia looked at Xander.

"When your father asked me to keep an eye on you," Xander clarified. "You were already at the top of my list because of your progress on the Gauntlet, but when he asked me to monitor you and was uncommonly vague, it solidified the likelihood in my mind."

Cecilia wrung her hands, her thumb brushing over her inner wrist as she tried to make sense of all the information.

"But I'm not a goddess. I feel no different. It's impossible," she said, looking at Xander. "You know Cato personally?"

Davide smirked. It was the same as Xander's smirk but with none of his warmth. "Our family has a long-standing relationship with both Endros and Cato."

Cecilia shook her head. The thought of living, breathing gods searching for her was terrifying. She wanted to deny it, but it answered all questions. It explained why she always felt so strange and separate from the world around her. It explained why she met one of the gods before, a secret she kept to herself simply because she thought it was the grief-stricken imagination of a six-year-old girl.

"My father—" She cleared her throat. "Leo Reznik knew?"

She thought back to his somber mood before she left. Leo knew what she was, and he never told her.

Cecilia looked to Rainer for reassurance that it was madness. She half expected that it was some sort of nightmare she might wake up from at any moment.

Rainer was perfectly still. He stared at her. He looked miserable, but not surprised.

Rainer knew.

Cecilia felt gutted, breathless with betrayal. She was the Lost Goddess. She'd been betrayed twice in a day by the two men she cared about most. Betrayed by the people who raised her, who now seemed like strangers. The truth sucked all the air out of the room.

Her heart beat wildly, whooshing in her ears. Her vision was blurry as she slid down the stone wall.

"Cece." Xander reached out to her, but she flinched away from his hand.

She dug her nails into her palms, forcing herself to focus on the physical pain.

She met Davide's eyes. "So, you want me to marry you so that you can have a bunch of little gods and goddesses to stomp all over Olney?"

The entire idea of it was absurd.

"Cece?" Xander sounded scared.

"You all realize how insane this is, right? I'm not a goddess. I don't have any powers other than my regular powers." She turned to Rainer. "How long have you known? Did you lie to me my whole life? Gods, I did not know you were such an excellent liar."

Rainer looked miserable. "I didn't know until four years ago, when we were sent out for the first time."

Rainer's sudden intense interest in mythology right around the time they'd started Gauntlet runs finally made sense.

"Your father told me. Cece, I wanted to tell you, but it seemed impossible. I thought we would do the whole Gauntlet, and nothing would happen, and we would go back and prove them wrong. According to your father, you needed to complete the Gauntlet to come into your full power—to become a goddess. That part of the story was true. I'm sorry. I should have just told you, but you were already so isolated. I thought it would make it worse."

Cecilia tipped her head back and sighed. "Gods! I am just so tired of men deciding what I can and can't handle!"

She was quiet for a few moments. She put her head in her hands and closed her eyes, but in the dark, all she could see was the well in the Cave of Longings.

Finally, she looked at Davide.

"Davide, I won't marry you. I'm definitely not going to have babies with you, and I'm certainly not going to help you destroy my kingdom."

"I'm not interested in what you want, Cecilia," Davide said.

She rolled her eyes. "How lovely! Lack of consideration for my wants and desires is number one on my list of things that make a great husband."

Davide sighed. "I think you're mistaking your position, Cecilia. I'm not asking."

She stood, trying to summon confidence she didn't feel. "I think you're mistaking your position, Davide. If I'm a goddess, like you say, I could kill you without even touching you. Who knows what my powers do? Even I don't, but I'm willing to find out to shut you up."

"No one would allow that. I'm the heir to the Argarian throne." Davide's face sagged in a scowl, but she felt his fear prickling out in the air around him.

"It's just the four of us here, and three of us *really* don't like you," she whispered.

Davide blanched. "I could hurt the guardian."

"He's pledged his life to the cause. He came here willing to die. Did you?" she asked.

Davide paused, studying her like he was finally seeing her clearly for the first time. "Gods, is she always this difficult?"

"This is nothing," Xander said. He looked at her with open adoration, but she still wanted to punch him.

"Fine, I'll kill my brother," Davide said, drawing his blade and holding it to Xander's throat.

Cecilia shook her head. "You won't."

"Why is that?" Davide taunted.

"Because we are already engaged and because I'm already pregnant with his child. You'll get the heroes for the kingdom. They just won't be yours, Davide."

"You proposed to my princess?" Davide turned to Xander with fury in his eyes.

"I did," Xander said, smiling at Cecilia.

"And she said yes?" Davide was indignant.

"Technically, she told me I was doing a terrible job proposing, but then she said yes." Xander's eyes lit up.

"And you still want to marry him even after he betrayed you?" Davide laughed in disbelief.

"Yes."

Relief broke on Xander's face.

"You may be a goddess, but you're also a stupid, vapid girl." Davide glowered.

"Yes, Davide. I have many facets—like a diamond," she said.

Davide fumed, and Xander coughed to cover a laugh.

"And you're pregnant?" Davide asked.

"Last I checked." She brought a hand to her belly the way she'd seen pregnant women do.

"The royal doctor will have to confirm."

"Obviously."

Xander looked very confused, but he followed her lead.

"How did this happen?" Davide asked.

"The usual way." Xander laughed.

"I explicitly forbade you from bedding her."

"I know, but I couldn't help it. She was very persuasive," Xander said.

Cecilia was vaguely aware of Rainer cringing in her periphery.

"How dare you defy me like this?" Davide's voice echoed against the stone walls.

"Mother and father didn't explicitly say *you* needed to marry her. They said one of us had to. So, I was doing what I was told by them. You were the one who decided that it should be you," Xander said.

Davide's face went bright red. "This is the one time you chose to be obedient to them?"

Xander shrugged.

"We'll see what they have to say about this," Davide huffed. He stomped out of the tower, slamming the door behind him.

When they were sure he was gone, Xander turned to her.

"Are you crazy? They are going to know you're lying right away," he said.

Cecilia shrugged. "Not necessarily. You can't detect a baby's heartbeat for a while, and if a doctor examines me, they will see that I'm not a virgin, so—"

"Gods, Cecilia! What have you done? With an Argarian Prince!" Rainer chided.

She shrugged. "It's not as if I knew at the time."

"I was onto him," Rainer huffed.

"You were jealous of him. That's different." Cecilia sighed.

Rainer threw his hands up in frustration. "Well, you shouldn't have slept with him, because now you might actually be pregnant."

"It's unlikely. I take a monthly herbal preventative tincture," Xander said quietly.

"I cast a monthly preventative spell," she said.

"Cecilia! Gods! Why?" Rainer looked genuinely shocked.

"Rain, I'm twenty-two, and I take it for this exact reason. Would you say the same thing if I were a man? No! You would urge me on like you do with your guardian friends. Why shouldn't I be prepared to have some fun?"

"Because you are a goddess!" Rainer huffed.

She glared at him. "As I recall, the gods have always been known for their wild sex lives."

Xander laughed, but Rainer just looked exasperated.

"What were you thinking?" Rainer asked finally.

"I wasn't thinking. I was feeling," she said. "Can I have a moment alone with Rainer?"

Xander nodded and left them alone in the tower.

"Cece—"

She held up her hand like a shield to protect her from forgiving him. "Don't. You're just going to listen and answer my questions. I don't want any of your excuses. What he did to me is horrible, but what you've done is *unforgivable*. You were supposed to be my best friend. My guardian. I was supposed to be your priority. Not my father. Not the kingdom. *Me*. You were the one person who was supposed to care about me first. How could you not tell me?"

The words stuck like shards of glass in her heart. Speaking them aloud seemed to give them more power to hurt her.

Rainer gripped the bars of his cell desperately. "I didn't know what to do. I was so shocked when your father told me right before we started going on Gauntlet runs. You had just turned eighteen. We spent every day together. I would have seen it. I am connected to your heart, for the love of gods. Even so, I thought it would just make you afraid, so I kept it to myself."

She futilely fought against tears. "I can't even put into words how much it hurts. Nothing I could say could make you feel even a breath of what I feel right now. It is savage. It's a new level of loneliness, and I've been a lonely girl my whole life."

She took a breath, pulling back desperately on the reins of her emotions.

"You've flaunted every relationship you've ever had in front of me. You've broken my heart over and over. I am used to it, but this is the deepest wound you've ever caused. It will always be there. I will always carry this scar, and nothing between us will ever be the same because of it. That is something we will both have to live with for as long as we do."

She opened up the connection between them completely and let her heart ache. He cringed the moment it hit him.

When he met her eyes again, it surprised her to see tears in his. Twice in one trip, he'd torn her apart. Twice in one trip, she'd needed to put herself back together. She wasn't sure she could. Her body felt like lead.

"Cece, I'm so sorry. I wish I could take it all back. I wish I could take away your pain," Rainer rasped.

"Just save it. Because I need my energy to figure out how to get us out of this nightmare, not to make you feel better for being a shitty guardian and a shittier friend."

She turned and stormed out of the room without looking back.

22

Cecilia exited the tower in a huff, the door slamming behind her with a dooming clang. Xander reached for her, but she slapped his hand away.

"I don't want to be touched right now," she snapped. "What happened earlier was a huge lapse in judgment, and it will not be happening again."

He nodded and stepped back, dropping his hands to his sides.

She felt strangely disappointed that he relented. This time the betrayal wasn't from someone else but her own body. She loathed and desired him in equal measure.

"I'm just—" She took a breath and looked at the ceiling.

The grief and all-consuming loneliness seemed to open an abyss in her chest. She blinked back tears.

"I'm exhausted. I can't do this with you right now. I need to make a plan," she said.

Xander's voice was gentle, prodding. "I know you're tired. I know I really hurt you, Cece, but I need you to do something."

Cecilia sighed. "What?"

Xander swallowed hard. "I need to bring you to my parents and introduce you in front of people as my fiancée. I need to let them know in private what's going on, and then I will leave you alone to rest."

"Xander, I couldn't possibly right now. I just found out that both of you have been lying to me. My whole life has been a lie. I can barely stand on my own two feet."

"I wouldn't suggest it unless it was necessary. I need to have that solidified to keep you safe. Endros is in the field, but I don't know where Cato is. Having you as my fiancée gives me more of a say in who has access to you."

Cecilia shivered, suddenly terrified at the prospect of meeting one of the living gods without access to her magic. She leaned her forehead against the cold stone wall. She bit her lip and squeezed her eyes shut, trying to keep herself from crying.

"Can you do it? You're going to have to be okay. You're going to have to seem like you're in love with me," he said.

She nodded, her eyes still squeezed shut.

"Not that I doubt you, love, but when we go in there, you're going to have to be fully all right, so why don't we let you take another minute to make sure?"

She felt an overwhelming surge of gratitude, but it tangled with her anger and betrayal, and she couldn't pull it apart again. All she wanted was to be comforted, to tuck herself into his arms and pretend he was the Xander from a few days ago who kissed her and held her all night like she was something precious and delicate, but indulging in a fantasy would only give him more opportunity to manipulate her. She refused to give him the chance again.

Cecilia took a breath and begrudgingly took Xander's hand. As they made their way through the corridors, Cecilia was struck by how bright the castle was. Where Olney Castle was dark and dreary, Castle Savero had large stained-glass windows on every floor that let in the bright light in a rainbow of colors. The doors were all intricately carved wood that showed stories from ancient myths, and fireplaces in each room kept out the chill.

The tapestries and paintings on the walls were bright and boisterous, unlike the solemn portraits hanging in Olney Castle. She tried to memorize their path as they went, a habit born out of her hunter training. A good hunter always had an exit plan.

"I know what you're doing, love, but it's unnecessary. I'll tell you whatever you want to know about how to escape," Xander whispered.

He sounded sincere, but then again, he'd sounded sincere since they met.

Xander paused in front of an ornate wooden door that showed a carving of Endros mid-battle. He knocked, and a deep voice beckoned them in.

King Damian Savero sat in front of a chessboard by large windows that opened up to a courtyard, an ornate crown balanced on his head.

Before Cecilia could take anything else in, a woman crossed the room and swept Xander into a hug. She leaned back and looked at him, holding his face in her hands. She was beautiful, with hazel eyes just like Xander's and dark hair neatly swept into a sophisticated updo.

"My darling boy! I heard you got back late last night, and I can't believe you waited this long to come greet us! We are so happy to finally have you back for good. We have missed you."

She hugged him again, and Xander looked both relieved and content.

"Mother," he said, pulling away from her. "I want you to meet someone." The queen turned to look at Cecilia. "This is Cecilia Reznik, my fiancée."

Cecilia stepped back and curtseyed. "Your Majesty."

"Aren't you beautiful?" Juliana said, tilting Cecilia's chin up to see her face in the light.

King Damian came over to join them.

"Your Majesty," she said as she gave him a stiff curtsey.

The king's appraising gaze slid over her before he turned his attention to his son.

"No wonder you wouldn't give her up to your brother. She could be Desiree herself." The king chuckled. Cecilia wasn't sure if it was a compliment to her or an insult to the goddess of love and beauty.

Xander's chest puffed in pride. "You should see her with a bow."

"An Olney lady who can shoot. I suppose that's the influence of your father. As I understand, few ladies of the Olney court are permitted to train in combat." Damian smiled.

"Yes, Your Majesty," Cecilia said.

She plastered a stiff smile on her face, the same one wore to every court event in Olney over the years. She pretended she was at one of those events instead of an enemy court in front of a King who wanted her to help destroy her home.

"In Argaria, we are happy to have women in our hunter army," Damian added.

Cecilia had heard rumors, though she'd never met a female Argarian hunter. Her father's army had very few women, and the ones who were there were outcasts. They were tough and twice as deadly as their male counterparts, but they suffered for it.

"We have female hunters and slayers, and women happen to make the best spies," Damian said. "Excluding women is almost as barbaric as bonding children to each other for life when they're too young to understand the bond or its permanence."

Cecilia bristled. Bonding was so ordinary in Olney she'd never even considered it strange that it happened so young. She didn't like the way the implication made her feel disempowered, when her closeness with Rainer had always made her feel strong.

"Nothing to say about that?" Damian taunted.

"No, sir," Cecilia replied. "I'm afraid I know little of how Argarian traditions differ, and I was raised to hold my tongue about things I haven't experienced and don't understand."

Xander cleared his throat and squeezed her hand, but she held the king's gaze.

She couldn't believe she was within striking distance of the enemy king with no weapon but a sharp tongue. Xander had a dagger on his belt, but she doubted she'd be quick enough to land a killing blow. Even so, killing the king would only put Davide in charge, and that would be short-sighted.

Eight other sets of noble eyes around the room were trained on her and Xander. It was not the time to make reckless choices. She'd have one chance to escape, and if she wanted her and Rainer to live, she needed to play nice for now.

"You've been away too long, Alexander." King Damian pulled Xander into a tight hug, which looked more like a performance for the audience of eyes than actual warmth. "You've done a great thing. Olney doesn't have a fighting chance. Endros is already rallying the troops, and now that you've brought this—" He cleared his throat, his gaze darting to the watchful eyes of the nobles in the room. "This talented witch into the fold. We can really break the will of the people of Olney."

"Why do you even want that? Is your aim to reunite the two kingdoms? To what end?" The questions shot out of Cecilia's mouth unbidden.

"I suppose you're worried about your father," Damian huffed. "If the huntmaster surrenders, he need not meet a vicious end. We'll make it quick."

As if killing her father quickly was a true act of generosity for his daughter-in-law.

"I will be known as the king who finally reunited the kingdoms. The Savero family will rule the entire peninsula."

Cecilia could read the subtext. It would give his family much greater ability to corner the world trade markets thanks to Olney's plentiful ports. Without the ongoing conflict to waste resources and make other kingdoms nervous about permanent trade deals, Damian would be lauded as a hero to his people and possibly even to her own eventually. Money had a way of manipulating even those with the strongest of convictions.

"You could just stop the war and focus on trade if that's the goal," Cecilia suggested sweetly.

King Damian eyed Cecilia as if unnerved by her ability to see through his plan. He fixed Xander with a glare. "She's more spirited than I expected for an Olney lady. I suppose that's why you've taken such a shine to her."

"Cecilia and I wish to be married right away, but we'd like to have a private audience with you both before we discuss details," Xander said.

The queen waved her hand, and the servants, lords, and ladies scattered.

Once all the doors were closed, and they were sure they were alone, the king spoke.

"Your brother is furious, Alex. He feels you tricked him," King Damian said solemnly, sitting back in a plush chair by the window. Juliana sat down next to him.

Xander sighed. "My brother is lazy and lacks forethought and follow-through. I'm not afraid to get my hands dirty."

A flush warmed Cecilia's neck and cheeks at his innuendo. She couldn't help thinking about all the things his hands could do. Though Xander sounded confident, she felt his doubt. She slid her hand into his and squeezed.

The king laughed, and the queen fought back a smile. He turned his gaze to Cecilia. "And you, Lady Reznik, you wish to marry Alexander? Even though it will mean using your power against your kingdom?"

"Must I be used for destruction?" she asked.

"Anyone who surrenders will be welcome to pledge loyalty to Argaria and the Savero family. If they fall in line, there's no need for bloodshed."

"How generous," Cecilia said tightly.

"I understand this must be uncomfortable for you, but it doesn't need to be," Damian said.

She looked from Damian to Xander. Xander squeezed her hand. She thought of the first time he kissed her, the moment he said he loved her, how good it felt to be close to him. She could not summon any actual memories thanks to the Unsummoner bracelet, but she clung to the feelings from her time alone with Xander to blot out the blinding betrayal.

"I want to marry Xander," she said.

Damian leveled a stern gaze at Xander. "Alex, you know this

wasn't what we agreed to. You agreed to bring back Lady Reznik for Davide."

"I know I messed up. I couldn't help falling in love with her," Xander said.

"Well, then it's going to be difficult to give her up." The king looked at him pointedly. He wasn't backing down. Of course he wouldn't. Davide was the heir. The oldest son. They needed their gods and goddesses to be heirs.

Cecilia felt lightheaded. Panic fluttered in her stomach. Xander ran a thumb across the top of her hand, pulling her closer to him.

"That's the thing. I can't. I won't give her up. There's something else—" Xander started.

Cecilia's head swam. The room felt too hot. She felt like she was suffocating. Her vision grew hazy, and her heart raced.

"Cecilia, dear, you look very pale," Juliana said.

Suddenly everything went white, and she stumbled. Xander's arms swept her up, and she leaned her head against his firm chest.

"My love," he whispered, his lips brushing her temple.

She blinked, trying to focus her gaze. She wanted to kiss him, but then she remembered where they were and everything that had happened, and then she wanted to punch him.

"Is she all right?" Juliana asked.

"Yes, she's fine, but this is what we were trying to tell you," Xander said, turning to face his parents. "Cecilia is pregnant."

Both of their eyes went wide, and she did not know what to expect from them.

"Alexander!" Juliana said sternly. "That is not how we raised you!"

"Juliana, what would you expect from a boy of mine?" Damian smirked.

"I'm sorry," Xander said, looking into Cecilia's eyes. "I saw the moonlight on her skin, and I couldn't help but fall in love with her immediately, and then I spent weeks trying to seduce her."

His gaze was full of desire, and she knew exactly what he was thinking about. She wanted to look away, but she was snared. When she finally turned away, she was certain she'd lost some part of herself to him she'd never reclaim.

"That certainly changes things—moves the timeline up," Damian said.

When Cecilia looked back at them, Juliana eyed her carefully, a knowing look on the queen's face.

"You can put me down now. I feel better," Cecilia whispered to Xander.

"I don't know. I'm enjoying holding you like this," he said.

The king and queen looked at each other. "Two weeks?" Damian asked. Juliana nodded.

Their quick agreement surprised Cecilia, but they probably assumed she'd be easier to control if she married the brother they thought she was in love with. They were in for quite a surprise if they thought Xander could wrangle her.

"You'll be married at sunset the Friday after next," Damian said.

A command. Not a request. The lack of consideration chafed her.

Xander set Cecilia back on her feet, keeping a supportive arm around her.

"And Davide?" Xander asked.

"We will make him behave himself." Damian chuckled as if Davide threatening to murder anyone who didn't do what he wanted was adorable.

"Cecilia, I would love to get to know you better. Could we have tea once you've settled in?" Juliana asked.

"I would like that, Your Majesty," she said earnestly.

They were the enemies of her people, but she wanted to get to know Xander's mother. It was all very confusing.

Juliana smiled. "For now, though, rest, dear. You're carrying the future of this kingdom."

Xander led her out of the room, and as soon as they were in the hallway, he swept her back up into his arms.

"Xander! Put me down!" Cecilia squirmed in his arms.

"I can't chance my love swooning again and hurting herself," he said, burying a kiss in her neck.

She tried to access her anger again, but it felt intangible. She struggled to her feet, and Xander led her back to her chambers, and closed them securely inside.

"What happened in the sitting room? Did you fake that to sell the pregnancy?" Xander asked.

"No, I just didn't feel well. I felt faint, and I thought I could breathe through it, but suddenly, I was going down."

He touched a hand to her forehead and cupped her cheek.

His eyes lit up. "You couldn't actually be pregnant, could you?"

"No, we already discussed this. I'm not. I'm just exhausted and overwhelmed. You said you were taking monthly herbal supplements to prevent such a thing."

"I am," he said. His face fell, and for a moment, he looked crushed.

"You're disappointed," she said aloud without meaning to.

His eyes went wide. "I'm not. I—"

"Go on. Lie to me again," she said bitterly.

Xander swallowed hard. "For a moment, I thought that might be something that would make you want to stay. I imagined what it would be like to see a child we created together. I bet she would have your beautiful eyes. Gods, I hope she would have your laugh. Basically, I would just want her to be a little version of you. She doesn't need to have any of me at all."

His face was so earnest and happy that she burst into tears. It was all too much. She was sure she hated him, though she was becoming less certain by the moment. Everything that had seemed so simple just days ago seemed impossibly complex. The black and white of her life twisted into a murky gray mess.

It forced her to confront the impossible loss that she hadn't even had time to process—a pain she shoved to the back of her mind violently as soon as it revealed itself. She remembered what she'd agreed to give up in the Cave of Longings, and the loneliness felt much too large, and she, too small. A ragged sob tore through her. She wanted to tell him—to share all the things that weighed so heavily on her heart, what it cost her to become a thing she never even wanted to be. The sharp, merciless edge of her sorrow tore through her like a dagger, and she fell apart.

"Love, it's going to be okay. I'm so, so sorry. Tell me how to help you," Xander whispered to her, smoothing her hair and rocking her against his chest.

She cried for a long time, heavy body-shaking sobs that seemed unending. When the sobs quieted to sniffles, Xander finally spoke.

"Cece, what happened?" He touched her cheek, and she leaned her hand into his palm, but she couldn't say it. "I am so sorry that I hurt you. I would take it all back in a second if I could. I hate myself."

"I have to tell you something," she said. Cecilia swallowed hard as she met his eyes. "Do you remember when I said that there was a cost with the Cave of Longings? An exchange—one that I didn't know or understand, but that I would ultimately have to decide at the moment if I could sacrifice?"

He nodded. She paused, her throat clogged with emotion. It wasn't that ignoring it could undo the exchange, but speaking the words made it more real.

"Cece, whatever it is, you know it won't affect how I feel about you."

She wanted that to be true. She took a shaky breath and tried to memorize the love on his face. The love that would change when he heard what she said.

"I can't have children." The words hung in the air like smoke.

Xander frowned. "How do you know? You haven't even been examined by the doctor yet," he said, completely thrown off. She watched as recognition broke through his confusion. "Cece, you didn't —"

"I did. I sacrificed my ability to have children to be the Lost Goddess, without knowing what I was giving it up for. I would take it all back if I could, though I had little choice. I thought it was accept or have my soul trapped there forever. Exchange magic is unpredictable. I thought I was just releasing magic back to the witches of Olney. I never thought I was going to be the powerful one."

The revelation shocked him into silence.

"I would understand if you wanted to go back on our agreement," she whispered.

Fear took root in her heart—fear that he believed what everyone in the kingdom of Olney was raised to believe: that if she couldn't have children, she didn't have any value as a wife.

Xander looked horrified. "My love, no. I don't want that. I just feel awful for saying all those things. It was foolish of me to get so carried away. Of course I would have loved to have children with you, but make no mistake, I will be just as happy with you and me. I just feel for you. Did you want to be a mother badly?"

She reached a hand to his cheek, and he kissed her palm and then the inside of her wrist. She felt breathless each time she thought of what she'd given up.

"I'd not had much time to consider it. I hardly feel grown enough to be a mother. I thought I'd have more time. I didn't realize it would hurt so much until I saw the way your face lit up. I can't give you something that you want, and that makes it hurt even worse even though I hate you."

"Oh, love, I'm so sorry that I made you feel that way. I love you very much. *You* are what I want the most. It just frustrates me that you had to sacrifice something that you wanted." He kissed the tears from her cheeks. He kissed her eyes, her lips, until she finally stopped crying. "What can I do?"

Cecilia shrugged. "Nothing. There's nothing to be done now. I just have to learn to accept it."

"I'm going to get you out of here. All will be well," Xander said.

She wanted to believe him, but he'd shattered the delicate trust between them. She couldn't understand how she could be so angry and hurt—how she could hate what he'd done to her—and still somehow feel a confusing swell of wonder every time he touched her. Cecilia was disgusted with how much she enjoyed his comfort, all the while telling herself that she was doing it to convince him she would trust him again, eventually. False hope would help her escape. But there had been nothing false in the way he touched her or the surge of emotion that made her chest feel like a mess of brambles.

"It's never going to be okay again. The entire foundation of my life has been ripped out in a day. I've lost everything. My family, my friends, my future, my identity. I don't feel like a goddess. I feel like a stupid girl who didn't realize that everyone was lying to her all her life. It's exactly what happened in the Cave of Longings. I'm alone and will always be that way—isolated. I've always been different, and now I always will be."

Xander stared. "Cece, what can I do? Do you want to see Rainer?"

"I don't know. He's my best friend, and he always knows what to do, but now all I see is the person who lied to me for four years. And I don't want to tell him, because he will never forgive himself for what this cost me. As mad as I am, I don't want him to hurt. I'm furious, but I can't really feel it, or I might blow up the godsforsaken castle with my new goddess powers."

Xander opened his mouth and closed it.

"Xander, there's nothing to say. All I can do is try not to fall apart. I've been unsuccessful so far." She laughed bitterly. "I don't see a way out of this, but maybe there's a way to still prevent a war and save lives, at least. It's never the people who start these conflicts who perish in war. It's all the people under them they send to the slaughter—normal, everyday people—hunters, witches, and guardians. I can't cause that kind of destruction on top of everything else. It would be too much."

Xander sighed. "I am going to hate myself for saying this. I think we should see Rainer. He might have a plan. I know you are mad, but three minds are better than two."

As reluctant as she was to agree, she had no better ideas.

23

Rainer was waiting for her, pressed against the bars of his dingy cell, looking weary. His eyes looked especially bright in the dim room, as if they absorbed all the light the stone walls refused, and the effect was devastating.

"Cece, I'm sorry—" he started.

Cecilia held up a hand. "Don't. That's not why I'm here."

He looked wounded, but she didn't care. She wanted him to hurt like she did, even though she knew she'd instantly regret it.

"We are officially engaged, and the wedding is in two weeks," Xander said.

Cecilia didn't miss the way Rainer flinched, clenching his hands on the bars of his cell. He looked miserable and frustrated.

"Well, at least that means you don't have to marry Davide," Rainer offered.

"Yes. At least there's *that*," Cecilia said coldly.

"That said, we have bought very little time, because there's a bigger issue." Xander looked at Cecilia, but she just looked at the stone floor. "Cece?"

"What is it?" Rainer asked, reaching for her through the bars.

She took a step back so he couldn't touch her. "The problem isn't just that I'm not pregnant now, it's that I can't get pregnant."

"Right. Because of the prevention spell, but you can just stop taking it, Cece." He looked over at Xander, who shook his head.

Cecilia cleared her throat. "Rain, remember when we were talking about the Gauntlet? The readings said that the exchange gets more costly as you go and that by the time you get to the Cave of Longings, the price might be too high?"

She finally looked up at him, and he understood. Recognition stole over his face as he felt her grief.

"No, Cece." Rainer's words were breathless.

She fought to keep her voice even. "I didn't even know what I was buying with my sacrifice, Rain. If you had told me, I might have chosen differently."

Rainer looked horrified. His hands flexed and gripped the bars over and over.

"So we are here for a plan, and you better have a damn good one," Cecilia rasped. "We have precious little time, and I need to prevent a war and keep myself from becoming a weapon for the enemy."

Rainer's focus was clear in the determined set of his jaw. He turned away from the bars and paced the cell, running a hand through his hair as he muttered to himself.

Rainer mumbled something imperceptible. "There's something about the exchange wording. Hold on, let me think."

He paced some more before he came to an abrupt stop.

"*When entering the Cave of Longings, know that you can refuse it. The cost will be high for certain. But the price is only paid once you use it,*" Rainer said. "Cece, have you used your goddess abilities?"

"I don't think so. How would I know?" she asked.

"I guess it would just depend on if you summoned anything. It's hard to say if it works the same way as your regular powers," Rainer said.

Cecilia held up her wrist with the Unsummoner bracelet. "I haven't. Why?"

"Because the deal isn't sealed until you use the gift you've been given," Rainer started. "So, in theory, you haven't paid the price yet because you haven't used the gift."

Xander leaned into the wall, relief plain on his face, though she couldn't tell if it was for her or to assuage his own guilt. She had never been so grateful for Rainer's intense focus on mythology and how obsessively he studied all materials about the Gauntlet.

"So all you have to do is not use your powers," Rainer confirmed.

"That could be tricky behind enemy lines," she said.

"Good thing you're engaged to the Storm Prince," he countered morosely.

She nodded. "So I'm not technically fully a goddess yet. I'm still mortal."

Rainer nodded. "If what we read in the books is true."

"That makes sense with what I was told," Xander interrupted. "We understood from Cato that you might have a hint of your goddess power but that until you completed the Gauntlet, you would remain fully mortal until you tapped into your power."

She swallowed hard. "So until I accept my powers, I could still be hurt—or killed."

Rainer looked warily at the two of them. "Can we have a couple minutes alone, Xander?"

Xander nodded and left the tower.

Rainer reached for her. "Cece, I'm so sorry. There were so many times I wanted to tell you. We spent every day together. It seemed impossible that you could be the Lost Goddess. It was so counter to everything we'd been taught. Oh gods, don't cry."

Frustrated tears streamed down her cheeks. "Why did my father tell you and not me?"

Rainer reached for her hand, and she reluctantly let him take it. "He told me when you turned eighteen, and we went on our first Gauntlet run. He wanted me to know that you might be more of a target if anyone had figured it out. Apparently, the huntmaster was a friend of your birth mother, Selene. When the war broke out, she and Clastor wanted to hide you. Since the Rezniks couldn't have children of their own, it seemed like a solution that would make everyone happy and keep you safe if they died. Apparently, Rosalee expected she'd be raising you alone since your father was the second-in-command of the hunter army. That's why they invited Clara to come and stay. Her husband was in Zelden Novaris's battalion and had been killed in the battle to hold back Endros's forces. They thought that helping Rosalee raise you would help her grief."

Cecilia recalled the only bedtime stories her father had ever told her. They were all about Selene Carrick and Clastor. She could still hear Leo telling her the story of how Selene Carrick used all her magic until it was spent, switching to her bow when she was exhausted. How Endros dealt the killing blow to Clastor, but not before Clastor wounded both Endros and Cato with a cursed blade, hurting them badly enough that they'd need years to recover. How Clastor's daughters, Sayla, Adira, Aelish, and even Desiree, had helped the Olney hunter army beat Argaria back over what was now the dividing line between the kingdoms. Her father had told every story in such vivid detail, it should have been clear that he was there fighting alongside them. Everyone said Leo Reznik was a war hero, but Cecilia had never thought about what war they referred to, which only backed up what Xander had said about Cato's manipulation making people look away from inconvenient details. She could not believe that his magic could make people certain that both the war and the Gauntlet were so much older.

She swallowed hard around the revelation. She could not get used to the idea that Rosalee wasn't her mother and Leo wasn't her father—they were strangers.

"The huntmaster knew that Endros and Cato likely had spies in Olney. I doubt he realized how much they'd infiltrated—gods, after Xander—anyone could be a spy." Rainer shook his head in disbelief. "Understand, when he told me all of this, I still thought what you did, that we'd complete the Gauntlet, and the power would just be released to all the witches of Olney. I really thought he was over-reacting."

Rainer squeezed her hands.

"Leo made me swear not to tell you because he wanted you to get to live a normal life as long as you could. He loved you, and he didn't want you to worry," Rainer said.

"I need a plan, Rain. I'm so lost." She knelt, leaning her head against the bars.

"Do you want to marry Xander?" he asked.

"*Really?* That's where you're going to start?" Cecilia couldn't hide her frustration.

"I'm not trying to be callous. I'm trying to assess the least catastrophic plan, and I know you two are close."

It should have been an easy no, but somehow it wasn't. Pain clouded Rainer's expression, and she tried to keep her face neutral. He brought a hand to rest on hers on the bars.

"He really did ask me to run away with him," Cecilia said. "I said yes when he proposed, but it was before all of this, and now I just don't know anymore. All I know is how much everything hurts. I'm afraid I might implode at any moment into this bottomless pit of grief. Either way, I don't want to get married so far from home in front of strangers who hate my people and me. I don't want to be used."

Rainer kissed the crescent scar on her hand. Then her inner wrist. She never noticed how intimate the gesture was until Rainer felt like a stranger. He did it all the time—after dances or as he was sneaking out of the cottage in the morning. Now it felt like rubbing salt in a raw wound.

She ripped her hand from his grip.

"Gods, I wish I could take it away, Cece. I'm so sorry. I know I really hurt you, but I will do my best to get us out of this. We're still a team, right?"

He reached out to her through their connection, but she could offer nothing but grief.

"I don't know if we ever were a team," Cecilia murmured. "This taints our entire history. I look at you and taste poison. I see someone who pretended to be my best friend while lying to me for *four years*. I see the person who cost me everything after promising his life to take care of me. And as much as I feel rage and grief, as much as I can barely even sit with the betrayal of it, it kills me more that I might not be able to save you."

Rainer sighed. "I've never been like you. I've pretended to be brave my whole life, but I'm not actually brave. I couldn't walk into those caves, not knowing what to expect. Why do you think I memorized every passage in every book for every cave we were going to? Why do you think I made you repeat each step of our trips over and over? Why do you think I still insisted on doing story time even though we're grown up? It wasn't because you were worried or scared. It was because *I* was." He took a breath, running a hand through his hair. "I don't want you to marry him."

Leaning his head against the bars, Rainer squeezed his eyes closed.

"I'm going to try to get this all out, and it's probably not going to be pretty, so bear with me. It kills me being in here while feeling how nervous and scared you are and not being able to stand beside you while you face it all." His voice was raw. "It kills me that I can't tell if you want me to talk you into or out of this. I have always known what to say to support you, but I'm at a loss. I wish I could offer you something else, but I'm trying to be realistic. We both love a fairy tale, but this is real life."

Unsurprisingly, Rainer made such an emotional decision so logical. That was what he always did, but it wasn't what she wanted from him now. She didn't want her guardian. She wanted her friend.

He reached his hand through the bars and touched her cheek. "I wanted to tell you what you were so many times, but every time, I didn't know how to say it. I didn't think you would ever forgive me. There were just so many mistakes, all stacked on top of each other. I couldn't undo one without the entire tower of lies coming down."

"And you didn't trust me enough to forgive you."

He hung his head. "I didn't. And that's my biggest mistake. The biggest one I've ever made. It's what separates you from everyone else in the world, Cece. You're so compassionate and forgiving."

Cecilia didn't want to forgive him. She didn't know if she could, but there was a part of her that could never stay mad at him for long. "All of your options were bad options, Rain."

"Like yours now."

"Yes. So, as someone who has been there, can you tell me what to do?"

Rainer sighed. "I can't, but I can listen. I don't trust Xander at all. Regardless of what he thinks he feels for you. You're my priority. If your option is Xander or Davide, I suppose Xander is the lesser of two evils in that he at least seems mentally stable, even if he is a conniving liar. But if we get out of here, you might be expected to go back and marry someone else. You wanted the power to choose for yourself. This might be your only shot. Do you love him?"

She barked out a startled laugh. "He betrayed me."

"That's not a no."

Cecilia shook her head and sighed. "I don't know how I feel. I was right on the edge, and then all of this happened, and now I think love is a risk I can't afford."

"Do you love me?" Rainer's voice was so quiet, his eyes searching.

Her eyes locked with his. "No."

A smile tugged at his lips. "Liar."

Cecilia looked away. This was dangerous. Maybe more dangerous than anything that lay outside the lockup doors. Her heart was still raw and unprotected, and she wasn't sure it would survive another blow.

"I think he's your best bad option," Rainer said finally. He took a breath, running a hand through his hair. "I don't want you to marry him. No one has ever been good enough for you in my eyes, but you deserve to choose."

She shook her head and laughed. "Do you know what I wished for when we watched the meteor shower?"

Rainer stared at her.

"I wished for the power to make my own choices. I guess it's a classic case of be careful what you wish for. What about you? Did yours come true? What did you wish for?"

Rainer swallowed hard as he met her eyes. "I can't tell you."

She felt into their connection, but Rainer kept the door between them solidly closed.

Cecilia studied his face, looking for a sign that she should hold on to one last hope. She was uncertain if she would ever really give up on Rainer or if she'd be doomed to a lifetime of trying to make him want her enough.

Finally, she turned on her heel and left, ignoring him calling after her, happy he couldn't follow.

24

Cecilia struggled against the tight bodice of her dress as she pulled the bowstring taut before letting it go. The arrow hit the chamber door with a satisfying *thunk*. Her hair might have been perfectly styled and her dress might have been constricting and uncomfortable, but it didn't prevent her from making a perfect shot.

"Unbelievable. Right through the eye of that sheep." Teddy chuckled.

Cecilia lifted the blindfold, taking a peek at her shot in the farm landscape on the door. "I win!"

"That is an unparalleled gift you have, Lady Reznik."

"Cece," she insisted. "I think it's an improvement to the door. A sculpture of my own."

"*Cece*, how is it you have such uncanny aim blindfolded?"

"Well, Teddy, I think it's entirely possible that your training program is *that* inferior."

The hunter laughed. She'd taken a liking to Xander's friend. Despite her best efforts to hate him, Teddy was warm and brushed off all of her righteous anger and snide comments. He enjoyed finding harmless ways to cause trouble around the castle, and it didn't hurt that he snuck her whiskey to ease her nerves before bed or before court interactions.

He was a softy and either felt confident that she wouldn't try to escape or was unaware that she kept an inventory of any relevant information he'd let slip over the week and a half since she'd arrived.

Cecilia took a sip of the whiskey in her teacup. "I'm fairly certain I could beat the top archer in Argaria drunk and blindfolded. You all have terrible form."

"Even Xan?" Teddy teased.

Cecilia rolled her eyes. "He's passable."

"You spend a lot of energy trying not to like him."

"I can't see a better use of my energy at the moment," Cecilia quipped. "It seems old hat for most married couples. Maybe I'm trying to get a head start."

"You don't believe in love matches?"

"I lack the naïveté that would let me love the liar who betrayed my trust and dragged me into enemy territory. I know he's your best friend and all, but you have to stop trying to sell me on him. The man has been inside me. If *he* can't convince me to trust him, I'm not sure you have a better chance."

Teddy's cheeks blazed. "You're not like I expected."

Cecilia took two more quick shots with the shabby bow that Teddy had snuck her. "And what did you expect?"

Teddy shrugged, running a hand through his golden hair. "Not sure. I expected you would have escaped through one of the passages by now."

Cecilia arched a brow, her gaze darting around the room before falling back on Teddy.

He held up his hands. "Forget I said that. There aren't any passages in this room anyway."

She laughed at the terrible lie, watching his eyes dart to the tapestry on the far wall.

Teddy cleared his throat. "What I meant to say is, Xander has always preferred intense women, but you're different. Softer."

"Softer?" Cecilia asked, her voice going shrill.

"I mean it as a compliment."

"Teddy, I'm liking you less and less with every word," she teased, pointing the dull side of an arrow toward him.

"I think you're good for Xan. You don't take his nonsense, but you're soft enough that he wants to take care of you. I've never seen him so doting with someone. You know, I had a feeling about you from the first letter he sent us about you."

"Don't bullshit me, Teddy. I like you too much to let you lie to me."

He rolled his eyes. "It's not a lie. How long are you going to be mad at him?"

"Forever," she suggested. "Maybe longer. Apparently I'm an immortal goddess, so I suppose it remains to be seen how long I can hold a grudge."

"But he loves you," Teddy insisted.

"I'm unaccustomed to such romantic notions from a hunter," Cecilia taunted.

Teddy shrugged. "I see nothing wrong with being hopeful. The world is dark enough."

Cecilia grinned. "I think I'm starting to understand the dynamics here. You're the cheerful optimist. Xander is the charming liar. And Evan is the grumpy, serious one holding it all together."

Teddy barked out a surprised laugh. "That's shockingly accurate, though I think you could make a good case for Xander being an optimist as well."

"I'm inclined to agree since he expects to win me over still." Cecilia sighed.

A sharp knock on the door interrupted them, and Xander strolled into the room.

"I'm here to escort my beautiful fiancée to tea," Xander said. "Gods, isn't she lovely, Ted?"

Cecilia rolled her eyes. "Save your flattery for someone impressed by it."

"I seem to remember a time when it worked wonders on you," Xander said. There was a threat in his eyes that sent a flood of heat through her body. He took in the arrow marks on all the furniture. "Having a little archery session?"

Teddy grinned. "Cece was bored."

"Can't have that," Xander said with a wink.

Cecilia threaded her arm through his, letting him lead her into the hall.

Once they were out of earshot of Teddy, she looked up at him. "What am I walking into?"

"I had breakfast with my mother today, and she's excited to speak with you. We've put this off as long as possible with the wedding in just a few days. I'll stay for the first few minutes so I'm not totally throwing you to the wolves, but after that, you'll be on your own."

Cecilia drew up short. "What if she doesn't like me?"

She knew it was stupid to worry about an enemy queen liking her. Still, Juliana was also Xander's mother, and deep down she wanted that approval, even if she was planning on escaping the first chance she got.

Xander took her face in his hands. "Cece, she will love you as much as I do." Then he lowered his voice. "I wish I could kiss you right now—maybe more than kiss you." She looked away, and he laughed. "I love how you blush even when you're angry."

Cecilia felt calmer by the time they made it down to the sitting room. A servant announced them, and they joined Queen Juliana in a beautiful sunlit room overlooking the gardens. Most of the flowers in the gardens were in bloom. No doubt it was earth witch magic that kept them in bloom in such a chilly climate. She curtseyed and tried to remember all of her court manners.

"Cecilia, it's good to see you have some color back in your face. How are you feeling?" Juliana asked.

"Much better, thank you, Your Grace. I was tired from my ordeal when we first met. I'm quite embarrassed it's taken so long to recover."

"Nonsense, you made a lovely first impression. I'm sure my son has told you I'm an expert judge of character," Juliana insisted.

"He has."

Juliana smiled at Xander, and her love was so apparent, it made Cecilia miss her own mother, or at least the woman she'd believed to be her mother.

"You must tell me about how you two met," Juliana said, taking a sip of her tea.

Cecilia looked at Xander. "My love?"

Xander grinned sheepishly. "Mother, she's trying to protect me because it's a bit of a scandalous story. I was being a bit of a rake."

"You often are, Alexander." Juliana gave him a disapproving look, but Cecilia could tell she was trying not to smile.

"Well, I paid off a hunter who won her father's solstice contest so that I could have the honor of dancing with her, and then I paid the musicians to play a Reldan so I could hold her close."

"Xander!" Juliana chided.

"Then when I met her again in the wild, she was bathing."

Juliana looked horrified.

"Mother, it's fine. She made up for it by throwing a dagger at me."

Juliana gasped.

"In my defense, I was just in a bathing gown, and he was a strange man. I could tell he was a hunter and assumed he was there to kill me. My guardian was gone, and I was frightened," Cecilia said.

"Then she continued to attack me." He laughed, smirking at Cecilia.

"For the love of the gods, why didn't you tell her who you were?" the queen asked him.

"She mesmerized me. A beautiful woman who fought so fiercely. I wanted to see what she would do." Xander squeezed Cecilia's hand and planted a kiss on it. "Then, three hunters happened upon us, but she took two of them out before I could even pick up my bow."

"Really?" The queen seemed more intrigued than upset.

"Gods! She was magnificent. I hadn't even seen her up close with a bow yet. I think that's when I really fell in love with her." Xander winked at Cecilia, and her cheeks burned, thinking of the position she'd been in during their last ride through the woods. She squirmed in her seat, and Xander beamed at her.

"Then what happened?" Juliana asked.

"She tried to resist me for weeks, but eventually, I won her over." Xander looked so proud of himself. She wanted to roll her eyes, but she forced herself to smile instead.

"I couldn't help myself," Cecilia said plainly, surprised at how much she meant it.

Juliana looked back and forth between them and smiled. "Clearly, you're quite smitten with each other. Now, why don't you leave us ladies to chat?"

"All right," Xander said, standing abruptly. "You two have fun." He leaned down and planted a long, sweet kiss on Cecilia's lips, taking full advantage of her need to pretend to be loving and devoted. She was so surprised she nearly fell out of her chair, but Xander held her firmly in place.

"Alexander!" His mother laughed, swatting at him. "Behave yourself!"

"I'm sorry. I couldn't help myself."

Cecilia tried to contain how flustered she felt.

"I've never seen him so happy," Juliana said.

Tears welled in Cecilia's eyes, and she quickly blinked them back.

"Oh dear, are you well? I understand it's been quite a shocking couple of weeks for you," Juliana said.

Cecilia nodded quickly, wiping the tears away.

"Are you certain this is what you want?" the queen asked her. "Please speak plainly. Let us have no secrets here."

"Why do you care what I want?" Cecilia asked.

Juliana's face grew serious and knowing. "Because, dear, all mothers want their children to be happy. It's clear that Alexander is quite in love with you, but if you don't feel the same—if your only plan is to pull him close and use him—I couldn't bear that."

Cecilia saw the queen in a new light. She was a mother first and a queen second.

"If you are just using my son the way the king intends to use you, I'd prefer you accidentally escape." Juliana held her gaze.

Cecilia couldn't hide her surprise. She swallowed hard, considering the offer. Even if Juliana was willing to let her escape, she doubted that goodwill would extend to Rainer, and she wouldn't leave without him. She thought hard about what to say. The queen's emotions showed sincerity, but Cecilia wasn't foolish enough to rule out the possibility that it could be some kind of test.

"Honestly, I have had my world shaken the past few days, but I love Xander. He makes me laugh even when I don't want to—even when I want to cry. He never tries to force me to be something I'm not and sees me just as I am." The words were an admission to herself as much as Juliana. Cecilia didn't know why she was talking so much, but she couldn't stop herself once she started.

"I had my doubts the day we first met. Alex has always been a handsome, charming man but not a serious one, as I'm sure you know. He's had a bit of a wandering eye. Still, I knew he felt something the first time he wrote to us about you. I didn't even need to see his face. Mothers always know. But you were at war with yourself when we met you. I wasn't sure if you were just trying to do the right thing. Now I see it."

"Does that mean you approve?" Cecilia asked.

Juliana looked surprised at the question. "Do you need me to?"

Cecilia sighed. "I suppose I don't, but it would mean a lot to Xander. I know these circumstances are not at all what I'd imagined for myself, but watching the two of you this morning—I wish my own mother were here to meet him—" She blew out a breath. "Well, the woman I thought was my mother."

"Mothers are the ones who raise us. They don't have to be the ones who birth us. Don't forget that, Cecilia. I'm sorry for your loss," Juliana murmured.

"It was a long time ago."

"Still, no girl should have to get married without her mother." Recognition lit Juliana's eyes. "Tell me, what can we do to make you feel you have some part of home at the wedding with you? Is there a certain flower you like? We can get whatever you need."

Cecilia thought for a moment. "It would be nice to have your blessing. It would mean a lot if Rainer could be there. He's my best friend, and we grew up together."

Juliana's face was tense for a moment.

"I'm sorry. That's too much, I know," Cecilia said.

She looked down at her hands in her lap. She rubbed her thumb over the inside of her wrist, trying to settle her mind. "I like peonies and roses. My mother used to grow them in her garden. I remember helping her water them as a little girl."

Cecilia grew quiet, gazing out the window. She was messing everything up. She wouldn't even be passable as a lady, let alone a princess.

"Your Majesty, I'm sorry. I know I don't have proper manners, and I don't know your customs and traditions. Clearly, I have a lot of catching up to do. I'll probably always be a woman who speaks whatever is on her mind when she should be silent. Many people will find me offensive and inappropriate. I am certain I'll make a lot of mistakes, but I promise I'll care for your son."

Juliana smiled warmly. "Well, that is good to hear. Not everyone will like this marriage. There are those who would not think twice about harming Alexander. Endros and Cato, the remaining living gods who inhabit this court, are fickle and dangerous, and they have an interest in you. I know they will hurt Xander if he stands in their way. Beyond that, many of my own subjects think Xander has been away too long and is more Olney than Argarian. Worse, our enemies stretch beyond just Olney. There are relatives of ours who want to usurp this throne if given the opportunity. My husband's brother, William, and his son, Vincent, are a constant threat along with this ongoing conflict with Olney. Xander will always be in danger, and you may be the only one to protect him from these threats."

Cecilia nodded.

Juliana's face softened. "There will be good times, too. Don't let these frightening ones scare you off. I think you two will be good for each other." She paused. "You should ask to see his art."

Cecilia's eyes grew wide. "Xander is an artist?"

Juliana nodded. "He pretends it's just a hobby, but he sends me a drawing every time he sends a letter. I think art has been an outlet for him all these years he's been alone."

The picture his mother painted softened Cecilia's heart more than she would have liked. Maybe he had the soul of an artist, but he'd still lied to her.

"I would love to stay and chat longer, but my work is never done, and with your wedding so soon, I have much to do," Juliana continued. "I will leave you with this. Alexander speaks so highly of you. He says you have courage, and I hope that's true. You're going to need it. It's difficult to be a foreign woman in this court. Courage is an asset you will need to rely on regularly. The courage to speak up and the courage to stay silent even when you don't want to. I hope that you have the wisdom to know the difference."

There was no threat in the queen's voice. Just honesty.

"I will see you at your engagement ball tonight. There are so many people eager to meet you. I'm sure you'll put your best face forward."

Again, the words came as more of a reminder than a threat.

Cecilia curtseyed and watched the queen go, worrying that she was in over her head but unwilling to accept defeat.

25

Cecilia turned from side to side, smoothing her hands down the cinched fabric of her dress. As she twisted, the light caught the silver thread in her dress, giving the illusion of a starry night in a scarlet sky. The sweetheart neckline, off the shoulder sleeves, and leg slit for ease of access to the dagger Xander had finally returned to her put a lot of her figure on display. While she knew Xander would love it, she wasn't so sure about the entire kingdom seeing so much of her.

The engagement ball was likely her best chance at escape. Although she was one of the central participants, she'd been to enough court events in Olney to know how chaotic they became as the evenings wore on and the wine flowed more freely.

Tugging at the neckline of the dress, her clammy hands sticking to the fabric, Cecilia tried to calm her racing heart. She'd met plenty of lords and ladies of the court at afternoon tea, but tonight she and Xander would be formally introduced as a couple, and she dreaded all the attention.

There was a light tap on the door.

"Cece, it's Teddy. Xander asked me to escort you down to the party."

Cecilia opened the door and let him in.

Despite her best efforts to keep Teddy at a distance, they'd become fast friends. He'd be easy enough to shake since he'd already decided he liked Cecilia. Evan, on the other hand, watched her like a hawk. He would be harder to evade.

Teddy grinned. "You look elegant."

"Oh, Teddy, are you always this much of a flirt?" she teased.

He blushed and held out his arm for her to take.

"So tell me, what am I about to walk into?" she asked.

"Which version? The honest version or the one that will make you feel better?" Teddy asked.

"I think I've had enough *harmless* lies for one lifetime."

He nodded. "I expect you'll find many of the ladies of the court here are opportunistic. You'll be popular, but it's best to remember that most of them are just vipers jockeying for status. Who wouldn't want to be friends with the new princess? I'm sure you'll have to play nice, but they can be tedious. It helps that they won't know until after the wedding that you're the Lost Goddess."

"Are any of them nice?" Cecilia asked.

"Lady Eloise Spellman is nice enough, though her father is an absolute thorn in the king's side. She's so charming you'd have no idea her father owns half the land in Argaria. Lady Tanya McGraph is kind and seems to avoid politics, and she's also quite beautiful." Teddy smiled.

"Oh, *really*?" Cecilia said, giving him a pointed look. Teddy's cheeks pinked. "And does she have any suitors?"

Teddy grinned. "Perhaps she will soon." He cleared his throat. "Anyway, I'll be with you the whole time. Xander assigned me to your protective detail, so you better get used to me. If you get overwhelmed in the crowd, just let me know, and we can step out for air."

She felt a surge of gratitude for Xander anticipating her needs. Despite everything that had happened between them, she was relieved that he wanted her to feel as comfortable as possible.

"Will Davide behave?" she asked.

Xander had insisted that Davide was harmless, but the older prince felt like an ever-present threat.

"Hard to say. He'll take any chance he can to get under Xander's skin. I'll keep an eye on him, though. Don't worry about it."

"Was he ever nice?" Cecilia asked. "Xander described him to me as charming and kind."

Teddy frowned. "Yes. They were close as children. You'd think the bitterness might have started when Xander was nine and started getting attention for being the Storm Prince. But it didn't really get bad until he left to go undercover in Olney at fourteen. Every time Xander came home to visit, it was worse. Xander hasn't had luck mending things."

They walked around another corner, and she spotted Xander and Evan at the end of the hall. He leaned against the stone wall with his back to her. Evan had warmed to her slightly, though she still felt his distrust every time he was close. He stood eye to eye with Xander. The two had similar builds and mannerisms. It was clear they'd spent a lot of time together training. Evan's hair was lighter, but his skin was darker, and his eyes were a warm brown to Xander's hazel. He took in everything, but with far less humor than Xander. There was always a crease of worry in his brow that reminded her of Rainer.

Cecilia understood. He was Xander's best friend, and he regarded her with the same skepticism that Rainer reserved for Xander.

Evan smiled tightly as Xander turned. She'd frozen him out the past few days, refusing to see him for anything other than meals and only speaking to him when she needed to.

Xander looked starved for the sight of her. His eyes glanced over her face and then down her dress, following the slit all the way to the ground, his grin growing wolfish.

"You look stunning. Evan and Teddy, can you just keep an eye out for a second?"

Cecilia gasped as Xander pushed her up against the wall, planting a passionate kiss on her lips. Her hands clenched his tunic like claws, but she didn't push him away. She had every intention of sneaking out during the party, and the kiss would be their last.

He took his time, like they weren't in a hallway that anyone could walk into. He reached a hand down, skimming her leg through the slit in her dress, and she pushed him back.

"Xander, we're in public," she said in a harsh whisper, biting back an involuntary smile.

"Perhaps we should skip the party. I'd like to have you to myself in this dress. I knew it would look spectacular," Xander whispered.

She rolled her eyes. Truthfully, she might have preferred that idea to the enemy court's scrutiny, but she had no intention of letting him know that. Evan cleared his throat, and they turned to see Damian, Juliana, and Davide walking toward them.

"Good evening, Your Majesties," Cecilia said, bending into a curtsey.

Juliana gave her an approving look. Damian nodded, but Davide sneered at them.

The king and queen were announced, then Davide. Then Cecilia and Xander were introduced as the prince and soon-to-be princess.

Cecilia gripped Xander's hand tightly, terrified of falling. Thousands of blood-red roses flanked the staircase and matched the enormous bouquets on every table in the room. The stairs opened to a ballroom with white marble floors and large windows draped with red and gold curtains. She felt the weight of every eye in the room bearing down on her as they descended.

Xander gave her hand a reassuring squeeze as they reached the bottom of the stairs, and he led her through the crowd. He pulled her close, wrapping an arm around her waist. It was just the two of them in the middle of a large marble dance floor.

"Try not to look so terrified," he whispered. "This reminds me of the night we met."

"I hate everyone looking at me," Cecilia rasped.

"Oh, love, I assure you they're all looking at me," he said with a wink. "The rogue prince returned home—wealthy, strong and extremely good-looking."

"And so modest," Cecilia quipped as the music began, and Xander started to lead her through the steps.

Xander's eyes lit with mischief. "You can tell me, you know?"

"Tell you what?"

"That I'm a better dancer than Rainer." He smirked.

She laughed. Rainer had confidence and loved to show off, but he didn't have Xander's grace.

"You're a better dancer."

"You just agreed with me. Should I be worried? Are you feeling all right?" Xander taunted as he dipped her.

"Well, you can't *always* be wrong." She grinned as he spun her again.

Xander pulled her closer. "I wish I could kiss you right now," he whispered before spinning her one last time and dipping her as the song ended.

When he brought her back up, he bowed and kissed her hand, and the crowd clapped, and she didn't know what to do other than smile at him like an idiot.

"I have to go mingle with some guests, but Teddy will stay with you. I'll be back in a while," Xander whispered.

She gripped his hand hard, unwilling to let him go. "What am I supposed to do?"

"Talk to people. You're charming. I know my people will be as in love with you as I am by the end of this party." She gave him a doubtful look as he kissed her hand again. "Trust me, Cece."

Then he and Evan disappeared into the crowd.

Within moments of his departure, a group of over-preened ladies descended on her. Teddy handed her a glass of bubble wine, and she gave him a grateful look. The ladies asked her questions about her life, Olney court traditions, questions about the prince, and how they fell in love.

Talking to them was exhausting. She felt their contempt, resentment, and jealousy. Apparently, the story everyone at court had been told was that their prince, who had been away for years, was home and had fallen in love with an Olney witch. They blamed the swift wedding on his impulsive nature, but she didn't miss the murmurs that buzzed around her, suggesting that she must be pregnant.

The women brought up all matter of tedious topics as Teddy had warned her they would. But when their conversation shifted to discussing King Damian and his mistress and how he snuck her in and out through the passages by the prison lockup that conveniently led to the stables, Cecilia perked up. The ladies of Argaria had the same loose tongues as the ladies of Olney. All she had to do was sneak upstairs and break Rainer out, and then they could flee together. She grinned as she turned, searching for Teddy, but instead came face to face with Davide.

"Lady Reznik, would you like to dance?" he asked.

Teddy stiffened in the corner of her eye. She was sure she couldn't say no with so many people watching so closely.

"Please? I'd just love to get to know my sister-to-be."

She placed her hand in Davide's, and he led her to the dance floor. She searched the room for Xander with no luck. Davide wrapped an arm around her waist and took her hand.

"I have to admit I underestimated your cleverness, Cecilia."

She smiled sweetly at him. "You wouldn't be the first man to do so."

"I expect not. How do you think this is going to work? You think you and Alex can just play out this little 'young and in love' nonsense, and everyone will fall for it?"

"It seems to be working so far. Usually, the truth is effective."

Davide scoffed. "You can't possibly convince me you really love him after everything he did to you. All the lies and manipulation. The way he seduced you in the gardens in Olney."

She'd assumed Xander had kept that bit of intimacy to himself. The fact that he hadn't chafed her.

"Love isn't logical, Davide, but I doubt you would know that."

Davide grew quiet, but his eyes said everything. He thought she was a complete fool.

"Has it occurred to you he could still be pretending? Playing the sweet prince who's enthralled just so that you'll stay here. Maybe he plays along so he can keep fucking you. Who knows? It sounds like he enjoyed that plenty, but Xander's always had a wandering eye, so we'll see how long he can keep up the charade."

Cecilia searched the room for Xander.

"Can't find him, can you?" Davide grinned.

Fear crept into her chest, making it impossible to take a deep breath. "What did you do to him?"

"Me? I did nothing, Cecilia. He's probably with Nessa. She used to be his first stop every time he came home to Argaria. I'd have to go drag him out of her apartment. Those two could go for hours—days sometimes. Old habits die hard, but I'm sure you'll get used to it. All royals do. She will be a great consort for Alex's considerable appetite." He paused and chuckled at the look on her face. "I'm certain you weren't foolish enough to expect that you could be enough for him. He's always been rather insatiable in that department."

Heat rose on Cecilia's cheeks, and she tried to hide her humiliation. Jealousy twisted her stomach in knots, which made her even more furious because she wanted to feel nothing for Xander. She wasn't foolish enough to ignore Xander's past, but she hated the envy she felt when confronted with it.

"He wouldn't do that to me," she said.

"Why? Because he's *so in love*?" Davide scoffed. "Please! I know you're young, but you must be smarter than this. He's using you because he knows what you are. He'll use you to make me obsolete in the line of succession."

The music shifted, and recognition tore through her. She narrowed her eyes at Davide. He and Xander were more alike than either of them thought.

"Don't worry, I'll be happy to lead you through a Reldan. Maybe I can still win you over." He winked at her, and just for a second, she could see a bit of Xander in him.

As Davide pulled her firmly against his body to start the dance, she spotted Xander in the ballroom doorway, his face stormy as his gaze locked on her and Davide. Evan stood behind him, and next to him was a beautiful dark-haired woman in a black dress with a plunging neckline that showed off her ample breasts.

Davide dipped Cecilia into a backbend. She was uncomfortable with how close their bodies were and how low Davide's hands had drifted on her hips, pulling her flush against his body. Over his shoulder, she saw Xander making his way toward them. The pretty, dark-haired woman followed him.

Irrational jealousy swelled in Cecilia's chest. She didn't care who Xander spent his time with because he was just a means to an end. She felt nothing for him, and she was leaving.

"I told you he was with her. I also heard he was meeting with Cato earlier," Davide said, noting her gaze locked on Xander.

Cecilia choked on her surprise. "The god of manipulation? Is he here?" The prospect of meeting a living god both thrilled and frightened her.

Davide's lips quirked into a sly smile. "I promise you don't want to meet him or his father, Endros. You'll find it's best to avoid their attention until we need to march you into Olney to crush your people."

Cecilia met Davide's hazel eyes. "I know the way men like you look at a woman like me. I'm small and pretty. You think that means you're the aggressor, but you have no idea what you've done. You've brought an Olney fox into your little Argarian hen house. Everyone sees a helpless girl. I see a kingdom poised for destruction. No one uses me. If they think they have the upper hand, it's only because I let them."

Davide frowned. "You're surrounded and collared thanks to that bracelet. The only way out is through my brother or me."

Cecilia smiled sardonically. "Oh, Davide, I thought you were supposed to be the smart brother."

Davide's eyebrows shot up. The song ended, and she curtseyed. As soon as she turned, Teddy took her elbow, handed her another glass of bubble wine as he guided her toward the courtyard.

The air outside was chilly, but Cecilia was grateful to be away from the bustling party.

"Are you well?" Teddy asked. He pulled off his cloak and wrapped it around her shoulders.

"I'm fine. He's just a bully, and I've dealt with plenty of those in my life."

"You were bullied?" Teddy asked, surprised.

"Oh yes. I was half the age of my classmates when my magic showed up, and I couldn't control it. They were cruel to me, just like hunters were cruel when I excelled."

Music kicked up again inside, and Cecilia's eyes darted to the door.

"Overwhelmed?" Teddy asked.

Cecilia nodded. "I've never been to a court event without Rainer."

"Do you miss him?"

Even Xander hadn't asked her that. She missed Rainer desperately—or perhaps she simply missed the idea of him. Twice in the space of a few days, Rainer had reminded her that they weren't on the same page, and she struggled to tell which parts of their relationship were real and which were imagined. Still, she hadn't realized how hard it would be to be away from him because they had never spent so long apart. As furious as she felt, Rainer's absence was painful, like she'd stretched their bond so uncomfortably taut.

"Yes. He's probably crawling out of his skin up in that cell."

They were quiet for a moment as she sipped her bubble wine.

"Who was the woman following Xander around?" Cecilia tried to sound casual and failed.

Teddy shifted uncomfortably from foot to foot. "That was Nessa. She and Xander used to be involved."

"How involved?" Cecilia asked.

Teddy bit his lip and looked down at his feet. "Intimately. For several years."

"Years!" She choked on her wine. Xander had been in a relationship with someone else that spanned years.

"Yes, but only twice a year when he was home for a month, or the twice a year when she visited him."

Cecilia shook her hands like she could shake off the jealousy. "So Xander had a quarterly sexy vacation with a long-term girlfriend?

"It was different," Teddy assured her.

She shook her head in disbelief. "How do you know? Davide made it sound like they were very attached and that Xander is just manipulating me."

Teddy blew out a breath that spun into a little white cloud. "I know because I see the way he stares at you from across the room like he can't believe you're real. He has never once looked at Nessa like that, and he's only mentioned her in passing, where with you he was effusive in his praise. Don't let Davide get under your skin."

She rubbed her thumb over the red skin where the Unsummoner bracelet chafed, a constant reminder that she was powerless in an enemy court. Renewed determination swelled inside her. Leo Reznik had made damn sure that she never relied too heavily on just her magic. She was resourceful, and she would find a way out.

"Cece?"

She whipped around at Xander's voice.

Teddy slinked away to give them space.

"Hi."

"Hi? What did my brother say to you? You looked upset," Xander said, winding one of her curls around his fingers.

"Just the usual. You're using me. Pretending to be in love with me."

"You know that's not true, Cece. I know you feel how much I love you." He placed her hand over his heart. She hated feeling it and hated the way her heart stirred in response.

She frowned. "I know. He also told me about Nessa."

Xander paled.

"That was quite a dress she was wearing. You two looked friend-ly," Cecilia said coldly.

Xander tilted her chin. "While it brings me a certain thrill to see you jealous, I feel nothing for her. I never did. That relationship was only ever purely physical, and it's been over for some time."

She narrowed her eyes at him. "So you would be fine with me having a purely physical relationship with someone else?"

"Gods, you are pretty when you're angry."

"I always look pretty," she said, jerking her face out of his hands and turning away from him. He laughed and wrapped his arm around her waist, tucking his face into her neck.

"That's true, but tonight in this dress, you take my breath away." Xander kissed her neck. She jumped away from him. "I'll give you the chance to make me forget I ever knew Nessa later on." His eyes heated, but his words stoked her anger.

"I'm not interested in being your palate cleanser, *Your Highness*. I have more people to meet."

The fight was a convenient excuse for more than one reason. It would make it easy to avoid him the rest of the night, but she also wanted to hang on to the lie that nothing compelled her to stay with Xander. The truth was harder to swallow because she knew that the deepest betrayal she'd suffered so far was that of her heart.

Cecilia caught a smirk on Evan's lips as she breezed by him into the warmth of the party with Teddy on her heels.

She stalked through the crowd, talking to courtiers impatiently, and pretending to sip her wine but instead dumping it in centerpieces when no one was looking so she could give the illusion of celebrating while keeping a clear head. It was a trick she'd learned from Sylvie their first season at court. When Teddy was distracted by another hunter, she stole several hunks of hard cheese, apples, and bread from the banquet tables, tucking them into the pocket of her dress so that she and Rainer would at least have some supplies for their trip.

"Teddy, I think I'd like to head up to bed early. This has just been so exhausting."

Teddy nodded, and she threaded her arm through his, careful to make sure he bumped into a passing lady so that he wouldn't notice when Cecilia lifted his dagger. Once they were out of the crush of the crowd, she could breathe easier, but her heart raced as they wound their way up the stairs and nearer to her target.

"Oh, is this the library? I've been dying to see it," Cecilia said, guiding Teddy into the room at the turnoff for the prison lockup.

"Yes, this is the royal library," he said, turning away from her to look around the magnificent room. "There are volumes here from—"

Cecilia smacked the back of his head with the pommel of the dagger, and Teddy crumbled to the ground. She cringed, hoping she hadn't hurt him too badly. He was unconscious, but his pulse was strong, so she patted his head and stole the rest of his weapons. Then she ducked out of the room to free Rainer.

26

Teddy's short swords and dagger rattled at Cecilia's waist as she raced breathlessly down the hall. She took the familiar twists and turns until she made it to the prison hallway. It was darker than the rest of the castle, and just one guard stood between her and Rainer.

The cold stone at her back snagged the delicate material of her dress as she assessed the easiest way past the guard. A fight would make too much noise, and she'd rather not leave a body that would send the castle into high alert. If she wasn't cut off from her power, it would have been much easier to do this quietly. Still, she was unwilling to risk using her goddess power and completing the exchange.

Instead, she stepped out into the light.

"Excuse me, sir. I'm afraid I've taken a wrong turn. I'm looking for the guest wing," she said, twirling a loose curl at her neck.

The guard sidled up to her. "You want to turn left and then—"

She brought the pommel of the dagger down hard on the back of his head, and he stumbled. Cecilia smacked him again, and he slumped against the wall. Catching his arm, she stumbled under his weight, struggling to get him into a chair across the hall. Then she stole the keys from him and ran into the prison hall.

Rainer was waiting for her. "I felt you were close, but where—" He looked beyond her as if expecting Xander.

She dashed to the door of his cell and worked on finding the right key for the lock.

"It's just me. Your white knight, here to save you," she said with a grin.

Rainer shook his head, rubbing the bridge of his nose. "Cecilia, this is reckless, even for you."

"Would you rather I wait around for someone here to decide they don't like their prince marrying some foreign witch and take a crack at killing me? I'm cut off from my magic and you. At least if we do this, we have each other. Now shut up and let me rescue you."

Rainer fought off a grin as she pulled the heavy barred door and hugged him.

"You're well?" Rainer asked.

She wrinkled her nose. "I'd be better if you didn't stink so bad."

"Unfortunately, I didn't receive the same hospitality as the new Argarian princess," Rainer said with a sardonic smile.

She unbuckled the short swords from her waist and gave them to Rainer.

"What about you?" he asked.

She gestured to her dagger on her thigh. "There's a crappy old bow in my room. That's our next stop, so I can put on some heavy clothes."

They ducked down the hall, hiding in the library, where Teddy was still unconscious on the floor, as a guard patrol passed before making their way back to her room. Rainer set about trying to clean up quickly in the washroom while she ducked into her dressing room and pulled on leggings.

"What's the rest of the plan?" Rainer asked as she wrapped the cheese she'd stolen from the party along with some apples from the table in her room in a gauzy scarf and tucked them into a leather satchel.

"The rest of the plan is to go steal some horses and ride hard."

Rainer shook his head, eyeing the bow that she'd been using for shooting games with Teddy earlier that day. "You can work with that old thing?"

"I can work with anything," she said with a confident grin.

Rainer's gaze snagged on the leggings peeking out from the slit in her dress. "Go finish changing. We have to be quick."

She ducked back into the closet and grabbed a tunic. Before she could put it on, death whispers howled through the bedroom.

"Rain!" Stepping out of the closet, she saw him pinned against the wall by two hunters.

"Hold still." A woman's voice was a sharp command in her ear. Cold steel pressed against her throat.

Cecilia froze, her eyes darting to the mirror across the room, which reflected the woman who'd been following Xander around the party.

"Nessa," Cecilia breathed.

Nessa grinned. "Ah, I see my reputation precedes me. Let's make quick work of this. Take off your clothes, guardian."

The two hunters let Rainer go, but he hesitated until Nessa pressed her blade harder against Cecilia's neck. He tugged off his tunic and undershirt, tossing them aside, revealing a broad muscular chest and stomach. His skin was tanned and flawless despite years of combat, thanks to Cecilia's healing magic.

Nessa clicked her tongue. "My, my, lucky Lady Reznik, bedding two such handsome men."

"I'm not," Cecilia huffed.

Rainer glanced from her to the two hunters.

"Don't bother, guardian. We're too well trained to let you escape, and if you pull anything, I'll just slit your witch's throat and she'll be dead before she hits the ground."

Rainer stilled. His eyes locked with Cecilia's, and a rush of panic tore through their connection.

"Keep stripping, then get into bed. I'll help you with your dress,

Cecilia," Nessa taunted, popping several of the buttons on the back of the dress.

"What is the endgame?" Cecilia asked.

"That your guardian killed you in a fit of jealousy when he found out you were really going to marry Xander."

Cecilia scoffed. "Xander would never believe that."

"It doesn't matter what he believes. It matters what everyone else believes. I get you out of the way. I buy myself a favor with Endros, and when Xander needs comfort, I'll be there waiting."

"You made a deal with Endros?" Cecilia asked.

Nessa sighed heavily. "Yes. He doesn't care for King Damian's plan to use you against Olney. There's too much opportunity for you to change your mind and switch sides. Easier to take you off the board. His goals align with mine."

Rainer unbuttoned his pants as the door burst open and Xander, Evan, and a rumpled Teddy stumbled in.

"What the fuck is going on?" Xander barked, looking from a half-naked Rainer to Cecilia and Nessa.

The second of surprise was all Cecilia needed. She elbowed Nessa, simultaneously bringing her other hand up to block the blade, but her hand slipped as the blade sank into the inside of her left wrist. The pain was blinding as she twisted away. Blood slid down her arm, pooling on the stone floor, filling the air with a metallic scent. Cecilia felt dizzy.

She knew from the way the wound pulsed with her heartbeat that she'd need to work fast. She forced herself to concentrate in time to block Nessa's attack and countered by punching her in the face.

Nessa struck back with a kick and a slash with her dagger, but Cecilia kicked the blade away, so they were fighting hand to hand.

"You tricked him. He only wants you because you're a goddess. You used your magic," Nessa taunted.

The words hooked into Cecilia's heart, speaking to a fear she had never voiced. Even though she hadn't used magic on him, some part of her was afraid that Xander wouldn't love her if she wasn't a goddess.

They fought viciously, and Cecilia worried about the amount of blood she was losing. The men moved around them, battling the hunters who'd come with Nessa.

"He must have a thing for huntmasters' daughters." Nessa laughed.

The revelation hit her like an arrow. She knew the name was familiar when she heard it before. She was fighting the daughter of Lukas Ducrane, the Argarian huntmaster, Vanessa Ducrane, Cecilia's Argarian counterpart.

"He fell in love with me long before I was a goddess, but I'm not just the huntmaster's daughter." Cecilia laughed, trying to sound calm as she threw another jab. "I'm also the daughter of Clastor."

Saying it out loud summoned new confidence.

"You're just another whore who let Alex between her legs," Nessa said. "Did he taste you, *goddess*? That man is so gifted with his tongue. He used to make me sing when he was between my legs—"

Cecilia punched her before she could finish.

Nessa wiped the blood from her lips and laughed. "But not as much as I made him sing when I was between his."

Cecilia felt possessed. She flew at the huntress, tackling her to the ground. She grabbed for her throat. Her rage made her sloppy, and Nessa flipped her on her back.

They'd fallen by Nessa's blade, and she snatched it, pressing it down toward Cecilia's heart. Blood rushed in Cecilia's ears.

The death whispers rose like the roar of the river rapids. The wound on Cecilia's wrist bled profusely, making her hands sticky. She slipped, and the knife nicked her chest.

Then Xander yanked Nessa off of her. The huntress went flying, her head smacking the wall hard. She slumped over, unconscious.

"Cece?" Xander knelt beside her, taking her wrist in his hand and tearing off the sleeve of his shirt to wrap her wound.

"I'm all right," she rasped, still breathless from the fight as he helped her to her feet.

He shook his head. "I never expected Nessa to be so jealous."

Cecilia shook her head. "I don't think she was jealous. She said that Endros put her up to it."

She explained what Nessa had told them about her plan for Cecilia and Xander and Endros's intentions. By the time she finished, Evan looked pale.

"Did you know?" Xander asked.

Evan shook his head. "My spies had some notion that his plan might be a slight departure from the king's, but nothing like this."

Xander's gaze lingered on him, but Evan held his hands up in surrender. "You've not liked Cecilia from the beginning."

"I swear, Xan." Evan rubbed the bridge of his nose. "She's a tiny, over-preened lady with a bad temper and a penchant for getting into trouble. Of course I don't like her. She makes you distracted and reckless. I dislike anyone who makes you act more foolish than usual, but I wouldn't hurt her."

Cecilia smiled sardonically. "By all means, don't hold back. Tell us how you really feel, Evan."

Rainer looked like he was trying not to laugh as he pulled his shirt on. "Funny, I've thought all the same things about your prince."

Xander crossed the room, looking at the two other hunters they'd knocked out. "You know them?"

Evan shrugged. "Just as her minions. You know Nessa. She likes to dangle possibilities in front of hunters for their allegiance, though I'm not sure why it works, because as far as I know, she rarely, if ever, follows through."

A grunt on the other side of the room stole their attention as Nessa grabbed a dagger that had landed beside her and launched it at Cecilia.

The blade came so fast that Cecilia only had time to suck in a breath. Before it struck her, Xander slammed into her side, sending her sprawling on the stone floor. When she pushed to her feet, she turned and found the blade embedded in Xander's shoulder.

Cecilia crossed the room in a fury and plunged her own dagger into Nessa's chest. The huntress's dark eyes met Cecilia's, and she let out a harsh laugh as she mumbled something.

"What's that?" Cecilia asked.

Nessa grinned, blood gathering at the corners of her mouth. "I said, why aren't you dead yet? The poison from my blade should already be in your system."

Cecilia's eyes flew to her wrist, and she stumbled back as Nessa let out a wet cough and slumped against the wall.

"Get Magdalena!" Xander yelled.

Teddy disappeared out the door as Evan helped Xander to a chair, and Rainer caught her around the waist and guided her to the bed. Cecilia's thoughts felt foggy, and her breathing wouldn't settle from the fight.

"Cece?" Rainer's hand patted her clammy forehead. "Xander, we need a healer."

Cecilia reached up and brushed her thumb over the crease in Rainer's brow. "I found a worry, but I'll fix it in a hurry."

Xander appeared on her other side, his face creased with fear. "My love?"

"I'm fresh out of worry fixes," she murmured. She wanted to sound teasing, but her voice sounded so weak.

Blood seeped from the dagger still embedded in Xander's shoulder, but he acted as if nothing had happened, taking her bloody hand in his and kissing her wrist.

Suddenly, all of her rage seemed terribly foolish. It didn't protect her from loving him. It only made them both suffer. Now she was going to die, having only admitted her love for the one person who wouldn't love her back and refusing the man who'd quite literally taken a knife to the chest to save her.

Tears welled in her eyes. "I'm sorry," she mumbled, squeezing Xander's hand.

"Shh, no apologies needed, love. Just stay calm. Magdalena will be here soon, and she'll fix you right up."

"Poisons are hard, Xan." Her words came out slower and more slurred than she wanted as she shivered.

Evan picked up Nessa's dagger from the floor and sniffed it. "Smells like Angel's Chariot." He bent over Xander, looking at the blade in his chest. "That's yours, right? Not one of Nessa's?"

Xander nodded as a woman burst into the room with Teddy on her heels. She took in the bodies on the floor and Cecilia and Xander on the bed.

"Oh dear," she murmured as her gaze settled on Cecilia. "Do we know what it is?"

"Angel's Chariot," Evan replied.

The healer rested her hand on Cecilia's forehead and then felt her pulse. "There's too much in her system right now for me to do a direct pull. I need a living thing to transfer the poison into."

Rainer fumbled with their satchel, pulling out the bundle of apples, and Magdalena got to work.

The healer cut a chunk of Cecilia's hair in offering and murmured the words of a spell to remove the poison. She held one hand on Cecilia's chest just above her slowing heart and held an apple in the other hand. As she whispered the words of the spell, the apple withered into a black husk. She repeated it with each apple until they were all black.

Cecilia didn't need her confirmation it wasn't enough. It was becoming harder to stay conscious. Her body ached, like her muscles had been clenched for hours with no relief.

"I need something else," Magdalena said.

"I'll go to the kitchen," Teddy offered. His voice sounded far away, and the room grew dimmer.

Magdalena shook her head. "She doesn't have enough time for that."

"Put it in me," Xander said.

"Absolutely not!" Evan scoffed. "I know you love her, but that's insane. Magdalena, talk sense to him."

The healer shrugged. "There's no sense where love's involved. If a Savero prince bids me to do something, I must."

Evan threw his hands up. "Even if he's a self-sacrificing idiot?"

Xander shook his head. "It's not insane. You can go get more produce from the kitchen. I heal faster. If there's only a little left, Mags can pull it out and put it in me."

"You heal faster than the average person, Xander. You're not a god," Evan said.

Magdalena shrugged. "He's right. He can at least contain it until you bring me more produce, but Cecilia doesn't have much time."

Rainer squeezed her hand. "I can feel it," he whispered. "I can feel our bond trying to tug free. Cecilia Juliet Reznik, you better not let go. I did not drag you across two kingdoms for you to die here now." His eyes were glassy with unshed tears. "Don't go where I can't go."

Cecilia choked on a laugh. She'd said those words to him so many times when she wanted to tag along on some guardian activity when they were younger.

The healer met Rainer's eye. "Keep pulling on her. Keep her tethered here while I work."

A sharp tug hooked in her chest, and she instinctively rubbed her sternum. "Not so hard," she mumbled.

Teddy darted out of the room again to rush to the kitchen.

Magdalena placed one hand on Cecilia's chest and the other on Xander's and began murmuring the words of the spell again.

Cecilia turned her head, her gaze locking with Xander's.

"Stay with me, love. I know you won't admit it, but you want to," he whispered.

It felt like they were the only two people in the room, like he could see the words she'd tucked away in her heart. Despite Magdalena's ministrations and Evan and Rainer sitting so close, she was focused only on Xander's hazel eyes and the warmth of his hand in hers.

"Keep looking at me, Cece. Yours are the most lovely eyes I've ever seen, and I don't want to see anything else right now," Xander rasped.

Cecilia's vision sharpened. Sweat beaded on Xander's brow, and his skin grew ashen. His hand trembled in hers as the room seemed to grow brighter, her heartbeat quickening.

"Why did you try to leave when I promised to get you out?" Xander asked.

"Why would I trust you?" she asked, the words more hurt than angry.

Xander sighed. "I'm sorry that I ever hurt you. If I could do it over, I would do everything different. I would tell you the truth from the beginning and put myself at your mercy. Cece, I would sweep you off your feet and run away with you to a place where you could be anyone you want to be. I will never let anyone hurt you again. I love you so much."

The emotion in his voice and the glassiness of his eyes struck her speechless as strength surged back into her body. Magdalena pulled her hand away from Cecilia's chest. Cecilia rolled over and kissed Xander.

She put everything she felt into the kiss, as if she could lure him from death's doorstep with the promise of more. Her fingers threaded through his hair. It was a testament to how bad he felt that he couldn't even lift a hand to get in a quick grope.

"Don't you dare die on me, Xander," she whispered against his lips. "I hate you so much, but I'll hate you more if you die."

His lips drew up in a satisfied smile. "You are the most beautiful liar I've ever laid eyes on, but I'll let you have your lies."

She did not know how Xander knew what she felt. Maybe he felt it in the desperation of her kiss. Maybe he was bluffing. Either way, she was unwilling to admit it still. She could not sacrifice her power to him twice, could not get so close again. Her heart might have wanted to jump in without a second thought, but her pride was too wounded for her to be open in the same way.

Xander looked to Evan. "How about you, spymaster? You like to hoard secrets. Do you know her secret?"

Evan's gaze moved from Xander to Cecilia and then back to the door. "Where's Teddy? He should be back by now."

"Evan?"

Evan grimaced at the prince. "I think she's way more trouble than she's worth and repeatedly proves that she can't be trusted. Is that the secret?"

Cecilia didn't blame Evan for distrusting her, but Xander had betrayed her first.

She brushed Xander's hair back from his damp forehead, and his eyes focused before going unfocused.

"Anything you'd like to tell me, Goddess?"

"Yes, you look terrible," Cece rasped.

"Another lie. I'm certain there's never been a more handsome dead man." Xander chuckled breathlessly. "Do you know what might make it hurt less?"

"Oh gods, now you're making me ill," Evan quipped.

Cecilia kissed Xander again until her heart thundered and the tears she was holding back streamed down her cheeks.

"I'll never tire of that," Xander said breathlessly. "Marry me."

"If this is a proposal, it's a terrible one." Cecilia laughed, wiping away her tears.

"You're right. I should be on both knees and begging, but alas, I'm quite incapacitated."

Cecilia looked at Rainer, whose brow was pinched in concern. He tugged on their bond. He knew the truth and was waiting for her to admit it.

Magdalena's nervous gaze darted to the door as Teddy burst in with a basket of produce. She went to work immediately, pulling the poison into the fruit until the large basket was heaped with blackened fruit.

Cecilia waited, gripping Xander's hand in hers.

"Why isn't he healing?" Cecilia asked, taking in Xander's still-bloodless lips.

Magdalena shook her head. "The poison does damage. He was already wounded. It might be too much for him to take on. The next few moments are critical."

Cecilia felt furiously powerless and hated the healer's resignation. "Do something! He's the prince, for the love of the gods," she huffed, holding up her wrist with the Unsummoner bracelet.

The healer pulled out the dagger, brought her hands to his chest, sending more healing into the wound. It closed beneath her hands, but Xander still looked like he was on death's doorstep. His trembling grew even more severe.

"Please, my fierce, stubborn Cece, let me hear it just once," he pleaded. "I can't imagine hearing anything better my whole life."

Guilt twisted Cecilia's gut in knots, but still she could not speak the words. She finally understood why people called it falling in love. Loving Xander was something she'd done by accident. It wasn't until she was midair, powerless to do anything to stop her momentum, that she realized what was happening.

Xander's body gave a great shudder, and suddenly he grew still.

"Xander?" She shook his shoulder, but he didn't move. "Don't you dare."

He still didn't move, and tears stung her eyes as a surprised sob burst up from the center of her chest. Cecilia felt breathless, a great sinking feeling settling in her stomach.

"I love you, you brave idiot! Are you happy now? *I love you*, Xander." She sobbed. "I love you, and I'm such a fool to feel that way and even more foolish not to tell you until you're gone."

She hung her head, silently sobbing.

Suddenly a hand squeezed her thigh. When she blinked the tears from her eyes, Xander was grinning at her.

"Oh my gods, you were pretending! You snake!" she barked.

The color slowly returned to his skin, and he laughed. "To answer your question, I'm happier than I've ever been, Goddess. Now kiss me or I'll let myself die to spite you."

She kissed him tentatively until he brought his hand to the back of her head and pulled her closer.

"I feel better already." Xander sighed as he pulled away. "Although do you know what would really get me back to full strength?"

Cecilia's cheeks heated. "Don't you dare. You've already done enough for one day."

"Evan, what did I say to you after Cece stormed off at the party tonight?" Xander asked.

Evan shook his head. "You said, 'That woman is in love with me. She just won't admit it to herself yet. I'm going to wear her down.' "

"Oh gods, he'll be insufferable now." Cecilia sighed. She turned to

Magdalena. "Thank you."

The woman looked exhausted and completely spent, but she unbound Cecilia's wrist and healed the cut there. "It will scar because of the poison, but I did my best."

"I truly can't thank you enough," Cecilia said.

Magdalena looked affectionately at Xander. "Of course. I wasn't about to let the first baby I brought into this world make his way out so soon. Please, Your Highness, rest until tomorrow and rebuild your strength."

"We have a bigger problem right now. Cece is clearly not safe in your court. We need to leave," Rainer said, taking a step toward the bed.

Evan crossed his arms. "Yes, you do."

"We all do," Xander corrected.

Evan huffed out a breath. "You cannot be serious, Xan."

"I am, and I'm the prince, so what I say goes. I need to get my lovely fiancée to safety, and we need to inform my father that Endros has other plans in mind."

"He's right, Evan. I don't like it either, but if Endros has turned against the family, we could use a goddess on our side," Teddy said. "Not to mention we don't know where Cato stands, not that we could even trust him."

Evan nodded. Cecilia was impressed at how Teddy tempered both Xander and Evan with his earnest enthusiasm.

"I'm sorry about your head, Teddy," she said.

The guard waved her off, though she saw the assessment in his gaze that said she'd not get the drop on him again.

Evan rubbed his temples. "I cannot believe I'm going along with this."

"But you are because you're the best spymaster I know," Xander said with a smirk.

Evan rubbed the bridge of his nose. "I am because otherwise you will get yourself killed and waste all my hard work these past few years. Tomorrow morning, Teddy will accompany Cecilia down to the stables, and she'll say that she wants to surprise Xander with a ride, and Teddy and I will be accompanying them. Then she'll pretend to 'visit' with Rainer's horse but will instead get him ride-ready. I will take care of supplies, food, water, weapons, and ensuring a smooth path past all guard posts. Rainer will have to remain in prison until tomorrow so as to not raise suspicion. I already tied up and hid the guard that Cecilia incapacitated. Xander, your only job is healing so you're up to a long ride."

Rainer lingered beside Cecilia's side of the bed, still tugging on their bond to check that she was all right.

Evan turned to Rainer. "Rainer can come back to my room, bathe, and change into warmer clothes so he'll be ready for the trip. Ted, you'll guard the door for now?"

Teddy nodded.

Finally, Evan turned his attention back to Xander. "Rest, Xan. Seriously." He met Cecilia's eyes. "Let him rest."

Cecilia threw her hands up. "As if I'm the instigator."

Xander wrapped an arm around her waist and pulled her down to sit beside him. "I promise I'll be on my best behavior." His tone made it clear he had no intention of doing such a thing.

With that, the group left Cecilia and Xander alone. She fidgeted with her hair nervously.

"Afraid to be alone with me without that wall you constructed between us, love?"

"Yes."

"Come to bed," Xander said, patting the pillow on his other side.

She climbed over him and laid her head on his chest, listening to the sound of his heartbeat growing stronger by the moment.

"I know I tease you a lot, but I love you very much."

"I know," Cecilia sighed.

"And you love me very much."

"I love you a little," she whispered.

Xander gave her behind a squeeze. "Nonsense, you only have one way to love, and it's fully. It's one of your finest qualities."

Cecilia snuggled into him, allowing him to be right for once without argument.

27

The stable hands scurried about, rushing to fulfill Cecilia's request for a surprise ride for the prince. They were all too happy to have her duck away into Zeke's stable for a visit. The morning was chilly but bright, the sun cutting through the stable windows and dancing over the muddy floor.

Zeke perked up when Cecilia stepped into his stall but seemed agitated by Teddy's presence. She patted the horse's side and fed him an apple.

"Good boy. Rain misses you. Are you up for some exercise?" She murmured as she set to brushing him down.

"Good morning, Lady Reznik. How is my sister-to-be this morning?"

She turned. Davide stood in the doorway, backlit by the bright morning sun. Teddy tensed, bringing his hand to his sword.

"Calm down, Reynolds. I'm not here to hurt her," Davide said with a laugh.

Teddy looked unconvinced, but Cecilia waved him off.

"What can I do for you, *brother*?" Cecilia asked, continuing to brush Zeke.

"You know, sometimes I forget how common you are, but seeing you in here taking care of a horse reminds me of where you really belong."

"Charming, as always, Davide." She sighed. She kept her gaze on Zeke, watching Davide and his guards in her periphery.

"I'm here because I heard a rumor," Davide started.

She smirked. "I didn't think you would be one for court gossip."

"Normally, I'm not, but this was an interesting piece of gossip. It seems a witch has spellbound my foolish little brother. He's got it in his head that he wants to run away with her and her guardian."

"That's ridiculous. Rain isn't even Xander's type."

Davide chuckled.

"I would advise you to ignore idle court gossip," Cecilia said, briefly making eye contact with Teddy.

"I know what really has my brother so strung out. It has nothing to do with magic and everything to do with what's between your legs," Davide said.

Cecilia stopped brushing Zeke and turned to look at him. "I see that being crude runs in the family."

"And I suppose being a slut runs in yours, daughter of Clastor."

Teddy flinched, but Cecilia laughed. Davide looked surprised by the reaction.

She turned back to her work. "What do you want, Davide?"

"I wanted to offer you some advice: stay here and fall in line. You can continue fucking my brother with the same reckless abandon, and you'll have some immortal Savero heirs to help our kingdom crush Olney."

"Or?" She struggled to stop fidgeting. Her body was full of nervous energy that she would normally spend on magic.

"It would be foolish to assume that Alex was the only person undercover in your court," Davide started. "You have already seen how close my brother got to the huntmaster. Are you really expecting that we don't have people in place to assure your compliance? Your father is getting up there in years. It would be a shame if there was some sort of accident."

Cecilia froze. Her whole body went still as she tried to quiet the roar in her ears.

"Cece?" Teddy whispered.

She turned to look at Davide. It took everything in her not to reach out to her power for the explicit purpose of smiting him.

"Even you could not make a difference in time," Davide said. "You will stay here, or your father will meet an untimely end."

"I have no reason to believe you," Cecilia argued.

"And yet you also can't disprove what I'm saying. Are you willing to risk it? Do you really think we would have allowed the prince of Argaria to be undercover for years without supervision?"

Her mind sorted through her father's closest advisors, trying to call up anything suspicious.

"You have a dear aunt as well, right? Clara? I'm sure you worry for her."

Cecilia paled. "Why are you doing this? You hate me."

"I find you common and distasteful, but you are a necessary evil. At least you'll make handsome, powerful heirs for the Savero family," Davide said.

She was suddenly grateful that they had let nothing about her bargain from the Cave of Longings slip, as it was likely the only thing keeping the Savero family on her side. It seemed that Davide had a different agenda than the king and queen, and Endros, but it still relied on her ability to have children.

"And if you get any ideas, remember that we still have your guardian," Davide said. "I promise if you cause any trouble at all, I will make his death slow and painful. I understand you can feel each other's pain."

Davide grabbed her hand and wrenched her wrist back. She cried out in surprise. Teddy grimaced, his hand still on his sword. Cecilia held up a hand to ward him off. He couldn't hit the heir to the throne, and neither could she. Davide's two guards were just waiting for them to make a move.

"I will peel the skin from his body and have a healer keep him conscious until he begs for death. Tell me—would you feel that?

Would he feel it if I broke your hand right now?" Davide asked, squeezing her hand.

"No," she grunted.

Davide laughed. "So brave. Let's test that theory. I have a guard with him now. Let's see how he reacts."

Davide crushed her hand in his, her bones snapping under the pressure. Cecilia couldn't stop herself from crying out from the blinding pain. She sucked in air, staggering away from him.

"You'll marry Xander on Friday like the luckiest common whore in all the land, and you'll keep your mouth shut. That will keep your father and your guardian safe. Tell me you understand, Lady Reznik." He smiled as she turned to face him.

"I understand," she gritted.

"Good." Davide turned on his heel and walked toward the stable doors.

"Davide," Cecilia called after him, cradling her broken hand. He turned to look at her. "Maybe not today or tomorrow, but someday soon, I will pay you back for this. You may have protection now, but I'd be happy to show you how the common folk handle their disputes."

Davide pursed his lips and stalked away. As soon as he was gone, Teddy rushed to her.

"We need to go see the healer. How bad is it?" Teddy asked. With the adrenaline of the moment gone, she felt the full extent of the pain.

"It's fine," she hissed.

"You're sweating, and you're very pale. Can you walk, or do you need me to carry you?"

"Teddy, please don't fuss. Let's go."

She smiled weakly, despite the way the pain twisted her stomach. She closed Zeke into his stall, and they walked back into the castle. On the way back inside, they ran into Evan, who walked them to the healer and then left to get Xander and check on Rainer.

The healer quickly mended her hand, and the relief was instant.

A few minutes later, Xander burst in with all the fury of a summer storm.

"My love, are you all right?" Xander asked.

"I'm fine. I just feel for Magdalena having to fix me two days in a row. It wasn't bad," Cecilia lied.

Magdalena patted Xander's shoulder. "Your Highness, she had five broken bones in her hand. No doubt it was painful and likely still numb from the healing. I offered her a tincture to help her rest, but she says she needs to stay sharp."

"Thank you, Magdalena. I'll stay with her," he said.

Magdalena left the room.

Xander's brow creased with worry as he looked down at Cecilia. "Cece, I'm sorry. I should have been with you. I made you a promise last night, and I didn't keep it."

"Xan, it's my fault. I should have—" Teddy started.

"You couldn't have done anything, Teddy." Xander sighed. "Davide is the heir to the throne. You would've been executed. You did the right thing. It was stupid of me not to realize he would do something."

"Please don't fuss. I'm more concerned about my father and Rainer. I've never broken a bone, so Rain is probably beside himself. When the time is right, I'll pay Davide back," she said.

Xander finally smiled. "Gods, I love when you make threats."

"You're disturbed."

"Probably," he sighed. He leaned in close to her. "Teddy, look away."

Teddy turned away from them, and Xander kissed her. He wound his hands through her hair and drew her closer. When he pulled away, he brushed his lips to her hand so tenderly it brought tears to her eyes.

"It's just tingly and numb right now. It will fade in an hour," she said.

He was already looking toward the door when Evan appeared.

"Rainer is fine," Evan said. "A guard came in to watch him. Rainer didn't understand why until he felt your pain. He panicked, but he is fine now. I've given him the means to defend himself, just in case. He's very wound up, though. It wouldn't be a bad idea to stop by and let him see for himself." He looked at Xander. "Obviously, this changes our plans."

"It does," Xander said. He ran a hand through his hair in frustration. "I should have known."

"Do you know who the undercover hunters are in Olney?" Cecilia asked, looking from Evan to Xander.

"I only know of one. He was my personal guard. Avery Bernard," Xander said.

Cecilia gasped. "Gods! He's my father's third-in-command!"

"I know, but he's an honorable man. He was there to keep me safe. He wasn't a spy, and he's never had love for Davide. I doubt he would—"

"Would you bet my father's life on it?" Cecilia challenged.

She couldn't keep the panic and frustration out of her voice. Evan and Xander looked at each other.

"I wouldn't take any chance with your father's life, but I do trust Avery. Evan, do you have any contacts?" Xander said.

Evan practically laughed at the question. "Of course I do. I will work on getting a message to the huntmaster from someone he will trust. Don't worry. We will ensure your father is aware, and as I understand it, he is a formidable man, despite his age."

"Well, he certainly likes to think so," she scoffed.

Cecilia couldn't remember the last time she saw her father spar with anyone full force. She knew he took great pains to do his own training in private, out of view of any prying eyes.

"Xander," Teddy interrupted. "Your brother also verbally insulted Cece in front of his guards. You should prepare yourselves for him to continue to disparage her character and her—"

Cecilia almost laughed, watching Teddy struggle with the wording.

"Gods, Teddy, relax! He's trying to say that your brother made some accusations about my virtue."

"He used much coarser language," Teddy huffed.

Xander looked at Cecilia, and she couldn't contain her laughter.

"Well, he suggested that I'd bewitched you with what's between my legs." Cecilia laughed.

"He might be onto something there. So, what do we do now?" Xander asked, looking over at Evan.

"We don't have the numbers right now to do anything before the wedding. I know it's not ideal, but it would be safest to wait until after. I need time for my message to reach my contacts in Olney and Commander Reznik. We need time to sneak Rainer out and get him somewhere safe. Once you're married, the paranoia should die down, and security should be laxer," Evan said.

"Are you sure? Even given my *condition*?" Cecilia asked skeptically.

"Yes, even so. Appearances are important, and they can't exactly tell the guards they don't need to worry because the new princess is already pregnant. During your honeymoon would be ideal, as you'll have more privacy than you will once you return," Evan offered.

Cecilia felt like the walls were closing in. Her stomach bottomed out when she thought about being a princess. The despair that she felt the day before roared back. As if he was reading her mind, Xander turned to look at her.

"Could you give us a few moments alone?" he said, dismissing Evan and Teddy. "Cece, I know this isn't what either of us hoped for, but I meant what I said. I will never make you be something else. I love you, and I want you to be happy. It's fast, but we can pretend the wedding here never happened. I don't want you to feel pressured. I know we are doing things a little out of order, but when we get back to Olney, I would love to court you properly."

"But we'll already be married," Cecilia said, trying to keep her voice calm and even.

"I hate the idea of you being forced into this. I want you to marry me because you love me, and I know you don't feel ready. That kills me. But I love you, and there's not a doubt in my mind that I want to marry you."

"Xander—"

He held up his hands. "I know you think I hardly know you, but I promise I will put my whole heart into getting to know you better. I fell for you so fast it doesn't feel strange to me at all."

"I meant what I said before. I want to marry you, but I fear the expectations and the pressure it will put on our relationship when it's brand-new." Cecilia sighed.

"You let me worry about that."

"Gods, we're going to have to have this awful impersonal ceremony, aren't we?" She was embarrassed to admit that she hoped for something more intimate.

"It seems that way, though I wish I could give you the wedding you want."

"Honestly, I've never even thought about what kind of wedding I would like. I never imagined it would be a huge ceremony from a culture I don't even know, surrounded by people who think I'm an evil witch with magical lady bits," she said.

Xander burst out laughing. "They are magical." He pulled her into a tight hug. "I'm going to fix this for you. I love you."

"I love you, too," she sighed, leaning into him. Having him close eased the fears that screamed in the back of her mind.

"Xan, I want better choices. I want to not always be making the best bad choice."

"Then we will build a world together that has better options for everyone."

28

After tossing and turning all night, Cecilia woke the next morning exhausted. All she could think about was the strange impersonal ceremony she'd been walked through by Queen Juliana the day before. Although she was worried about remembering everything, she was most concerned by the fact that Argarian tradition required an invasive custom of having a witness to the wedding consummation. She kicked off the covers and sat up, hoping to find something to do to chase the fears from her mind when a light tapping on her door drew her attention.

"Cece, come to the door, but don't open it all the way and don't look at me," Xander said in a loud whisper.

She cracked the door.

"Good morning," Xander said. "Just reach your hand through."

"Why are you acting so strange?" she asked as he enveloped her hand in his.

"It's bad luck for the bride and groom to see each other before the wedding," Xander replied.

"The wedding isn't until tomorrow."

"That's our Argarian wedding, my love. I had an idea—"

"Oh gods, what is it?" she asked. Cecilia's heart couldn't take many more surprises.

"I think you're going to like it." He stroked his thumb over her hand. "I was talking with Rainer."

"What!"

"Shh! Keep your voice down. I was talking to Rainer because I had an idea that I thought might make you smile, and I love when you smile." He hesitated, anxiety buzzing around him.

"You're nervous," she whispered. She couldn't think of a single time she'd ever felt him so nervous.

"Yes, I am."

"Now I really want to look at you," she said.

"Please don't. It's bad luck. I've already done this badly twice. I know tomorrow is our big fancy wedding. You're putting on a brave face, but I know our customs feel strange and impersonal to you. We have so little control right now over anything. I thought that maybe at midnight tonight we could have our own wedding, so that no matter what happens tomorrow, we will have something that is personal and just for us. Rainer offered to officiate since he's licensed to officiate Olney weddings."

Cecilia had laughed in Rainer's face the previous summer when he decided to get certified so he could officiate a guardian friend's wedding. Now the knowledge seemed practical.

Xander kissed her hand. "I was hoping you would let me do this for you. I always loved how the intended chose their own words in Olney weddings. You deserve to have the wedding that you dreamed about since you were a little girl."

"Gods, you're such a romantic." Cecilia laughed, blinking back tears. "And to be clear, this is the first time I've ever thought about my wedding."

Xander chuckled. "Of course, my mistake. Much too busy shooting hunters with arrows to worry about a wedding."

"Obviously." She laughed.

"I wanted to ask you, and this is going to be clumsy because I have my eyes closed, and you can't see me, but I'm getting down on one knee."

His knee hit the ground with a thud.

"Cecilia Reznik, will you marry me tonight at midnight? Will you let me spend the rest of my life trying to drive you as crazy as you drive me?"

All at once, she felt like her heart might burst. The rush of love was so strong she leaned against the doorframe for balance. It felt so easy.

She wanted him. The man who wanted more for her when she was afraid to want it for herself, who worshipped her mind as much as her body, who was just on the right side of cocky and lived his emotions as large as she did. Xander empowered her. He looked at her and saw her for who she truly was. Though her mind could come up with plenty of reasons to decline, Cecilia had always been victim to the whims of her heart.

"Yes. I'll marry you."

Xander kissed her hand.

"Thank gods, because I already ordered the seamstress to make you a dress, and it was quite expensive on such short notice." He stood, releasing her hand. "All right, love. The seamstress will be up momentarily, and Teddy will come to get you later tonight. Sena will stop by to help you with your hair."

"All right."

Xander was quiet for a moment.

"Cece, I love you."

"I love you, too."

Even though things were moving much more quickly, a strange calm settled in Cecilia's bones.

———

It took the seamstress and three of her apprentices the entire day to make the dress. The fabric was the typical icy light blue of all Olney wedding dresses. It was a detail that touched Cecilia's heart. The sleeves draped off the shoulder, and the bodice and skirt had an organza overlay embellished with hundreds of tiny white flowers in intricate swirls.

When Cecilia put it on, she felt like a princess for the first time. Her hair hung loosely around her shoulders in curls, but the front had been twisted back from her face. She'd never felt more beautiful in her whole life, and to add to her calm, Magdalena had stopped by earlier in the day and removed her Unsummoner bracelet and healed the raw skin of her wrist.

Cecilia had no intention of using her magic and solidifying the exchange she made in the Cave of Longings, but it was a relief to be able to sense it again.

"Prince Xander sent presents and a note," Sena said.

Cecilia opened the box. In it were dozens of small white, star-shaped flowers; a beautiful silver, sapphire, and pearl hair comb; and a bird-shaped note that she carefully unfolded.

––––––

My Love—

Here are some stars for my Moon Goddess. These flowers are called Stellaspo Tenebiso. It's an Old Argarian word, but it translates roughly to a "hope in the dark." They always make me think of you and the night we met. The fairy tales say they only grow on the old battlefields where a cause felt especially hopeless, and many fell believing in their cause, anyway.

You are my hope in the dark. When I saw you in the moonlight by the river, I felt like I was shocked back to life. I never wanted love, but before I even understood what was happening, I was falling for you, and I never stopped. You brought hope back to me when I thought I lost it, and you make me believe in the impossible.

The flowers are said to bring good fortune to a marriage, so they are an Argarian wedding tradition. I thought you could put them in your hair or your bouquet or whatever you want. (Look at that! I'm already giving up trying to tell you what to do.)

The other present is on loan from my mother. She said that she under-

stood Olney tradition requires something old, something new, something borrowed, and something blue. This is old, borrowed, and blue, and she wore it on her wedding day. I believe she wanted you to know that she approves of you.

I can't wait to see you. I know you are going to be so beautiful it will probably stop my heart, so please do your best not to kill me.

Love, Xander

—————

Cecilia looked up at Sena, blinking back tears.

"That's so romantic," Sena swooned.

"It is," she said, dabbing her eyes.

"Oh! Don't cry. You'll get all puffy," Sena chided.

"I know," Cecilia laughed, fanning her face and trying to get a grip on her emotions.

Sena placed the comb and then took her time tucking the flowers through Cecilia's hair.

There was a knock on the door, and they heard Teddy's voice. Sena let him in.

"You look like a princess," Teddy said. "Are you ready?"

She nodded and took his arm. She tried to keep her breathing even and calm as they walked. The castle was so quiet late at night. When they reached the main hall, they ducked into a secret passage, with Sena trailing behind them. They followed Teddy through the passage's twists and turns until they reached the ground floor kitchen exit. They crossed the courtyard quickly and wound down behind the old cemetery along the cliffside. Castle Savero was poised precariously on the steep cliffs high above the Bay of Endros.

Waves crashed against the rocks far below the path, and Cecilia looked out at the way the full moon shimmered on the water. It reminded her of the night she met Xander by the river.

Finally, they reached an old temple on the bluffs.

"Wait here," Teddy said as soon as they stepped into the vestibule.

"Don't come out. Xander will kill me if he sees you before you're coming down the aisle."

Sena fussed with her dress, and a moment later, the door of the chapel slid open a crack, and Rainer sneaked through. He stopped in his tracks like he'd been stunned.

"Rain!" Cecilia threw her arms around him, and he pulled her into a tight hug. He drew back to look at her.

"Gods, Cecilia, you've never looked more beautiful," he breathed.

Her heart fluttered, and she felt so overwhelmed. She wanted to cry all over again.

He must have seen it on her face. "Don't cry. This is a happy day for you."

For you. Did that mean it wasn't for him? She wanted to say something, but she couldn't bring herself to speak. Her eyes raked over his freshly shaven face, neatly combed hair and intricately embroidered tunic that was clearly borrowed from Xander. The fabric pulled tight over Rainer's chest and arms, though he seemed unbothered by the poor fit as he stared at her.

"You are my best friend and the person who I care about most in the world." Rainer's voice broke. He fought to hold himself together. "I will always do what's best for you. I know you think I hate Xander, but I'm coming around."

"He has that effect on people."

She felt torn. A part of her still wanted Rainer to tell her not to marry Xander. Standing there, the love for him she'd buried came surging to the surface. Some reckless part of her held out hope that Rainer would come around, even after all this time, even though she loved Xander.

She had always thought love was a simple thing. You loved someone, or you didn't, and you could only love one person at a time, but she was recognizing how naïve she'd been. Love was much more complex. She thought her heart was divided between them, but perhaps it had simply grown to contain more. She could barely breathe as Rainer spoke again.

"So it seems," Rainer said begrudgingly. "That's not what I wanted to say, though. I know that nothing I could say would deter you because you are a smart and passionate person who always goes after what she wants. Cece, I have always admired that about you, and I'm glad you've stuck to it. I know you think I don't pay attention and that I never cared about love, but I was always fascinated by what made people think they could spend their entire lives together."

Cecilia swallowed hard. Rainer took her hand in his, brushing his thumb over the inside of her wrist.

"I wanted to know how they could be certain in the face of the unknown. I said something about it to my mother once, and she said that no one is ever certain. They take what they know and what they feel, and they try to make the best choice based on that, and every day you decide to keep loving that person. I see the way you are with Xander. I see what he's done to make you happy, even when everything is falling apart. A good marriage is really about finding someone who will make the best of bad situations with you. That's where you really get to see what someone is made of. Xander spent the day planning this for you and is risking getting into a lot of trouble to make you happy."

Cecilia nodded, trying to clear the overwhelming emotions that clamped down on her throat.

Ask me to wait. Ask me to run. Ask me to be with you.

She tried to brush the unwelcome thoughts away, but the part of her that had been in love with Rainer for so long had deep roots. She tried to convince herself loving him was a product of the magic that bonded them together. Magic had already spoiled so many good things in her life. Loving him was a bad habit—one she needed to break herself of if she wanted to be happy.

She was about to marry someone else, and she deserved joy.

"I'm saying that I think, whatever happens, Xander will put you first, and I guess that's something I can get behind," Rainer said. He sounded sincere, but apprehension snaked through their bond.

He pulled Cecilia into another hug and kissed the top of her head.

"Are you ready?" he asked, offering her his arm.

She tried not to think about the fact that she had only ever imagined him waiting at the end of the aisle for her. She tried for a moment not to want him.

It didn't work. The love she felt for Rainer was impossible to ignore, even with someone wonderful waiting for her, but she'd made her decision. All she had to do was move forward and accept it.

Cecilia took a deep breath, and she let go of Rainer in her mind. She released him. She pushed him out of her heart to make room for someone else who wanted to take up that space.

"Yes. I'm ready," she whispered.

"Not just yet," a voice from behind them said. There in the doorway, bathed in moonlight, stood Queen Juliana.

29

The silver light of the moon illuminated Queen Juliana's plain servant's clothing. She'd clearly disguised herself to be there.

"Your Majesty?" Cecilia said, curtseying.

"You didn't really think I would miss my son's wedding, did you?" Juliana asked. "I understand it's an Olney tradition for the mother of the bride to walk her down the aisle."

Cecilia nodded. Rainer stared slack-jawed at the queen.

"I know your mother has passed, but I wouldn't want my daughter walking down the aisle without a woman who cared about her happiness and wished her the best," Juliana said, taking Cecilia's arm.

Rainer backed away, ducking into the temple. Sena fussed with Cecilia's dress and then looked at them expectantly.

"I'm ready," Cecilia said, hoping that saying the words would make them true.

She felt like she was in a fairy tale. Despite the immensity of her loss. Despite the grief that seemed to be her constant companion now. She was happy.

"Don't forget to look at his face when he sees you," Juliana whispered.

Sena slid the door open to the beautiful temple. Behind the altar, moonlight streamed in through the glass windows, and Cecilia could faintly hear the waves crashing on the cliffs far below them. They'd lined the short aisle with flowers and candles that cast a warm glow through the dim temple.

And there, at the end of the aisle, was Xander Savero, the Storm Prince—a man she'd willed herself not to love, but her stubborn heart had proven immovable. He looked painfully handsome in a navy tunic and pants, with his dark hair neatly combed and his hazel eyes locked on her.

Xander looked stunned—like he'd turned to stone. He didn't move, didn't blink, didn't breathe. Cecilia walked toward him, trying to commit every detail of the moment to memory: the beautiful temple, the thoughtful gifts, but most of all, the way Xander looked at her like she made his world stop.

When she finally reached him, Juliana kissed both of their cheeks and then placed Cecilia's hand in his.

Finally, Xander spoke. "Cece, you look beautiful on a normal day, but tonight there are no words that do you justice."

He kissed her as if no one else was there. Rainer cleared his throat.

"It's not time for that yet," Rainer whispered.

Xander reluctantly pulled away. "I'm sorry. I couldn't help it."

Rainer started the ceremony by binding their hands together. He said the traditional Olney opening blessing. Cecilia could barely concentrate. She was nervous about remembering what she wanted to say. Everything she'd come up with didn't seem right. The words seemed too small and trite. Xander squeezed her hands as if to remind her to relax.

When they finally reached the vows portion, she took a deep breath and spoke. But she didn't say the words written on the paper she'd worked on all day. Instead, she shared the words that came to her at that moment.

"Xander, I choose you today and every day, not because you are the easy choice but because you're the hard one. You have always pushed me to pay attention to what I want instead of what everyone else expects of me, and now we're standing here getting married, so I feel like maybe listening to you was a mistake."

Xander laughed.

Cecilia continued, "I'm here today not because I need to be but because I want to be. You see me exactly as I am. You've pushed me to be myself, and you won't accept anything less. You haven't assigned me your own wants or desires or made me feel inadequate. You loved who I was in the dark when I was afraid to step out into the light. Despite all of my best efforts not to, I love you. A wise man once told me that a good marriage requires finding someone who can make the best of a dire situation with you. You have done that every day since we met. So today, I promise to love you, fight with you and for you, and to do my best to make the best of all of our bad situations." She slid the ring onto Xander's finger.

Xander swallowed thickly, his eyes shining in the candlelight. She brushed her hand over his cheek, and he kissed her palm.

"Gods, you always have to outdo me, don't you?" Xander swallowed hard. "Cecilia, I've heard yes all my life. When you're born a prince, you get used to hearing that word, but the first thing you ever said to me was no. Actually, it was 'no, that's stupid,' and since then you've continued to push back against all of my nonsense."

She grinned as he continued.

"You make me want to be a better man. You make me want to listen, but best of all, you see me as I am. Even after I betrayed you and broke your heart, you forgave me. You taught me to forgive myself when I thought I never could. You're so compassionate, and you care so much about everything. I don't know how you don't sleep all the time from the weight of it all, but I love winding you up and watching you go off. You're the person I want to fall asleep with every night and wake up with every day. You're the only person I want to go on adventures with, and, gods, do you make me laugh. I am so unworthy of the love and understanding you have given me, but I promise to try as hard as I can every day for the rest of our lives to deserve it. I promise to love you through whatever storms may come, to comfort you, to treat you as my equal in all things, and to do my best to give you everything you could ever want."

Xander slid the ring onto Cecilia's finger and kissed their bound hands. She blinked back tears.

"Let no one break the bond you've made here today in front of these witnesses," Rainer said, the words tying their binds in a bow. "May the gods bless this union and make it fruitful. May they bring abundance to your doorstep, ease to your days, and peaceful rest to your evenings."

Rainer unbound their hands and handed each of them one end of the tie.

"It's up to both of you to keep your end secured. The world may try to rip you apart. You may want to let go. But it's always going to be up to you to keep the bond alive," Rainer said, looking from Xander to Cecilia. "Do you promise to hold on to that bond and not let go?"

"I do," they said in unison.

"Then, by the power granted to me by the Olney Monarchy, I now pronounce you married. You may kiss," Rainer said.

Xander pulled Cecilia into his arms and kissed her in a way that was not at all appropriate for a temple, but she was so happy, she didn't care. Their small entourage clapped.

She looked around the moonlit temple, and her heart was so full she didn't mind that the world she'd known had burned to the ground.

She ceased to care that the girl she'd been no longer existed. She just wanted to be *this* girl now—one who gave herself over to love, even when she was afraid, even when there were reasons not to, even when it felt impossible.

Love was the last hard thing worth having. Love was something she didn't mind being bad at. Love was the thing that grasped her hand when she stood on the edge of the abyss of her grief and pulled her back, kissed her softly, and helped her lay down her burdens.

Xander hugged his mother. Rainer hugged Cecilia, and then he kissed the top of her head before he disappeared with Evan, Sena, and Teddy.

"Go wait outside, dear," Juliana said to Xander.

Queen Juliana took hold of Cecilia's hands. "I always wanted a daughter, but I had so many complications with Alexander, I could never conceive again. I hope we'll have a relationship. You seem well suited to each other, and I expect you'll have a good marriage. I only have one thing to ask."

"What's that?" Cecilia asked.

"He's always been a reckless boy, and seeing him today—seeing both of you this way—he will always put your safety first. He will do anything to save you. I know he would lay down his life to protect you, but I beg you, please don't let him. Being royal means that you'll always be a target. Even from my Davide. He's my son, and I love him, but he is power-hungry and manipulative. Endros, maybe even Cato, have clouded his sweet disposition. Please be careful where Alex isn't. He hides a tender heart behind all that charm. Don't let him fool you."

Cecilia nodded.

"And Cecilia, I know I'm not your mother, but if she were here today, I think she would want you to know that you look beautiful. I'm sure she'd be incredibly proud of you. I think that she'd be happy that you married for love. It's a rare thing for women in our world."

Cecilia nodded and blinked back tears as the queen gave her a hug. At that moment, she missed her mother fiercely.

She stared at the simple gold band on her left hand as they walked down the aisle. It was strange that something so small could be so significant. From one moment to the next, her future was tied to someone, and yet she didn't feel trapped as she'd feared she would. She just felt overwhelming love.

Xander and Evan were waiting for them when they stepped out into the night. Evan took the queen's arm and led her back toward the castle.

Xander took Cecilia's hand and led her up a path that wove in the opposite direction.

"Where are we going?" she asked.

"Evan thought we could use a little privacy for the evening after you were so vocal the other day. There are old high priestess quarters over here that have been converted into a guest suite for visiting dignitaries," Xander said.

"But won't we be expected to be in our rooms?"

"Cece, if you think there is any way that I am letting you out of my sight when you look this beautiful, you're crazy."

The small building came into view, and she ran up to it, about to open the doors, when Xander swept her up into his arms and carried her across the threshold. He placed her back on her feet and barred the door, and only then did she turn and see the enormous wall of glass overlooking the sea far below the cliff's edge.

"Gods," she whispered. Through the wall of windows, she could see the full moon's silver path cutting across the waves.

"Do you like it?" Xander asked.

She walked toward the glass, taking in the view.

"It's stunning. I've never seen a window this big. It's the entire wall. It puts my cottage to shame." She turned around and found Xander staring at her. "What?"

"It's just you, in that dress, in the moonlight, as my wife—it's perfection."

She smiled at him, and he wrapped his arms around her and spun her around so they could both look at the view.

This is what love does. It opens you up to happiness that feels like your heart could burst, she thought.

Xander kissed up her shoulder and neck. She leaned into him, overwhelmed by the sensations in her body. "Thank you for today. I can't even tell you what it meant to me. There really aren't words for it." She craned her neck to look at him, tears welling in her eyes.

"Oh, love, I didn't want to make you cry." He kissed away each tear.

"No, they're happy tears. I wasn't lying when I said I'd never thought about my wedding until the day you asked me in the cabin. I hadn't even considered it. No one asked what I wanted, and it wasn't a priority, and today was what I didn't even know that I wanted. I couldn't have dreamed of something more beautiful or meaningful to me."

She turned to look at Xander, pressed to her tiptoes and kissed him.

"So what do we do now?" she asked.

"Well, I don't know about the Olney traditions, but with the Argarian tradition, usually the bride and the groom consummate their marriage," Xander said with a wink.

"Oh?"

He spun her around, gathering the hem of the dress. "Gods, this dress has about a thousand buttons. We might have to go for a shortcut."

"But what if I have something pretty on underneath this dress?" She laughed, batting his hands away.

He raised an eyebrow at the prospect. "That's intriguing, but I suspect there's nothing as pretty as your skin, love."

She flushed as he laid her back on the bed. He gathered the skirt and drew it up, kissing up her inner thighs. He froze.

"Cece?"

"Yes?"

"There's nothing under here."

She giggled. "That's what I was trying to tell you."

He peered up at her from over the layer of silk and tulle with a huge smile. "What a very pleasant surprise."

Before she could say anything, he dove back between her legs, and she squealed. Each stroke of his tongue sent a fresh wave of pleasure through her. She squirmed as the tension built quickly within her. He was so exceptionally good at it.

She breathed in quick gasps as the tension coiled inside of her. Xander's hands pressed her hips to the bed, forcing her to stay still as tiny shocks shot through her. Her whole body was charged and waiting to explode, the wet slide of his tongue sending her over the edge. She screamed his name as the tension burst into a million little sparks of pleasure. When she finally stopped shaking, Xander smiled up at her.

"Let's get that dress off," he said, helping her back to her feet. Her legs still felt shaky, but she stood still as he worked on the buttons.

"Godsdammit! This is going to take an hour," Xander said. He kissed her neck, pulling her against him, and then she could feel him hard against her.

"I guess good things come to those who wait."

He settled back to the task of undoing the buttons. "I know we have the benefit of being alone tonight, but I have to give an answer in the morning for who you'd like to witness our consummation tomorrow. Have you given any more thought to who you'd be comfortable with?"

Cecilia met his eyes in the window reflection. Her mouth went dry thinking about someone watching them. It was less the nudity than the intimacy that made her uncomfortable. "I don't know anyone here."

"I could ask my mother—"

"How will I ever face her again if you ask her?" Cecilia said, her cheeks burning just from thinking about it.

The only person she knew in the entire kingdom was locked in the tower as a prisoner, and thinking about Rainer watching her made her feel a whole different type of heat.

"Personally, I'd love to keep the sight of you to myself, but it will go a long way in people accepting the legitimacy of the marriage." Xander muttered a curse as he fumbled with the buttons. He had made little progress. "Are you terribly attached to this dress?"

"You are out of your mind if you think I'll let you harm this masterpiece," she said.

Xander laughed and went back to the buttons. Finally, he reached a point where she could shimmy out of the dress, and she stood before him in the moonlight.

"This reminds me of the first night I kissed you." He smiled.

"I wasn't naked then," she said.

"Yes, but I could see almost everything I can see now."

"And you stared like you're doing right now."

"Is that a problem?" he asked.

"No, I would simply prefer that you stop staring at me and do something."

Xander laughed as he tugged off his shirt and pants.

"Something like this?" he asked, sweeping her up so her legs wrapped around him as he pressed a long kiss to her lips.

"That's a good start, but I'd like more," she whispered.

He grinned at her and then bent forward. He was inside her before they even hit the mattress. She gasped at the familiar fullness. He rocked against her, and she met each movement. She felt familiar lightning weaving through her, from her heart through her veins, and then on and on down her body. It seemed to pass between them like a crackle through the air. She wanted to lose herself in the moment and the overwhelming sensation of him. It felt so good to stop pretending, to use the energy she'd spent trying to hate him to love him instead.

"I love you, Xander."

"I love you, Cece." He kissed her tenderly.

When he pulled back, they both found a new urgency. Their hands were everywhere, frantically trying to touch more. She pressed harder against him as he drove into her, eager for more. She wanted to be completely connected to him. Something strange and supernatural seemed to be happening.

Once again, she felt like she had called in lightning from all over the world, and all at once, they both tensed, and the lightning sensation struck them both. They were left panting and clinging to each other. In their time together, she'd never felt anything so powerful and intense. Her legs trembled as she tried to slow her heartbeat.

Xander wove his fingers through her hair, kissing her slowly. The air still crackled around them like it did before a storm, and when he touched her cheek, there was a little spark.

"What was that?" he asked.

She shrugged.

"Just magic, I guess," he whispered.

She wondered if it was the storm in both of them bouncing off one another. Magic recognizing magic. Like calling to like. Was that why she always felt like there was lightning whipping through her when she was with him?

He lay down next to her, pulling her into his arms. "So far, I really like being your husband."

"So far, I really like being your wife, but you have plenty of time to make me regret it," she teased.

"Oh, love, any part of my heart and soul that weren't yours are now." Xander sighed.

She giggled. "You're so dramatic."

"You think I'm joking, but I am definitely not, love. That was incredible."

She flushed at the compliment. Nothing took the edge off of the bottomless want they had for each other.

Clearly he'd been holding some part of himself back in case she changed her mind and backed out. Now that she was his, every bit of self-control Xander had was gone. Cecilia also felt herself let go of whatever control she'd been clinging to.

She was Xander's, and he was hers. So each time he woke her as the night wore on, she was happy to indulge him.

"I think you're going to kill me," Xander mused, flopping down beside her. "I'm going to die from wanting you too much or being too happy. Is that possible? It feels like it is."

"There are worse ways to go," she said as her eyes fluttered closed.

The weight of her exhaustion finally pressed down on her, stronger than the desire for more. He scooted closer to her, running his fingers idly over her collarbone.

As they lay there for a long time talking, Cecilia felt satisfied and even a bit excited for the future. Any doubt that had entered her mind earlier that day was gone. She wove her fingers into Xander's, the moonlight shining on her wedding band. No matter what obstacles they faced, she knew Xander would be on her side.

30

Urgent kisses roused Cecilia from a heavy sleep. First along her collarbone, then up her neck, to her lips, as she finally blinked her eyes open.

"Wake up, love. I know you hate the early morning, but I need to show you something." Xander kissed her forehead, and then her eyelids, and then her lips. She frowned at him in the dark.

"It isn't past ten. I'm not getting up," Cecilia groaned. "I need my beauty sleep."

"No, you absolutely do not," Xander murmured against her shoulder. "You're already much too beautiful. If you get any prettier, it might kill me. I promise you don't even have to get out of bed, but if you don't open your eyes and sit up soon, you will miss it."

Cecilia sighed heavily. Satisfied exhaustion pressed on her, but she sat up. Through the glass, the sun was about to rise on the horizon. Dawn painted the room in the lilac shade of first light.

"I thought you'd like to watch the sunrise. Before you yell at me, I already made you a cup of tea, and it's loaded with a truly alarming amount of sugar and some lemon and mint, just the way you like."

She grinned as he handed her the cup of tea and sat down behind her. He wrapped his arms around her and kissed her bare shoulder.

They watched color scatter across the sky as she sipped her tea. It reminded Cecilia of one of her mother's paintings of an abstract sunrise. The spectacular view and the beauty of the morning took her breath away. They watched the scene play out in silence, and Cecilia felt contentment like she never felt before.

Xander stood suddenly, taking her empty teacup away and turning toward her. "Are you mad at me for waking you, love?"

"A little," she said.

His face drew into an exaggerated frown. "Oh dear. It seems I've already upset my wife. That's not a good start. How can I make it up to you?"

Hearing him call her his wife sent a thrill through her.

"Perhaps just apologize. You should probably familiarize yourself with the concept."

"No, that's not it. I know—"

With no warning, he yanked her to the edge of the bed and knelt down between her legs, dropping his mouth between her thighs. She let out a surprised curse.

He laughed. "I don't think that is a word princesses should say."

"And you are a paragon of princely behavior?" she panted.

Xander arched a brow. "If this isn't princely behavior, I don't want to be a prince."

He went back to work until she moaned his name and ran her fingers through his hair. It didn't take long before she cried out as her climax ripped through her. Xander kissed her inner thighs and pushed her back on the bed, moving over her.

"I've been thinking about doing this for hours," he whispered. As he settled himself between her legs, there was a knock on the door.

"Not a good time. I'm trying to get very intimately acquainted with my wife, Evan!" he shouted, kissing Cecilia.

"I'm sorry, Xan, I wouldn't be here if it wasn't extremely urgent," Evan said through the door.

Xander sighed heavily. He hopped up from the bed, tossing Cecilia a robe and shrugging into his own.

"What is it?" Xander asked, opening the door.

Evan walked in.

"Apologies." He nodded at Cecilia. "Good morning, Princess."

"What's going on?" Xander asked impatiently.

Evan looked around nervously. "There's no delicate way to say this. Your parents are dead."

All the air seemed to rush out of the room.

"What?" Xander stared at his friend.

"A maid found them this morning."

Time seemed to stall. Cecilia couldn't keep up with the twists and turns of the past few days. She placed a hand on Xander's back to steady him.

He looked pale and lost. His face was unreadable. "This has to be Endros's doing."

"My spies say it was your brother's doing, though it could certainly have been directed by the god of war. If Endros was already at odds with your father on how to deal with Cecilia," Evan said. "The timing of it on your wedding day makes me suspect Davide isn't acting alone."

Cecilia stared at Xander wide-eyed. His brother was clearly violent. He'd broken her hand. But the thought that he could actually kill his own parents sent a chill through her.

"He planted evidence to make it seem like Rainer did it. Though that may benefit us since we broke him out of the tower. You know what this means, Xan," Evan said.

Xander cursed under his breath. "It means Davide is king, and he's willing to eliminate any threat to the throne."

"And you're the biggest one right now. We need to get both of you out now," Evan said.

"But we aren't a threat," Cecilia insisted.

Xander took her face in his hands. "My love, you and I both know that, but Davide only speaks one language, and that's power. I am the only other one with a legitimate claim to the throne. He sees you as a threat because you are a goddess who loves me."

"It goes beyond that." Evan gave Xander a pointed look. Something unspoken passed between the two.

Xander met her eye again. "Davide doesn't know that we are married, and he's the king. He could choose not to recognize our marriage."

There was something he wasn't saying, but her mind was spinning too fast to puzzle it out.

"What Xander isn't saying, because he doesn't want to worry you, is that if Davide wants you for himself, as he did with the original plan, we wouldn't be able to stop him from taking you or anything else he wanted," Evan said solemnly.

The words made Cecilia's blood run cold. She was no stranger to the type of violence Evan suggested. Every woman in the two kingdoms, and likely the rest of the world, was aware of that specific brand of savagery. She'd seen the echoes of it in women in Olney when she volunteered at the healer's clinic. It was the reason her father had been so insistent that she learn how to fight in the first place.

If Davide caught her, she'd be forced to lose. She would never allow that type of harm to befall her, which meant that she'd be forced to use her powers, solidifying another loss. Either way, she would sacrifice something she couldn't get back.

"Where will we go? What about Rainer?" Cecilia asked.

"Rainer is waiting for us with Teddy and the horses. They are the only two people I trust to make this journey with us. As for where we will go—I expect you would still be welcome in Olney, Cecilia. Perhaps you can ease the way for your new husband," Evan said.

She nodded, and Xander's brow pinched.

"Not that I want to be king, but can I really leave our people in Davide's hands knowing what we know about him and Endros now?" Xander asked.

Evan shook his head. "I don't like it either, but if we're dead, we can do nothing to help. Our best chance is seeking help from Olney. Assuming, of course, they don't kill us on sight."

"How much time do we have?" Xander asked.

Evan's mouth formed a grim line. "Not much. You two should get dressed quickly."

"The only thing I have is my wedding dress, and I can't ride in that," Cecilia said.

"I had Sena pack for you." Evan handed her an absurdly large satchel, and she ducked into the washroom to change.

Cecilia changed in a rush, braiding her hair as she emerged. Xander handed her a fur-lined cloak. She took one last longing look at her wedding dress, devastated that she couldn't bring it with her.

"I will find a way to get it to you in Olney. Don't worry." Xander tucked the dress into a closet by the door, and then they ran out into the morning sun.

Xander led her over to her horse and gave her a boost, then mounted his horse, and they were off. Cecilia was happy to be reunited with her bow and a quiver stuffed with arrows.

"We expect company soon, so be ready," Evan called over his shoulder.

"Remember, no magic, love," Xander reminded her. "I will take care of all the summoning."

She nodded. It felt good to ride again, but even the frigid air and the freedom of riding weren't enough to make her feel fully alert. She was exhausted and nervous about the journey. She kept looking over her shoulder to see if they were being followed.

"Incoming!" Evan yelled from the front.

They slowed. Over the horizon came a group of five hunters. Cecilia was ready. She fired off a shot, hitting the closest one in the eye. Xander matched her shot with another hunter, who went down quickly. Arrows arced through the air, and they all ducked. She came back up shooting, quickly taking out two more hunters. Evan killed the last one.

"You're an excellent shot, Princess. Xander understated your talent," Evan said.

"He's just jealous." Cecilia laughed.

"I have always asserted that my wife is a woman of many, *many* talents," Xander said, winking at her.

Heat rushed to her cheeks, and Evan rolled his eyes.

"Wait!" Cecilia shouted. "We should take their sweaters. They think they are looking for the prince and the princess and a couple of hunters, but we could disguise ourselves as Argarian hunters and blend in."

"I don't know if that would work," Rainer said skeptically.

"Think about it. Xander isn't at court often. Very few people know what he or I look like. Only the lords and ladies and a handful of hunters have been at the events this week," she said.

"It's not a bad idea, at least while we are this deep in Argaria," Evan said as he and Xander hopped down, pulling the sweaters off of the fallen hunters and tossing one up to each of them.

Cecilia stored her fancy cloak and rolled up the sleeves on the much-too-big sweater as she met her husband's eye.

"What?" she asked.

"I'd just forgotten for a moment how lovely you look in red," Xander said.

She rolled her eyes. "Is this really the time to flirt? You've already won me over."

"I told you before, I will always make time to flirt with you," Xander quipped.

"Are you two going to be like this the whole trip?" Rainer asked morosely.

Xander shrugged. "What do you expect, McKay? This is our honeymoon."

They rode for the rest of the day without incident. The few times they ran into hunters, their disguises held up, and no one really paid them any mind.

"There is a cabin coming up in the valley ahead where we can stay for the night," Xander said.

"How do you know?" asked Rainer.

Cecilia's cheeks heated, thinking about how Xander had made love to her on every surface in the place.

"We stayed there on the way to the Cave of Longings," Xander said, grinning at Cecilia.

By the time they reached the front door, a light snow was falling. Cecilia was exhausted. She hopped down from her horse, and her legs nearly buckled beneath her as she stumbled to the door.

As soon as they were safe inside, Rainer got to work starting a fire. Evan and Teddy took an inventory of their supplies and supplemented them with some he found in the cabin. Xander summoned a storm to lay down fresh snow and cover their tracks.

When he finally came back inside, he pushed Cecilia against the wall, kissing her with a ferocity that stole her breath.

Evan cleared his throat, and Xander drew back, resting his cheek, still cool from the icy mountain air, against hers.

"Just wanted to make sure you remembered you aren't alone," Evan said.

"I promise I'd have given her a far more scandalous greeting if I'd forgotten you were here," Xander said, tucking a kiss into Cecilia's neck before reluctantly pulling away.

She caught his hand in hers, noticing dry blood caked on his palm. "What happened to your hand?"

Xander shrugged. "I think I cut it when I was removing equipment from one of the hunters as we were leaving Argaria. I didn't have time to stop and check until now, though I'm sad to say, I ruined my favorite pair of gloves."

He tossed the oxblood leather gloves onto the table. Cecilia fumbled through her bag until she found her aid kit and pulled out a needle and thread meant for stitches, before grabbing the damaged glove and sitting down to mend it.

"Love, I did not know you would be so domestic. Here I thought you hated needlework," Xander said, his eyes lit with delight.

"I said I didn't like needlepoint, learning to stitch has its practical uses."

Xander sat down next to her and watched her work a line of even stitches in the thin leather until she'd mended it.

"There's something wonderful about you taking care of me like this," he whispered. "I know you like to be known for your sharp edges, my love, but don't hate me for enjoying the softer side of you as well." Xander brushed a kiss to her temple.

She languished in Xander's attention, surprised at how comfortable she felt in the role of wife. For all of her apprehension, she'd yet to feel stifled or trapped by her marriage to Xander. Despite the somewhat strange and urgent circumstances, she felt at ease with him.

She took Xander's hand. "Now let's fix you."

"But you can't summon to heal me," Xander argued.

"I'm not going to. *You* are."

He appraised her skeptically.

"Xander, if you are a storm witch, it's likely that you have the power to heal, too. Did you never learn?" she asked.

He shook his head.

"That's okay. I can try to teach you. In Olney, it's one of the first magics they teach witches, so it might take a couple tries, but you'll get it. It's not a serious wound, so you should be able to fix it easy enough." She cradled Xander's palm in hers, using alcohol and cotton to clean the wound. "So when you reach out to your storm magic, what do you feel?"

Excitement sparkled in Xander's eyes. "It feels like a prickling lightning feeling."

It was exciting to have a partner who understood how magic beat like a pulse through the body, how it felt both natural and other-worldly.

"For me, healing feels cool and tingly, like putting peppermint oil on the skin," Cecilia said. "You want to reach out for your magic and go past your storm magic to something that feels like that. Then you focus on the wound and imagine it knitting back together."

Xander's brow furrowed in concentration as he stared down at the wound. After a moment, he squinted, tilting his hand in the light to search for progress. He frowned when he found none.

"It's okay, try again," she whispered.

He focused and took a deep breath, his eyes narrowing on the wound. The edges of the cut gradually drew in toward each other until only a faint pink mark remained. Xander's eyes went wide in surprise.

"You did it! You'll need to eat extra tonight to make up for using all that energy, but as you get more practiced, you will learn to be more efficient," Cecilia said with a grin.

Xander swept her into a hug, spinning with her in his arms. "You are an excellent teacher, love."

She leaned into him, savoring his warmth. It was minor magic, and it would take him a while to master more complex injuries, but she understood his sense of triumph. Magic was exhilarating, especially when it was new. She closed her eyes and leaned her head on Xander's shoulder.

When she blinked her eyes open, she found Rainer watching intently. A crease formed in his brow, his mouth pinched in a grim line. She knew she shouldn't feel guilty for being affectionate with her husband. Rainer had all but tossed her in Xander's waiting arms. Still, she was hyperaware of how Rainer's shoulders hiked up to his ears every time Xander touched her.

Anger bubbled in her veins. Rainer had literally married her to someone else. He had a chance to speak up. She practically begged him to, and instead, he helped Xander plan a surprise wedding, so he had no right to be angry.

Clearly he didn't care what he had a right to, because as she pulled Xander into a kiss, a sharp spike of jealousy burst through their connection.

Cecilia drew back and rolled out her shoulders, as if she could shake off the guilt his reaction sparked. Her love for Rainer hadn't faded, so she locked it away in a hidden chamber of her heart and prayed it would disappear.

Rainer's gaze was a heavy weight on her shoulders as she moved around the cabin. She prayed Xander wouldn't notice. If he did, he was good enough to not say anything.

Xander seemed better able to compartmentalize than she and Rainer. Despite the loss of his family and the overwhelming shift in circumstances, he seemed remarkably focused as they settled into the cabin.

Later, after they'd eaten, Xander excused himself and walked out into the night. Cecilia followed. He stood in the clearing, staring up at the sky. His breath came out in little white puffs, and for a moment, she stared at how handsome he was. She smiled when he turned to look at her.

"If you want to be alone—" she started.

"I always want your company." He smiled.

She wrapped her arms around him from behind and slid her icy hands up the hem of his shirt.

"Can I put my hands here?" she whispered as he jumped.

"You can put your hands anywhere you like, love."

They were quiet for a moment, and she pressed her ear against his back, listening to his heartbeat.

"I know it's a silly question, but are you all right? You haven't said a word about your parents," she whispered.

"I don't know. It doesn't feel real. Maybe I should have seen it coming. I've always been outplayed by Davide, but I never thought he could do this. I'm disappointed in myself."

Cecilia moved around him so that she could see his face.

"My father loved chess," Xander started. "When we were young, he made us play all the time and not like a nice parent. He played to win and crushed us hundreds of times until we learned. I wanted to be good at it so badly. He loved it—said it was a king's game. It's all about strategy. Have you ever played?"

She nodded. Her father taught her when he was teaching her battle tactics from *Siege and Strategy*, a book on war games.

"Well, he made us play for hours. Sometimes against him or other elite players and then each other. Davide was always better, but I worked my ass off. I learned everything I could about the game, and I finally got to the point where I thought I could beat him. I was so close about ten times, and he would bait me and then crush me. It was demoralizing. All it did was remind me how ill-suited I am to rule, not that I wanted the responsibility. And the past few days have felt like that all over again. I feel like I'm twelve years old again, getting trounced by him. I might have always been the better soldier, but he's always been the strategist. He is always one step ahead. It's not just him. There's also Endros, the centuries-old god of war, whose goals seem to align with his. That's what truly terrifies me."

The pain in Xander's eyes broke Cecilia's heart. In one violent action, he'd lost both his parents and his brother. She threw her arms around him, and he picked her up into a hug. She held tight as he tucked his face into her neck. He stood there, crushing her body against his.

"I'm so sorry. I was very set on not liking your mother, but she was so kind it was impossible not to," she whispered.

"I suspect she was surprised how much she liked you as well," he said, leaning his forehead against hers.

"Is there anything I can do?" she whispered.

"Just having you here. Knowing that you understand the loss. That's a comfort I'm not sure I deserve." He kissed her, placing her back on her feet. "I need to give you something. After the ceremony last night, my mother gave me this. I was supposed to give it to you at our official wedding today. She wanted both of us to know that she approved. For you, it was showing up and walking you down the aisle, but for me, it was this."

He held up a beautiful diamond and sapphire ring.

"I know you don't know what it means. It's a family heirloom that's been passed from queen to queen through the generations. My grandmother didn't pass it to my mother until she had Davide. It was a very big deal for her to give it to me, so you could wear it. It means that you're my family now," Xander whispered, his voice rough with emotion. "My mother said you have a good heart—" His voice broke, and his eyes were glassy. "She said that you have a good heart and a forgiving nature and that the world will look at you like that makes you weak. They will take advantage of it, but I should never take it for granted."

Xander took her hand and slid the ring on her finger. "Even she could tell I didn't deserve you." He laughed and kissed her hand.

"Yes, you do," she said.

"I don't, but I'll never stop trying," he said.

She wrapped her arms around him and held him for a few long moments. The only sound was the wind in the trees on the edge of the clearing.

"Do you want to go back inside?" Cecilia asked.

"I thought maybe we could stay here and look at the stars for a few more minutes," he said.

She twisted in his arms, leaning back against him as they gazed up at the beautiful sparkling sky.

They lingered for a long time, Xander pointing out fake constellations and making up myths about them like he had when they were alone in the wild before. They stayed there until Cecilia swayed on her feet from fatigue and Xander's fingers were stiff and cold before going inside and falling asleep in a tangle of limbs.

———

Cecilia woke from a dream of an arrow lodged in Rainer's heart. She choked on a scream as she shot up in bed. Immediately, Xander was holding her. Evan looked over at her from his perch by the window.

"Something's wrong," she rasped. She looked around the room wildly for Rainer. She finally took a deep breath when she saw him looking back at her, his green eyes drowsy with sleep.

"What is it?" Rainer asked.

Cecilia closed her eyes and listened. "Death whispers. They're faint, but they're there."

"You can't summon," Xander said, panicked.

"I've always been able to hear them. I'm not summoning anything. I've just always been able to sense spirits and those whispers," Cecilia assured him. She listened again. It was subtle, but they'd definitely become louder and slightly more insistent.

She jumped to her feet. "We have to go."

They packed their supplies in a flash and rushed off as first light lifted the veil of darkness from the surrounding woods. They hoped to ride all the way through the Godswoods by nightfall.

Cecilia pulled on her fur-lined cloak to warm herself, though she knew the chill she felt wasn't from the cold. It was from fear. The death whispers faded behind her, but they left her with the distinct feeling that they could run as much as they wanted, but there was nowhere to hide.

31

The snow had stopped falling but still lay thick on the trail, making for a difficult morning ride. They finally stopped for a break in the late afternoon, the horses and their riders desperate for rest. They weren't making the time they hoped to, and the idea of resting in the Godswoods for the night instead of in Alstairs on the other side of them made Cecilia uneasy.

She was about to grab her canteen when an arm snaked around her waist, turning her before pushing her up against a tree. The kiss shocked her down to her toes as his hands wandered greedily over her body. When he finally pulled away, she was grateful for the tree behind her because she thought she might fall over.

"That was excessive," she mumbled.

"I promise, it wasn't. I'll show you excessive later, love." Xander winked.

"I think it's *excessive* how you kiss her like you've been separated for years instead of a couple of hours every time you get off your horse," Evan huffed.

"You don't have to watch, Evan," Xander quipped.

Evan crossed his arms. "Well, when you do it a foot off the trail, we kind of do because, clearly, you're not paying attention to anything except the princess's lips. Someone has to make sure you don't get one or both of you killed."

"I think that's the first time I've ever seen royals kiss. If that's how they do it, I guess I understand why I haven't seen it in public," Teddy teased.

Heat crept into her cheeks as Xander laughed. Rainer fussed with a map, his eyes snagging Cecilia's.

"I suggest not looking if you don't want to see me kiss my beautiful wife that way, because I'm never going to stop doing it. I'm the prince, and I'm in charge. What I say goes," Xander said.

"Technically, you're a refugee fleeing a coup," Rainer grumbled.

"That's fair, but I still can't help myself," Xander said.

Xander sat down with Teddy and Evan, discussing workable options for their route through the Godswoods, and Cecilia made her way over to Rainer.

"You okay?" she asked.

They hadn't spoken since the wedding. She'd hoped she'd feel different once she was married, but her heart was immovable, still fluttering when Rainer met her eyes.

"Yes," Rainer sighed. "This wasn't what I had in mind for you."

"What do you mean?"

He frowned, avoiding her eyes. "I thought marrying him would keep you safe, not make you more of a target."

"If you knew then what you know now, you would have told me to do something different?" she asked.

Rainer reached over and tucked a stray hair behind her ear. "I don't know."

Instead of feeling the conflict that she usually felt in their connection, she felt deep regret in him. She placed her hand on his.

"We chose the best option to get us home safely. All we can do is make the best of it now," she said.

He stared at her, his gaze dropping to her lips briefly. Desire pulsed through their bond. She froze. Teddy looked over at them at that exact moment, and she wrenched her gaze away from Rainer's as Xander sat down beside her.

Rainer cleared his throat, fumbling with the map. "So we'll be camping in the Godswoods tonight."

"As I recall, you quite enjoyed the ride through the Godswoods last time, love," Xander teased.

A flush rose to her cheeks as she remembered the way he'd pinned her up against the rock and kissed her.

"The Reflection Forest was tricky before, but when you passed through the Godswoods last time, you weren't a goddess," Rainer said. "Those woods have powerful magic. They say that the gods used to roam there, and their spirits still do. It might pull on you, Cece. They might try to bait you into summoning."

"I won't," Cecilia said plainly.

"You don't know that."

"I do," she said. Rainer sighed and gave up the fight.

As they settled in to eat, Teddy couldn't contain his excitement.

"I've always wanted to swim in the Adiran Sea. Is it true that the heat makes the sand on the beaches too hot to stand on?" he asked.

"It's true," Cecilia answered.

His enthusiasm lifted Cecilia's spirits. Although Teddy was twenty-five, he had a youthful exuberance and wanderlust that made him seem younger. It became clear quickly that although the circumstances of their trip were bleak, Teddy could make the best of any situation. He'd never left Argaria and thrilled in traveling farther than he ever had before.

"I've heard there are lemons the size of your head there!"

Teddy's smile warmed her heart. She was looking forward to showing him around Olney.

"There are. They make the best lemon cakes in the world," Cecilia said.

Teddy's eyes lit up as he asked her question after question about the small villages in the Olney outskirts. She told him about Olney City and the solstice and equinox festivals.

Cecilia found his constant questions a relief. It was the only thing that kept her mind from Rainer's words and the death whispers. She made an excuse about needing to refill her canteen and walked off toward the stream. Despite eating, she felt shaky and tired. The lack of sleep, the fear for Rainer's life, the hard ride, all of it pressed down hard around her, but she forced her feet to move one after the other.

When she got to the stream, she filled her canteen and sat on a nearby rock. She tipped her head back and closed her eyes, feeling disconnected. Summoning would focus her concentration and connecting with her magic always made her feel more calm.

She took a breath as she tried to clear her head. Instead she felt Rainer's proximity and turned to find him leaning against a tree a few yards behind her.

"Doing all right?" Rainer asked. He looked as tired as she felt.

"Just tired," she lied. *And lost and overwhelmed and happy and terrified all the time.* She hadn't even realized it until then, but loving Xander raised the stakes. It gave her one more thing to lose when she really couldn't afford it.

"I know something is bothering you. You don't have to tell me, but I want to remind you I'm here. And if you don't, I'll sit with you," he said as he sat down next to her.

"The last time I was really alone was the night I met Xander, when you left me alone to bathe. I've had no time to gather my thoughts. I have been reacting for weeks, and I feel exhausted. It's all pressing down on me now. I haven't even had time to process half of what's happened, and now we are going home. I'm going to have to face more people I love who have lied to me my whole life." She blinked away tears.

Rainer placed his hand on hers. When she looked at him, she saw her pain reflected in his eyes. Her immediate instinct was to make him feel better, but the wounded animal part of her wanted him to feel it. She wanted to reach out and take a swipe at anyone who had put her in this situation.

"Would you have done something differently?" Rainer asked.

The question surprised her. "I think I wouldn't have let us split up."

Rainer looked haunted. "I think that too. All the time."

"Rain, would you have told me what I was?" she asked. "I think I would have always felt the obligation to finish the Gauntlet. I spent my whole life thinking that magic was worth it, no matter the cost. I wanted to protect my father. Even at the moment I made the exchange, I decided it was worth it. But I never wanted the magic for myself. I wanted to help our people and be free, not be their savior." Her voice broke.

Rainer slid an arm around her, and she leaned her head on his shoulder. It felt comfortable, like coming home. His arms had been a shelter to her for as long as she could remember. They helped her off the ground at training, boosted her up rocky cliffs, and they spun her around the dance floor. He'd cleaned her wounds and wiped her tears. He'd also left her alone with Xander and let her walk into a trap.

The grief was wild. It tried to claw its way out of her chest. It threatened to surface right there in the middle of the woods.

"What does it feel like?" Rainer asked.

"All of my magic feels so different. Spellwork feels like outside magic—like it's coming from somewhere else and requires an external exchange like blood or hair. Summoning feels like inside magic, like I can pull the outside world elements in, or with memory use my own mind, but it runs off of my energy. I'm always aware of how much I'm using when I summon. I can feel it draining me. But this goddess magic feels like—" She paused, searching for the right words. "It feels like there's a vast energy source on the other side of a dark wall. But it doesn't feel like I'm borrowing from nature or my body. It's entirely mine. Even if I pulled the wall down, it feels like I'd be trying to funnel a river through a walnut shell."

Rainer gave her hand an encouraging squeeze as she continued.

"All witches have a sense for magical things. The same way I can feel a magical object or the spellwork at the caves, I can sense it in me now. Madame Costello, my summoning teacher, used to say this thing in class. She said there was a type of fear that was really just wisdom—smart scared, she called it. And she'd say a wise witch knows when to be the smart kind of scared. It's when you're confronted with something you have neither the will nor the training to control. That's what this feels like. Something too powerful for me to fathom. So I am smart scared."

Rainer's silence was frightening. She couldn't look at him, afraid she'd see the same fear on his face that she felt. It was one thing to be afraid of her own power, but it was something else entirely for Rainer to be afraid of her.

"Of course, Madame Costello also said I should have been smart scared about most of my summoning as a child, so maybe smart scared isn't such a bad thing for me to feel," she joked, trying to break the tension.

She finally met Rainer's gaze, and he opened their connection, sending calm through. "I've seen you do a lot of amazing things, Cece. You will figure this out."

His thumb stroked soothingly along the inside of her wrist over the fresh scar from her fight with Nessa. She didn't share Rainer's confidence, and she doubted he would sense the magic, but she was relieved that he didn't look the least bit afraid of her.

Rainer stood, helping her to her feet. "We should head back. We have a ways to go before nightfall."

They joined the rest of the group and took off into the afternoon.

As the shadows grew long, they finally entered Olney territory, tossing off their Argarian sweaters in anticipation of Olney patrols and warmer weather since they were out of the Argas Mountains. The benefit of not having to stop at a bunch of caves was that they could take a direct route back, and it went much faster than Cecilia had expected.

Since the kingdom's territories shifted along the neutral lands, there was no official marker for the boundaries between kingdoms, but Cecilia noticed the shift from Argaria to Olney. It was clear in the wildflowers that bloomed along the road's edge and the tinge of humidity that hung in the air. Even without being in Olney City, the brightness of the kingdom blossomed all the way out to its border villages. The trees were lush and bright in their greenery. In a day or two, they'd be close enough to smell the sea air. Cecilia hadn't realized how much she missed it until that moment.

As the sun set, they settled in to camp in a copse of trees in the Godswoods. On her first ride through with Xander she'd been so distracted, first by the adrenaline of having narrowly escaped a group of hunters, and then later by his kisses, that she'd missed the eerie beauty of the mystical forest. Ivy vines climbed up silvery tree trunks, winding their way through a lush canopy that occasionally dropped dead leaves that ground down to sparkling silver dust. The forest floor was littered with swirls of it that reminded her of a painting of the sea back in her cottage.

Cecilia's bubbling sense of anxiety had calmed to a steady whisper under a horde of warring emotions. Apprehension about finally facing her father back in Olney. Fear that she'd be letting the kingdom down if she didn't make her final exchange and use her goddess gifts to protect her home. But most of all she felt relief to finally be just a five-day ride from home and safety.

32

Cecilia's eyes shot open, certain that someone was calling her name. It took a moment to adjust to the darkness. She sat up, shocked to find herself alone in the same place on the forest floor where she'd fallen asleep. It instantly reminded her of Rainer's warning about the magic of the Godswoods.

She came to a crouch, searching the surrounding area, and had the distinct sense of not quite being asleep or awake, but somewhere between the two.

"Cecilia." The whisper came on a gentle breeze, the voice familiar.

She held completely still, straining to hear it again.

"Cecilia."

She jumped to her feet, dagger in hand as she followed the voice down a small trail away from their camp. As she crested a hill, she saw a man sitting down by the river. Both his presence and body were imposing. Silver threaded through his brown hair. He turned to look at Cecilia.

Even if she didn't recognize him from statues and paintings in Olney, she'd know who he was. Clastor, the god of all matter.

"Daughter." She walked toward him, and Clastor took her face in his hands. "You're all grown up."

"How is this possible?" she asked.

"This is the Godswoods, Cecilia. It's old magic—a liminal place for those of us who have ascended and moved on from the realm to move more freely," Clastor said.

Her eyes went wide with panic. "Am I using my magic?"

Clastor shook his head. "I suspect you know now that your birth mother was an ancient and powerful memory witch—Selene Carrick." Clastor's eyes got a faraway look in them. "She wasn't afraid of power, hers or mine. You were her idea. She wanted a child more than anything, even if she knew she wouldn't be here to see you grow. She wanted you to have everything, and she thought you had the best chance of bringing peace to the realm. When Cato suggested I leave some of my power in the caves of the Gauntlet, we thought it might be the best way to trick him into thinking I was weak, and also create an easy way to bind your power until you would be old enough to handle it. It would help hide you from Endros and Cato. That way, if we failed in the war, you'd still have a chance."

Cecilia rubbed her thumb along the inside of her wrist, trying to process his words. "Did you know you were both going to die?"

Clastor's eyes filled with grief. "I didn't, but your mother was close with Raven Whitewind, the same seer who bonded you with your guardian. I suspect Selene consulted her and didn't tell me. Otherwise, I don't think she would have made plans with Leo and Rosalee to take you. Selene and Leo were close, and she knew they had been struggling to conceive for several years. Leo was only second-in-command at that point, so he had a better chance at survival, and he ended up taking up the mantle in that last battle when so many of us fell."

He grew contemplative. "Selene assured Leo that most of your magic was bound and that any that showed up before you were of age and had completed the Gauntlet would be attributed to you being a witch."

Cecilia knew she should listen. She didn't know when she'd get another chance to learn about who she was, but she was furious.

"But you left me alone. I spent my whole life feeling like an outsider and not understanding why I felt so different."

Clastor grimaced. "I'm sorry. We didn't realize our mistake until later. Selene was so enamored with you, I was afraid she wouldn't let you go. Believe me, we didn't want to leave you. But Selene was adamant that it was the only way to protect you and Olney. It broke both of our hearts, but I wanted you to figure out who you were on your own before everyone's expectations were thrust upon you."

Cecilia sighed. "So you used Cato's promise to make it seem like the War of the Gods had long been over?"

Clastor nodded. "Gods are bound by the deals they make, so he had to. Little by little, everyone in the two kingdoms came to believe through his manipulation that the War of the Gods had happened centuries earlier than it did and the Gauntlet had been going on since. The only exceptions were King Hector Teripin and your parents, who knew the truth."

Apparently, Davide Savero had been telling the truth. The power to manipulate on such a grand scale astonished and terrified her.

"I wounded Cato in the battle, but his talent is unparalleled, and he had to follow through on his deal with me. This type of mythology takes root fast. Storytelling is powerful, as you well know. He started with the elders and historians and created a few 'ancient' books, and that was that. Everyone assumed all the older Gauntlet duos had perished in pursuit. It was tidy."

"Are humans that predictable?" Cecilia scoffed. "Even if there weren't generations of duos dying, there were still twenty-three years' worth killed by enemy hunters or accidents in the field."

"It was a calculated sacrifice to keep you safe and protect the future of Olney." Clastor paused, and his face softened. "You mustn't be angry with Leo, Cecilia. He thought he was protecting you by not telling you."

"Don't tell me how to feel," she snapped. The force of the words surprised her, and for a moment, she thought he might be offended, but he just laughed.

"You sound just like Selene." He chuckled. Then his face grew serious. "You're unwell. You should accept your goddess powers."

"I won't," she said firmly.

"Why not?"

"Because I can't pay the price for it."

"Power always comes at a price, Cecilia. You know this. All magic requires an exchange," Clastor chided.

"But this is one I cannot pay."

"It's because of Alexander Savero?"

It surprised her that it looked like Clastor disapproved.

"It's because they asked me to pay an impossible price without even knowing what I was buying," Cecilia said. "Everyone in my life lied to me, and I found out at the same time. I wanted to take back the choice that was taken from me."

"But not using your magic has made you weak," Clastor said. "It's why you feel so unwell. When a witch is cut off from their magic, it's painful. It's like a sickness, but there's no need to wither. You don't need to stop summoning. You have always been a witch, Cecilia. Summoning won't cost you that price you can't pay. Only reaching across and accepting your goddess gifts will. I'm sure you feel the difference."

She'd always thought about magic in terms of what it cost her and not what it did for her. Cecilia's last Gauntlet run had centered on her giving things up, but Clastor's words reminded her that her magic also gave back to her. It soothed her. It was familiar and vital to who she was. She hadn't realized how much until she was without it for so long.

"It feels like a dark wall with something terrifying on the other side," Cecilia whispered.

"A little fear is healthy. It shows you understand the responsibility."

She watched Clastor's face, looking for herself in his features, but the harshness in the fix of his jaw and brow made it difficult to see herself in anything but the color of his eyes.

"That goddess power will call to you. It will tempt you. You'll feel the bloodlust. There will be moments when you will feel it just beyond your grasp, and it will get harder to resist it. It's like an addiction when you try to fight it off. It will grow stronger until you accept it."

Panic clenched in her chest. "How will I change when I let it in?"

"You will feel it. Your body will buzz with it, and it will be hard to stop once you start. Your gifts are meant for war, and war is here. Do you fear them?"

"I fear the sacrifice. I never wanted immortality. I just wanted a simple life." She sighed.

"Life rarely gives us what we want. It gives us what we need."

Cecilia felt humiliated by the tears in her eyes, as if she were a petulant child throwing a tantrum.

Clastor frowned. "The prince will love you whether or not you can have children. He's already told you that. He's weak and foolish, but he loves you."

"Xander might be foolish, but he's not weak," Cecilia said.

"It's sweet that you love him, but he will never be your equal."

Her eyes narrowed on her father. *How dare he show up after years and tell me how to live my life?*

"I want him anyway."

Clastor sighed. "You know, we counted on your being half-human to ground you in this world and give you compassion, but I've always worried it would give you too much. You surprised me by not choosing your guardian. He's smart and compassionate. I thought he was a better match. Why do you think we made sure you had such a powerful connection? I told your father to pair you with the kind one."

The kind one. Rainer. The words pulled back the memory of when she'd first met him, and it filled her with a longing so strong she was worried it might tug on their bond and wake him.

"Well, if that was your plan, you should not have picked such a rule-follower," Cecilia said bitterly.

"It's okay to love them both. I have loved many at once. You may take after your dear old father."

"I'm *nothing* like you." Her words were full of venom. The rage and hurt that lived deep in her heart sprung to life.

"You're more like me than you think, Cecilia. When your mother died, it broke my heart. We'll be separated forever, me in the Otherworld with the gods and her in the Underworld with the humans. I made you as you are so you'd have the power to save the ones you love."

"I don't want to be special or immortal. I just want to be with him." Even as Cecilia said the words, she wasn't certain which *him* she meant.

"Don't be silly. You'll still be mortal, but without aging. You'll live a much longer life and be much harder to kill, but not impossible," Clastor said crossly.

"And how did you feel living without my mother?"

Clastor's face softened, and he ran a hand through his hair. He looked like he was fighting some internal war with himself. She sighed.

"I'm sorry," he whispered. Clastor looked defeated. "I didn't mean for it to be this way."

"Then help me now. Tell me there's a way out. My husband wants —I want children."

She'd not even admitted it to herself. It felt like too much to say out loud. Now that she had, it felt like a wish lost to the wind.

"I'm sorry. I wish it could be another way. I knew there would be a price to the magic since you had to earn your magic, unlike the rest of us who were born into this world with all of our gifts. The witches were in charge of the exchange, and they did not explain to me what it would cost. If there was a way out, I swear I would tell you, but I don't know one. Your mother was the strategist, so while I'm sure she had her reasons, she didn't share them with me. You can hold it off for a while, but eventually, the call of that goddess power will be too much, even for your stubborn nature. Power calls to power. You can't be that close to it and not reach out to touch it. It's in our nature to take that which calls to us. You know well the way your summoning power calls to you. The ache you feel without it now is what it is to have that within reach and not grasp it."

Tears streamed down Cecilia's cheeks. She sighed in frustration. Everything was happening to her. She wanted to be proactive, but all she'd been able to do so far was react to terrible circumstances.

"I never wanted power."

"You did," Clastor started. "We gods hear wishes, you know. And when you were watching the meteor shower at the beginning of your trip, you wished for the power to make your own choices. The world has taught you that, as a woman, you don't deserve power. This world has taught you that you only deserve it if it suits someone else's agenda, but you were born for power. You wanted the power to make a change in the world. You have the will to use it. Don't be ashamed. Power is your birthright. The world will try to make you forget that. You must remember it always."

Cecilia sighed, wringing her hands in frustration.

Clastor pressed on. "Cecilia, the dagger that you carry is a gift from me and Selene. It is a Godkiller, blessed with a special spell. It can kill any living gods, but if the moment comes and there's a loss you truly cannot survive, you can have the one you can't live without stab you through the heart. You will die, but they will live. And then you will ascend to be with your real family and me. I would prefer that you live a long and happy life, so think hard before making such a sacrifice."

Cecilia nodded, overwhelmed by the information. That explained why Leo had been so adamant about her keeping it on her all the time.

"Be careful with Endros, the god of war, and his son, Cato, god of manipulation and influence. Be vigilant. Don't try to outmaneuver Cato. You won't succeed. Let him outmaneuver himself. And as for Endros, his biggest weakness is the same as all fighters, his hubris."

She stared at Clastor, trying to absorb the idea of two gods conspiring against her.

"I have to go now, but I and your siblings will be watching over you. You can call on us when you need our help, and where we can, we will. However, we need to keep the balance in the world, so our powers as ascended gods have their limitations in this realm. All of us combined are less powerful than you are here. Use your wisdom and compassion. Those were your mother's gifts."

He stood quickly and kissed the top of her head, and then disappeared into a puff of mist.

Something broke open in Cecilia, and she was pulled back into the abyss that had existed since the Cave of Longings. She felt powerless to stop the momentum of her life. She pulled her knees into her chest and cried for all she was helpless to stop herself from losing.

33

It took Cecilia most of the day's ride to calm down from her run-in with Clastor. She decided not to share with the rest of the group until she knew how she felt about it.

Once they stopped in the evening, she explained that she could still summon and that not using her magic had been part of the reason she felt so faint.

Still, some part of Cecilia felt morose and resistant to summoning anything. She wasn't sure how the magic she'd missed so much suddenly felt hollow. She was tired of exchanges, and the thought of summoning anything brought her nothing but grief. On top of that, she was afraid she'd accidentally push too far and connect with her new power.

Xander and Cecilia sat off to the side, away from the other three men and the fire. The rest of the group let the newlyweds have small moments of privacy, though she suspected they were tired of Xander's very public and aggressive displays of affection. Part of her was a little embarrassed by his lack of shame, but another part of her loved that he couldn't keep his hands off her. After so many years of only being pursued because of her status, it was thrilling to be the center of such focused attention. She wondered if Xander would always be like that or if he had noticed Rainer's eyes on her during their travels and that was the reason he was so eager to stake his claim to her so publicly.

Either way, Cecilia was happy to have alone time, even if the other three men were still close by.

"Cece, you must summon. I saw the way you wavered when you got off your horse earlier." Xander sat next to her, running a finger along her jawline.

She brushed his hand away. "I'm fine."

"Do something easy. Show me a memory."

Cecilia placed her hand in Xander's, and he closed his eyes. She hadn't shared her powers with him much, and he resisted her memory powers reflexively.

"Relax, don't fight it. Just let me into your mind and watch. You'll like it. I promise," she whispered.

Both their minds lit with the memory of their first morning in Argaria when she'd been furious with him, and he'd taken her up against the wall. When it was over, she slid her hand away, and she smiled at the look on his face.

"That was very naughty, Cece. I won't be able to stop thinking about that," Xander whispered.

"That was kind of the idea." She smiled. She straddled his lap and kissed him.

The soft kisses became heated and consuming. She rolled her hips, and he groaned against her lips. He kissed down her neck, forcing her to bite her lip to keep from making a sound.

"You are making it very difficult to not ravish you right here." Xander sighed. She laughed at the desperate tone of his voice. "I wish we weren't in the middle of the woods, running for our lives."

The exhaustion, fear, and nonstop running had fried her nerves. All she wanted was to feel good, even if it was temporary. She wanted to be alone with him for a week or a couple of weeks. They'd had so little alone time together so far, and nothing was guaranteed.

She wasn't sure if it was desperation or the thought that they might not make it all the way home. She unbuttoned her pants. Xander watched, wide-eyed as she rolled off him, shimmied out of her leggings, and settled back on his lap with a blanket around her waist. Her hands fumbled for the button of his pants. He gasped at her touch as she wrapped her hand around him.

She lowered herself slowly onto him, biting her lip to keep from moaning.

"Love, you are full of surprises," he whispered. "Are you sure you're going to be able to keep quiet?"

She shrugged as the air filled with the smell of a storm and the clouds churned in the distance, not to bring rain but to cover the noise.

"I'm going to try," she whispered.

Then there was no more talking. She moved on him. His hands were everywhere, desperately seeking her skin. She rocked against him, and he met every movement. She buried her face in his neck to muffle her moans.

His storm kept thundering nearby, covering up her gasps and whimpers. The lightning built overhead and inside her. Xander pulled her into a kiss right as she fell apart, and he followed right behind her.

They stayed there, still connected, hearts pounding, skin flushed with pleasure, breathing the same air. Xander brushed a kiss to her temple.

Over Xander's shoulder, Cecilia glanced at the other men who were camped around the fire with their backs to her. Rainer was frozen in profile. For a moment, she wondered if he'd felt something through their bond, but he never turned all the way around to look at her.

She snapped her eyes back to Xander, who looked at her adoringly.

"You couldn't be more perfect if I dreamed you. I love you." He kissed her cheek, and she giggled, squeezing her arms around him. "It goes without saying that I very much prefer you half-naked and with your legs wrapped around me, but you should probably get dressed in case of company."

She pouted as she rolled off of him, quickly sliding back into her pants. Xander immediately pulled her back into the same position and went right back to kissing her in the same desperate, feverish way as before.

"Gods, you have to stop, or we're going to keep doing that all night. You're the one who told me to put my pants on," Cecilia whispered.

"I immediately regretted it." He nipped at her earlobe.

She laughed. "You just love a challenge."

"I particularly love the challenge of getting you naked and listening to all the wonderful sounds you make when I touch you."

Those words unraveled her resolve. Xander felt her falter, and he brought his hands to her arms, trying to still her.

"You're right. We should get some rest. Tomorrow is another long day, and while I would love to keep doing this all night, and I would definitely find it to be worth it, I know you need rest, love."

He led her back to the others and tucked her into sleep, wrapped in his arms.

She was about to drift off when her eyes shot open, and she looked ten feet in front of her, finding Rainer staring right back at her. She knew the feeling that was coming through their connection because she'd felt it for so long herself.

Icy jealousy poked through their bond. He held her eyes for a long time, and she felt a whirlwind of emotions. She couldn't settle on one feeling because there were too many. Relief that he was jealous. Anger that he thought he had a right to be. Grief that he'd let her go and still wanted her. Sadness that she had never had a chance with him. Satisfaction that he felt what she had for so many years.

She sent comfort through the connection. She watched his eyes the moment it hit. The slightest peace settled over his face, and one corner of his lips kicked up in a half smile. He closed his eyes.

Cecilia drifted off peacefully but woke up a short time later from a nightmare of hands around her throat, like the darkness itself was strangling her. She fought, but she couldn't pull the hands away.

She woke up screaming. Her throat was raw. All four men were on their feet, startled and confused.

"Cecilia, what happened?" Xander asked gently, brushing hair out of her eyes. She looked at all the concerned faces of her friends staring down at her. Her hair clung to her clammy skin.

"I don't know. It was a bad dream," she mumbled. "I'm sorry for waking you. I don't know what happened."

Teddy nodded and went back to watch duty, and Evan settled back into sleep, but Rainer waited. He closed his eyes and brought his hand to his heart. She knew he felt what she did, something rumbling in their connection. It was swirling, and it felt like anxiety and hunger mixed together.

"Do you need something to eat?" Rainer asked.

"I don't know," she mumbled.

She felt something ravenous inside her, but she didn't think it was physical hunger. Clastor's warning came back to her. It had to be the goddess power reaching for her.

Cecilia stood up abruptly. Rainer and Xander moved to go with her, but she waved them off.

"Give me a minute," she rasped.

She walked into the woods and barely made it out of their sight before she vomited. She held her hair back from her face, leaning against a tree. Resting her head back against the rough bark, she took long deep breaths, and the hungry, sick feeling faded.

"Cece?" She turned and met Rainer's worried face. Even in the dark, she could see the furrow of his brow. He offered her some water. "What is that feeling?"

"I don't know," she lied. "I should feel better since I summoned a memory tonight with Xander."

"What can I do?" Rainer asked.

"You can let my husband be the one who comes to find me." She sighed. She didn't want to hurt Rainer, but she was too exhausted to be nice. He needed to get used to letting someone else comfort her.

"He's busy sulking that you waved him off. I wanted to make sure you're all right."

"I'm fine now," she said, making her way back to camp.

Rainer snagged her arm at the edge of the woods and turned her to face him.

"Cece, tell me what's going on. I know you're lying," he whispered. He tucked a stray hair back behind her ear and let his fingers linger on her neck. "Talk to me."

"I can't do this with you right now. I need to sleep. I'm exhausted," she mumbled.

Rainer held her gaze, his eyes like a snare she couldn't shake free of.

"Rain, could you feel—earlier?" She couldn't seem to form the question to ask if he'd felt what happened between her and Xander earlier in the evening. She couldn't concentrate with him still touching her neck.

It was clear from the look in his eyes he knew exactly what she was talking about.

"I felt it. I didn't know what it was at first. I haven't felt it that strong before, but I guess since you weren't very far away..." Rainer shut down the bond between them, and she didn't know whether to be grateful or frustrated.

"I'm sorry. I never felt it from you before."

Rainer smiled weakly. "You don't need to apologize for being happy, Cece. I know there's something else going on, so don't change the subject."

She pulled out of his grip. When she turned toward camp, she found Teddy watching them. She smiled and pretended like everything was normal as she sat back down next to Xander.

"Love, are you all right?" Xander asked as he pulled her close.

"Don't you start, too. It was just a bad dream," she huffed, lying down and tugging the covers around her.

"You were screaming your lungs out, Cece. You probably woke everything in a five-mile radius. I'm trying to give you the benefit of the doubt, but I'm worried about you."

"I just need to get some sleep, and I'm embarrassed that I woke everyone up with my crazy nightmares."

Xander smiled down at her and kissed the tip of her nose.

"When you want to talk about what's really going on, you know I'm here for you, and I love you," he whispered. "And if you want me to do what I've done in the past to make you feel better, I'm happy to."

He winked at her. She rolled her eyes, but she secretly loved it. She tried for sleep but tossed and turned all night, afraid falling back into a deep sleep would allow her goddess powers to sink their claws into her again.

———

Morning light brightened the dark greens of the forest to emerald as Cecilia helped pack up their camp. The forest air smelled like dew and wildflowers.

"Strange storm last night," Evan said, smirking at Cecilia as he packed his blanket on his horse.

She flushed, realizing Evan's hunter's hearing meant he knew exactly why that storm was conjured.

"You know how it is this time of year—quick weather changes," Xander said, smirking at his friend.

Cecilia was cranky after sleeping so poorly, and she still hadn't been able to eat much. Rainer fussed over her, offering her bits of bread and apple until she swatted his hand away. He sighed and walked by Xander to pack up his horse.

"Good luck with that. She's in a wonderful mood this morning," Rainer grumbled, loud enough that she could hear him.

"Love, why are you giving Rainer a hard time? He's trying to make sure you're taking care of yourself. I thought you would be in a better mood considering—"

She gave Xander a scathing look that warned him not to finish that sentence.

"Don't start with your nonsense this morning, Your Highness." She sighed.

He swept her up into his arms and kissed her cheek.

"Cece, I'm here if you want to talk about it," Xander whispered.

"I don't want to. Now put me down and let's get on the road. You're holding everyone up," she huffed.

Xander set her back on her feet and kissed her forehead before helping her up onto her horse. He mounted his own, and they started to ride.

"If you're still in a bad mood later, I'm sure I can make you feel better," Xander said.

She tossed a small, stale crust of bread at him. "Next time, it will be an arrow, Your Grace. Don't make Evan have to defend you for your stupid mouth."

"Feels like something I've been doing my whole life. This time I might let you have a free shot, Princess." Evan smirked.

"Traitor," Xander huffed at Evan. "I think you enjoy my big mouth, Cece."

"Not nearly as much as you do," she quipped.

Teddy and Evan both laughed, but Xander wasn't deterred. He was always trying to draw her out, even when she wanted to hide away. He wasn't satisfied to let her blend into the background. Cecilia enjoyed being drawn out into the light, even if it felt unnatural.

Xander flashed her a teasing grin. "My love, what did you say to me the night we first met in the garden when I asked what I should call you?" Xander asked.

"Not for you," she said with a grin.

"Oh gods, no wonder he liked you so much," Evan quipped.

Cecilia laughed. "You should have seen him. He was so opinionated. He even told me how I should wear my hair."

"Yes, but you wouldn't have been talking to me out in the garden, trying not to cry, in the first place if Rainer hadn't tried to ruin your night." Xander leveled his gaze at Rainer, and she saw with clarity that the jealousy between them cut both ways.

"You were kind of overbearing. I probably should have known then that you were royal." Cecilia sighed.

"Well, I said I wanted to be a prince that first night. Still, you came back again the next night to talk. You couldn't get enough," Xander gloated.

She really wanted to shoot him with an arrow to knock him down a few pegs. A flesh wound, nothing catastrophic.

"Gods, you look so angry right now," Xander said.

"Ugh, Xander, give it a rest."

She gave him a look that mercifully stopped him from saying anything else. They rode in silence for a bit before Evan sidled up next to her.

"Are you also here to give me a hard time? Try to force more food on me?" she asked.

"No. I was going to congratulate you because I've never seen him shut up that fast," Evan said.

The hunter finally seemed to be warming up to her.

They rode quietly the rest of the morning, enjoying the scenery. When they stopped for lunch, Rainer still monitored her food intake like an overbearing mother, continually handing her more to eat. She finally felt hungry again, so she didn't mind as much.

"How does your bond work?" Teddy blurted.

"Our bond?" Rainer asked.

"I've been watching you two, and I've heard things about bonded witches and guardians, but we don't do that in Argaria. I've always been curious about how it works beyond just feelings," Teddy said.

His gaze bore no judgment. Rainer and Cecilia looked at each other, and she shrugged.

"Well, there are practical uses for it, like knowing if she's in danger or how close she is," Rainer started. "Right now, I can tell she's uncomfortable with me saying all of this. We've never really talked about it to other people. And now she's annoyed at me for sharing that."

Cecilia slapped Rainer's arm, and he laughed.

"Where do you feel it, and how do you tell what's hers and what's yours?" Evan asked.

"I feel it right here." Rainer tapped his sternum. "Almost like it wraps around my heart. That's what it feels like to you, right?"

Cecilia nodded.

"If she needs me, I'll feel it like a quick tug in my chest. I feel her pain and can choose to take some of it on so she feels better. If we're both upset, it's almost impossible to tell the difference between our feelings, but in general, her emotions have a distinct quality from mine. They're much more intense, and Cece has her own baseline feeling."

"And what does Cece feel like?" Xander asked.

Rainer closed his eyes, and she felt him pulling on their connection, trying to open it more.

"Even when she's in a bad mood, like today, she feels hopeful. She feels like lying in the sun on a warm day, like being warmed from the outside in. There's nothing she doesn't feel intensely. It can be overwhelming sometimes." Rainer hesitated for a moment. "And I hope she won't be mad at me for saying so, but she also has a persistent undercurrent of loneliness."

Cecilia had never given Rainer credit for truly seeing her. Tears pricked in her eyes. She'd spent years wanting him to see her, but he'd missed nothing. She did not know that he could feel her near-constant loneliness. There was always a sense of separation, a persistent emptiness, even with Rainer. She'd hoped marriage would change that, but it persisted.

She stared at Rainer. He looked back at her with such open adoration that for a moment, she forgot anyone else was there.

"And what does Rainer feel like?" Xander asked Cecilia, interrupting the tense silence.

The question felt like a test that was impossible not to fail. She closed her eyes and felt into their bond anyway.

"Rain feels like when you laugh so much, your stomach hurts. He has this levity that's comforting. There's a steadiness to him and his emotions—a confident sense of certainty that's always there. He feels this genuine warmth and honesty. He feels like coming home after being away too long."

She hadn't meant to say the last part out loud. It felt too personal. She spoke again, trying to settle her nerves. "And there's always an undercurrent of anxiety. He's a worrier."

It surprised her to see a light flush on Rainer's cheeks. His warm fingers brushed hers lightly as their eyes locked again.

No one had ever asked so many questions about their connection, and discussing it felt strangely intimate. They'd rarely talked about it, even to each other. It felt numinous. Hard to define and more difficult to give voice to. It was something felt more than spoken.

"I've never realized how hard it is to describe the essence of someone until now," she said as she wrenched her gaze away from him.

"What else does the connection do?" Teddy asked.

Teddy was so earnest, but Cecilia could tell that Xander was over the conversation. Guilt swelled as she tried to imagine what it was like for him to see that kind of intimacy on display between his wife and another man.

But Rainer was wrapped around her heart, and he'd had sixteen years to tuck himself in deep. She couldn't throw him out in a matter of days. It would take time, and she wasn't sure she even wanted to throw him out in the first place.

"We can send each other feelings or comfort. So if Rainer is stressed, I can try to send him peace. If I'm sad or in pain, he can try to take some of it," Cecilia answered.

"That's amazing!" Teddy gushed. "I've never seen that kind of magic, but watching the two of you is interesting. You can see it almost right away. Was it always like that?"

"No, in the beginning, it was really overwhelming and confusing," Rainer said. "We were so young, and Cece has always been so passionate. She feels other people's emotions, not just mine. So I had to learn how to shut her out until I knew how to handle it."

"Do you shut each other out now?" Evan asked.

"Sometimes," Cecilia said. "But the bond protects me, so if I'm feeling something really strong, it will automatically open up so that he can check on me."

"That sounds nice—always having someone there," Teddy said, smiling.

"Sometimes it's nice, and sometimes, like today, for example, it's really annoying because he won't stop fussing," she said as Rainer tried to hand her another chunk of cheese and an apple. He smiled at her, and she couldn't help but smile back.

After a breath, she forced herself to look away, since everyone was watching.

"That sounds like a lot. I don't think I would like to feel everything Xander does," Evan said thoughtfully.

"I'm sure you wouldn't. He's probably busy feeling impressed with himself all the time," Cecilia teased.

Xander shrugged. "You claim you don't like it, but here you are committing treason with me, so don't feed me that bullshit, Evan. And as for you, love, I know you like it."

She rolled her eyes, but she let him kiss her for an inappropriately long time right there. She was a little dazed when he stopped.

"I don't know, Xan. I think it's possible that she just enjoys kissing you," Evan taunted as they packed the horses up.

"He might be onto something." Cecilia laughed.

"I'll take what I can get." Xander sighed as they prepared to ride out again.

Her husband acted casual, but she could sense jealousy brewing beneath his calm demeanor. She only hoped they made it to Olney before it boiled over.

34

The horses stirred restlessly as they approached the tree line at the clearing's edge. Fog hung heavily over the field, the gray sky above doing little to light their way in the warm afternoon.

Rainer held up a hand, forcing them to pause and wait to check that it wasn't a trap. The group watched the woods around the clearing for a few minutes, looking for any movement. Neither Xander nor Evan picked up any hint of enemies in the tree line on the other side of the clearing, but the strange quiet sent a shiver down Cecilia's spine.

"I'll go first. As long as it's clear, the rest of you follow. Teddy, you guard Cece," Rainer said. He started into the meadow.

Cecilia felt a pervading uneasiness. The normal forest sounds were absent, and even the quiet din of the spirit world was shockingly silent in a way she'd never experienced. She could feel spirits nearby in vast quantities, but they didn't move or make a sound.

"I don't like this," Evan whispered.

"Something doesn't feel right," Cecilia agreed. "It's too quiet. There's nothing. It's almost like someone made all the spirits silent."

She sucked in a sharp breath as recognition tore through her. "Oh my gods. There's a death summoner!"

Cecilia had never seen a death summoner at work, and she only vaguely understood her own ability. She'd only met two other witches who could summon death in her time in Olney, and she'd learned little about the power because it frightened her. She instantly wished she'd taken more time to learn about it.

It was too late to stop Rainer. He was halfway across the field, and an invisible force stirred the woods on both sides of the clearing. Cecilia cursed and took off at a gallop. Xander, Teddy, and Evan all called out to her to stop, but this wasn't a battle with men yet. It was a battle with spirits. Cecilia was the only one who could help.

She rode hard, yelling to Rainer. He turned around to look at her, confused. The spirits raced toward him, an army of gray shadows. She rode harder before jumping down from her horse next to Rainer, the shock of the landing reverberating through her body.

Cecilia reached out beyond memory, fire, earth, tides and the storm. She reached out to the power she didn't like to touch—the cold thing—death.

She held up her hands out to both sides, trying to hold back the tide of spirits rushing toward them. She was vaguely aware of the other three men riding up behind her, but this was a blind battle for them. Only she could fight this enemy that appeared in various flickers of gray and white. She was grateful she'd finally been able to eat so she had some energy, because she was going to need it. Rainer hopped down next to her.

"What is it, Cece?" Rainer asked, looking at her straining.

"It's death."

Rainer's eyes went wide, and he paled as he looked around, trying to spot an invisible opponent. The other three men had caught up to them, and the five of them stood facing outward in a tight circle.

"How do we stop it?" Rainer asked.

"There has to be a death summoner nearby. In the woods. Have Xander hit the periphery with lightning. I'm going to break the connection to the summoner," Cecilia said.

She focused on the hoard of spirits circling them. As she held them off, her power drained at an alarming rate. A flash of lightning brightened the sky over the clearing.

Death didn't whisper anymore. It screamed. Cecilia winced at the torrent of sound that only she could hear.

She followed a thread of energy between the spirits, like a string of light connecting to someone hidden in the woods.

"There!" she said, pointing to the woods to their left. "Light it up, Xander, and hurry. I don't know how long I can hold them back. All of you stay close."

She slowly pushed the spirits back, widening the circle around them, but it was hard work. She was burning through her energy too fast—shaking and sweating through her clothes. Cecilia brought her hands down to the ground and sent a tremendous burst of energy at the same moment that Xander struck the summoner.

The spirits were suddenly free, scattering back to where they came from. Cecilia knelt, panting.

"Are you okay, Cece?" Teddy asked, kneeling beside her.

"Yes, but there are living people coming now. One of the spirits warned me," she mumbled.

Teddy helped her to her feet. She picked up her bow and quiver and slung them over her shoulder.

"What can I do, Cece?" Xander asked.

"Keep the storm going. You're much better at controlling the storm than I am, but I can pull lightning from it if it's already there," she said.

"Love, you're flushed. Are you sure you're all right?" Xander brushed her sweaty hair back from her face and gave her a quick kiss.

"I'm fine. Focus," she said, turning back to the woods. "Rain, how close is the nearest waterway?"

"Just beyond the tree line to our right," Rainer replied. "Are you going to summon it?"

"If I have to." She sighed, turning back to the trees.

They were terribly exposed in the field, but they'd be defenseless if they retreated. They had no choice but to stand and fight. The first hunters appeared at the edge of the woods, and she and Xander pulled lightning from the clouds, striking along the tree line. The other three men shot arrows at anyone who managed to get through. The flood of Argarian hunters kept coming.

The tides were Cecilia's weakest summoning, and she'd already used more of her energy than she would have liked. She was a little worried she would drown all of them, but she needed to take as many hunters out as efficiently as possible.

"Stand behind me," Cecilia yelled to the rest of them.

Teddy refused. He knelt in front of her, bow in hand. She knew Xander made him promise to protect her as her princess guard, but she didn't want him to get hurt.

To her left, Xander engaged with the few hunters who had sneaked through the line. He fully lived up to the Storm Prince hype as he cut through opponents with ease, never once losing his grip on the storm. Magic and close combat pulled the mind in different directions, but Xander made it look effortless to fight and summon at once.

Still, they were outnumbered, so Cecilia reached out to the tides and pulled hard. Water crashed through the clearing. She pushed it toward the forest full of enemy hunters. She kept it away from the five of them.

"Xander, hit the water," she yelled over the storm.

He grinned at her and brought a huge bolt of lightning down into the water. The air filled with the sickening smell of charred flesh. It turned Cecilia's already roiling stomach, but their plan worked. Every hunter at the tree line went down.

The charred tree trunks smoked and sizzled as Cecilia used the last of her power to pull back the tide and send the water back to the river. She stumbled, and Rainer caught her.

"I'm fine, just tired," she said before he could ask.

He smiled at her. "You and Xander saved us," Rainer said. He looked both jealous and relieved.

Xander knelt beside them. "Cece, you are brilliant. You're all right?"

She nodded.

"Good, because I need to yell at you for being so reckless and running out here on your own. You're a princess now. You can't run into the middle of a battle alone." Xander looked so stern that she almost laughed.

She was so relieved that they were all safe that instead of arguing, she kissed him.

"You are going to be the death of me." Xander sighed.

Evan and Teddy came back from briefly scouting the woods.

"Looks clear. But we should try to move out quickly," Evan said.

Xander put his weapons back on the horse. Cecilia tried to settle her stomach. She turned back toward the woods and came face-to-face with a hunter with his bow trained on her.

Time slowed. Rainer screamed her name. Cecilia grabbed her bow, but before she could grasp an arrow, she was hit hard. She landed on the ground, the wind knocked out of her. She blinked, unable to comprehend the scene.

Teddy lay next to her with an arrow through his chest. She looked up at the enemy hunter, drawing an arrow. Evan took the man down before she could flinch. Cecilia crawled to Teddy.

"You saved me, Teddy," she said.

"I did," he breathed. His face was twisted in agony.

"It's all right. I'm going to fix it," she soothed.

Evan knelt down next to her. "What do you need me to do?"

Cecilia's vision blurred with tears. "We need to get the arrow out, and then I can try. Evan, I don't know if I can—"

She knew she couldn't heal it. It was a vicious wound that she'd struggle to fix on her best day, and she was so tired she could barely stand. Evan carefully removed the arrow, and she placed her hands over the wound, but her power sputtered out. She couldn't summon anything else. Xander knelt down next to her.

"I saved her, Xan," Teddy choked.

"You did. I'm so grateful. You did exactly what I asked you to. She's the most precious thing in the world to me," Xander said. "But you are a close second, so I need you to hold on."

Cecilia swallowed a sob.

"You're a good friend, Ted. The best. Maybe I can fix it. Remind me how to do it, Cece. Talk me through it," Xander whispered.

"Reach past the storm. Remember, it's cool and tingly." She let Xander concentrate. She saw the moment he connected to it. "Then bring your hands to the wound. Both sides. Push the healing in. Imagine it knitting everything back together."

She lay down next to Teddy and held his hand while Xander worked. Blood pooled around them, and she tried to shove away the thought that the healing wouldn't work if he'd lost too much blood.

"Don't cry, Cece. Tell me about the Olney court ladies you were saying would like me," Teddy said, forcing a smile.

"A handsome hunter like you?" she started, blinking away tears. "You would do very well. You're foreign, so that certainly brings some intrigue. I suspect my friend Sylvie would like you. She's so beautiful, I mean, irritatingly pretty, and she's the life of the party, but she's super picky. I think she would like you, though. You're very genuine. She always has men falling in love with her, but I know she would like you because you're kind and brave, and you have an honest face."

"Do you think she would go to a ball with me?" Teddy asked. He shivered, and his breath sputtered.

"I know she would," Cecilia said.

"My love, I don't think I can do anything else. What can I—" Xander's voice broke. "How can I help?"

"Keep healing, but try pulling the pain. It will hurt you temporarily, but it will help him," she said.

Xander looked wrecked, his eyes wide with helpless fear.

Teddy's hand tightened around Cecilia's. "Cece, I don't think I'm going to get to swim in the Adiran Sea."

She shook her head as tears streamed down her cheeks. "No, you're going to be fine. We'll go for a swim together. You'll love it. We'll have a picnic on the beach and swim all day. I'll show you our favorite sea cave. Then we'll take trips to all the magical places in Olney. Heartwood Valley, the Wailing Woods. We'll go to the Fall Equinox Festival. I'll save you a dance. Forget Xander. If you hang in there, you can have all the dances. I'll dance with you all night. He's not that great of a dancer anyway."

Teddy laughed and winced. "Cece, I'm sorry. That sounds wonderful, but I won't make it, and you know it. I wanted to tell you something, but you have to come close."

Cecilia saw the moment the wave of pain relief hit him. His face relaxed, and the crease in his brow softened. He smiled. She leaned in close because his voice was a whisper.

"I wanted to tell you that you're really brave. You're brave how you fight, but you're braver how you love—with your whole heart. I understand why he fell in love with you. Don't lose that. Even if it hurts. Don't let them lose it either," Teddy whispered.

She nodded with tears in her eyes as Evan and Xander moved to take her place in front of their friend.

Even on death's doorstep Teddy managed to smile at his friends. "Don't look so grim. I'll be seeing my father soon." He let out a shuddering breath. "Ev, don't take everything so seriously all the time. The world won't fall apart if you aren't there holding it together every minute. You're like the stern older brother I never wanted."

Evan gave him a tight smile as Teddy turned his gaze on Xander.

"Thank you for taking my pain, Xan," Teddy rasped. "Don't be so reckless. You're not just a spare prince. You were always more than that, but now you're a husband and a best friend, and our people are going to need you."

Xander looked wrecked by the words.

Teddy took a breath in and out, and his chest didn't rise again.

Xander sat back on his heels, his shoulders slumped in defeat, his eyes shining with unshed tears. Evan tapped his fingers on his forehead, lips, and heart in silent prayer before placing a hand on Xander's shoulder.

An oppressive weariness settled into Cecilia's bones. Teddy was so young, so excited to see the world. It was his first time away from Argaria. He didn't deserve to die, especially not saving her.

For a moment, they stared in disbelief at their fallen friend. Then, Cecilia got up, drank some of her witch tea, and walked into the woods. She found a pretty spot by a bed of wildflowers. She drank more tea and used a sputtering bit of earth magic to create a grave. Then, Evan and Xander picked up Teddy's body and gently laid him to rest.

Cecilia was on the brink of fainting from using too much power, so they all pushed the dirt back into place with their hands.

Rainer held up a flask. "To a good man who did my job when I could not. I'm grateful for his courage." He handed the flask to Cecilia.

"To Teddy who snuck me whiskey in teacups and was good enough not to hold it against me when I knocked him out and tried to escape. I'm grateful for his relentless optimism," she said, taking a sip and handing the flask to Evan.

He stared at it for a moment before speaking. "To Ted, who gave the best advice and never gave up on trying to make his friends laugh, no matter how stoic they were. I'm grateful for fifteen years of his friendship even if he never stopped talking." Evan took a long gulp and passed the flask to Xander.

Xander blew out a long breath. "To Teddy, whose letters brought all the color of home to my world miles away and who always picked up where we'd left off like I'd never been gone at all. I'm grateful for his persistence." Xander gulped down the whiskey and nodded, wrapping an arm around Cecilia to guide her back to the horses.

There was nothing else to do but keep riding on toward Olney City.

Their victory felt hollow. Teddy had been the first person other than Xander to make Cecilia feel welcome in Argaria. He never stared at her or felt afraid of her. He was curious, and he asked thoughtful questions. She kept looking to Evan and Xander, waiting for one of them to say something, but they just looked shocked by the sudden loss.

When they finally stopped for the night, it was much too quiet. Cecilia could barely focus on the grief around the gnawing of the goddess power. It was worse than it had ever been. It felt like an insatiable hunger. Like she could eat for days, and it would never be enough.

She knew Rainer felt it, but she was too tired to close the connection, and it was probably too strong for her to hide anyway.

"What *is* that?" Rainer finally asked.

Xander and Evan looked confused.

"I don't know," she mumbled.

"Liar," Rainer huffed.

"Is this some weird connection thing?" Evan asked.

"Yes," they said in unison.

"It's been getting worse," Rainer said solemnly. He studied her face as if the answer would be written there. "It feels like hunger and anxiety and something else. I don't recognize it."

"Maybe I'm tired and hungry and anxious."

"You've barely eaten anything," he argued.

"I'm not—"

"Hungry. I know. That's why I'm confused. Do you want me to take some of it?" Rainer asked.

Her instinct was to say no, but she wondered if maybe it would at least take the edge off, like when he took the pain from her.

"Okay," she sighed.

Rainer held her hand and closed his eyes. Cecilia felt the moment he pulled on the feeling because the relief was instant. The tension released from her body.

She threw her arms around him and squeezed him.

"Thank you," she whispered.

"Cece, that feels awful. Are you going to be all right?" Rainer asked.

"Of course, but I need to get some sleep, or I'll be as cranky as I was this morning," she said.

Xander helped her set up for bed. He lay down, facing her. He brushed his fingers over her cheek.

"Xan, what can I do for you? Do you want to talk?"

Xander shook his head. "I don't know what to say. It doesn't quite feel real. For now I want to focus on the road ahead. Do you want to talk about what's going on with you?"

"Not yet," she said. "I'm sad. I really liked Teddy. I really thought we were in the clear. We're so close to home."

"I know, love. I did, too. I assigned him to you because I knew he had a better temperament for you than Evan. I knew you would like him. You know, it's a great honor for a hunter to protect a royal and to die in service. In Argaria, it's one of the highest honors," Xander said.

She was slowly beginning to see that Xander struggled with grief, tucking it behind anger, jealousy or lust, the edges of it always in the background of whatever emotion he was willing to show.

"I would think it would be a greater honor to live." She sighed.

Xander caressed her cheek. "Cece, Teddy knew what he was signing up for, and I am immensely grateful to him because he saved you. He wanted to meet you even before I brought you back. The last time I came back to visit six months ago, he wouldn't stop asking questions about you. I really—" He swallowed thickly. "I really appreciate that you showed me how to help him." His face grew serious. "You saved the rest of us today. You are too brave for your own good. I thought my heart would stop when you charged into the clearing. Please never do that again. I wasn't trying to stop you from fighting. I just wanted you to have as much cover as possible, Cecilia. I cannot lose anyone else I love. I won't."

Cecilia kissed his hand. "I'm sorry. I didn't mean to frighten you. I have never seen the spirits attack before, and I panicked."

"Because you were worried about Rainer." Jealousy swirled around her husband.

"Yes, wouldn't you have charged in to save Evan?" she asked, staring him down.

Xander sighed. "I suppose."

"I would have tried to give more notice, but there were so many of them. I didn't know what would happen when they attacked. I don't know if their touch kills. If it was just hunters, I might have done things differently."

"Doubtful."

"Well, hopefully, we don't have to find out. Now, do you want to keep talking about Rainer while you're pressed up against me? Do you want to be mad, or do you want to kiss me?" she asked.

He sighed and pulled her into a kiss. They clung to each other in the dark like the love between them could ward off trouble.

PART IV:

THE PUPPETMASTER

35

The raw ache of the goddess powers returned as Cecilia woke in the morning. Everything felt heavy. Even the surrounding forest seemed to sit in silent vigil of Teddy's death. Clouds blotted out the sunshine, and birds in the canopy above seemed to sing a quiet, mournful tune.

Xander cornered Cecilia as they packed for the day's ride.

"I know you're not ready to talk about what's going on with you, but I'm ready when you are," he whispered.

He played with a curl that had escaped her braid.

"I'll tell you everything once we're home." She appreciated his patience but wasn't even sure how to begin to explain. "How are you this morning?"

"I know it's wildly inappropriate," Xander started, "but after yesterday, I'm feeling a little on edge. I want to give you a proper send-off before I can't touch you for hours."

Xander's eyes darkened. Cecilia peeked around to see how close Evan and Rainer were. They were either too busy to notice, or pretending to be.

"What do you want?" she stammered.

"I want to put you up against that tree and kiss you senseless."

Xander kissed her with feverish intensity. All Cecilia's anxiety, fear, gnawing hunger melted away as his lips met hers and his hands moved over her body. He lifted her so her legs wrapped around his waist, and kissed her until her mind was blissfully empty. When he finally put her down, she was shaky and dazed. Xander's eyes were bright with lust.

"That was more than a little inappropriate," Cecilia mumbled.

"I wanted to make you feel good. Did I succeed?"

"It was adequate," she quipped.

Xander's eyebrows shot up. "Oh, *really*? Well, I could try again."

"Please don't," Evan groaned.

Xander leaned in, his lips grazing Cecilia's ear. "Love, when we are home safe, I'm going to make you feel so exceptionally good. All of Olney will hear you screaming my name. You're never going to say the word *adequate* again."

Cecilia was speechless as Xander helped her onto her horse, gave her a pat on her butt, and sent her off.

Being solidly in Olney territory didn't put the group at ease. Teddy's death was fresh in their minds. Cecilia scanned the forest constantly, listening for spirits.

Rainer rode quietly beside her.

"What would have happened if the spirits had reached us yesterday?" he asked quietly.

"I don't know. Best-case scenario, they fight us, and I'm the only one who can see them. I don't even want to think about the worst case," she said with a shiver.

Rainer nodded. "Thank you for saving me again."

"I like being your knight in shining armor," Cecilia said. "I know you're the one who's supposed to be saving me, but I'll let it slide."

Rainer's grin made her stomach dip, and it startled her how the simplest things could make her feel like she'd made no progress in escaping the unrelenting pull to him.

They rode through the warm morning at a slower, more cautious pace.

Cecilia expected to feel relieved being just a two-day ride from home, but she felt exhausted instead. The ache of the goddess powers was relentless, and by midday she needed to stop and rest.

As they were tying up the horses, Cecilia felt a swirl of energy around them. A velvety voice cut through the silence.

"Good afternoon, little goddess."

Cecilia whipped around. Two of the most handsome men she'd ever seen were sitting on a rock not ten feet away. The taller man's raven hair fell over his forehead. His eyes were a pale, icy blue. He had a strong jawline and a mischievous smile.

"Didn't mean to scare you," the tall man said.

Cecilia blew out a breath. Beside her, Xander, Rainer, and Evan had all drawn weapons.

It took her a moment to recognize the man, but an old knowing settled into her bones. Her goddess powers reared up as if begging to be claimed, and she gritted her teeth, reminding herself of what she'd lose. She brought a hand to her stomach, trying to calm the roiling nausea.

"Cecilia Reznik: the one who got away." He laughed.

She blanched. Until hearing it from the mouth of the god of death, she wasn't certain how close she'd come to dying two years earlier.

He arched a brow. "Oh, come on. You can't get behind some dark humor?"

"Grimon," she said with a tight smile.

"Very good! I wasn't sure if you would recognize me. It's been a while." Grimon laughed.

"*That* is the god of death?" Xander mumbled. "He's so—"

"Handsome?" Cecilia suggested.

Xander raised his eyebrows. "Really, Cece?"

She giggled at Xander's overt jealousy. The god of death looked equally amused by the exchange. His eyes glowed with power.

"Most people expect me to be scary, but it's much easier to lure people to the Underworld when you're nice to look at."

Nice was an understatement. Xander crossed his arms, looking from Cecilia to the god, and Rainer took a step toward her.

"We used to spend some time together," Grimon said. "Remember, Lady Cece?"

"Cece," Rainer said, his voice tight.

"I assume if he was here to kill me, I'd already be dead," she said.

"That's true." Grimon laughed.

The sound sent a shiver down Cecilia's spine, but not an unpleasant one.

"I thought you'd be happier to see me considering I was your first crush and all," Grimon continued.

"Your first crush was the god of death?" Evan said in disbelief.

"Can you blame me?" She laughed. "I was young, and he was so handsome and nice to me."

"I thought I was your first crush," Rainer said absent-mindedly.

Cecilia tried not to laugh at the surprise on his face.

"If he's Grimon, then who's that?" Xander asked, pointing to the second man.

The other god had the same raven hair and startlingly bright hazel eyes that flickered like flames. Cecilia couldn't meet his gaze without blushing.

"Samson," Cecilia murmured, looking down at the ground.

When she looked into Samson's eyes, her skin felt too hot and tight for her body. A shiver ran through her. The god of lust gave her a look that set her blood on fire, putting Xander's heated looks to shame.

"Old Clastor, he always was a vain motherfucker." Samson smirked. "I suppose that's why he made her so lovely."

Cecilia pulled her hair away from her neck, trying to cool down.

Samson winked at her. "Brainy, beautiful, and deadly. A triple threat and a very wild one."

Cecilia's knees felt weak.

"Tone it down a bit, brother," Grimon said quietly. "She's still mortal."

"I can't help it. She's just my type," Samson said, licking his lips.

"Everyone is your type," Grimon huffed, rolling his eyes.

Samson looked back at Cecilia. His smoldering gaze made her feel naked.

"Do you mind?" Xander said.

Cecilia stifled a nervous giggle.

"Ah, the young Storm Prince has stolen your heart from your old love," Samson said, nodding at Rainer. He walked behind Cecilia and laid a hand on her shoulder. "And yet they both still want you desperately," he whispered in her ear. "Perhaps we have more in common than I thought, Goddess."

Samson's power was a gentle caress on her skin. It filled the air with the scent of vanilla and tobacco. It rushed through her and opened her up to what Xander and Rainer felt for her. The lust made her dizzy.

"Easy does it." Samson laughed, catching her when she stumbled.

"What do you want?" Xander asked.

Samson walked around Cecilia and stared into her eyes, and she couldn't tear her eyes away.

"Prince Savero, she has scandalous thoughts about you. She greatly appreciates your—talents. She lets you do such naughty things to her. Hmm, and yet you still long to compare his kisses to your guardian's. Wicked, greedy little goddess. I enjoy being in your head. I think we should be friends," Samson said, sliding a hand down her arm, leaving goosebumps in its wake.

"Get out," Cecilia said, looking away. She tried to slap him, but she missed and stumbled.

Samson caught her arm. "Why is she so weak?" he asked.

"Long story," Rainer mumbled.

Grimon stared at Rainer in a way that unnerved Cecilia. She wondered what he saw. Finally, he looked at her and smiled.

"Heard you had a run-in with a horde of spirits," Grimon said.

"I did," she said.

"How did you stop them?"

"Luck."

Grimon laughed at her honesty and pulled out a picnic basket. Xander gave him an incredulous look.

"Relax, Your Highness. It's just a picnic. Your wife is skin and bones," Grimon said.

Xander sheathed his sword and sat next to Cecilia.

"You want us to have a picnic with you?" Evan asked, staring at the two gods in disbelief.

"We aren't here to hurt you. We wanted to see what all the fuss was about. It's not every day you get to meet a new goddess—especially one who is also a witch," Grimon said. "Tell me, little goddess, why don't you access your power?"

Cecilia's cheeks burned under the intensity of Grimon's gaze. "That's personal."

Grimon smirked. "I like you, Cecilia. You have very little fear. You've always been that way. You've really piqued his interest."

"Whose interest?"

"The Trickster."

Cecilia's blood ran cold.

"He's very interested, and that asshole has tricked me more times than I can count," Grimon said. "I'm curious why you make him so nervous."

"Cato hasn't even met Cece," Xander said. His expression was inscrutable. His emotions were a swirl of fear and anger.

Cecilia frowned as Grimon continued.

"You've met before. You'll probably meet again soon. He can't help himself. Curiosity always gets the better of him."

Cecilia shook her head. "But my father didn't tell me I'd met him. Only to be careful of him."

"Your father doesn't know everything, Cecilia," Grimon said. "Cato has a way of sneaking between realms and between consciousness to get to who and what he wants. You probably met him before your powers awakened and didn't recognize him."

Cecilia searched her memory, but nothing stuck out.

"Come on, little goddess," Grimon taunted. "Gray eyes, dark hair, scar on his right eyebrow, mischievous smile."

"My dream," she whispered.

"Not quite a dream, I suppose," Grimon said. "What did he want?"

Grimon's distaste for Cato was obvious on his face. Samson's scowl echoed his disgust.

Cecilia pulled up the memory. "He said he wanted to get to know me."

"And what did you tell him?"

"That he was creepy."

Grimon and Samson chuckled, and Cecilia grinned at the insanity of making the gods of death and lust laugh during a picnic in the forest.

"But if he's not on our side, why did he save us in the Reflection Forest?" Cecilia wondered aloud.

The look of shock on Rainer's and Xander's faces reminded her that she'd never told them what happened there.

"Who can say why the Trickster does what he does, but it's always motivated by his own best interest," Samson said.

Grimon poured a glass of wine and waved a hand over it. Cecilia took it skeptically.

"It will help with your symptoms, Cecilia."

She took a tentative sip.

Grimon looked at the others. "Will you really turn down hospitality from a god?"

They all moved at once. Both kingdoms considered it bad luck to turn down offerings from a god, though Cecilia had always thought that was more metaphorical. Rainer and Evan sat down and helped themselves to the feast.

"Why are you helping me?" Cecilia asked.

Grimon's smile was disarming.

"Most people turn to me when they need something, but you've been talking to me since you were young," he said. "Do you remember?"

Cecilia finally allowed the memory from childhood to pop into her mind. She hadn't known what she was as a child, but Grimon must have.

"I remember you as a little girl, walking on the beach, talking to me about your mother," Grimon said, the moment he described flickering in Cecilia's mind. "You didn't ask me to bring her back. You just asked me to take care of her. You talked to me about the spirits who asked you for things. You were always asking me to take care of the ones you ran into—especially the lost ones. You have a big heart, little goddess, but there's little room for heart in what you'll have to do to survive. You don't even know the trouble you're in."

"You prayed to the god of death when you were a little girl?" Evan asked.

"Who would you pray to if you started seeing spirits?" Cecilia replied.

Evan shrugged.

"She knew there was nothing to fear. She understood what most wise adults don't." Grimon sighed.

"And what's that?" Xander asked.

"That he doesn't control who lives and dies," Cecilia said, staring into Grimon's eyes. "Only the fates do. His job is simply to act on their instruction, to shepherd the dead and to take care of the spirits who have crossed."

Xander, Rainer, and Evan were dumbfounded.

"Is that true?" Rainer asked.

Grimon nodded. "It's easy to make me the villain. Truth be told, I'm probably the least violent of all the gods. People assume because I can't just keep people alive that I want them dead. There's a balance between the worlds. If I kept a person alive, someone else would have to die. I can only return spirits who are in between, and even then, they must *choose* to go back."

"So why are you here?" Evan asked.

"Technically, Samson and I are supposed to remain neutral in all godly affairs, but I have a personal score to settle," Grimon said, turning to Cecilia. "Are you feeling better? You don't look as pale."

The gnawing in Cecilia's stomach had eased, and she actually felt hungry. Before she could reach for a sandwich, Rainer handed her one.

"Your soul bond is fascinating and very rare," Samson said.

"We know it's rare," Rainer said.

"Yes, but do you know how rare? There's never been a god or goddess with a soul bond," Samson said. "No one knows what it means, but it certainly makes things more interesting. He has a direct connection to your heart. He shares your burdens and your grief."

Samson took a swig of wine, ignoring the dirty look Xander gave him.

"You know what they say about soul bonds, right?" Samson continued. "How they always seek each other out? How they can't stand to be apart? He feels such a deep longing for you."

"Are you trying to make this the most awkward lunch ever?" Cecilia huffed.

Samson laughed.

Grimon stood and offered Cecilia his arm. "Relax, feisty little goddess. This is nothing that we all don't know. Will you walk with me?"

She looped her arm through Grimon's and followed him down the trail.

"It would be best if you accept your power sooner rather than later. At least now it will be your choice to do so. Later it might not," Grimon said.

"None of this has been my choice," Cecilia said coldly.

"That may be true, but you can either throw a tantrum about it or accept it. You can't delay forever. You've always been a goddess. Your powers were just bound. When you accept the exchange—when you embrace the full power—you'll have a whole new set of gifts and abilities."

"What will happen?" she asked.

Grimon shrugged. "Your senses will be heightened. You'll see, hear, smell, and taste things like you couldn't before. Powers you already have will be stronger. New powers will show up."

"Why do you care?" she asked.

"Because there is trouble coming for you, and we are old friends,

Lady Cece. War is coming. It would be best for you and your kingdom if you were prepared."

"And you care about Olney?" She laughed.

Grimon frowned. "I care about Endros. That vapid warmonger is starting another one of his ridiculous wars, and you could be the one who stops him."

"Shouldn't you like the god of war? Doesn't he send you lots of souls?" Cecilia asked.

"No, Cecilia. Endros and his wars upset the balance between worlds. It's an overwhelming number of souls entering at once, and it creates problems," Grimon said. "There's not enough people working intake. It just gets very messy."

"You want me to accept my goddess powers so you can avoid staffing problems in the Underworld?" Cecilia said, scowling at Grimon.

"It's much more complex than staffing," he said. "It upsets the balance between realms. I don't think you want to know what it looks like to have too many souls to process. Especially after what you dealt with the other day with that death summoner."

Cecilia shivered, thinking about it.

"I know why you don't want to access your powers," Grimon said. "It's a shame it will cost you so much, but your sickness will just get worse until you accept them. You're wasting away."

She clenched her fists and said, "I'm not ready yet."

"You better get ready soon. I know it isn't fair. Cultivate that anger," Grimon said quietly. "Hold on to that rage for when you discover where to direct it."

"What does that mean?"

"It means eventually you will figure out who deserves the brunt of your righteous anger, and when you do, use it."

"Must you all be so cryptic?" she asked.

"I suppose it's part of my allure," Grimon said. "Those of us who are ascended gods are not permitted to give you all the answers. We can give you pieces, but none of us can offer the full picture. You must put that together yourself. It's part of the laws of nature and the balance between worlds. It's an exchange of sorts. You're still corpo-real, and you will be once you accept your powers. You need the veil that keeps you in your body as a living god. Those of us who are ascended don't have that problem, but we're much weaker in this world."

"Well, it's terribly annoying." Cecilia sighed.

"Can I offer you some advice from a very old god to a brand-new goddess?"

"I suspect you'll give it to me whether or not I want it," Cecilia said, raising an eyebrow.

Grimon laughed and nodded. "Love is a powerful thing," he said. "Some would say the most powerful thing. But it can be a poison, or it can be an antidote. It's important to know the difference."

Cecilia rolled her eyes and said, "That was appropriately vague."

"Then let me be direct. Your husband walks a fine line between love and obsession. I'm sure you've felt it. I don't even need to touch him to feel it, and Samson knew it before we even got here. You've already seen once that there is more to him than meets the eye."

Cecilia took a step back. "You think he's lying to me."

"I think he hasn't been fully honest. What he feels for you is real, but it's dangerous. It can be twisted," Grimon said.

"And what do you suggest I do about that?"

"From what I understand, you have a unique ability to persuade him to do just about anything you want. Use it. Withhold what he wants so badly." Grimon winked at her, and she flushed.

He turned and walked back toward the picnic. "Secrets often seem harmless, little goddess. But it's important to remember that even the most seemingly harmless secrets can devastate. You have a tender heart and two men who love you. Love can make you power-ful, or it can make you weak. You get to choose."

As they neared the others, Grimon's gaze fell back to Rainer.

"Why do you keep looking at him?" Cecilia whispered.

Grimon's face was neutral, but she felt a heaviness in the air around him. "I wish I could tell you, Cecilia, but that's not allowed. Take my advice. Accept your powers sooner rather than later. Free will is the antidote to the whims of fate. Do you remember what the seer asked when you met her all those years ago? The day you were bonded to Rainer?"

"She asked if I seek love or power. It's the same thing Cato asked when I met him."

"And what did you say?" Grimon asked.

"Love."

"Love is power, Cece. At least it is to those who know how to use it," Grimon said, looking at Rainer again. "Sometimes power can save those we love."

"Do you know what my powers are?" she asked.

"There's some speculation, but until you accept them, it's just gossip. Clastor has always been tight-lipped about the gifts he gives his children, and yours, in particular, were shrouded in mystery."

"I feel like I've had enough surprises for one lifetime." Cecilia sighed.

Grimon smiled at her. They walked the last few feet in silence.

Cecilia's mind spun with Grimon's words. *Should I just accept the power now? Is it inevitable? Is something wrong with Rainer? Could my powers save him if there was?*

"We must leave you now," Grimon said, breaking her out of her reverie.

"Do we have to?" Samson moaned as he ruffled Evan's hair.

Evan looked like he wasn't sure if he wanted to run away or lean into the touch.

"Remember what I've said. Be wise about the deals you make with other gods. Exchange is a tricky thing. Sometimes that which seems harmless does the most damage," Grimon said, bringing her hand to his lips.

Her companions could only stare as the god of death smiled and kissed the inside of her wrist. His lips made her skin tingle in the most pleasant way.

"Stay safe, Lady Cece," he said.

Samson reached for her, but Grimon swatted his hand away.

"No fair. I want to kiss her too," Samson whined.

"I don't think she needs that right now, brother. She already has too many loves as it is," Grimon teased.

He threw an arm around Samson and led him into the woods, the scent of burnt cinnamon, tobacco, and vanilla wafting in their wake.

Cecilia looked at her wrist. The sunlight showed a faint outline of Grimon's lips on her skin, like a tattoo. It was a shade lighter, with an iridescent sparkle.

"Well, that's terrifying," Evan said. "What do you think it does?"

"I think it's a blessing," Rainer said. "In some of the old mythology books, they talk about the gods granting favors with a kiss."

"Are you well?" Xander asked.

"Much better," Cecilia said.

Xander eyed the kiss of death on her wrist suspiciously.

She smirked. "You're jealous."

"Of my wife making heart eyes at the god of death? Of course I am! You were practically drooling," Xander teased.

"Can you blame me?" She rose on her toes and gave him a peck on the cheek before going back to her sandwich.

"Did he say anything interesting?" Rainer asked.

"Just the usual cryptic stuff. He suggested I accept my powers sooner rather than later. He thinks Endros is working to inspire war between Argaria and Olney, and he doesn't want that because, apparently, it overwhelms the Underworld with souls and throws off the balance between realms. Grimon is under the impression that I can do something about it."

"Can you?" Evan asked.

"I don't know. I don't know what my powers will be, so it's hard to say."

Evan met her gaze. "Maybe you should just—"

"No," Xander said emphatically. "That will not happen. It's Cece's choice, and none of us will pressure her to decide anything."

Xander squeezed her hand. Though she appreciated his confidence, she didn't share his certainty. She would do anything to keep the people she loved safe.

"We should head out," Evan said, standing up to gather the horses. "We're about a day's ride from Olney City if we push."

Everything that Grimon said swirled in Cecilia's mind as they rode through the afternoon. She trusted him. Their goals were aligned. She considered reaching out to her power right there, but immediately flashed back to the way Xander's face looked when he talked about having kids. If there was even a chance she still could, she had to hold out for him. Maybe she could give up on herself, but she couldn't take that dream away from him, not when she still had the power to fight.

Cecilia was lost in thought as they crested a hill.

So lost she'd missed the whispers nagging at her for the last mile. When they got louder, she realized what they were: death whispers.

"Wait!" Cecilia yelled.

Her eyes darted to Rainer, who was out front, but it was too late. Arrows arced through the air, striking Rainer, knocking him from his horse.

36

The moment Rainer fell was the worst moment of Cecilia's life. If there was any part of her that truly believed she'd stopped loving him, it was gone the second the arrows hit him.

She didn't even realize she was screaming until Xander turned to make sure she hadn't been hit as well. She was off her horse in seconds, standing over Rainer, leaving Evan and Xander to deal with the hunters in the trees.

An arrow protruded from Rainer's neck and one from the right side of his chest. He made horrible choking noises.

He's dying.

The thought stole the breath from her lungs. Panic seized her as she remembered the way Grimon stared at Rainer as if he knew he'd be seeing him soon. Cecilia's heart leaped into her throat.

She pulled the arrow from his neck first. Blood surged from the wound. She covered it with her hands as Rainer's eyes fluttered.

"Please don't leave me, Rainer." Cecilia repeated the words like a prayer. She prayed to the gods as she healed his wound. She bargained. She offered to trade anything.

The goddess power beckoned to her, the dark wall keeping it out threatening to shatter. Rainer's eyes shot open, and he grabbed her wrist as if he sensed her intention.

Her hands were covered in blood, but the wound in his neck was almost healed. Another moment and it was done. She carefully wiped the blood from his mouth with her sleeve.

"Cece," Rainer whispered. "Don't do it. I won't be the reason you give in to it."

"And I won't be the reason you die today. We're so close to home. You're coming back with me. You have to come back with me. Rainer, I *need* you."

Rainer's hand came to his sternum, and he winced against the tug of their bond. She rarely used the word with him because a need required a guardian's response. It was selfish of her to use it, but it was also true.

"There's nowhere else for me, Cece. Just with you." The words were a ragged whisper on Rainer's lips. He placed a hand on her cheek.

Evan knelt beside them, fresh blood on his sword from fighting off the enemy hunters. He lifted the arrow and sniffed the tip. "Angel's Chariot. Cece, these are poison arrows."

Her eyes went wide. "We have to get the other one out."

"Can you heal the wound?" Evan asked.

"I don't know. The last one took a lot, and then I have to get the poison out. I'm not good with poisons. You saw back in Argaria. I could accidentally pull it into my body. I—"

Tears blurred her vision as she tried to remember the words Magdalena spoke for the poison spell back in Argaria. But she'd been wearing an Unsummoner bracelet, and she was so weak that the memory was patchy.

Xander knelt beside her. She checked him frantically for wounds.

"I'm fine," Xander whispered. He cast a nervous glance at Rainer. "Can you fix him? Can I help?"

She looked from Xander to Rainer, and she could barely see him through the tears. She was furious and frustrated. The death whispers tormented her as they grew louder.

"It's the whispers, isn't it? I feel your fear," Rainer rasped.

She shook her head, but he knew. "No, it's not. It's totally quiet," she lied. "I need you to fight, Rain. *Please.*"

The words sparked her determination. If she was going to ask Rainer to fight, she had to fight too. Cecilia took a deep breath and centered herself. She grabbed the other arrow and yanked it out. Covering the wound, she pushed past all her fear and panic, blocking out the death whispers, drawing on her healing power. She pushed past where she thought she could, to the limits of her power—so hard that she felt the goddess power just a breath away as if the wall had become nothing but a sheer silk curtain.

It was agony. She stitched the blood vessels and muscle and skin back together. Sweat dripped from her nose. Her whole body ached and shook with the effort, but she refused to stop. Finally, it was sewn back together. There was a scar, but he was whole again.

When she looked up, Rainer was pale. His skin was clammy. His eyes fluttered, looking past her like he couldn't totally see her face, then focusing again.

"It's the poison," Evan said solemnly.

"Rain, I'm begging you—please hold on. Please stay. Don't go where I can't go." She held his face between her hands.

She looked down at his beautiful green eyes and realized he was crying. Her chest was impossibly tight.

"I'm sorry, Cece. I couldn't see it—not until now. You're everything. If I could go back, I'd choose you every time. I love you so much."

If Xander or Evan were surprised by the revelation, they didn't react. Cecilia thought she'd been the only one carrying the weight of secret feelings, but now it was clear they all bore the burden.

Rainer brushed his fingers over her cheek. "You gave me so many chances. I'd go back. I'd give it all up for you." His eyes sharpened on hers. "There has never been a moment when I wasn't breathless with love for you. I was made to love you, Cece."

Then, to her surprise, he kissed her.

Right there, in front of her husband, Rainer McKay kissed Cecilia

Reznik, the Princess of Argaria, the Lost Goddess, his best friend. He kissed her like he'd been born to the task and he didn't care who either of them were or who was watching. Rainer kissed her like he was dying and he wouldn't get another chance. His tenderness unraveled her.

She met him with every part of her that wanted to hear those words for so long. Her heart raced, and her blood sang in her veins—her body a perfect harmony of sensations conducted by a deep, potent longing.

I was made to love you, Cece.

It felt like coming home to somewhere she'd never been before but never wanted to leave. Rainer smelled like the intoxicating fresh linen and ocean air and lilac smell she loved so much. The kiss was desperate and hungry, born from a deep need that had been repressed for so long, but as it went on, it became slower, softer, more languid.

Every brush of his lips was like remembering a piece of something long forgotten. Cecilia couldn't stop chasing it, as if trying to grasp on to a dream the moment after waking. On and on, she followed that familiar feeling, his taste seeping into her bones.

The tension in her body melted away all at once, replaced by a pulsing buzz of pleasure beneath her skin. Her heart raced so fast that she worried for a moment that the thrill of kissing Rainer might actually kill her, too. The pleasure of it snaked through her body, coiling and uncoiling.

For a few minutes, it was just the two of them. Two friends who loved each other, kissing like they might never get to do it again. Two hearts trying desperately not to break. Two lost souls trying to cling to a thread of hope.

They were both shaking when he finally pulled away. Tears streamed down Cecilia's cheeks, heart cracked wide open, all the love pouring out at once.

Rainer's breath rattled in his chest, but he smiled.

A sob ripped through her. *What good is it being the daughter of the gods if you won't help me?* Rainer's eyes fluttered. She saw the pain on his face and felt the pain in his heart.

Help me. Help us, please. I will do anything. Please help me save him. Please help me fix him, she begged any god who would listen.

Suddenly everything stilled around her. The forest was silent. Rainer, Evan, and Xander were all frozen. She sat up and looked around and saw him. Jet black hair, gray eyes, cocky smile.

"You!" Cecilia said. "What are *you* going to do to help?"

"I take it you've figured out who I am. You should be mindful with rogue prayers. You never know what god might answer."

"Cato."

"At your service. How can I help you, Cecilia?" Cato asked.

She crossed her arms. "Save Rainer. I don't know how you are going to do it, but if you're here, you must know how."

"Didn't your father warn you about dealing with me?" he taunted.

"Were you spying on me in the Godswoods?"

Cato grinned. "I'm always spying on you. Like I said, I've been waiting a long time for you."

"Can you save him or not?"

"I am the trickster god, little dove. I can do anything. Pulling one over on the god of death is no exception."

"And he'll be as good as he was before? None of your trickster nonsense," she huffed.

"No tricks for you. I will ask for a favor in the future. A life for a favor is a good deal."

"What kind of favor?" Cecilia asked.

Cato shrugged a shoulder. "I'm not sure yet."

"You can't just do this for me without a favor?"

"Would you trust me if I did?" he asked, smiling mischievously.

Cecilia blew out a breath. "No, I wouldn't. Fine. But the favor can't involve hurting anyone, and the favor can't be me."

"Do you agree?" Cato's eyes lit with triumph.

"I agree."

"Gods seal deals with a kiss."

She frowned at Cato and sighed. "Fine."

He slid a hand up her neck and pulled her into a gentle kiss. It was just long enough to make her curious and leave her wanting more for reasons she didn't fully understand. His lips quirked up, and recognition washed over her.

"You don't actually seal deals with a kiss, do you?" she groaned.

"We don't." Cato laughed. "But I couldn't help myself. There must always be a small trick in my deals, or everyone will think I've gone soft."

He placed a vial in her hands. "Have him drink this. It will draw the poison to his stomach and make him very sick. He will still need a healer when you get home to fix the lasting effects, but this will save him, and he will heal once they work on him."

"Thank you," Cecilia said, blinking back tears. "I won't forget this."

"Don't worry. I'll remind you next time I see you. You don't have to wait until you're in trouble to call me. See you soon, little dove." Cato winked at her.

She looked down at Rainer, and when she looked back, Cato was gone. She was standing over a very confused Evan.

"How did you get over there?" Evan asked.

"Magic," she said, settling back down next to Rainer. "Rain, you have to drink this. It will not be pleasant, but it will fix you."

She helped him sit up and held the vial to his lips. Once he'd downed the whole thing, she rolled him onto his side and held his head in her lap.

"He said it would make Rain sick, but it would fix him. We'll still need to get him to a healer when we get back, but this will work for now." She ran her fingers through Rainer's messy hair.

"Who is 'he'?" Xander asked.

Cecilia met his eyes. "Cato."

"Love, that could just be poison." Xander looked wildly around the woods like he'd be able to spot Cato himself.

"Why intervene if Rainer was already going to die? It wouldn't make sense." Cecilia tried to sound confident.

Rainer was curled into a ball, his breathing shallow. "I don't feel good," he rasped.

Cecilia rubbed Rainer's back and brushed the hair back from his clammy forehead. He writhed in pain, and she held her hand against the back of his neck, trying to soothe him.

Rainer whispered her name repeatedly, like a prayer. She hated watching him suffer, so she looked at Xander.

"What did it cost, Cece?" Xander asked.

She frowned. "I'm sure I'll find out soon."

Xander looked like he wanted to say something else, but he kept his mouth shut, looking down at where her hand rested on Rainer's skin. Jealousy swirled in the air around him. She knew they would probably fight about everything that had transpired between her and Rainer later, but she pushed the thought from her mind.

Finally, Rainer started to wretch. He threw up for an absurdly long time. When he finished, his color looked marginally better, but he still looked like he was on Grimon's doorstep.

"We shouldn't stay here tonight. It's a poor position to defend. We probably can't make it back to Olney tonight, but we can't stay here," Evan said.

It took a lot of heavy lifting from Evan and Xander to get Rainer onto Zeke with Cecilia. Once he was there, he wrapped his arms around her waist and leaned forward, curling his face into her neck. He was still dazed from the medicine, but she was comforted by the steady rhythm of his breath on her neck.

She followed behind Evan and Xander at a distance.

"Rain? I need you to promise me something," she whispered.

"Anything, Cece."

"Crescent promise you will never lie to me again like you did about the goddess thing. Never keep something important from me."

Rainer sighed, placing his left hand over hers on the reins. "I crescent promise I won't lie to you ever again."

"Even if you think it's for my own good, or it could save me."

"Even if I think it's for your own good." He hesitated. "Even if I think it could save you."

"I need you to promise not to make any deals with Cato. I know I'm going to regret that. Even if he says he can save me."

"I promise," Rainer said.

"I need to feel like I have one person I can trust completely," Cecilia admitted.

"What about Xander?"

"I've known you much longer. I trust you more than anyone else in the world." She didn't say that Grimon had put new doubt in her mind about Xander. "Were you scared?" she whispered.

Rainer tightened his arms around her waist. "I don't remember. I just know all I could see was you when I closed my eyes, and I thought I was going to die. I saw every moment we spent together. I saw the way you smile in the morning when I'm sneaking out, and you know you don't have to be awake yet. I heard your laugh when you beat me on the archery range. I saw my whole life, and the only thing I wanted to see was more of you. It wasn't enough. I wanted to hold you every night, kiss you every day. I saw all the things I wanted to do that I hadn't yet—all the things I let stupid rules keep me from, and I thought the regret alone would kill me."

She tried to hold back the flood of emotions. She tried to push the image of Rainer dying out of her head.

"Thank you for saving me. I'm sorry I kissed you in front of your husband," Rainer whispered. "And also, I'm not sorry at all. I'd almost die all over again to kiss you like that." She felt him smile against her neck. "I kissed a princess."

She giggled through her tears. "I'd really like to shove you off this horse right now for telling me all of this now."

"I know." He tightened his arms around her waist. "I can wait for you. I was made to love you, and I'll never stop."

The words called forth a flood, and she couldn't hold back anymore. Tears poured down her face. They were exactly the words she'd wanted to hear for so long. Fate was cruel to bring them forth when she was happy with someone else.

She didn't try to stop the tears. All of the broken things in her came to the surface at once as she sobbed with her best friend's arms wrapped around her while she carried him home.

She thought she was done with wanting Rainer. Thought she had given him up weeks ago when he told her he would never give her what she wanted. She remembered the grief and loneliness, her longing like a blade slicing through her.

She'd surrendered that dream and burned it on a pyre in her mind, but as Rainer dozed against her shoulder, she knew that hadn't settled it.

Her love for him was a phoenix. She watched it burn, but now it rose from the ash reborn, a different form, and yet somehow still the most familiar thing in her life.

I was made to love you, and I'll never stop.

Cecilia wondered if the fates were trying to tell her she was made to love him too.

37

The sun beat down as the group crossed through Olney farmlands, the heat a constant reminder of how close they were to home. Rainer was still too weak to do much. He rode through the day, dozing on Cecilia's shoulder.

Xander was uncharacteristically quiet, as he had been since the afternoon before, and his somber mood set Cecilia on edge. She had been too afraid to bring up her kiss with Rainer, but she felt the tension seeping in ever since.

Xander's anger rose off him in waves, but she didn't know if it was directed solely at Rainer or also her. When they stopped for lunch earlier in the day, Xander shifted when he was helping Rainer down from the horse and let him tumble into the dirt.

Cecilia had seen nothing but satisfaction on Xander's face when Rainer looked up at him and said, "I deserved that."

But he'd yet to say anything to Cecilia, and she had a sneaking suspicion she'd feel less guilty if he did. As if his anger leveled at her would somehow lessen culpability for not just kissing Rainer but still being in love with him.

Bringing it up to Xander felt needlessly cruel. If he would not address it, the least she could do was sit with her guilt.

Thankfully, she had little time to think about it before they reached the familiar rows of houses at the edge of Olney City. The relief she felt when they finally reentered the city just as the sun was setting was overpowered by the fury she'd spent days packing away. She knew she'd have to face her father soon. But first, she and Rainer needed to do their final Gauntlet closing ritual.

Evan and Xander helped Rainer down and were ready to walk him to her father's house, but she stopped them.

"Just help him over here for a second," she said, walking to the stable entrance, where they'd stood weeks ago before they left. Rainer smiled, even as he wavered on his feet. He pressed his hands into hers, palm to palm and crescent scar to crescent scar.

Rainer smiled. "Once upon a time, there was a guardian—"

"And a witch—"

"Who completed their last Gauntlet run—"

"And they lived happily ever after," she whispered.

Tears streamed down her face when she pulled him into a tight hug. She let all the fear, worry, grief, and exhaustion go and hugged her best friend, who'd ridden all over the two kingdoms with her. The true magnitude of what they'd done finally hit her.

"I'm so proud of you," she whispered to Rainer. He pulled back, and she could see in his eyes what those words meant to him.

After a long moment, they turned to Xander and Evan and walked up the path to the Reznik estate.

————

Cecilia stood in the greenhouse doorway, staring at her imposing father. Her hands were poised on her hips as if facing down a naughty child.

"My little storm!" Leo Reznik's face lit up when he saw her.

The nickname startled her, sucking the fire out of her stern facade. She needed her anger to get through this confrontation. *He's not your real father. He lied to you your whole life.*

"Dad," she said, allowing him to sweep her into a hug.

She relaxed for a second into the embrace of the man who raised her, taught her to hunt, made her a warrior behind the disguise of a lady. He set her down and studied her face carefully. Searching for something he didn't find.

"That's a lot of blood," Leo said, looking at her shirt.

"It's Rain's. I'm fine."

Still, his eyes searched her arms for a wound. Finally, his gaze shot over her shoulder to the three men behind her.

His eyes locked on Evan, growing wider as he sniffed the air. "Cecilia Juliet, have you brought an Argarian hunter into my home?"

Cecilia placed a hand on his chest. "Did you get our message? This is Evan Farlan."

The huntmaster nodded warily.

"I have a lot to tell you, and you have a lot to tell me—a lot you left out of your stories," Cecilia said.

A wave of regret passed over his face. "Of course," he said gruffly, his gaze darting back to her companions. "Rainer!" He pulled Rainer into a hug. "What's wrong with him?"

"He was hit with poison arrows. I've done my best, but he really needs a more experienced healer. Of course, he insisted on coming here first to help," Cecilia explained. "As if I'm the stubborn one."

Her father nodded. His eyes passed over her husband. "Xander! My boy, it's good to see you. I see you succeeded in bringing my daughter back in one piece. She didn't give you any trouble?"

"None that I wasn't happy to get into," Xander said.

Cecilia gave him a dirty look before turning back to her father. "Dad, I have good news and bad news. Which do you want first?"

"Cecilia, you know I always prefer to get my bad news on the heels of something positive."

She hesitated. Xander gave her an encouraging smile.

"Good news is that I got married." She held up her hand, showing off her wedding band and Queen Juliana's ring.

Leo's eyes went wide, and he took a step back. "Cecilia!"

"To Xander."

Xander stepped forward and put a hand on the small of her back.

Her father's face was inscrutable. She felt the swirl of emotions around him—confusion and anger, tinged with joy. Her father had a temper, but when it came to her, he knew when not to bother with a battle. What was done was done.

He looked at Xander, who shifted nervously beside her. She knew her father loved him as a hunter, but that didn't mean he thought he was good enough for his daughter. In her father's mind, Xander was still below her station, but she could tell Xander was desperate for his blessing.

"Xander." The huntmaster pulled him into a tight hug. Then Leo turned back to Cecilia, taking her hands in his. "You've always been one to laugh in the face of tradition, but did you have to run off and get married without me?"

"I can show it to you," she said.

She closed her eyes, took his hand, and shared the memories, both hers and Xander's, careful to leave out any hint of their location or images of the enemy queen. When she opened her eyes and looked up at her father, there were tears in his eyes.

"You were so beautiful! Gods, I wish your mother could have been there to see it." Leo pulled her into a tight squeeze. She leaned her head on his shoulder. He let her go and stepped back, looking back and forth from her to Xander. "So, what's the bad news?"

She carefully positioned herself between Xander and her father.

"Promise to stay very calm?" She said it softly, like she was approaching a wild animal. His eyes darted over her shoulder to Xander. "You know him as Xander Merleen, but that's not his real name. His real name is Prince Alexander Savero."

The huntmaster's eyes grew wide, and his face turned red as he looked at Xander. "Cecilia Juliet Reznik! You married the Prince of Argaria? Our enemy! Have you lost your mind?"

"You're the one who trained him under your wing all these years," she scoffed.

"You! You've done this. Some strange magic!" Leo tried to push past Cecilia to get to Xander, but she stood her ground.

"Dad, calm down. I knew who he was when I married him. There was no magic involved. I love him."

"Sir, I love Cece very much. I apologize for not asking your blessing," Xander started.

"Don't speak to me, Savero! I asked you to keep an eye on her, not seduce her!" He turned on his heel, pacing back into the greenhouse. "Cecilia, why would you do this?"

"To prevent Davide Savero from becoming an unbeatable enemy, Dad. To save Olney. Because I was blindsided by finding out that I'm the godsdamned Lost Goddess. I had to make a choice. Actually, I had to make quite a few hard choices to protect *you*."

She reconnected with her anger, and it felt good. Her father clenched a fist at his side, but he stayed quiet.

"I fell in love with Xander before I knew who he was. And then I found out who he was, and I still said yes when he proposed, because I love him. You taught me to be assertive, to go after what I want, but then made it clear that I'd be coming home to a choice you made for me. I made a choice for myself instead. No point arguing about it now."

Her father just stared at her.

"It's easy to say that I would have decided to do this differently, but I don't think that's true." She reached for Xander's waiting hand. Holding it made her feel stronger, more like herself. It wasn't so much that he lent her strength as he reminded her of the strength she already possessed.

"He loves me, and I love him. I know you saw it in the memory. We have a plan, or at least the beginnings of one. He protected me when I couldn't protect myself. I need you to trust me. I need you to give this a chance, and you might not be inclined to, but I'm asking you to because you owe me."

Leo looked down at the floor, ashamed.

"Which brings me to my next bit of bad news that we should probably talk about alone."

Cecilia turned into Xander's arms.

"Are you sure you don't want me to stay?" Xander asked.

"I'm sure. Will you help Rainer get up to the healer? Take Evan to your old place. I'll meet you outside when I'm done."

He searched her face for a moment. When she smiled, he kissed her forehead and turned to help Rainer out of the room.

She faced her father. Leo suddenly looked much older. As much as she was furious with him and wanted to hurt him the way he hurt her, some small part of her felt guilty for wanting to. Finally, he spoke.

"I think a part of me always thought you would marry Rainer. The two of you were so clearly in love with each other. That's why I turned down all the offers for your hand. Every time someone approached me about it, it just felt wrong."

The words shocked Cecilia and completely threw her off course. "But that's forbidden—" She stumbled on the words.

"But it would have made you happy. Once you were the goddess, who would tell you no?" Leo asked.

The revelation scalded her. She thought she was prepared for this, but she'd somehow miscalculated. "Why didn't you tell me?"

"I wanted the two of you paying attention on this last trip, not all over each other," Leo said, shaking his head. "I know he spent every night with you."

Her eyes went wide. "You do?"

"I'm the huntmaster, for Clastor's sake! Of course I knew what my own daughter was up to. I let it happen because no one knows how to love and care for you better than Rainer. I saw it as you grew up. I knew he would never do anything you didn't want him to. I trusted you to make your own decisions. You are so much like Selene and Rosalee in that way. Headstrong and stubborn, and you keep your own counsel."

Cecilia could hardly breathe. Her father ran a hand through his hair. His weariness was clear in every movement.

"When Rainer looks at you, he sees nothing else. It's been that way since he met you. That is why I let you be paired with him to begin with. It's why I let you have an inappropriately close relationship with him your whole life. Even when you were young, the two of you used to sneak off to the cottage and fall asleep telling stories.

However necessary it might have been, marrying someone else is a pretty big surprise. I see the way you look at Xander and the way he looks at you. You love each other. But it's not the same as how Rainer looks at you. I know because it's the way I looked at your mother."

The question scared Cecilia, but she asked it anyway. "How does he look at me?"

"He looks at you like you're the very air he breathes. Like he could never get enough of you. So I'll ask once because you're my daughter and I love you. I will get you out of this mess in a second if that's what you want. Do you want me to have the marriage reversed? There's a strong case for proving you were under duress. I know it feels like so much choice has been taken from you. Let me give this back."

He looks at you like you're the very air he breathes. Like he could never get enough of you.

Cecilia drowned in the words, uncertain what to say. She thought of Rainer's confession when he was dying. She thought of how it felt to think of living without him.

"You don't have to decide now—"

"Dad, I made a promise. You taught me to be a woman of my word—to never make promises I can't keep. There is no going back, I can only move forward. I love Xander. He's kind and funny, and he drives me crazy, but I love him."

"And you don't still love Rainer?"

Cecilia threw her hands up. "Of course I do. I always will. But he only realized his mistake when he thought he'd lost me. He couldn't see it until I was all but gone. Xander looked right at me, and from the first time he saw me, he couldn't get enough. He chose me over his family—an impossible choice—but he made it easily. He's done nothing but honor me and put me first. He lets me be me."

Her father smiled weakly. "Well then, I suppose I should call you Your Highness now."

"You better not." She laughed. "Dad, why didn't you just tell me I was the goddess? Do you have any idea of the heartbreak you could have saved me?"

"I wanted you to have a chance to be a normal girl for as long as possible. Cecilia, I always loved you like you were my own. You are my daughter just as much as you are his. You were always my daughter first. You still are. I think a part of me didn't want you to transform."

"Well, I haven't," she breathed. "I haven't used the power yet, so technically, I'm not the goddess yet."

"Why not?"

She fought hard against the tears that threatened. A lump formed in her throat and threatened to choke her. For a moment, she couldn't look at him. "Daddy—"

His eyes went wide at the name she hadn't called him since she was a child. She tried to grasp onto the rage she'd felt earlier, but it slipped through her fingers like sand. She took a deep breath.

"The exchange for the power. It's a price I don't think I can pay. I'm trying not to. If I knew what I was buying with my sacrifice, I wouldn't have. If I accept my full powers and become the goddess I was meant to be, I will lose my ability to have children." Her anger evaporated into silent tears.

Her father looked as if she had slapped him. He was speechless.

"Now I am fighting with this thing like I'm in the grips of a relentless addiction. I don't know how long I can hold it at bay. We're being pursued by Davide Savero and his army and maybe Endros. I married Xander, but Rainer finally wants to be with me, and I'm just—gods, I'm just so exhausted. I don't want to save the world. I just want to be a normal girl. How can I save the kingdom? I can barely save myself," she sobbed.

Leo hugged her, and as she cried in his arms, she felt like she was back to being just the huntmaster's daughter, as if she'd come full circle.

They held each other for a long time as they both tried to fathom the gravity of a loss she hadn't yet suffered. Together, they'd weathered the loss of her mother. Nothing prepared them for that, the same way nothing prepared them for this loss. A lifetime of exchanges had done nothing to prepare the Rezniks for the sacrifice it took to accept that type of power.

38

Even with her eyes closed in focused meditation, Cecilia felt the moment Xander shot up in bed looking for her.

They'd rushed into her cottage the night before, eagerly bathing and then falling into bed together. Cecilia expected to sleep heavily thanks to finally being back in her bed, but she tossed and turned, chased from sleep each time she found it by nightmares of Rainer being struck with arrows and falling from his horse.

She understood Xander's panic. It was barely dawn, and she was awake and out of bed. She tried to ignore the feeling of his heavy gaze on her and focus on the words she silently repeated to keep her grounded and contented to her body: *Sky above. Earth below. Me right here.*

But as the sun rose, casting the lilac light behind her eyelids orange, she gave up.

"I know you're awake and staring at me," she said, blinking her eyes open.

Xander frowned. "I think the real question is, what is my wife, who hates to get up early, doing up at dawn?"

"I woke up and couldn't go back to sleep."

It surprised her how smoothly she lied. Still, Xander read it on her face. He always saw her so clearly, even when she was trying to hide. She loved him for it.

"Were you praying?" he asked.

"I suppose it's a bit of a prayer. More to myself than the gods, though."

"Love, I've been trying to give you the space to work whatever this is out on your own, but I'm worried."

She sighed. "I know. I can feel that too."

"Do you want to tell me?"

"No."

"Will you please tell me? Whatever worries you have, let them be my worries too."

"I don't want them to be your worries." She sighed.

All day and night, the goddess power clawed at Cecilia, scraping her with its talons, begging her to claim it and solidify the exchange she'd agreed to. The more it went on, the more she felt hopeless. Her resistance felt futile, but how could she admit that to Xander?

Frustration painted his face. "Well, it's not up to you. We agreed to be a team on all things. Talk to me, Cece. Tell me what's bothering you so much. Don't think I haven't noticed how you barely eat. I see how you wake up in cold sweats from nightmares. I've seen the edginess since you shared memories with me back on our journey. What's going on?"

Her frustration evaporated, and her shoulders relaxed. She crossed back over to the bed, and he wrapped his arms around her, kissing her softly.

"Whatever it is, you can tell me. I hate to see you go through it alone," he whispered.

She hesitated still. "The goddess power is close. I don't know how to explain it or when exactly it started. I don't know if it happened because I started summoning again, but I know it got really intense around then. Each time I summon, it's like the wall between me and my power crumbles a bit. I can feel it all the time, just out of reach. Like even though my summoning is different, it's magic, and it wants to reach out to other magic. It's always there, waiting. I cannot seem to shake it no matter what I do. The only time it ever goes away is when I'm here with you."

"Well, I guess you have to just stay in my arms forever," Xander said.

"I wish that I could." She smiled. "I'm afraid that I can't hold it off. I'm doing my best, but it is relentless. I feel it in my bones, under my skin, like a humming. It calls to me like a siren song that I am afraid I'm not strong enough to resist."

"So you pray?" he asked.

"I repeat a phrase to myself over and over until it stops, or at least recedes. It reminds me I'm here, and I'm human. Xander, I'm really afraid of it. I don't know what it is, and it feels dark —" Her voice broke, and tears rolled down her cheeks.

"Not possible. There is no part of you that isn't brilliant and shining."

She blew out a breath. "Be serious."

"I am serious. Look, I'm no stranger to the dark. I'm not afraid of it, and I'm definitely not afraid of any part of you. I love you, whether you are at your best or your worst, no matter what happens."

"But what if I give in? What if I become the goddess?"

Xander looked baffled by the question. "Then you become the goddess, and we figure it out."

"But I won't be able to have children, and you want them."

He cradled her face gently in his hands. "There are many ways to be parents. We will find a way to make it happen if you want, but I will live the rest of my days a happy man with just you and me. That is truly what is in my heart."

"What if it changes me? Power can corrupt. What if it makes me dark and scary?" she sobbed.

"Have I ever told you what you smell like?"

"Xan, what does that have to do with anything?" she asked, exasperated.

"Bear with me here. I promise I have a point. Have I ever told you what you smell like with my enhanced hunter's senses?"

"Lemons and lavender. Summertime."

"Yes, but it's more specific than that," Xander said. "I smell the lavender buds at the peak of their season, mixed with the pollen of other wildflowers. I can smell the salt of the ocean on the stems. I can smell the sunlight on the rind of each lemon, plump with juice. You smell like everything bright, beautiful, and vibrant in the world. It's a smell that suits you better than I could have ever imagined. Cece, you are hope embodied. I meant what I wrote on our wedding day. You are a light in the dark. I am certain that whatever you become will reflect who you are as a person, and that is a goddess I would like to meet."

Sometimes Xander's intensity startled her, but it simply felt romantic at that moment. She'd always struggled to let anyone take care of her, but with Xander, she found it easy.

He was too good to her, which only made her guilt worse.

Cecilia had been waiting for the other shoe to drop. Waiting for Xander to yell or rage. Waiting for him to notice that she hadn't been nearly as distraught when he'd almost died to save her life back in Argaria.

"Are we going to talk about what happened in the woods?" The words came out in a rush of breath.

Xander held her gaze. "What's there to say? The man thought he was dying. Can't say I wouldn't like to get a few shots in when he's ready to be back in the fighting ring, but it was just a kiss, right?"

Cecilia swallowed hard. "Right."

"Feeling guilty? Hoping I'll offer absolution, love?"

"I want you to forgive me for kissing another man when you're my husband."

Xander cocked his head to the side. "And if I can't?"

Cecilia frowned, suddenly angry. "If you can't, I'd urge you to search your heart again. After all, I forgave you for taking me to bed while lying to me about who you and I were."

Xander shook his head. "Can you really say it's forgiven if you wield it like a dagger in every fight?"

"I married you, did I not?"

"Did you have another choice?" Xander countered, his brow

pinched, eyes blazing. She'd never seen him look so angry, at least not at her.

She cupped his face in her hands. "Of course I did. I married you because I love you, Xander. I could have waited until the next day and been free on my own."

Xander threw his hands up. "You didn't know that at the time."

Cecilia took his hands in hers. "But I could have pushed it off instead of having a deeply personal and romantic ceremony with you."

The raw doubt and fear on his face unnerved her. He was always so confident.

"Will you kiss him again?"

Gods, she wanted to. The phantom of the kiss still lingered on her lips. *There has never been a moment when I wasn't breathless with love for you.* Those words from Rainer's lips carried so much weight.

"No," she said, her voice strong with conviction.

It wasn't exactly a lie. She had no plans to, though she couldn't say for sure that if the opportunity presented itself, she'd be strong enough to pull away. Maybe a good marriage required exchanging small lies to keep the peace.

The goddess power churned in her stomach, and she winced under the strain of the stress of it.

"Come here, love. I'll make it go away," Xander whispered as he pulled her into his arms.

All the tension eased from her body. Xander kissed her until she stopped worrying. She'd never been more grateful for the way his kiss ignited an insatiable flame in her that drove her well beyond distraction and the way his touch made her feel so grounded and aware of every nerve in her body. She felt fully human.

She let him make love to her all morning until she floated off blissfully to sleep again, and though he never explicitly said he forgave her, there was forgiveness in his touch.

39

Cecilia blinked her bleary eyes, adjusting to the dim light as she and Xander stepped through the threshold of Olney Castle. After two days of doing little more than walking on the beach, eating, and spending most of their time in bed, they were forced back into the real world by a royal summons.

Whether Cecilia felt up for it or not, in a few moments, all eyes would be on her, the new Argarian princess and secret goddess, and her handsome prince. She had a major bone to pick with the king, no matter how exhausted she felt.

Once she confessed what the exchange for her power cost her the night she got home, her father admitted how complicit King Hector Teripin was in the lie of the Gauntlet. Cecilia knew the king was eager to figure out what her powers were. She wasn't sure what the king was expecting when he summoned her, but he wouldn't be met with the same meek girl who'd left weeks before.

She thought of all the duos they had known that had perished in pursuit of the Gauntlet, and it reinforced her resolve. Hector Teripin had known the truth, and he allowed hundreds of Olney children to grow up training to be warriors to fight to complete a Gauntlet when he knew who Cecilia was since birth. Argarian hunters or accidents in the field might have caused their deaths, but the king bore just as much responsibility.

No full-out war had come while she was finishing the Gauntlet. Evan confirmed Argaria had been waiting for Cecilia being fully in their grasp before they set out. Those plans had clearly shifted since their sudden departure from Argaria. King Davide Savero was marching toward Olney with several battalions of men, and Olney scouts could not figure out how he was making his way around their patrols.

Xander pulled her to a stop before they reached the throne room. The effect of him clean-shaven in his Olney hunter uniform was devastating. She couldn't stop grinning despite her nerves.

"Love, if you keep smiling at me like that, I am going to throw you over my shoulder and take you back to bed." The words sent a burst of heat to her cheeks. "Gods, I love that I can still do that."

He gave her a quick kiss before pulling back to meet her eyes.

"How is it right now? Scale of one to ten?" he asked.

"Five." It was more like an eight. A fine sheen of sweat coated her skin, but Xander didn't challenge her.

"Are you sure you don't want to wait?" he asked.

"We can't wait, Xander. Your brother is already on his way, perhaps with Endros himself. We have to at least help sort out this bit of madness." She sighed, lacing her fingers with his and tugging him down the hall.

When they stepped up to the doors of the throne room in Olney Castle, all eyes were on Cecilia. She hesitated in the doorway, but Xander squeezed her hand.

"We can still turn back," Xander whispered. "I might be a prince of nothing, but I don't mind throwing what little weight I have around for you."

"You know there's no turning back now. If we run into any trouble, I will summon a wall of fire to get us back to the door," she whispered.

She held her head high as they walked into the room hand in hand.

Her gaze landed on her father, who stood close to Hector's side. Even he looked nervous.

"Lady Cecilia Reznik and Prince Alexander Savero of Argaria."

As they were announced, a hush went over the court. The room was so quiet she wondered if everyone could hear her heartbeat banging in her chest. She curtseyed, and Xander bowed.

"Lady Reznik. It seems you've been busy," King Hector bellowed.

"Yes, Your Majesty."

"Do you care to explain yourself?" Hector asked.

"Not really," she said.

There was an exchange for betrayal. The lies she'd been fed her whole life made it impossible for her to contort herself back into a woman bound by duty. The appeasing daughter, the compliant witch, and the tamed lady of the court were gone. They were unbound by the tug that unraveled the tapestry of her life. She would never again be powerless to men who ruled with fear.

Xander coughed to stifle a laugh. His gaze heated like it always did when confronted with her defiance and her sharp tongue. Murmurs and gasps filled the room.

Cecilia caught Rainer's eye. He looked pale, and his anxiety buzzed through their connection. She sent him a thread of calm, and his face relaxed.

"Excuse me?" Queen Elena looked flabbergasted.

"Apologies, Your Majesties. I meant that this is quite a large audience to discuss so much about my personal life, and it makes me rather uncomfortable," Cecilia said.

"Well, Lady Reznik, we wouldn't have to if you hadn't run off and married yourself to an Argarian prince." King Hector was not a man quick to anger, but she felt the seething rage behind his words.

"An Argarian prince who spent the past eleven years as a valuable member of your army," Cecilia said. "It seems we've fallen for the same deception, Your Majesty."

The room went silent and so still, Cecilia wondered if a fire witch had sucked all the oxygen out.

Queen Elena shattered the heavy silence with a laugh. Everyone jumped in surprise. "She's not wrong, dear."

"Cecilia, I think Their Majesties would just like to know what transpired," the huntmaster said, his face grave.

"Well, what transpired was that you all sent the hunter you thought was Xander Merleen to assist Rainer McKay and me at our last few stops to finish the Gauntlet."

She locked eyes with Xander, and he smiled at her.

"I was resistant to any additional support, but Rainer had been captured by a pack of Argarian hunters. I knew I couldn't rescue him myself. So we did it together. We faced down eleven Argarian hunters and a slayer."

There were gasps of shock.

Rainer cleared his throat. "I was overpowered while I was momentarily separated from Cece—Cecilia. If Xander hadn't found her, I'm not sure what would have happened."

Cecilia gave him a grateful smile. Rainer tried to smile, but he looked scared, his gaze fixed on Raymond McKay, who looked entirely unimpressed with his son.

"Very sloppy, Guardian McKay. My bigger concern is how you could let her marry our enemy." Hector's anger had cooled slightly.

"It was my fault, Your Majesty. I take full responsibility. Cecilia is my charge." Rainer hung his head.

Cecilia sighed heavily. "No, I take responsibility because I'm a grown woman and quite capable of making my own decisions. For too long, this court has operated on outdated and ridiculous rituals that elevate men and subjugate women and that treat those of other classes as expendable. I'm a lady of this court, and I have only had the right to marry who I wish because I had the privilege of a father who gave me a choice. Everyone—women, hunters, common folk should have the ability to choose what they want based on their own values, not the archaic ones that have propped up this kingdom for centuries."

The stunned silence returned, and her father looked pale. His face was stoic. Anxiety pulsed around him.

"Well, you certainly came back from your journey spirited, Lady Reznik," Hector said.

Cecilia smiled sweetly. "I actually prefer Princess Savero now."

"Yes, perhaps you could explain that part," Elena said. Cecilia was grateful that the queen gave her grace, having been such close friends with her mother.

Xander squeezed Cecilia's hand. She was walking the line between disrespect and honesty.

She took a breath, and with Rainer's and Xander's help, told the rest of their story. When they were finished, Cecilia locked eyes with the king.

"All of my choices in life had been taken away in one day," Cecilia said. "I wanted to choose something for myself finally. So I chose Xander, and he chose me. If I could go back and do it over again, I would have done the same thing."

"Xander, were you tasked with this by your people? Winning the heart of the Lost Goddess?" Hector asked.

"No, Your Majesty. I was tasked to bring her to my brother so he could marry her, but I fell in love with her. It was impossible not to. I was gone for her before even I realized."

Xander looked at Cecilia in a way that made her knees weak. She felt uncomfortable with other people seeing the raw emotion on his face. She wanted to keep that for herself.

She looked around the room for friendly eyes among the women she'd grown up with. Sylvie looked amused, but all the other ladies of the court had eyes full of quiet contempt.

Not only had she married one of the most notorious playboys of the Olney court, but she was a princess who was so obviously adored by her very handsome prince.

"How do we know that you're telling the truth even now?" Hector looked frustrated, but Elena put a hand on his arm.

"Darling," Elena said. "One only needs to see the looks on their faces to know that kind of affection cannot be faked. What happened next? How did you escape?"

Cecilia swallowed hard and explained the rest of their story. How

Davide had murdered his parents, and they'd been forced to flee, how much they'd all sacrificed, especially Teddy.

"My husband might be an outsider, but he's lived in our court almost as long as his own," Cecilia said. "He may be the son of our enemies, but I've known him to be a kind person who wants what is best for his people. He doesn't want to be at war, and he's already lost enough."

The emotion of reliving their experience and the journey and the sharp ache that she fought off constantly had sucked the life out of her as she spoke.

King Hector rubbed his chin. The court was tense and silent.

"And what of your goddess powers?" he finally asked.

Cecilia didn't think it was possible for the room to feel more airless, but somehow the tension grew more oppressive.

"I have not accepted them yet."

The king scoffed, "Why not!"

"Because the cost is too high," she said quietly. "I'd be happy to share with Your Majesties privately, but I won't share in such a public forum."

She made eye contact with her father, and he looked down at the floor. She felt his shame from where she stood.

"So you aren't yet the goddess?" Hector asked.

"And I won't be." She tried to sound confident, but the words felt like ash in her mouth.

Hector scowled. "Not even to defend your people from a war you brought to our doorstep?"

"With all due respect, Your Majesty, I did no such thing," Cecilia said.

The room became deathly still. Xander stiffened next to her.

"This war has existed in one way or another since before I was born. Men insisting on proving their power is nothing new," Cecilia continued. She tried to tamp down her fury, but it reared up. "All of this could have been avoided if it wasn't in our culture for those in power to lie to everyone. This entire training program was built on deceit. If you had been honest from the beginning, I would have known what I was walking into. I would have avoided it, and we wouldn't be in this predicament now. I take no responsibility for believing a lie created to manipulate me—a lie that poisoned my entire life and ended the lives of countless others. You made children into warriors and sent them to the slaughter, chasing a Gauntlet you knew only I could complete. You may not have held the blade, but you sent them to slaughter at Argarian hands. I've done my part to mitigate the very real damage this kingdom has caused with its deception. I got myself out of Argaria. I married myself to their prince, hoping to bring peace. Freedom is expensive, and it seems the only one not to pay it's price so far has been you, Your Grace. I have done my part. Now it's time for you to do yours."

The words hung in the air, the entire court shocked by her boldness. Her anger was clarifying. It sharpened her words into a deadly weapon she was ready to wield against whoever required wounding.

Hector wanted to speak, but there was nothing to say. Fury surged around him, but he couldn't argue with her logic or pull her words back now. The entire court had heard.

"Very well. This isn't the end of our discussion, but we have much to consider with this new information. You may leave and continue to rest after your ordeal. We will summon you back for planning soon," King Hector said, waving a hand to dismiss them.

She and Xander turned and left the throne room, followed by Rainer and Evan. As soon as they were outside, Cecilia sucked in deep breaths. Her legs shook so badly she had to stop and let Xander steady her.

Before she could recover, Sylvie burst through the doors and hugged her. "You tricky little minx! You always have to show me up. I cannot believe you finished the Gauntlet and married a prince!"

Cecilia grinned at Sylvie, instantly forgetting her fatigue at the sight of her friend's joy.

"Sylvie, this is Xander," Cecilia said, gesturing to her husband.

"I know. We've met," she said.

Sylvie eyed Xander skeptically before her gaze settled on Evan.

Cecilia smirked as she recognized a spark of interest in her friend's eyes.

"And this is Evan Farlan."

Evan bowed and kissed Sylvie's hand, a gesture that Cecilia had never seen from him. His gaze lingered on Sylvie for an extra moment. It seemed the interest was mutual.

"Well, Cece, it's good to know you give all royals the same level of attitude. I'm glad that's not reserved just for Xander," Evan teased.

Cecilia's gaze snagged on Rainer, and in the light of day, the look of longing on his face was startlingly apparent. She averted her gaze as he, Evan, and Cal talked amongst themselves about the erratic and seemingly untraceable movements of the Argarian army.

Sylvie leaned in close enough so only Cecilia could hear.

"Cece, I would kill to have just one man look at me the way the two of them look at you. You've worked your way into quite a complicated little love triangle."

"Be careful what you wish for," Cecilia whispered.

Sylvie leaned away, pulling the rest of the group into the conversation. "Royalty looks good on you. You were amazing in there. So commanding. I love to see it."

Cecilia smiled tightly as her gut churned. "Hopefully, I won't regret it."

"I still can't believe you said all of that," Evan interrupted.

"What could he say to me? Being the Lost Goddess ought to buy me some respect. He lied to all of his people. A little verbal punishment is the absolute least he deserved."

Cecilia's eyes blazed from Evan to Rainer to Xander. When she saw the look on Xander's face, she froze.

"We should talk strategy this afternoon. I've been talking with other hunters and guardians," Rainer said.

"Later," Xander said, his eyes fixed on Cecilia's weary face.

"Could I borrow her for a few minutes?" Rainer asked.

Xander pinned Rainer with his gaze.

"Just to talk," Rainer said.

"I'm not her keeper," Xander said tightly.

Cecilia let Rainer guide her around the corner of the building out of sight of prying eyes. He paused for a moment in front of a statue of Zelden Novaris, the guardian who had once held off Endros's attack to allow Olney to prepare for battle. For most warriors in the kingdom there was no better example of honor and courage.

Cecilia reached up and brushed a hand over Rainer's cheek. "You look much better today."

"You look good, too." He smiled, his cheeks growing pink.

She hadn't seen him blush in a long time. Her fingers drifted over the scar on his neck, where the arrow had struck days before.

"Does it take away from my good looks?"

Cecilia smiled. "Scars are just reminders of the things we've survived. This is just a sign that you are stronger than the thing that tried to break you."

Rainer smiled at the words he'd said to her so many years before. He brought her left hand to his lips and kissed the crescent-shaped scar on her hand, the one he'd replicated on his own hand the day he'd spoken those words.

Rainer sighed. "I wish it was different. I wish I'd told you what I felt much sooner. Do you ever wish that?"

She swallowed hard. "I wished it every day for years."

"And now?"

"And now I'm confused. You told me to marry him and gave me your blessing. You sent me into his arms, and now you want to take it back? It's not fair, Rain."

She struggled to keep the tears at bay. Rainer cupped her face in his hands. There was so much love in his eyes.

"I wish I had never done that. I wish I had listened to you after the Reflection Forest. You gave me a chance, and I blew it—twice. I have so many regrets."

"And you will have to learn to live with them. I made vows to Xander—"

He sighed. "I know."

"I love him."

"I know."

429

"So, what do you want from me now?" she snapped. Her hands fastened around Rainer's wrists. She wasn't sure if she was holding him there or preparing to push him away.

"Whatever you will give me and also everything else." There was a desperation in his voice she'd never heard before.

She knew she should say something, but the words died on her lips.

"I will never stop wanting you—every part of you you're willing to give me," Rainer whispered.

It was so overwhelming. Cecilia wanted him to stop touching her and also wanted his hands everywhere. She wanted him to kiss her, and also, she wanted him to get as far away from her as possible. She wanted all of him, and she wanted no one else to have any of him. It was selfish, petty, and codependent. What they wanted was far too aligned, and that was dangerous.

"I shouldn't—" she started.

I shouldn't still want Rainer? I shouldn't be looking at his lips? I shouldn't have married Xander while I was still in love with someone else?

There was no denying her love for Xander. But there was also no denying that her feelings for Rainer were far from resolved.

Rainer looked at her lips and then her eyes, but he nodded and dropped his hands at his sides. Then he held them behind his back like he did not know what to do with his hands if they weren't touching her. He backed away, giving her space when she didn't want it—when she had no idea what she really wanted.

All she knew was she wasn't thinking about the gnaw of the goddess powers anymore, lost instead in how good it felt when Rainer touched her.

She dropped her head back and sighed.

"Did I make it worse?" he asked.

"No. It made it much better. I want—"

Rainer raised an eyebrow. "What do you want? Because I really can't tell anymore."

She sighed heavily. "Sometimes I wonder if what I feel for you is real, or if it's just because of the bond, or because someone told us we were a soul match. Do you ever think about how much is magic and how much is real?"

Rainer looked surprised by the question. "I've thought about it before. I know we're a bit codependent, and maybe that's unhealthy. When I was trying to talk myself out of wanting you a few years back, I really thought about it. I wrote a bunch of stuff down about it, actually."

Cecilia smiled. It was so like Rainer to make a list about something so hard to define and to analyze emotion like it was a battle strategy.

"When it comes down to it, even if I had never been paired with you. Even if we hadn't been bonded, I would have seen you," Rainer said. "I would have seen that you're kind to everyone. I would have seen the way you love so freely. You still would have scared the shit out of me because you're so brave and so open-hearted, but I have no doubt that I would have still fallen in love with you."

Cecilia stared at him, hardly breathing.

"Of course, I feel the pull to you. In some ways, I've always loved you," Rainer continued. "But what I feel through our bond enhances what I already feel for you. Trust me. I've spent two years trying not to love you. I don't think any magic is strong enough to withstand that."

"I hate the idea that this is one more thing in my life that magic might have poisoned," she said.

"Cece, watching you over this last trip showed me so much. Your compassion, even while you're suffering and grieving. Your willingness to forgive me, even when I don't deserve it. Your courage to face things that are terrifying and impossibly heavy. You never cease to amaze me. The bond is always there, so I won't know what it's like without it, but I know I would love you anyway," he said. His eyes were full of so much love, it was hard to hold his gaze.

"I would have loved you, too," she whispered.

They stared at each other, the air between them heavy with all the words spoken and unspoken. *I was made to love you, and I'll never stop.*

The words called forth a storm in her chest every time they floated into her mind.

Suddenly, the ache was back in her gut with a vengeance. She cringed around it.

"Let me take some of it, like before," Rainer whispered. "Share the weight with me. I can take it."

He slid his hand into hers expectantly. Cecilia hesitated for a moment but relented when he stroked the inside of her wrist. He pulled the pain right out of her. The relief was instant. When she blinked her eyes open, Rainer's face was pained. He took deep, shaky breaths until the pain passed.

"I'm sorry," she whispered.

Rainer shook his head. "You have nothing to be sorry for. It's already almost gone. It's not a big deal."

"It's a big deal to me," she murmured.

She wondered if she could actually continue this way. Perhaps it was as easy as sharing the burden with Rainer every other day or so. Maybe she could hold back the power after all. Maybe they could develop a system that would at least give her and Xander a chance to try to have a baby. Maybe she had to hold it off for a year or two. If they could do this every few days, she could endure it.

Maybe she didn't need to solve for the exchange as much as postpone it. Even that felt like taking back some of the control she felt she'd lost. It didn't make up for the choice being taken away from her, but it did place some of the power back in her hands.

"I think I could hold out if you did that every few days," Cecilia murmured.

Voicing it out loud felt dangerous—like tempting fate—but she couldn't help herself. Hope had been elusive ever since she'd set out on that last Gauntlet run. She needed to cultivate what she could now.

"Cece, I will do that every day if it makes you feel better. When you pass it to me, it's there for a moment before it dissipates. If it helps you, I can do it as often as you need." His thumb circled her inner wrist, as soothing as his words.

"What if I can't bear it? What if I give in to it?" Suddenly, she desperately needed Rainer's reassurance, certain that whatever darkness waited for her would turn her into someone Rainer couldn't love.

Rainer frowned. "What if you do?"

"What if it changes me?"

"It won't." He said it with so much certainty. She wondered how, after everything they'd been through, he still had access to that same sense of certainty.

"You can't know that."

"I know you," Rainer said. "Better than you know yourself sometimes. Whatever you become, I'll love you. You are stronger, kinder, and braver than anyone else I know. You've been going into the dark on your own since we were kids. I know that whatever happens, you will come out the other side still being yourself."

"But what if it's something terrible?" She was embarrassed by the desperation in her voice and terrified of how much she needed his reassurance. "Generally, the gods seem like assholes."

Rainer laughed. "I think you'll be different. Most of the gods didn't live mortal lives before they became gods. That's unique to you, and it's given you humility and compassion. You'll be a better goddess for it. I understand your apprehension, but you should know, I don't feel any at all. I have faith in you."

Rainer stepped back, letting his hands fall away from her skin. Cecilia instantly missed his warmth.

"You should go. We'll meet you at the cottage in an hour to talk strategy," Rainer rasped, finally breaking eye contact.

Cecilia nodded wordlessly and stepped back around the front of the building. As she took Xander's hand, she'd never felt so grateful that she had friends to borrow faith from when hers was elusive.

40

The Adiran Sea glittered in the sunlight like a chest filled with gleaming blue gems as Cecilia and Evan stood on the beach below her cottage. The humidity had waned, but the heat remained in the morning light, and she couldn't help but feel excited for autumn in Olney. Cecilia loved the season for its warmth and lack of humidity, bright days, and lovely blooms.

"I feel like I should be included in the planning for whatever is to come." Cecilia sighed, looking out into the surf.

"Cece, you need to trust that they will include you where you are needed," Evan said.

"Do you trust them to do that?" she asked.

Evan shrugged. "No, not really. They both treat you like you're a delicate flower, when you're more like an unsupervised powder keg rolling toward a fire."

Cecilia grinned. "Careful, Evan, if you keep being so sweet, I'll start to think you're actually warming to me."

The hunter let out a tentative laugh.

Davide and his battalion were two days out. War had finally come. Rainer and Xander were called away to meet with the huntmaster to discuss the impending invasion. Much to her frustration, they left

Cecilia with Evan for the day, and to avoid sitting in the cottage while he paced, she suggested a walk on the beach.

"Xander's trying to do what's best for you. You're his number one priority, and beyond that, you're technically my princess, so you have to accept my protection," Evan said.

"What about my people? My life is not more important than anyone else's. I should just get over my hang-ups, claim this stupid power, and stop trying to pretend it isn't inevitable." She dragged a toe through the sand.

"Your sense of responsibility is commendable," Evan said. "Let the men who brought the war to your doorstep take care of the mess they've made. Xander knew this was a possibility from the moment he insisted on marrying you. He's made a mess that neither you nor I can solve for him. You have to give him the chance to rise to the occasion."

Cecilia frowned. "How do you think Davide and his battalion have covered so much ground so quickly? If the scouts are to be believed, their route is impossible."

Evan looked warily out at the sea. "I cannot say, but there are rumors about Endros's and Cato's powers that might explain how they so easily made their way across the border and have moved freely within Olney."

"Care to elaborate?"

Evan frowned. "I'm still the Argarian spymaster. I deal in facts, not rumors."

Cecilia flung a shell from the sand into the roiling blue sea. War existed before her and would exist after her. She'd been reacting to an impossible set of circumstances from the beginning. She'd made a point to put the responsibility where it belonged when she spoke to King Hector and all the court. There'd been frustration and rumbling among the people since that day. Fair or not, she felt responsible.

"Evan, I never apologized to you. In hindsight, I should have just accepted the powers right away. I probably could have saved Teddy. I'm not even certain why I am fighting so hard now. It seems so foolish. I could make a difference."

She met Evan's gaze. The slightest flicker of grief appeared in his eyes and then vanished.

"Don't torture yourself. You made a difference. You saved the rest of us. I don't blame you, and Teddy wouldn't either. We've both known Xander for a very long time. Teddy made a split-second decision that I know he didn't regret. It was on me as much as it was on you. I checked the woods. I thought we were clear. We could probably all find reasons to blame ourselves, but it does no good. It's just grief talking."

Evan threw a shell into the sea and looked back at her. His eyes were world-weary and carried the wisdom of someone much older.

"How do we make peace with it?" Cecilia asked.

"If I knew, I would tell you, but that loss is going to hang out for a while. That's the price to be paid for caring, but it's not one I would trade. Xander and I were a unit for so many years, but we fought a lot. Teddy brought us into balance. He forced me to have more fun and could encourage Xander to practice his magic without letting him show off too much. I used to be so annoyed by his incessant chatter, but now I miss it." He ran a hand through his hair. "He used to tell me I could not control outcomes with planning alone. That all I can do is accept that life is chaotic."

"You make it sound so easy." She sighed, sitting down in the sand.

"It's natural when you're born of loss," Evan said, sitting down next to her. For the first time, Cecilia realized how little she knew about her husband's best friend.

"Why did you become a hunter, Evan?"

"Because it was the only option I had. My mother died in childbirth with me. My father was a favorite of King Damian's hunters. He died in battle shortly after I was born."

"I'm sorry you lost both of your parents so young," she said.

"King Damian took me under his wing. He made sure I had the best training from the time I was young. I trained with Xander. That's why we're so close. I learned how to be a hunter, and although we don't have guardians in Argaria, I was raised to protect him. Little did

I know the job would become mostly just protecting him from himself."

Cecilia grinned. "I can only imagine."

"I promise you can't," Evan said, shaking his head. "He was fiercely independent and always trying to prove he was more than just an extra prince. Davide was given so much time and attention from everyone, but when Xander asked for any, he was treated like he was too needy. Even Davide used to be so protective of Xander."

For a moment, Evan appeared to be lost in a memory. She thought about asking if he would share it with her, but there was an intimacy and trust required to share a memory that she wasn't certain existed between the two of them.

"Why is Davide so awful now?" she asked.

"Some of it feels unnatural to me, but I can't figure out the source. I used to think it was just that when Xander stopped that group of hunters at ten and earned the title of the Storm Prince, it pulled attention from Davide. It seemed obvious that Xander having magic when Davide didn't would even the field between them—both of them special in their own ways—but Davide was fascinated by it. The resentment didn't start until years later when Xander left for Olney. Maybe things would have been different if Xander had stayed in Argaria, though I think he would have felt suffocated there. Xander has really thrived in Olney. I think he needed the space and the freedom of not being a royal. Every six months when he came home to visit, he was better. His skills with a bow and in close combat are unparalleled now. I know he credits your father with that."

Cecilia sighed.

"Do you think he will be enough for you?" Evan asked, turning to look at her.

The question caught her off guard. "Excuse me?"

"Xander. Is he enough for you? He's my best friend. He'll never be able to walk away. He'll try to be enough for you the same way he tried to be enough in his family. Do you think you could be happy with him?"

She didn't blame Evan for asking it. A couple weeks ago, it might have been an easy yes, but she wasn't sure if she would have been lying to herself then or if she was now. She knew she loved Xander—felt it every time he looked at her, kissed her, every time she woke up to his smiling face. She also loved Rainer, and the pull to him was undeniable.

"I don't know," she finally said.

Evan said nothing. He just nodded, like he'd expected that answer. "We should head back to the cottage before Xander comes looking for you."

They climbed the cliff trail to her cottage. As soon as they got close, Cecilia could tell that something was wrong. The door was cracked, and when they pushed it open, there were signs of a struggle. A strange pine-and-leather scent hung in the air. Evan drew his sword and kept Cecilia behind him, searching the cottage.

Rainer and Xander were both gone, though it was clear it was recent since their tea was still steaming.

Cecilia tried to shove down the rising tide of panic that swelled in her chest.

"I didn't feel anything through the connection. How could I not feel anything?" Her hand came to her heart.

Evan went to the door and looked at the footprints in front of the cottage.

"Six sets of prints. They could have been overpowered. Maybe they hit Rainer in the head, and he was out cold?" Evan suggested.

"I should have felt the physical pain of that, though," she said.

She picked up a kitchen chair that had been knocked over as Evan lifted a teacup to his nose.

"Nightingale root. It's used as a sleeping tonic. Perhaps they were both unconscious."

"I don't know if that's a good thing or a bad thing," Cecilia said.

"Perhaps only Rainer was unconscious, and Xander tried to fight," Evan said.

Cecilia closed her eyes, trying desperately to reach across her connection for any sign of Rainer. She looked around the room frantically for a clue. Her gaze snapped on a note lying on her pillow.

———

I have the three men you love most. I'll trade them all for you, Goddess.
   Shores of Adira — Tomorrow — Noon
   King Davide Savero

———

Cecilia took off at a run. As soon as she entered her father's house, she knew he was gone. The door had splintered by the latch. Sword marks on some of the furniture showed the extent of the struggle. She screamed for her Aunt Clara and eventually found her tied up in her bedroom.

"Cecilia, thank gods you're all right. They came for your father with no warning at all. The door was bashed in, and there were too many of them. He couldn't fight them all off," Clara said.

"Is he well?" Cece asked.

"I think so. He didn't have any serious injuries that I saw, but I think they knocked him out. You know your father. He wouldn't give them the option not to fight. He's not one to go peacefully," Clara said, wiping tears from her eyes.

Cecilia hugged her aunt, and the two of them cried together. It took her a while to settle Clara down, but once she got her to bed and locked her in the house, she met Evan on the front steps.

"Xander will beat me bloody if I let you go." Evan sighed.

"I'll beat you bloody if you try to stop me," she said tightly.

"We need a plan, Cece. We can't just charge in there," Evan said. "And before you suggest it, you will not use the goddess power. Xander won't forgive me for that, and if you use it to save him, he'll never forgive himself for getting caught."

She sighed heavily. "So, what do we do?"

"We should leave soon, so we have time to scout the beach and figure out what's happening. If you conjure a storm, it could provide some cover for me to get close enough, and Xander could help without them noticing, assuming he's conscious."

439

"But I can't blast Davide if he's that close to the rest of them. The only one who would survive would be Xander. I'm not accurate enough with lightning to feel confident trying to hit him if he's close to the rest of them. I can try to draw Davide out, and once he gets far enough from the rest of them, I can use lightning, or you can use a bow. I'll hold his attention so he doesn't notice you. It might not be the best plan, but we'll go with what we have."

Evan nodded, considering it.

"I'll get my horse, Piper, and Rainer's horse, Zeke, saddled up for us. Meet you in the stables in twenty minutes."

As she threw some supplies in her satchel and grabbed her bow, she found her mind wandering to Xander. He'd kissed her that morning with reckless abandon before he left. She'd rolled her eyes at how excessive he was, but now she wished she'd put more into it.

She worried that might have been her last chance to kiss her husband, or if the night before was the last time she would hold Rainer's hand.

Cecilia shoved the thought away and hurried to the stables to prepare the horses. She didn't have time to let the fear in, not when the three men she loved most needed her to be smart. She looked forward to the day when she had the luxury of being proactive instead of reacting to each crisis as it arose.

41

The sun was setting, slicing the horizon with a bloody red line of clouds by the time Evan and Cecilia reached the Shores of Adira. They camped for the night in the brush on a cliff overlooking the beach.

Cecilia's skin was damp with sweat and coated with dirt from the hard ride. Her clothing stuck to her skin, making it impossible to get comfortable. She tossed and turned in the darkening evening. Evan kept a sharp eye on her as if expecting her to wander off and try to handle things herself.

When the light of dawn finally came, smoke of fires wafted through the sky in the distance. Evan estimated at least a battalion of hunters would be there, and they didn't have to wait long to find out. By midmorning, the battalion was in formation on the beach. There was still no sign of Xander, Rainer, or her father.

Cecilia paced restlessly as Evan continued to talk her out of just taking out the battalion right then with her goddess powers.

Waiting was a special kind of torture for Cecilia. The hours dragged as if weighted by her worry.

Finally, a little before noon, Davide appeared with three men in tow, each with their own guard. Something about his gait and confidence was different than it had been back in Argaria.

There he'd faked confidence and menace, but even from a distance, Cecilia saw the way his stride exuded power. There seemed to be a pulse of magic around him.

"Does Davide have magic?" she asked.

Evan shook his head. "No. Why?"

Cecilia stared at Davide. "I don't know. There's something strange about him."

She wanted to rush down to the beach, but Evan made her wait until they were in position.

"Remember the plan, Cece. You need to stick to it. Promise me," he said.

"I promise, but I take no responsibility if he doesn't do what we expect," she huffed. She made her way down the trail that snaked toward the beach.

As she crossed the beach, she watched whatever hope that she wouldn't show up disappear from Xander's face and got a rare glimpse of fear in his eyes. She smiled at him reassuringly.

Rainer didn't look surprised at all—only frustrated. He turned to look at Davide, no doubt trying to figure out a way to take him out despite his bound hands, feet, and gag. She smiled at Rainer and shook her head. She hoped he would feel confidence through their connection instead of her fear. She hoped he trusted that she and Evan had a plan. His eyes darted around the periphery of the beach, looking for her backup.

Finally, her eyes fell on her father. Leo looked ashamed and frustrated. She knew he was worried, but she just gave him a wink.

"*Princess*, I'm so glad you could join us. Just all of your favorite guys here waiting for you." Davide laughed.

"*Your Majesty*, if you wanted to have afternoon tea with us, you only had to come to call. No need to take hostages," Cecilia said, trying to keep her voice even.

Something about Davide's presence felt more stifling. The air around him felt heavy with magic, though Cecilia still couldn't put her finger on what was different.

"Did you truly come without backup? I knew you were brave, but I didn't think you foolish." Davide smirked.

Cecilia looked out at the sea. "I have all the backup I need from my sister."

Davide's eyebrows shot up, and his eyes narrowed on her as if he were searching for something. For a moment, his gaze flickered to the sea as if he were expecting her half sister, Adira, goddess of the sea, to step right out of the surf. It was a bluff, but she hoped one that would make him think twice about whatever he had planned, even if Adira was ascended and her power wouldn't be as potent as that of a living god.

"What do you want, Davide?"

"I want to make a trade. I'll trade all three of your men alive and well for you, Princess. All you have to do is come with me without trouble," Davide said. "I have an Unsummoner bracelet to keep you from using your magic."

It wasn't exactly what she and Evan expected to happen, but it was close enough. She and Evan agreed that she would go with Davide, and they would try to help her escape during the transition once her father, Rainer, and Xander were safely out of range.

"Fine," she sighed. "As long as they are all healthy and in one piece, I'm happy to make the trade."

Rainer and Xander both shook their heads, but her father looked resigned to it. Cecilia took a few steps closer to them.

"I'd prefer you give me a little more space until I let them go. I know how deadly you can be at close range," Davide said.

She backed away, keeping her gaze fixed on Davide. Once she was a distance away, Rainer's and Xander's gags were removed, and Davide instructed a guard to release the huntmaster first.

The hum of death whispers filled the air. Cecilia's eyes snapped to the three men. Xander and Rainer both had knives to their throats. She looked back and forth between them. Her father's ties were cut from his feet. She couldn't think straight as the roaring grew louder.

"No!" The word was out of her mouth before she could stop it as her father lunged.

She should have known he would do something like that. Her father's feet were free, but his hands were still tied. He rammed into Davide, but instead of going down, Davide stood tall like a stone wall. He grabbed Leo and plunged a dagger into his neck.

Her father let out a wet cough, his eyes wide and fixed on Cecilia.

Cecilia screamed, but it was a strangled sound. An arrow landed at her feet. She knew it was a warning from Evan not to overreact, but she was beyond reason.

The death whispers roared in her ears, and she finally surrendered to the pull of her goddess power.

42

Before her father fell to the ground, Cecilia called to the goddess power. She accepted the exchange without another thought.

It was a breath away, and it rushed toward her.

Finally, it whispered.

Strength flooded her body. There was a bright burst, like lightning, then smoke, and then she felt it rush through her like a flood of raw power. She wondered what it would be. What gift was hers to claim?

As the power surged, she finally surrendered to the dark abyss that lived inside her. She allowed it to swallow her. She bathed in it.

She was the sharp blade. She was night. She was the stillness before a storm. The wild edge of sorrow. The dark itself.

Her senses came alive like never before. She heard Xander whisper her name despite the distance between them. She saw the fear on the faces of the soldiers at the back of the battalion. She smelled the sweat in the air, tasted the ash. Her immortal body was alive and humming with power. Everything weak in her mind was turned to steel. Her will was unbreakable.

What was this strange power? Was it night? Grief? Death itself?

She didn't wait to find out.

She heard the last beat of the huntmaster's heart. It was too late to save him, but not too late to save the other two.

Rainer and Xander both called out to her. Her best friend. Her husband. Two loves.

No. Cecilia Reznik's best friend. Princess Savero's husband. Not hers.

She was a goddess, and the girl she was before was gone. Those men belonged to someone else. Still, she would save them.

She charged forward, carried by strength and speed that were new in her vibrating body. She raced toward the two men Cecilia loved most in the world. The two who were still alive.

She waved a hand, sending her power careening at the two guards with the knives to the throats of Cecilia's friends. Their eyes rolled back. They clutched their heads, screaming.

Rainer yelled to her, but she didn't listen. She heard the words, though she didn't want to. *Don't, Cece. Don't.*

He was talking to a ghost. Rainer pushed at the connection, wrapped around the goddess's heart, but she slammed the door shut.

The two Argarian hunters collapsed in an instant. They drooled, jaws limp, eyes blank—their minds reduced to nothing—but it wasn't enough. Her power no longer required a touch. She could wield it with just a look.

She moved past Xander and Rainer toward the battalion of hunters. She felt their confusion and their fear, and she enjoyed it. A hunter at the front drew his sword, ready to face her. She grabbed his gaze and used the same power to melt his memories like candle wax. He collapsed in a drooling puddle before his breathing slowed and stopped, the memory of who he was, all his training—even how to breathe—blown apart like dust in the wind.

Fear spread through the ranks. Some men turned to run, but most waited for a command from Davide. She stretched her powers wide like a net and froze them all. All of them were forced to hold perfectly still under the blazing midday sun. If they moved an inch or wavered, they would fall into the same madness as the men she'd already wiped out. Everything that made a mind worth having turned to ash. A brutal death without an ounce of blood spilled. It was tidy.

She smiled, but it was not Cecilia Reznik's beautiful smile that her guardian knew like the back of his hand or Princess Savero's smile that made her husband's knees weak. It was a hollow thing, an imitation of humanity. Because she didn't feel happy. She felt bored.

Death whispered, but this time it was a product of her power. She was its queen, and it, her servant.

Cecilia Reznik was gone. Princess Cecilia Savero was gone. They had both laid down their lives at the altar of grief to raise a new life. Goddess Cecilia.

In the back of her mind, she was aware of an even bigger sacrifice that savaged the princess the moment she decided to reach out to the power, but that was not her problem. She was not that girl anymore.

She was a breaker of minds, a bender of reality, a plague on memory. A Lost Goddess found. She was ruination.

She turned back to where King Davide Savero stood. Except he was no longer wearing the new king of Argaria's face. Instead, she saw Endros, god of war. It was a trick of godly magic. It seemed his son Cato's talent for manipulation extended to appearances. She knew as soon as she reached out to the power what he was, but she had more pressing concerns at the time. Now she was ready for him.

"Goddess Cecilia. That is quite a trick you pulled. Why aren't my men moving? What strange magic is this that kills them if they move an inch?" he asked, stepping toward her with his sword drawn.

Power emanated from his blade. She knew it was a Godkiller, just like her dagger, the weapon required to kill a living god. The same type of weapon she'd need to plunge into his heart to send him from her realm.

"Your men follow a foolish old god, and their minds are weak," the goddess said. "Tell me, old man, who helped you disguise yourself so well, and why would you do the bidding of the young king of Argaria? How the mighty have fallen to new lows."

Endros shook his head. "Of course. You're a goddess of mind and memory. It feels obvious since the Gauntlet relied on that magic."

He circled her, but she held perfectly still. She called to the storm. The old humble magic had its uses. All she needed was to stun him enough that she could end him.

"Cece, love. What are you doing?" Xander shouted over the building winds.

"Get Rainer out of here. You may be stormproof, but he is not," she said without looking.

She watched the way Endros moved. Her enhanced sense was new to her, but she felt the wrongness in him. The aura of power around him was dimmer than it should have been.

"You're sick," she said.

Endros's eyes widened slightly.

"How can that be? You're supposed to be immortal." She reached out to him with her senses. Regret and shame swirled around him.

"You don't know everything. You're still a child. And you're Clastor's child, which means you're proud and overconfident. I know more than you think about how we got here. He will find a way to use you as his own tool. He finds a way to use everyone," Endros taunted.

"Who?" she asked.

Lightning crackled in the air, thunder rumbled, and the wind was so strong that she was certain the only reason they could hear each other was because of their godly hearing.

"You know who. We are the last three living gods and the strongest powers in this realm. Cato pitted us against each other so there would only be two. I see it now. He knew you would be the only one with a chance to defeat me because you are a summoner, a goddess, and a hunter. You are a force of nature. That's why Cato likes you so much. You have a will of iron. He thinks he can break it."

"Cato is delusional. As far as he is concerned, I am unbreakable. I may as well be the goddess of stubbornness. I won't bend to him," she said.

Endros shook his head. His smile was bitter, and she couldn't tell who he pitied more.

"You've no idea the misery he plans for you, Goddess. He has a gift for it. He will bring you to your knees and enjoy it. People think I pull the strings, but that boy rules us all. Even when we think we're choosing, he's always choosing for us."

"I am not afraid of him."

"You should be," Endros said. "You're foolish to be so brave. He's in your life already. In ways you haven't begun to comprehend. He will bend you to his will, and the longer you fight him, the more he will enjoy it. There's no beating him. You will beg for it to end when he is done with you."

"I guess we will see about that. What did he do to you? How did he make you weak?" she asked, watching the old god falter.

"I made a deal with him, and he collected."

A chill shot through the young goddess.

Endros grinned. "You're a lot like your mother, Selene. But I killed her. And now I'm going to kill you."

Endros charged at her with his sword high, and she brought down a powerful bolt of lightning that struck his blade and jolted his whole body. He staggered back and went down onto one knee, but he did not fall.

"Cecilia!" It was the guardian's voice.

He couldn't be here.

"Xander, get him out of here! You can stay and keep the storm going, but he won't survive a lightning strike," she yelled.

She watched Xander lead Rainer away. He returned a few minutes later and kept the storm going. With him running the storm, she could pull from it as needed.

She summoned the tides. A huge wave came and knocked Endros onto his side. He sputtered, coughing up salty water.

"Say the word and we can end this now," she said. "You can stop attacking and leave, and I'll just tell Cato you died. I can make deals, too."

"He's my son."

She stared in disbelief. "He made you weak."

"I owe you nothing, Goddess."

"Suit yourself."

She continued to pummel him with the waves.

"The tides won't kill me," Endros choked.

"No, they won't. But they can incapacitate you and make you extremely uncomfortable."

"Perhaps your cruelty is better suited to Cato than I initially imagined."

She struck him with a large lightning bolt that sent even Xander stumbling backward. Endros lay flat on the sand.

"I thought you were a huntress. Why do you use just magic, Goddess?"

The goddess laughed. "You won't bait me into a game where you have the upper hand. The first rule of combat is to know your strengths. Are you getting senile in your old age?"

Endros scrambled to his feet. "I can see why he is so invested in you. You have a certain edge to you."

He surprised her, sending a dagger flying at her. She dodged it, but it sliced her left arm. She focused on the blade in his hand and summoned fire to heat it. It took Endros a moment to realize what was happening, but he was forced to drop the sword. He cursed, looking down at the brand on his palm. The moment of distraction was all she needed. His weakness made him slow.

She charged at him, pretending to stab her dagger into his neck. He grabbed her wrist, but the move left his body open, as she'd hoped it would. She dropped the dagger into her other hand and she slid it between Endros's ribs, piercing his heart.

His eyes went wide in surprise, and he stumbled backward, landing in the sand.

Xander slowed the storm, and Cecilia pulled back the tides.

Endros's breath sputtered. He looked up at her. His quicksilver eyes dimmed. "Not bad, Goddess, but I was already on my way. My boy will be another story. I agreed to lend Cato my power. He's going to be unstoppable."

"Any parting words? I'll be seeing him very soon," she said.

"Rest assured that me lying here was probably part of his plan. Maybe one I should have foreseen. You can't surprise him, Goddess. There's no one who doesn't owe him favors."

Endros took one last breath before the light disappeared from his eyes.

The goddess turned away from the dead god, toward the guardian and the prince at the edge of the beach. The girl inside her tried to claw her way back to the surface. It appeared she wasn't gone after all, simply hiding. When her eyes fell on the girl's dead father, grief swallowed her.

"Cece." Xander took a cautious step toward her, but something in her glare made him stop in his tracks. "It's me, love. Are you well?"

His gaze was fixed on a cut on her left arm.

"It's already healing," she said, staring at the skin knitting perfectly together without her using any healing at all.

The prince bristled. "Your eyes—" Xander said, staring at her.

"What about them?"

"They're glowing," he whispered, taking another step closer.

She flinched. If he touched her, the girl would come screaming to the surface, and she wasn't ready to deal with this yet. The girl wanted the oblivion of her husband's touch and the relief of his kisses. The goddess knew that might break her. She needed to protect the fragile girl.

"Don't touch me," she breathed.

Xander backed away.

"Cece!" Rainer ran to her, but she held her hands up.

"I'm fine, but please don't touch me," she said. "Either of you."

Again the girl was trying to claw her way to the surface, wanting to launch herself into her guardian's arms. She wanted to wrap herself around him, to be soothed and comforted. She wanted to fall apart, but the goddess would not let that happen.

Not yet.

So she turned to the hunter, who'd just stepped off the trail down to the beach. "Evan, I need you to get the huntmaster's body home. I'm fine, but I need some space," she said flatly.

Then she walked by all three men, climbed onto her horse, and rode back toward her cottage.

Not yet, she told herself.

In a moment, everything had changed. In a moment, she'd paid a price that she still wasn't sure the girl could live with. In a moment, she'd shut down some part of herself that she might never be able to access again. She should have felt relieved, but she just felt empty.

Alone. Alone. Alone. The word was like a blaring symphony in her ears the same way it had been in the Cave of Longings. She rode home without looking back.

43

When the goddess got home hours later, she took a hot bath and crawled into bed. She pulled on layers of clothing, unable to stop shivering. Her warmest pajamas and one of Xander's sweaters that still smelled like his skin. She piled blankets on top of her and curled into a tiny shivering ball.

Is this what it is to be a living goddess? Will I ever feel warm again?

And there in the quiet dark, alone as she had been the day she walked into the Cave of Longings, the goddess let Cecilia come back to the surface.

She cried for her father, who had loved her like she was his own. She cried for the men she killed on the battlefield. She cried for herself and the immensity of the loss she suffered after fighting it for so long.

As she lay alone in the dark, she chastised herself for every moment she ever felt alone before. She hated herself for every time she wanted someone to explain why she was so different. She would give it all up at once to go back to being a lonely witch.

What do you seek? Love or power? the seer had asked all those years ago.

Love. She'd known it without question. She knew it was the right choice then, but now she doubted it.

This is what love does. It cuts you down when you least expect it. It makes you do horrible, vicious things. It makes you run from comfort.

Cecilia knew that fear could make her a coward or a warrior, and she'd always chosen the latter. She had the scars to prove it. Now she wondered if she'd known the truth since she was eleven and received her first scar.

The worst wounds weren't the ones that left marks on her skin. The worst wounds were the ones that left marks on her heart, in a quiet place no one could see. She wasn't sure that this was one she could survive.

She cried until she thought her eyes would pop out and her body would shrivel up. And when she thought it might never stop, she fell into a dreamless sleep, knowing that all the power in the world couldn't save her from grief.

———

Xander and Rainer came back several hours after her. She woke to the creak of the cottage door. She didn't move from underneath her mountains of blankets. She peeked out as they tentatively approached.

"Love, can I hold you?" Xander asked.

"I don't know," she whispered. "Maybe just hold my hand."

She reached her hand out of her blanket cocoon, and he folded it between his warm palms. She could barely stand to look at the love in his eyes as he placed a soft kiss on the top of her hand.

"Cece, I'm so sorry about your father. He was a good man—"

"Stop, I can't," she said tightly. She pulled her hand back.

Rainer appeared in her field of vision, and nothing could have prepared her for his face. He looked wrecked. He sat down on the ground next to the bed.

"Rainy," she whispered. She sniffled, unable to hold back a rush of tears. She knew he understood best. Leo Reznik had been more of a father to him than his own.

"Hey, Cece," he whispered. "What's going on in there? How heavy is it?"

An old question that he hadn't asked in years. Not since the worst of the bullying when she was young. She would run back to the cottage after bad days and hide under the covers to cry until Rainer came to find her and asked her that question. Then he would lie beside her and hold her hand until she said it felt lighter.

Rainer looked at Xander for permission. He just nodded and scooted out of the way. Rainer tentatively climbed into bed next to her. "I'm just going to hold your hand. You don't have to talk about it. I'm just going to stay here until it feels lighter."

She nodded inside her burrow. She reached out her left hand, and Rainer placed his on top of her open palm, crescent scars lining up at the edges of their hands. For a few minutes, the only sound in the room was her sniffling.

Finally, Rainer spoke. "I was thinking maybe, since it was such a bad day, you could use both of us. How about if Xander goes to lie behind you? That way, we can both be here if you need us. We won't say anything. We'll just be here, okay?"

She shifted so that her head was out of the blankets, and she knocked some of them away to make room for Xander. He slid into bed behind her and curved his body around hers, his arm across her waist.

"Is this all right?" Xander asked. She nodded and relaxed against him.

After a few minutes, her sniffling subsided, and she let out a giggle that made both of them jump.

Rainer smiled. "What?"

"It's just weird having both of you in bed with me," she whispered. She was still crying, but the absurdity of lying there between the two of them wasn't lost on her, even in her grief.

"Maybe we should make it a regular thing," Xander said quietly, and she laughed again.

"Oh my gods, Xander."

"Love, I'm open to all ideas that will cheer you up," he whispered as he pressed a soft kiss to her forehead.

"What's the worst of it?" Rainer asked.

She blew out a breath. "The worst part is the choice was taken away again. Over and over, I've been told how powerful I am, and over and over I've had no control over the outcome. I've been forced to make impossible decisions. I don't know how to mourn what I've lost because I barely had time to want it."

Xander nodded, considering. "What can we do?"

"I don't know how to help," Rainer said.

Cecilia sat up. "War is still coming. That was just one battle. Endros might be dead, but Davide is still out there, and so is Cato. I will pull it together, but I just need to sit with this for now. If you want to help, keep an eye on Davide's movements. Figure out what's actually going on so that maybe we can get ahead of this for once."

Cecilia had won the battle, but in many ways, she felt that she'd lost a much more personal war.

AFTER

Rainer

L oose ringlets rustled in the sea breeze, rebelling against Cecilia's neat bun, drawing Rainer's attention to his three favorite freckles—a perfect constellation from her shoulder up her neck. He'd thought about kissing each one more times than he could count. He wondered what she would do if he bent over and did it now. Wondered why the impulse to do so was in no way dampened by the solemn occasion or his grief. Wondered if he would ever cease to feel relentlessly drawn to her.

She hadn't looked at Rainer once since she arrived on the beach. Instead, she stood beside Xander, his arm circling her waist.

Clearly, she was herself today and not the goddess. The changes came swiftly between the two, but they weren't subtle. The goddess did not like to be touched, especially not affectionately. Cecilia had explained it to Rainer as best she could as, "The goddess doesn't like Xander because he gets too grabby." Rainer and the goddess had that in common.

He sighed, noting a shift in the crowd as Raymond McKay wormed his way to the front row of onlookers to the left of the pyre.

His father gave him a subtle nod, but Rainer could read the disapproval in his eyes. He could practically see his father's mind turning over whatever counsel he'd spout off at the post-funeral feast about staying relevant to his goddess friend. Perhaps he'd chide Rainer for not letting him in on the most exclusive secret in the kingdom.

The best advice Rainer's adoptive father ever gave him was to avoid love at all costs. In hindsight, he realized the best advice from Raymond McKay was still terrible advice.

Love is a fool's errand. Love is the kind of foolish weakness that can bring an empire to the ground.

It was his father's idea of sage wisdom, and although Rainer couldn't stand the man, he still felt the frustrating need for his approval. The words took root in his heart.

Rainer looked at the huntmaster's funeral pyre. *Fight for her.* Leo's last words to Rainer battled with ones long ago planted by his father.

Over the past year, Rainer had never felt more at war with himself. Before their final Gauntlet run, he'd found it harder and harder to put the necessary distance between himself and Cecilia or to feign interest in other women. He found it nearly impossible to sleep through the night without her pressed against his chest.

Yet each day, he'd woken up and snuck out of her cottage and repeated seven words to himself as he walked home.

I won't fall in love with Cece.

The same seven words had echoed in his head as he wrote their story from the night before.

I won't fall in love with Cece.

And again when he went through his daily guardian training.

I won't fall in love with Cece.

It wasn't until afternoon training, when he'd meet up with Cecilia, that things would shift. He'd show her some new swordplay move, and she'd look at him, her bright blue eyes alive with excitement, and thank him. That was when he'd realize that he could repeat those words day and night, and it wouldn't make them true. That was when his mind shifted from a seven-word invocation to a painful revelation.

I am madly in love with Cece.

Laughable, considering he'd known deep down that was the case most of his life. His love for her was inexorable, winding its way through him even when he thought he was keeping it at a safe distance. Rainer quarantined the feelings in a secret compartment of his heart, but still, they spread.

Get some distance from that Reznik girl. It's good to be friendly. Her father is very important, after all, but you know well what ruin being too involved with her could create.

Had his father known then that she was the Lost Goddess, he would have surely encouraged his son to do the exact opposite. Rainer had been terrified of being banished and leaving Cecilia alone. Terrified to lose his connection to her that was so familiar and warm. Now Rainer felt incredibly stupid for ever trying to put any distance at all between himself and Cecilia.

Find a nice girl from a good family and marry her. Take care of her and show her affection. Show love when you need to, but never when you feel it. The worst thing a man can do is fall in love.

If he hadn't already known that he wasn't blood-related to Raymond McKay, he would have then. While Rainer liked to think he had dominion over his thoughts and emotions, he wasn't foolish enough to think it could stay that way forever. Worse, at least in his father's eyes, he didn't have the same impulse to seek power. Rainer sought recognition and acceptance. He wanted to live up to the legacy of his birth father, who'd been a great warrior who died in the War of the Gods. It was a private motivation that he didn't share with anyone, even Cecilia, for fear that he would fall short of his own expectations. So when Raymond McKay told him to avoid love, it was easy to convince himself he could, at least for the time being. He had other priorities.

Now those priorities had shifted in catastrophic ways. As a man who'd spent the entirety of his twenty-five years defining himself by his duty, he felt lost without it.

Rainer had always envied the way Cecilia refused to be shaped by any hand but her own. Her rebellion highlighted his compliance.

He'd spent so many years being sculpted by others' expectations, he found it almost impossible to create his own.

Although his vows to Cecilia were for life, she was now immortal and much less in need of his protection. She was a goddess, with a terrifying power, a witch with the ability to summon the elements, a huntress he'd trained for years, and now, a princess under the protection of the Storm Prince. Rainer's role as guardian and protector seemed superfluous.

With the Gauntlet complete and the shifting nature of guardians and witches in Olney, Rainer was unsure of where he belonged in the world, especially with no room left at Cecilia's side.

Xander

Waves lapped at the shoreline, the breeze off the Adiran Sea offering a reprieve from the sun high in the sky above. Xander glanced at the funeral pyre as sweat dripped down his back. Beside him, Cece shivered.

She was constantly cold since her transformation, as if the magic in her body sapped some of her natural warmth. At night, she trembled against him in bed, unable to sleep until he wrapped his body around her and soothed her with a spell.

Even that didn't bring peace for long. Cece was plagued by nightmares. She cried in her sleep, whispering Xander's name or calling out for Rainer in a way that shattered his heart.

Xander had never considered himself a very complicated person. He liked fighting, fucking, and besting anyone who challenged him. All he'd wanted in Argaria was to prove his worth as something other than a spare prince. He enjoyed being a spy and hunter, but the life he'd chosen for himself meant staying in the emotional shallow end. Since meeting Cece, he endlessly felt like he'd stepped out into the ocean too far and felt the seafloor fall away, realizing too late that he was in over his head.

Ten years spent spying taught him most people were worse when they thought no one was looking. But having watched Cece for a year before they officially met, Xander saw for the first time someone who was kinder when she thought she was alone. He saw the way she stealthily replaced the bow of a young hunter who'd been teased for his poor equipment. Watched when she sat in the queen's garden every Saturday morning staring at the roses, sometimes with tears in her eyes. She drew him in with her softness.

He felt a newfound desire to explore the depths, to show Cece more so that maybe, in turn, she would show him more. He felt things for her he'd never felt before—wild, dangerous things that he didn't quite understand how to wrangle. He'd never felt so possessive, but he'd also never been in love. It was mysterious and supernatural to him.

Xander had spent years hiding, but the moment Cece turned those expressive blue eyes on him, he had the distinct feeling she saw right through him. She enjoyed his overt excess and wanted what was hidden behind it, taking his hand in moments she sensed the specter of grief floating too close. She looked at him like she wanted to take care of him, like he was beyond her wildest imaginings.

Sometimes the raw vulnerability on her face forced him to look away because he knew he could not match it. Though his love for her opened him more than ever, there would always be something hidden in him. His secrets were so interwoven that one sharp tug might turn the tapestry of his life into a pile of string.

Now grief had descended on them like a heavy fog. Despite its sudden aggressive appearance in his life, with the loss of his parents and Teddy, Xander could not seem to find the words to comfort his wife because he did not know how to comfort himself. Cece's sadness was strange, quiet, and spun through with unspoken things.

Grief was isolating and consuming. It took everything he gave it and demanded more. Xander wished he could save her from its relentless assault, but he could do nothing but flounder beside her, his mouth crammed with words that seemed little consolation for all she'd lost. For all *they'd* lost.

There would be no children with Cece's wild dark curls and

bright blue eyes, not to mention how it would complicate the line of succession if Davide died in the war he was waging.

Worse, giving up their future children felt like giving up being tied to her in some permanent way. Marriage might have seemed enough back in Argaria, but that was before he watched Rainer kiss Cece in the forest.

Xander didn't deserve her. He solidified it in the cabin in the mountains and after, but he kept trying to prove himself wrong by being the answer to all of her problems.

He tightened his arm on Cece's waist as the newly appointed huntmaster stepped forward, holding a large torch, waiting for her to set the fire.

Cecilia

The torch crackled, a welcome reprieve from the whispers of the crowd. Cecilia felt all their eyes on her.

Just days before, she was all bluster in the king's throne room, insisting she wouldn't be their goddess. Now she felt the appraisal of the royal army and most of the court, wondering what to make of her mysterious newfound power.

Everything about her appearance was a little too perfect, her eyes too bright, her skin too glowing, her movements too sharp. People looked twice, trying to figure out what they were missing, their eyes recognizing magic without realizing it. She heard their whispers with her sharper hearing and sensed their fear. Still, she didn't blame them. She'd killed nearly a thousand men with a flick of her fingers, without a drop of blood spilled, their minds erased of every process that made living possible.

She sensed something else beyond the darkness inside her. Whatever was there, she was afraid to reach out to it. Afraid she wouldn't come back. Afraid she would lose everything she sacrificed for. Eventually, she might need it, just not yet.

Her whole life was a brutally cruel exchange she was fated to make.

The goddess reared up inside on a fresh wave of grief, but Cecilia shoved her down. *No, this is mine. I don't want to be here, but I will hate myself if I'm not.*

When the grief became too heavy, the goddess took over, like a sort of possession that allowed Cecilia to fade into the background and turn down the volume of her pain. It was impossible for her to explain how the goddess felt like her and also something else. She clung to the separateness to manage her guilt.

Cecilia finally lifted her gaze to the funeral pyre. Leo Reznik was shrouded on top, but she still knew his imposing figure under the white linen. Even in death, he seemed too big to fall. She kept waiting for him to stand and climb down.

Aunt Clara let out a quiet sob beside her, and Cecilia gave her hand a comforting squeeze. It was plenty warm out, but even in her heavy wool dress, Cecilia shivered, the new power slithering through her body like a winter breeze.

Xander brushed a kiss to her temple, an affectionate gesture neither appropriate for court nor the occasion, though she found it immeasurably comforting to have him beside her with quiet understanding thanks to his own immense loss.

He bent to whisper, "I can do it if you can't, love. Or Rainer will."

Rainer. She could feel his gaze on her, feel his presence close behind her, but she could not bear to look at him and see her grief reflected in his eyes. It was enough to feel him tugging at it, trying to share her burden through their bond.

Both he and Xander had hovered incessantly, putting their differences aside temporarily to help her, since that day on the beach. Now, just three days later, she could feel them both trying to prove their worth. Both men made vows to her. One pledged his life and his blade. The other pledged his heart for the rest of his days.

But the problem of her heart was small compared to all she still had to lose. Davide was regrouping. Cecilia owed a favor to the very god who pulled all the strings to get her to the exact place she was now, and she did not know how to protect the people she loved.

Worse, she wasn't sure if Cato was the biggest threat they faced, or if the people should be more terrified of her, a goddess who could wipe the minds of a battalion with a flick of her wrist.

She took the torch from the new huntmaster, the rough wood solid in her hand as she stepped forward, and the crowd seemed to take a collective breath.

Cecilia lit the pyre and watched her father burn, ash rising into the air, mixing with the sea, and a whisper passed her lips, "Remember."

Remember why she set out to finish the Gauntlet in the first place. Remember who deserved all of her rage, all of her vengeance, all of her power. She'd paid a heavy price for her freedom, and she intended to get her money's worth.

The Adventure Continues November 2023 in...

THE MEMORY CURSE

A goddess afraid of her magic. A prince without a kingdom. A guardian with an immortal charge.

Cecilia is struggling to adjust to her newfound powers, reeling from the loss of her father, and terrified of the favor she owes the architect of her misery, Cato. The Trickster God will use any means necessary to get what he wants and Cecilia is worried that she'll never be ruthless enough to beat him.

When Cato kidnaps Xander, Cecilia turns to the only beings who might be able to help: her godly half-siblings. But the gods seem more content to play games than assist her, as they send her on a series of seemingly unrelated tasks in exchange for information on the missing prince's whereabouts and Cato's weaknesses.

As Cato slowly rips her life apart, Cecilia may have to trade her last shred of humanity to save her kingdom and the people she loves.

The exciting next chapter in The Lost God Universe features all three character POVs and arrives November 30, 2023.

Until then you can join my email list for a prequel choose your own quest style story by following this link:
https://starsagespirit.ck.page/tlgprequel

Or get access to a BONUS chapter from Rainer's point of view by taking a screenshot of your review of THE LOST GOD on Amazon or Goodreads. Send the picture of it to thelostgodbonus (@) gmail.com and you'll get an email with Rainer's BONUS chapter.

ACKNOWLEDGMENTS

It takes a village to raise a book baby, and THE LOST GOD is no exception. It took fifteen drafts to get here and there are so many people to thank.

Creation is joyful and terrifying, so the first thanks go to Tanya Grant, who was the first person I trusted with this story. Thank you for being a rock-solid cheerleader from day one through the very end. Bless you for reading the early drafts when I was still learning how to write a book (not that I've stopped learning). It is not an understatement to say that this world would never have become what it is today without you.

The best friends bring you home to yourself when you get lost, but the best writing friends do that for your story. Thank you to my writing wife, Liz Leiby, for helping me bring this story back home to itself. Your late developmental changes were critical. Thank you for the accountability and for remaining endlessly patient while listening to all of my unhinged voice memos.

So much gratitude to my love, Mike, who not only listened to me talk about these characters for two years but also proofread the book, and made the map. Thank you for talking me down when I was scared and for not batting an eye when I handed you a full-length manuscript.

An immense thank you to my many early readers. This book took quite a few big revisions and I could not have done it without the fabulous feedback of Davis, Patty, Christa, Lauren, Melissa, Michelle, Flynn, Felicia, TR, Maureen, Ashley, and Megan.

Gratitude for all the writing friends who sat beside me and kept me accountable along the way. There were so many of you who helped with your presence and encouraging words.

Thank you to my wonder editor, Lisa Gilliam, for keeping my voice in the story and making it more clear. Thanks to my brilliant cover designer, Andrew Davis, for reading my word vomit of a description of the book and pulling a vision from it that blew me away.

Every writer should have a coven of witches ready to cast magic into the world. Thank you to Amanda, Ash, Christa, Davis, Nora, Patty, Scout and Winifred for all of your wisdom and for let me vent or ask random questions for my projects about herbs or tarot cards. I especially appreciate the help with publishing knowledge (Ash), technology (Patty), storytelling (Amanda), and astrology /marketing (Davis) has carried me through this process.

Thank you to my siblings, Colin, Alex, and Mary Kate, who listened to two prologues and told me which one they liked better and who are just generally, the best. And thank you to my parents for reading to us each night when we were little.

Thank you to all the friends and extended family who have encouraged this book, not realizing how much romance it contains. Hope you enjoyed chapters 16, 17, 20, 29, 30, & 33.

Gratitude to the writers who came before me, who let me find myself in their words. Reading has guided me through the darkest of times.

My greatest hope is that this story that has lived in my head for so long find it's way into hearts of readers, making them feel seen and understood. So my final thanks go to you, the reader, for taking a chance on this book. I am so grateful you are here in this world with me, letting me spin my story about love, memory, and connection.

ABOUT THE AUTHOR

The Lost God is Sheila Masterson's first novel. When she's not writing fantasy romance novels, you can find Sheila practicing yoga, or curled up reading tarot or a book. She lives outside of Philadelphia with her boyfriend and way too many houseplants.

 instagram.com/sheilareadsandwrites